THE
MOBILIZATION
OF SHAME

The Mobilization of Shame

A WORLD VIEW OF HUMAN RIGHTS

ROBERT F. DRINAN, S.J.

YALE UNIVERSITY PRESS *New Haven & London*

Set in Carter-Cone Galliard type by Keystone Typesetting, Inc.
Printed in the United States of America by R. R. Donnelley &
Sons, Harrisonburg, Virginia.

Library of Congress Cataloging-in-Publication Data
Drinan, Robert F.
The mobilization of shame : a world view of human rights /
Robert F. Drinan.
      p.   cm.
Includes bibliographical references and index.
ISBN 0-300-08825-6 (cloth : alk. paper)
  1. Human rights.   I. Title.
JC571 .D84 2001
341.4'81 — dc21   00-011312

A catalogue record for this book is available from the
British Library.

The paper in this book meets the guidelines for permanence and
durability of the Committee on Production Guidelines for Book
Longevity of the Council on Library Resources.

10 9 8 7 6 5 4 3 2 1

Governments should understand that the international *mobilization of shame* is not limited to governments which violate human rights directly, but also extends to those which refuse to take effective action in the IGO context. [emphasis added]

— Turkey campaign documents,
Amnesty International

CONTENTS

The chaos in Europe during World War II prompted a dream by the victorious powers—the United States, Russia, and Great Britain. That dream was the concept of internationally recognized human rights to be implemented by several international entities, most of which would be attached to the United Nations.

For fifty-five years that dream has developed in a wide variety of ways, some encouraging and many disappointing. Hardly any nation or multinational entity has rejected the dream or vision of internationally recognized human rights. But the question recurs: can a world of 191 very different countries be induced to comply with rulings handed down by courts that have worldwide jurisdiction over some of the most basic actions of all nations?

The simplest reply would be to say that the question is too cosmic, too vast, too imponderable to yield any single answer. What is certain is that the international community, in seeking to manage some 6 billion people, has to endure and to accelerate its efforts to bring some form of the rule of law to the world.

The broader, amazing story of how the family of nations has struggled to develop and inculcate human rights in the past three generations deserves to be told. It is a sprawling story with few spectacular victories and with many tales of neglect and defiance by nations dominated by dictators or generals.

The establishment of a catalog of internationally recognized human rights for the first time in the history of the world is a monumental achievement in itself, apart from the enforceability of such rights. But the creation of such a catalog engenders scores of other questions. Could the lack of enforcement of these rights lead to a cynicism among people everywhere as to the availability of the most basic justice? Could the weakness—even the impotence—of international machinery to guarantee human rights encourage the advent of military rulers who will seek to utilize arms in order to achieve what legislators and courts are unable to produce?

Other hard questions abound. But the rise and the worldwide acceptance of a growing list of human rights is a fact of primordial importance. Its impact is dramatically visible in the proclamation subscribed to by 171 nations at the June 1993 U.N. World Conference on Human Rights in Vienna (the Vienna declaration is reprinted in the appendix to this book). That conference was called together by the United Nations after the Soviet empire collapsed in 1990. The leadership of the United Nations knew that the end of the Cold War had made it possible and necessary to revisit the extraordinary work on human rights that had been carried out by the United Nations and its agencies since 1945.

The eight-day conference in Vienna, in which I participated as a delegate of the American Bar Association, resulted in an astonishing proclamation of the rights of humanity. Because the statement was agreed to by virtually every nation on earth, the document constitutes customary international law. This form of law develops when nations generally agree that a certain form of conduct is forbidden. Although an international tribunal or instrument may not be in place to prevent or punish the forbidden conduct, that activity is still deemed a violation of customary international law or, better, global law.

It is safe to say that the conclusions set forth in the Vienna declaration will continue to be accepted as binding on governments everywhere. The conclusions reached in Vienna will be cited by legislatures, by courts, and by scholars as edicts binding on everyone.

The Vienna statement is cited and explained in this book as the synthesis and epitome of all the proclamations made by the United Nations and its instrumentalities in the past fifty-five years. Indeed, the Vienna declaration contains some visionary and idealistic conclusions which have not yet entered into the public consciousness of the world — or even into the consciousness of some of its human rights activists. Nevertheless, these conclusions can still be regarded as customary international law because they have been agreed to by the vast majority of countries.

Some will feel that the thrust of the Vienna declaration should not be exaggerated or overinterpreted. After all, it is only an agreement by the representatives of nations that represent some 85 percent of the world's inhabitants. These observers are partially correct. The dreams of Vienna are not self-enforcing. But the extent of the consensus in the Vienna proclamation continues to be remarkable. For the first time in some fifty years — since the proclamation of the 1945 Charter of the United Nations in San Francisco by forty-eight nations — the world came together and after solemn deliberation boldly reaffirmed every human right agreed to by the United Nations and its agencies.

But has Vienna made a difference? Have all the pronouncements on human rights since 1945 really elevated the status of freedom and equality around the world? This book seeks to explain that question with dispassion and analysis. The basic assumption is that the acceptance and enforcement of basic moral norms elevates the standards of public morality and thereby enhances the dignity of all human beings. The law teaches and deters. Law may be a feeble instrument, but sometimes it works and the human family becomes less barbarous and more civilized.

The official declaration at the end of the conference in Vienna is the centerpiece of this book. This volume comments on economic and political rights, on the rights of women and children and on other topics, some familiar and some relatively new. All the declarations of human rights made in countless ways by world bodies prior to Vienna are not neglected here. They are summed up and incorporated in the final product of the unprecedented Vienna meeting.

At the opening of the Vienna conference China protested that human rights are a western construct and that cultural relativity should excuse Asian nations from some of the mandates of the human rights law built up by the United Nations and its ancillary bodies. But during the conference in Vienna this contention faded and was withdrawn. The Vienna declaration made it clear that human rights — civil, cultural, economic, and political — are interrelated, interdependent, and indivisible.

Similarly, the Vienna declaration gave a new and elevated acceptance to human rights as a product of international or world law. No longer could any leader scoff at the prescriptions of international human rights law as inconsistent with a nation's sovereignty. Indeed, the Vienna declaration ushered in a new era in the recognition of those human rights binding on all countries.

Vienna also signaled the beginning of a time when the quarrel was no longer about the content of individual human rights law, but rather about methods for their enforceability.

The 100 short paragraphs of the 8,500-word declaration of the Vienna conference echo, amplify, and clarify some of the key concepts in the U.N. charter. But the declaration adds to the charter. The Vienna statement insists, for example, that the right to development is an "integral part of fundamental human rights." A special place is secured for the least developed countries, "many of which are in Africa" (Article 9).

Other specific items are added. A plea is made to all nations, for example, to implement existing conventions "relating to the dumping of toxic and dangerous products and waste and to cooperate in the prevention of illicit dumping" (Article 11).

There is no priority given in the Vienna declaration to political over economic rights. Article 14 says, "The existence of widespread extreme poverty inhibits the full and effective enjoyment of human rights; its immediate alleviation and eventual elimination must remain a high priority for the international community."

The rights of women, migrant workers, persons belonging to ethnic or racial minorities, and the indigenous are given special attention. The document states, for example, that "gender-based violence and all forms of sexual harassment and exploitation . . . are incompatible with the dignity and worth of the human person" (Article 18).

The panoramic view taken of international human rights by the Vienna conference owes a great deal to the thousands of nongovernmental organizations (NGOs) who were present in Vienna and who had carefully worked to make sure that the major issues related to world law and human rights were taken up in the final document.

The conference in Vienna, which included all but a handful of the world's nations, was impressive (indeed, overwhelming), yet the question persists: Does the existence of ever more clear international norms on human rights have an effect on a world that has seen the massacres in Cambodia, Rwanda, and the former Yugoslavia? Despite the existence since the 1950s of global bans on genocide and the violation of internationally acknowledged human rights, the second half of the twentieth century may have been almost as bloody and violent as the first half, with its two world wars. One has, of course, the consoling thought that the crimes against humanity might have been even more barbarous if international law had not proclaimed the sanctity of human rights and made their violation an offense against world law.

It is not always possible to predict the effect of a law on human behavior. It can be assumed that society criminalized murder after Cain killed Abel, but murders have occurred ever since. The Kellogg-Briand pact in the 1920s outlawed war, yet World War II, with 30 million persons killed, was the worst conflict in human history. But in 1945 the nations of the earth pledged as never before to initiate a worldwide crusade to protect human rights. The document that contained that pledge is the U.N. charter. It was updated in the Vienna declaration in 1993. Can these norms be accepted and enforced? Can the protection of human rights be the public morality of the global village?

Part I

THE
UNITED NATIONS
AND
HUMAN RIGHTS

1

The paradox of the formation of the United Nations is that the original 48 nations and the 152 countries who have joined them since 1945 voted for the erosion of their own national sovereignty. It is indeed astonishing that the United Nations, which entered into force on October 24, 1945, was the beginning of the decline of a view taken of the state since the days of Grotius. The major presumption of the nations that signed and ratified the Charter of the United Nations was the conviction that world wars would continue unless nations pledged to transfer the power to make war to the Security Council of the United Nations.

The theory that war could be controlled by the United Nations — the very essence of the U.N. charter — was coupled with the co-equal idea that the United Nations would have to declare, implement, and oversee the observance of human rights on which there was world agreement.

The dream and vision of the United Nations were made real and concrete to the signatories because each of them learned in Article I(3) that by being a member of the United Nations that country agreed to become a partner in the task of achieving "international cooperation in solving international problems of an economic, social, cultural or humanitarian character." That objective was paired with the goal of "prompting and encouraging respect for human rights and for fundamental freedom for all without distinction as to race, sex, language or religion."

That sweeping language is still breathtaking. The obligations of the nations which joined the United Nations was made clear to them in Article II(2), which requires all member-nations to "fulfill in good faith obligations assumed by them in accordance with the present charter." The term "good faith" is a well-known concept in law which makes clear that nations must be willing and ready to comply with the duties they have agreed to perform.

The new vision of the United Nations and the solemn duty of nations to fulfill their obligations as members of the United Nations are even clearer in Article 55. This article asserts that the United Nations desires to create "conditions of civility and well being which are essential for peaceful and friendly relations among nations." This is an amazing goal and commitment; it is based, the charter reads, on the "principle of equal rights and self-determination of peoples."

It seems impossible to overstate the revolutionary nature of Article 55. It is in essence a pledge by the rich nations to create an economic system which would bring "conditions of civility and well being" to all countries. The drafters who wrote those noble words probably had little real understanding that in the next few years well over 100 nations would declare independence from the colonial powers that had conquered them and that consequently these new nations would ask for economic "conditions of stability."

It is clear, however, that the authors of Article 55 knew what they were demanding of countries joining the United Nations. These nations would be partners in an enterprise that would "promote higher standards of living, full employment and conditions of economic and social progress and development." If this part of Article 55 sounded like a utopian fantasy the nations, both rich and poor, which joined the United Nations did not protest. Article 55 promised even more: the new world organization would promote "solutions of international economic, social, health and related problems." In addition, it would advance "international cultural and educational cooperation."

All this is combined with the promotion of "universal respect for, and observance of human rights and fundamental freedoms for all without distinction as to race, sex, language or religion."

It is clear that the allied powers in the depths of World War II had a blueprint for the post-war period which can only be described as extensive, unlimited, and comprehensive. It is notable that the concept of human rights was not really mentioned in the charter of the League of Nations. Somehow that idea was born before and during World War II and became one of the seminal concepts in the U.N. charter.

The architects of the U.N. charter wanted signatories to fully comprehend their new obligations. Article 56 requires the countries to pledge "to take joint and separate action in cooperation with the United Nations for the achievement of the purposes set forth in Article 55." Each nation consequently agreed and indeed solemnly pledged as an oath or vow to act individually as a country but also in joint action with other nations and with the United Nations itself.

It is very difficult to come to some judgment as to the world's level of compliance with the solemn pledges they made pursuant to Articles 55 and 56 of the U.N. charter. In one sense the burdens of complying with Articles 55 and 56 are not very stringent. But if a nation took its obligations as a member of the United Nations seriously it would change its attitudes and actions in almost drastic ways. After all, a nation upon becoming a member of the United Nations agrees to participate individually and collectively in the remaking of the world because that is precisely what the United Nations set out to achieve. The charter affirms that for the first time in the history of the world all nations are equal and that all will pledge and promise to share their resources so that basic economic rights can be obtained by all the citizens of all countries.

The U.N. charter has been compared to the Articles of Confederation adopted by the thirteen American colonies. The states promised confederation, but it turned out that the federal government which they established was too weak to unite them. The Constitutional Convention in 1787 consequently did that by writing a Constitution with a strong federal government capable of compelling the states to subject their sovereignty to national standards.

The present U.N. charter shares the weaknesses in the Articles of

Confederation. It seems unlikely that those weaknesses can be corrected in the immediate future. But even without such a strengthening, the members of the United Nations have still pledged to work on their own and, through the United Nations, to promote basic economic and political equality among all the countries in the world.

The attitudes and actions of the United States toward the fulfillment of the objectives of the United Nations have always been central to the future of that organization. After all, it was the United States which was the principal architect of the United Nations. President Roosevelt undertook the principal initiative. President Truman signed the U.N. charter in San Francisco in the presence of representatives of forty-eight other nations. In addition, the United States agreed and even insisted that the United Nations be located in the United States.

This prime sponsorship of the United Nations by the United States has been a blessing and a curse for that organization. It has been a blessing that the United Nations has the prestige which it might not have had if it had been located in Geneva or The Hague. But it has been a curse because the United Nations can be victimized by the vicissitudes of American politics. The power of the United Nations indeed has been sharply curtailed in carrying out its basic responsibilities by the intensity of the decades-long east-west struggles between the United States and the U.S.S.R. Many of the United Nations' aspirations have been overshadowed by the Kremlin–White House tensions.

One of the basic ways in which the fundamental purposes of the United Nations has been frustrated is the separation of economic rights from political rights. The right to economic equality was basic to the U.N. charter and to the Universal Declaration of Human Rights. It was not separated from political rights. All the world's nations agreed to this. But when it came to implementing economic and political rights, the United States and the U.S.S.R. divided. The U.S.S.R. declined to sign on to guaranteeing freedom of speech or the right to demand elections, while the United States was reluctant to guarantee economic rights, which arguably were to some extent inconsistent with the principles of capitalism.

This struggle between the superpowers in the early 1950s is, unfortunately, underdocumented. It was and still is an invisible but enormously important struggle, resulting in 1966 in the creation of two separate covenants—one for political rights and the other for economic and social rights. These two covenants were agreed to by the requisite number of countries and hence entered into force in 1976.

If this split had not occurred, the enforcement of human rights might well have developed in essentially different ways. The u.s.s.r. and the Communist bloc would have been under the pressure of international law to allow elections, grant freedom to the press, and release captive nations from their colonial status. Americans and other capitalistic nations would have been under pressure to give health insurance and economic equality to millions of workers.

That was a part of the original dream of the U.N. charter and the Universal Declaration of Human Rights. It was made inoperative in part by the division between east and west and by the obduracy of the divided nations.

The United States finally ratified the Covenant on Civil and Political Rights in 1994. But, as mentioned above, the United States has never ratified the International Covenant on Economic, Social, and Cultural Rights, although President Carter signed it in 1978. In 1999, 141 nations had become parties to the Covenant on Civil and Political Rights and 144 parties to the International Covenant on Economic, Social, and Cultural Rights.

It is significant that the Vienna declaration made no distinction between political and economic rights. The "schism" between the east and the west was over in 1993. But the harm had been done: the split between economic and political rights had entered into the world's psyche. For the west—or at least for the United States—the lasting impression had been given that although world law guaranteed political rights like religious liberty and freedom of the press, economic rights such as entitlement to a living wage and health insurance were in a second tier.

It is not entirely clear how important this division is. But it needs to be stressed that there is no historic, legal, or international reason for any distinction between political and economic rights. It should, however, also be noted that the economic demands made by the International Covenant on Economic, Social, and Cultural Rights need not be guaranteed by any nation immediately but only as resources become available. But this concession does not mean that economic rights are less important or urgent than are political rights.

The vast explosion in the past fifty years in judicial rulings and academic literature concerning human rights inevitably raises questions about the ultimate definition of what is a human right. The question has been around since the Biblical question "Am I my brother's keeper?" The plea for human rights is as old as the demand made by Moses of Pharaoh, "Let my people go."

The remarkable and unprecedented consensus on the definition of human rights came together in the words of the U.N. charter and the very specific guarantees of the Universal Declaration of Human Rights. Although those documents make no direct reference to a supreme being as the ultimate origin of the inalienable rights of every human being, the language of both documents reflects a deep agreement on fundamental values.

The preamble of the U.N. charter speaks of the "dignity and worth of the human person." It insists that all nations must practice "tolerance" and "live together in peace with one another as good neighbors."

These values are very familiar to all Americans and to some extent to the peoples who live in democracies. But in 1945 and even more today these values are universally accepted. They are totally consistent with the values spelled out in the U.N. charter. They are the philosophical basis for the rights set forth in Article 55 describing "higher standards of living, full employment and conditions of economic and social progress and development."

One has to wonder whether the success of the United Nations as an organization would have been assured if the moral and spiritual values underlying the charter had been spelled out more clearly. One also must ponder on a continuous basis whether the assertion of human moral values has in fact influenced individuals and nations. The assumption must be made that the violent civil wars have had some impact, because the adoption of the U.N. charter addresses the question concerning what ideals should be followed on a global basis.

The Universal Declaration of Human Rights also reflects a broader agreement on some of the fundamental questions about the nature and origin of human rights. This document repeats the basic concept that "all human beings are born free and equal in dignity and rights," proclaiming boldly that all peoples should "act toward one another in a spirit of brotherhood," and that all human beings "are endowed with reason and conscience."

Nations have not protested over the past fifty years the inclusion of that profoundly meaningful word "conscience." It seems clear that the Universal Declaration of Human Rights has been the most important legal document in the history of the world. Scores of constitutions and thousands of laws at the national level have been modeled after pronouncements of the Universal Declaration.

In 1992 the Scandinavian University Press issued a volume entitled *The Universal Declaration of Human Rights: A Commentary*. It was edited by Asbjorn Elde and Theresa Swinehart, academics in Scandinavia. The volume, which includes thirty essays on each of the articles in the Universal Declaration, reminds us of the immense range of rights in the declaration and their potential impact.

A reader of the book from Scandinavia as well as anyone who peruses the ocean of literature on the Universal Declaration has to wonder how a document of such moral strength with such compelling consensus underlying it could have been so neglected by so many nations over the past fifty years. Undeniably, the very existence of all these moral standards and proposed rights has had a salutary effect on the enjoyment of human rights throughout the world. Indeed, the moral decrees of the Universal Declaration have become to an astonishing extent the law of almost all the nations that have become independent countries after their decades as colonies of the capitalistic world.

It undoubtedly would be worthwhile to explore further the premises and presuppositions of the authors of the U.N. charter and the Universal Declaration of Human Rights. But the nations present at the Vienna conference in 1993, after an initial raising of the question of the universality of human rights, have seemed satisfied to accept the suppositions of the writers of these two documents.

While a discussion or a debate about the moral or metaphysical assumptions of the Charter of the United Nations and the Declaration of Human Rights might be useful, there appears to be a relatively settled feeling that the broad acceptance of the idea of human rights as universal is adequate to continue to make human rights enforceable. But some academics and observers, dismayed at the appalling failure of many nations to guarantee human rights, feel that a clarification of the morally compelling reasons for compliance might be a useful task in encouraging countries to comply. These advocates of human rights, however, bump up against the imponderable — and perhaps almost the insolvable — question of why some rulers shamelessly violate human rights and defy international law. Can laws, penalties, or threats deter rulers who are prone to such conduct?

Because answers to these questions are so difficult, it follows that we need more exploration of the psychological, moral, and historical reasons tyrants resist law. Often these tyrants are supported by the military under their command. The U.N. charter is strong on promoting and protecting human rights. But it is also emphatic in promoting new worldwide checks on military power. It is therefore a mistake to separate the human rights aspect of the charter from its demands for a new international order based not on military force but on the rule of law.

The United Nations, to be sure, has sought to control arms and curb military dictators. Again, the United States has an imperfect record. During the Cold War, for example, it formed its own military alliances, often supporting anti-Soviet dictators with bad records on human rights. Even after the plain need for such alliances ceased with the collapse of the u.s.s.r., the United States has continued to sell arms to countries without an adequate evaluation of their record on human rights. Indeed, the United States in the period following the Cold War has become the world's top supplier of weapons of war. To point out that these weapons do or can lead to a denial of human rights is to state the obvious.

The dream and the drive for international human rights for everyone sometimes seems impossible to implement. There are too many impediments. It almost seems that the underdeveloped capacity for democracy in former colonial nations has to be reversed before the idea of human rights can be said to be succeeding. It also appears at times that multinational corporations are imposing such heavy debts on Latin America and in Africa that goals such as universal education and the right to health care cannot be achieved in the foreseeable future.

All these problems were known to the groups at the World Conference on Human Rights in Vienna in 1993. Some individuals within these groups appeared in ways to be dreamers and idealists who tended to overlook the harsh realities of living in poor or recently liberated countries. But if that charge can be made by the enthusiasts for human rights in Vienna it can also be leveled at the forty-eight nations who were the original sponsors of the United Nations in San Francisco in 1948 and the countries that signed the U.N. Declaration of Human Rights in Paris on December 10, 1948.

It is probably true that all these persons were dreamers of a higher order than were the authors of the Magna Carta, the Declaration of Independence, or other proclamations created for the citizens of any nation. The authors of the U.N. charter and the Universal Declaration of Human Rights wrote for a whole world — a universe never before linked by an international law binding on all countries.

If there is discouragement at the results after fifty-five years of the existence of the United Nations, it could be countered that the progress and advancement in the area of human rights since 1945 has actually been more spectacular than might have been expected or even imagined.

Those achievements could have been more substantial, however, if the United States had not expressed a disinterest in economic rights. This disinterest is clear from the fact that it has never even attempted to ratify the Covenant on Economic Rights. If the United States had not distinguished between political and economic rights, the principal areas of contention in the world today might well have been the rights of poor people to food, shelter, and medical care.

The third world nations made constant appeals to these rights in repeated calls for the right to development. For forty years, underdeveloped nations had little official support in this area from the United States. The dismal statistics today on poverty, hunger, and illiteracy in sub-Saharan Africa and Asia might be radically different if the attitudes of the United States had been different.

It is apparent that the global struggle for human rights for the whole world that began in 1945, as world movements go, is very young. In addition, the population of the earth has practically doubled since 1945. Much of this increased population resides in newly liberated, desperately poor countries. Their number increases by almost 100 million persons each year. Even in more stable situations it would be difficult to bring them the economic and political rights proclaimed by world law that ought to be their heritage and their legacy.

But world law proudly and openly proclaims that the majestic rights declared to be the valid claims of every human being cannot be compromised away or denied or overlooked. The assertion of those rights is emphasized again and again by diplomats, jurists, human rights activists, and politicians.

Will those assertions be agreed to and implemented in the twenty-first century? That probably is the central question facing the human family. But its answer does not depend alone on the enforcement of the international law on human rights. Even if the enforcement were vigorous, law cannot prevail unless there is an acceptance of it at a deep level. The passions and violence that could arise in the twenty-first century are almost totally beyond prediction. Terrorists, new nations, millions of refugees, and violent hordes seizing land and property are all possible. These frightening prospects emphasize once again the need to reassure the poor and dispossessed of the truth that their internationally recognized human rights to economic equality are in the process of being fulfilled. If the 2 billion poor people of the world have no reasonable assurance that they will have a decent life for their families, they will do what desperate groups have often done in human history.

The virtual certainty of mass uprisings if the world does not move toward some type of economic justice for all is one more reason the economic rights promised by world law have such primordial importance.

The chapters that follow chronicle how the world in the past fifty years has moved to carry out the solemn promises made in 1945 and 1948, and in dozens of covenants on human rights made by the United Nations and its affiliated agencies. But the fulfillment of these rights will not bring stability and justice to the human family unless the startling disparity between the economic status of rich and poor nations is diminished.

2

THE U.N.

COMMISSION ON

HUMAN RIGHTS

The original dream of some of the founders of the United Nations was to place a mechanism to implement human rights in the charter itself. But this concept died somewhere in the process. The Charter of the United Nations did, however, specify that there should be a commission on human rights. This is the only agency specifically authorized by the charter.

It may be that in 1945 the actual authorization of any unit designed to activate human rights was unusual, even amazing. The concept of human rights has developed so unbelievably in the past fifty years that it is easy to forget how obscure, even threatening, that idea was in 1945. The colonial powers of the several European nations seemed to be intact. Even the United States would not liberate the Philippines until July 4, 1946. The idea that some 100 nations colonized by England, France, Spain, and other nations would be liberated in the name of self-determination and human rights was almost unthinkable to the framers of the charter of the United Nations. The authorities of those countries who signed the U.N. charter in San Francisco probably had little idea of the consequences of the establishment of the U.N. Commission on Human Rights.

Indeed, even the persons appointed to represent the original members of the U.N. Commission on Human Rights seemed unclear about whatever mission the United Nations intended to give them, or at least they did not follow that mission during the first twenty years of its existence. To be sure, it had helped draft the twin covenants concerning political and economic rights. But every attempt to have the commission receive petitions about violations was rejected until 1966.

This is difficult to condone or even explain because in all those years, the western bloc of nations had a comfortable majority in the United Nations. And there was certainly an abundance of complaints to be heard from the Soviet Union and the "captive nations" in Eastern Europe.

The United States resisted any attempt by the U.N. Commission on Human Rights to hear individual complaints. As early as 1947 petitions on behalf of the 13 million Americans of African ancestry came to the commission. It seemed clear that the United Kingdom, France, Belgium, Portugal, and the other colonial powers shared America's fears and prevented the commission from receiving petitions concerning the denial of rights clearly contained in the Universal Declaration of Human Rights.

The best explanation of the silence and inaction of the U.N. Commission on Human Rights is set forth by Philip Alston in *The United Nations and Human Rights: A Critical Appraisal,* published by Oxford University Press in 1992. Professor Alston, an Australian who is now the chairman of the U.N. Committee on Economic, Social, and Cultural Rights, pulls together virtually everything known about the evolution of the U.N. Commission on Human Rights. But even the magisterial account of Professor Alston leaves the reader with the question of why the major powers of the world could permit the United Nations' top agency for human rights to remain on the sidelines for so long.

In 1967, the U.N. Commission on Human Rights ended its hands-off policy and authorized action to identify specific human rights violations. An expansion of this policy adopted in 1972 brought some 200,000 to 300,000 petitions each year. Typically, they were generated by nongovernmental organizations and concerned some very difficult and notorious situations. An excellent book by Professor Howard Tolly, Jr., *The United Nations Commission on Human Rights* (Westview, 1987), records the struggles over the jurisdiction of the commission. Yet, despite the attempts of the commission to designate specific violations of human rights, its record has to be described as disappointing.

But the resistance of the U.N. Commission on Human Rights to becoming a judge and an arbitrator on human rights complaints demonstrates graphically that until very recently, nations have assumed that their sovereignty is inviolate and that no international concept like human rights can in any manner alter the way they conceive of their rights and privileges. Indeed the way countries cherish, magnify, and idolize their sovereignty is probably the major reason the idea of internationally recognized human rights is still widely perceived by politicians and diplomats as the enemy of their power.

The United States added significantly to this excessive nationalism in an announcement by Secretary of State John Foster Dulles in April 1953. He stated that the Eisenhower administration would not seek the ratification of the U.N. covenants on human rights. Dulles was motivated to take this position in order to defeat an amendment to the U.S. Constitution by Senator John Bricker, the Republican from Ohio, which would have amended the Constitution in order to prevent any U.N. covenant on human rights from becoming the "supreme law of the land" (as set forth in the Constitution) after being ratified by two-thirds of the Senate.

By this and other actions the Eisenhower administration reversed the momentum toward an enforceable international bill of rights that had taken hold of the world since the acceptance of the U.N. charter in 1945. It is arguable that the United States has never completely reversed the Eisenhower position on human rights. Virtually all treaties, for example, proposed by any administration for ratification are not self-executing and do not become the law of the land until they are passed by both houses and signed by the president.

But since its period of abdication (1946–1966), the U.N. Commission on Human Rights has become a responsive and important forum for the development of human rights. Provisions were eventually authorized for hearing complaints on a public or a confidential basis.

In fairness to the Commission on Human Rights, however, the world half expected it to be an international criminal commission, a court that could award damages and an agency that could bring the attention of the world to the hideous violations of human rights that were occurring almost everywhere. The U.N. commission was ill equipped to accomplish any of these laudable goals.

In his book, Professor Alston urges several reforms on the procedures followed by the Commission on Human Rights. They are all commendable, but the massive political will needed to transform the commission is not apparent. Crippled and inhibited by its own history and machinery, it seeks to accommodate the needs and aspirations of its members, whose number is now up to fifty-three. It is now overshadowed a bit by the visibility of the U.N. High Commissioner for Human Rights, a post finally established in 1995 after years of debate and postponement.

The U.N. Commission on Human Rights acted creatively in the 1980s by establishing a task force to focus on such issues as disappearances, systematic torture, and mass executions. Reports multiplied, presumably some dictators were deterred, and standards for government conduct were elevated.

Other initiatives by the commission are ongoing, and some are successful. They include seminars, advisory services, monitoring, fellowships in Geneva, and the dissemination of public information. Obviously the most important of these initiatives is education.

Every examination of the activities of the U.N. Commission on Human Rights over the past fifty years indicates that its activities have been spasmodic, uneven, and heavily reliant on the political events and currents in the world.

But it can also be argued that in the past few years, since the collapse of the Soviet empire, the U.N. Commission on Human Rights has taken on a new life. Suddenly everything looks different in the world of human rights. The commission has been freed of the necessity to denounce the U.S.S.R. on every occasion. Free also of the urgency to denounce apartheid in South Africa, the commission is aiming at new horizons.

The new energy and the renewed vision of the Commission on Human Rights were evident at the U.N. World Conference on Human Rights in Vienna in 1993. The ambassadors of the newly inaugurated Clinton administration were there as well as delegates from the newly liberated countries in central and eastern Europe. Indeed participants in the Vienna conference wanted to feel that the first fifty years of the intellectual human rights movement had been superseded by an entirely new era in the development of democracy and human equality.

One of the central reasons for the collapse of the Warsaw Pact and the surge in the development of human rights had been the amazing increase in the number of nongovernmental organizations devoted to human rights. The U.N. charter was among the first of all international organizations to accredit NGOs. Although the machinery to grant consultant status to NGOs is cumbersome and slow, the number of groups with consultant status is constantly growing. Their impact and their importance could and should be the basis for a definitive study. To be sure, some of the NGOs lobby for causes that are nationalist, even extremist in some cases, but the overall work and thrust of NGOs is the advancement of human rights and democracy. These groups are active in Geneva and have a significant impact on the deliberations and the votes of the U.N. Commission on Human Rights.

The Commission on Human Rights was the first world organization devoted to human rights. It has been replicated in part by the European Court on Human Rights in Strasbourg and the Inter-American Commission and Court in Costa Rica. But the commission has no juridical powers, nor can it fine or penalize nations—except in the realm of public opinion.

The new changes and improvements in the procedures of the U.N. Commission on Human Rights are self-evident. But like other sprawling entities within the structure of the United Nations, it is not easily susceptible to change. It does not have a powerful executive in charge, and its mission and mandate are not as precise as they could be. Yet, the amazing fact remains that an agency which had virtually abdicated its principal duties for the first twenty years of its existence is now an articulate advocate for the defense and enhancement of economic and political rights. More poor nations will be seeking to become members of the U.N. commission, and more private organizations will be asking to have the commission direct its attention to the rights of the disabled, the indigenous, children, and all groups not receiving those rights which international law and the Vienna convention have promised them.

No one can accurately predict what newly perceived rights will gain the attention of the world. In the United States, for example, the newly decreed rights of the disabled as guaranteed in the Americans with Disabilities Act have, ideally in large part, been accepted. The rights of all persons including children to be free from sexual harassment has been recognized. These rights have suddenly attained a status close to the rights of the blind or of visually impaired persons, which were universally recognized decades ago.

Because of the unpredictability of how certain rights suddenly flower, it may well be that the U.N. Commission on Human Rights has achieved far more than is visible at the moment. The commission began its work for the disappeared and the tortured at a time when the world was unaware of or not sensitive to these groups of victims. In thousands of reports and press releases the commission made known its work, and scores of rapporteurs sensitized millions of people to the evils of unjust dictators or governments that were deaf and blind to violations of human rights.

The Vienna conference appears to have finally created the momentum and international will to establish the office of the U.N. High Commissioner on Human Rights. This long-pending institution, recommended by virtually every nation including the United States, was implemented in the mid-1990s. How it coordinates with other U.N. agencies is not clear. The articulate presence of Mary Robinson, the former president of Ireland, as the high commissioner gives prominence to the importance of human rights, but her statements have no binding juridical power. Some human rights specialists hope or dream that the high commissioner could be the "czar" of human rights. But the sprawling and frequently changing international human rights scene is not amenable to neat juridical boundaries.

The U.N. Commission on Human Rights is less well known than other U.N. agencies, like the World Health Organization, UNESCO, UNICEF, and the Food and Agricultural Organization. The missions of these groups are tangible and concrete. In contrast, the act of voting on the abuse of human rights is unpleasant, controversial, and unattractive to most audiences. In judging the record of the commission, moreover, it must be noted that the world's attitude toward the abuse of human rights has recently become much more sensitive to reports on such abuses. Some of that sensitivity is due to reporting and education and the relentless energy of the commission itself. It has been in the forefront of the human rights movement. In the coming decades, as the world becomes more aware of the preciousness of human rights, the role of U.N. Commission on Human Rights may expand its decrees and its findings have an importance in public opinion that is hard to even imagine.

3

ECONOMIC

EQUALITY

FOR ALL

The 1945 Charter of the United Nations, the Universal Declaration of Human Rights, and the International Covenant on Economic, Social, and Cultural Rights (CESCR) contain the astonishing dream and declaration that everyone in the world should have basic equality and economic rights. That dream has been endemic in human history. But it had never before been acclaimed in a document promulgated to be accepted by every nation on earth.

The brutality of World War II and the inhumanity of the treatment inflicted by the colonial powers on the nations they occupied combined at the end of the war to prompt the world community to compose and promulgate the CESCR. It is an amazing document. Is it naive? Is it a Socialist concoction? Is it a manifestation of guilt over the conquest and occupation of over 100 nations by the European colonial powers?

The document on economic rights, now ratified by 150 nations (but not the United States), is amazing. It guarantees the right to work, the right to join unions, and a qualified right to strike. Fair wages are assumed, and periodic holidays with pay are mandatory. Mothers are guaranteed "special protection" before and after childbirth including "paid leave." Signatories to the treaty are required to guarantee "adequate food, clothing and housing." Even more demanding is the requirement that governments offer a "continuous improvement of living conditions."

To be sure, the covenant requires governments to fulfill their obligations only in ways which are consistent with the "maximum of a nation's available resources." But every government is urged—even commanded—to adopt "legislative measures" which carry out the objectives of the CESCR. It is astonishing to see how the more than 150 signatories of the CESCR, put in force only in 1976, have undertaken responsibility for the compelling duties imposed on them by international law and are presumably seeking to carry out the promises they made to the world and to their own citizens.

Some observers—especially in the United States—have treated the CESCR with scorn and derision. Some anti-Communist hardliners suggested that the dreams and demands of the CESCR are Socialist manifestos. The implication is that the attainment of economic equality, however desirable, imposes no duty on governments to bring it about.

The thrust of the economic covenant is directly the opposite. It clearly requires the governments which ratify the CESCR to live up to their solemn obligations. Apparently, the framers of the CESCR do not approve of unregulated capitalism and are very serious and determined to compel governments to redistribute a nation's resources in ways that maximize the potential for real economic equality.

One of the most difficult problems in assessing the intended effect of the CESCR is the speed of compliance expected of poor nations. The treaty makes it clear that it does not expect the impossible of nations with limited resources. Similarly, it does not demand that governments require banks or private companies to challenge their traditional ways of operation. The treaty is hortatory, not mandatory.

The vast, almost impossible task of supervising compliance with the CESCR has been given to the Committee on Economic, Social, and Cultural Rights. Established in 1979, the committee regularly receives reports from the signatory nations. Many countries try to report as completely as possible. But the problem of compliance depends upon the basic philosophy of the nations' rulers in charge of the economy. Does a poor agricultural country seek to attract foreign corporations in order to manufacture consumer goods and thereby generate revenue for the government? Or does that nation seek to capitalize farming so that crops for export are generated? The central question, of course, is whether the committee has a right to direct and advise nations to proceed in specific ways in order to maximize their compliance with the objectives that they promised to uphold when they signed the CESCR.

Philip J. Alston is now the chairman of the U.N. Committee on Economic Rights. His essay of thirty-five pages contained in the volume *The United Nations and Human Rights* is one of the best descriptions of the committee, which has awesome but also amorphous responsibilities.

A reading of all the reports of the committee that supervises the implementation of the Covenant on Economic Rights conveys the overwhelming impression that a relatively small committee has the almost unmanageable task of assisting nations as they seek to fulfill the promises they made when they ratified the treaty, which requires them to provide their citizens with the basic rights of a modern welfare state. The members of the committee do not have the expertise or mandate to change economic policies of a small nation like El Salvador. If the committee feels or even knows with some degree of certainty that El Salvador has adopted a policy which enriches the bankers but impoverishes the farmers, the most that it can do is offer recommendations to the authorities in the responding nation assessing the potential or future impact of the policy issue on the overall objectives of the CESCR.

It may be that the Committee on Economic, Social, and Cultural Rights will become bolder in its objectives in the same way that the U.N. Commission on Human Rights developed. It is clear to everyone associated with the U.N. agencies that seek the implementation of human rights that additional cooperation and collaboration among all the agencies is essential. Nations are now required to fill out extensive forms in order to comply with the demands of several U.N. bodies. There is clearly overlap among these units. The Committee on Economic, Social, and Cultural Rights, one of the youngest of all U.N. bodies, regularly asks for information already furnished by countries to other U.N. bodies. In addition, it is not clear how the committee will treat copious statistics on the economy, the labor force, and the literacy rate of a particular country.

If the task is so vast and so complicated, the question arises about the usefulness of the Committee on Economic, Social, and Cultural Rights. The world struggled over that question from 1945 to 1966, when the two treaties on political and economic rights were finally agreed to by the United Nations. That debate continued during the ten years before the covenants in 1976 entered into force with the required number of ratifications.

In the years to come, it will almost certainly be the less developed nations that will seek to obtain rulings from the Committee on Economic, Social, and Cultural Rights that will be favorable to the economy of these nations. The forty years of struggle waged by the underdeveloped nations for the vindication and fulfillment of the right to development, then, will be reenacted in that committee.

The expandable concepts in the CESCR can suggest that the rich nations have a duty to share their resources with poorer nations. In other words, the logic would go, all nations are fellow signatories in a noble enterprise to give basic economic equality to every person. As a result, nations with more resources have some duty to assist the less endowed nations that have promised to make the objectives of economic equality attainable.

This concept is to some extent implicit in the philosophy and structure of the World Trade Organization. That unit seeks to maximize and equalize trade among all nations. The most powerful nations have some obligation of sharing their expertise with all countries, rich and poor. At least indirectly, the ultimate purpose of the World Trade Organization is the same as that of the CESCR — the elevation of the tragic living standards of the 6 billion people in the global village.

In a certain sense, the Covenant on Economic, Social, and Cultural Rights is the least successful of all of the endeavors of the United Nations. But paradoxically it may be the most meaningful and potentially successful of all of the aspirations of the United Nations. The goals of the CESCR are what humanity needs most. Political rights such as freedom of the press and religion are important, but over 3 billion people are in desperate need of food, work, medicine, and education.

For the first time in the history of the world a global body has responded to the cry for basic economic equality. Some 80 percent of the world's population have ratified that treaty and have solemnly promised to work for the objectives of a covenant that is truly sweeping in its aspirations and demands.

The fact that the United States remains outside that global effort can only be detrimental to the reputation of the United States and to the potential of the U.N. committee that supervises the implementation of the CESCR.

Fifty or one hundred years from now, will the demands of the Covenant on Economic, Social, and Cultural Rights be routinely accepted by lawmakers as binding obligations under international law? Will the rights to food, medicine, and education be as accepted as the duty of every nation to punish pirates and ban slavery? That is the hope of the visionaries who came together to write the CESCR. The vision of that group was restated and re-ratified in the final declaration of the World Conference on Human Rights held in Vienna in 1993.

The same nations that agreed to accept the CESCR in 1966 and 1976 once again proclaimed their promise to work for economic equality. When Vienna is added to previous declarations, it seems safe to say that the promises and commitments of the economic covenant are customary international law.

A treaty is a contract between nations. In addition, a treaty is a promise by each signatory that it will faithfully carry out the objectives of the covenant.

For centuries the human race has aspired to eliminate hunger and famine and to control deadly diseases. For the first time in the history of the world those objectives have become attainable.

The Covenant on Economic, Social, and Cultural Rights is a noble expression of the age-old dream — along with the basic steps which nations must follow — to eliminate hunger and conquer disease.

The dream is noble. Its attainment will depend upon the level of moral energy the world's leaders will extend to it. Participation of the United States through ratification of the CESCR would be enormously beneficial. The absence of the United States can only be foreboding.

4

THE

UNITED NATIONS

AND POLITICAL

AND CIVIL RIGHTS

If you want to see the dimensions of the global earthquake contemplated by the U.N. International Covenant on Civil and Political Rights (ICCPR), imagine a world of 185 nations that adhere to and follow the directives of the same document on civil and political rights now ratified by these countries.

The legislative history of the adoption of the Covenant on Civil and Political Rights has not been researched. The covenant is the result of the deep grief and guilt of the victims of World War II, as well as the anxieties of the colonial powers as they saw their empires dissolve in the 1950s and 1960s. Article 1 reflects that anxiety by proclaiming that "all peoples have the right of self-determination."

The Covenant on Civil and Political Rights also recognizes that, despite the separation of the covenants on political and economic rights, they are linked and inseparable.

If most nations had begun to enact the prescriptions set out in the ICCPR on March 23, 1976, the date the covenant had entered into force, the world situation today would be very different. First of all, there would be elections. Article 25 makes it clear that there must be universal and equal suffrage, "genuine and periodic elections" conducted by "secret ballot." There would also be a universal ban on all discrimination on "any grounds such as race, color, sex, language, religion, political or other opinion, national or social origin, property, birth or other status." Clearly, this covenant outlaws any inherited social system, such as in India with its caste system.

It is significant that the outline which was finalized in 1966 did not ban discrimination based on age, physical or mental disability, or sexual orientation. One likes to think that the concept of equal protection which is at the core of the ICCPR has developed and expanded in the view and the conscience of the human race.

Careful analysis of the words of the Covenant on Political Rights is especially important because the United States ratified the ICCPR on June 8, 1992, and the covenant entered into force in the United States on September 8, 1992. Even though the Senate's reservations, understandings, and declarations are lamentable, the fact that the United States has finally ratified the visions of the ICCPR is surely one of the most significant events in the story of the international human rights revolution, which began in 1945 with the adoption of the Charter of the United Nations.

The ICCPR, like the Universal Declaration of Human Rights, asserts forcefully in Article 23 that the "family is the natural and fundamental unit of society and is entitled to protection by society and the state." No marriage, furthermore, "shall be entered into without the free and full consent of the intending spouses."

But the covenant does not include the directive in Article 26(3) of the Universal Declaration of Human Rights that "parents have a prior right to choose the kind of education that shall be given to their children." This clause was inserted on behalf of Catholic parents in Europe, Muslims in Islamic countries, and minorities everywhere in order to protest "l'ecole unique," which tended to be the rule in France and elsewhere prior to the onset of the twentieth century.

For some years the advocates of pluralism in elementary and secondary education in the United States have employed Article 26 as a part of their argument. To date it has not been successful. But the differences between the view of the 150 nations that have ratified the political covenant and the prevailing view in the United States on aid to church-related schools of less than collegiate rank demonstrate dramatically the need for (or the fear of) a world standard that in some cases could be different from the norm established by legislative or judicial measures in the United States.

A graphic example of such a disparity can be imagined on the issue of abortion. The views on abortion reached by the majority of nations that subscribe to the Covenant on Civil and Political Rights could well be different from the arrangements set forth in 1973 in *Roe v. Wade.*

The majority of countries could reach the conclusion that women should not be allowed to have an abortion except for serious medical reasons in the first three or four months of pregnancy. Theoretically the United States should be prepared to accept and adopt the collective decision of the vast majority of countries. Such a decision by most nations would be termed "customary international law." Obviously there would be dissenters in the United States and elsewhere. Those individuals would be protected by the reservations made by the U.S. Senate in its ratification of the ICCPR.

But the issue is broad, complicated, and difficult. Are nations expected to yield some part of their sovereignty when they ratify an international treaty on human rights? On some sensitive point, are they required to yield their view because the world has reached a different conclusion?

That is the issue that will not go away. But the ICCPR tends to finesse that problem. It sets out those legal and moral truths on which there appears to be a consensus around the world. But it is not always clear whether the Covenant on Civil and Political Rights is expressing a new consensus or whether some nations or some nongovernmental organizations have persuaded U.N. officials to adopt a policy that does not yet constitute a world consensus.

That may be the case in the covenant's approach to the death penalty. The document in Article 6 does not ban capital punishment but it certainly discourages it. The document states firmly that "nothing in this article shall be invoked to delay or prevent the abolition of capital punishment." The covenant stipulates that the death penalty can be rendered only by a competent court pursuant to a clear pre-existing law; it cannot be imposed for crimes "committed by persons below 18 years of age and shall not be carried out on pregnant women."

On some issues, the ICCPR appears to be more progressive than American public opinion or even world opinion. Echoing the U.N. document of 1955 entitled "Standard Minimum Rules for the Treatment of Prisoners," the Covenant on Civil and Political Rights (Article 10) asserts very forcefully that the "penitentiary system shall comprise treatment of prisoners the essential aim of which shall be their reformation and social rehabilitation." That philosophy appears to be really at odds with the dominant approach of federal and most state officials in the past several years in the United States; their aim is to penalize and punish prisoners rather than to reform or rehabilitate them.

The Covenant on Civil and Political Rights is overall very modern and progressive in its orientation. It includes the presumption of innocence, the right not to testify against one's self, the right to counsel of one's own choosing, and the right to compensation by those who have been victims of a miscarriage of justice.

Privileges associated with the right to speak, to practice religion, and to hold opinions without interference are strongly protected under the ICCPR. Indeed, the nations which have publicly pledged their allegiance to the treaty have had few quarrels with its provisions.

The framers of the Covenant on Civil and Political Rights propose two methods of enforcement: the optional protocol, and the U.N. Committee on Human Rights.

A total of 95 nations have agreed to the optional protocol. This gives the citizens of these nations the right to file a protest against their own government. The petitioners must first exhaust their local remedies, obtain supporting documentation, and expect a long process before any adjudication is finalized. Theoretically the concept of the optional protocol is attractive. It is contrary to the outdated policy that no subject can sue the king. A world tribunal is now in place under which any person can have a day in court and prevail against any local government official in any faraway land.

The plan sounds wonderful. It has great potential. A century from now it might be a routine way for citizens with legitimate complaints to obtain a just result — or at least they could be heard.

The fact that the millions of citizens in Germany during World War II had no place to complain haunts the west. How could this have happened? On a continent with a highly developed court system, the inhabitants of a large and sophisticated nation had no access to world public opinion or to tribunals anywhere! The mechanism of the optional protocol was designed to prevent the impotence imposed on German citizens and all the millions of other persons victimized by dictators who had immunized themselves by banning the press and closing domestic courts to all complaining prospective plaintiffs.

The entity designed by the Covenant on Civil and Political Rights to hear the petitions alleging violation of the rights protected under the covenant is the U.N. Committee on Human Rights. Unfortunately, the work of this group is little known. Its sessions are not covered by the press, and its responses and reports to the signatory countries receive little publicity.

Currently, seven human rights treaties are in effect, and the states or nations that have ratified them have agreed to submit periodic reports on their compliance. It is encouraging to think that each of these monitoring units is a sleeping giant and that its reports will soon, ideally, become items of worldwide discussion. After all, these supervisory entities evaluate the performance of countries in explosive topics like the rights of women, the ways children are protected, the extent of racial discrimination, and the global ban on torture. Unfortunately, little is known about the first submission by the United States to the U.N. Committee on Human Rights after the U.S. Senate ratified the Covenant on Civil and Political Rights.

The committee that monitors compliance with the ICCPR is made up of members chosen by individual countries because of their competence in the field of human rights. Since the ratification of this covenant by the U.S. Senate, the United States for the first time has a representative on the committee that monitors the ICCPR. He is Professor Thomas Buergenthal, a survivor of the Holocaust, a human rights expert, and a former member of the Inter-American Commission on Human Rights, which convenes in Costa Rica.

The first report submitted by the United States pursuant to its duties under the Covenant on Civil and Political Rights was carefully crafted by the State Department and affiliated agencies. It is a 250-page document, filed in July 1994, that acknowledges America's problems but offers a candid and honest appraisal of how the United States is striving to cope with its new responsibilities. Drafted by John Shattuck, assistant secretary of human rights in the Clinton administration, the report openly admits to the "bitter legacy of slavery" but seeks to vindicate the efforts of the United States to eliminate segregation and prevent discrimination. The report does concede, nonetheless, that while 11.6 percent of the white population is living below the poverty line, 33.3 percent of African Americans and 29.3 percent of Hispanics fall below the poverty level.

The Shattuck report is possibly the most comprehensive and candid document on the state of civil rights and civil liberties ever to have originated from a high level of the American government. But it refrained from rejecting views issued by the Supreme Court and the executive branch. It is, as a result, hedged and cautious in some of its conclusions.

Even though the human rights community has the highest regard for John Shattuck, who was active in the American Civil Liberties Union and in Amnesty International prior to his appointment, human rights activists in the United States before and after the Shattuck report continue to be critical. In a joint statement by Human Rights Watch and the ACLU it was pointed out that the ICCPR mandates that each signatory to the covenant provide an effective remedy for violations of covenant rights and that these remedies be enforced. In the view of Human Rights Watch and the ACLU, the United States has not corrected those conditions in the area of education, housing, and race relations which are not in compliance with the demands of the ICCPR.

The NGOs are also critical of the Shattuck report. Native American rights groups complain that they are still plagued by abuse and discrimination. Amnesty International, women's groups, labor unions, and the advocates of children's rights have also entered statements to the effect that governments in the United States have not complied with the new obligations it assumed when it ratified the International Covenant on Civil and Political Rights.

In reaction to America's first submission on its compliance with the ICCPR, the comments by the U.N. Commission on Human Rights were also blunt and, on some points, harsh. Although the actual response of the commission was routine (every country receives a standard reply), in this case the response expressed the regret that America's first submissions contained too "few references to the implementation of covenant rights at the state level." The commission, in rebuking the United States for the extent of its declared "reservations, declarations and understandings," added, almost brutally, that it believed "the United States has accepted what is already the law of the United States." This is precisely what critics in the United States agree on. The White House, first of all, constructed a treaty that is *not* self-executing, which means that its promises are not effectively the law of the land unless they have been passed by both houses of Congress and have been signed by the president. In addition, the reservations, understandings, and declarations make it clear that despite America's acceptance of the covenant, its final obligations do not go beyond what American courts have already held to be the meaning of civil and political rights. The U.N. Commission on Human Rights is therefore correct when it points out that the United States, despite the ratification and its report on compliance, has not agreed to do anything not already required by U.S. law.

The U.N. commission has had other sharp criticisms of the United States. It has lamented "the large number of persons killed or wounded or subjected to ill treatment by members of the police force" and the "easy availability of firearms to the public." It has criticized laws that have criminalized "sexual relations between adult consenting partners." It also has openly urged the adoption of "affirmative action" and flatly stated that in connection with disputes over affirmative action for minorities and women the "obligation to provide covenant's rights in fact as well as law be borne in mind." The commission concluded its long series of recommendations by urging greater public awareness of the provisions of the covenant, adding that the legal profession should be particularly aware of the guarantees of the covenant "in order to insure their effective application."

The encounter between the United States and the U.N. Commission on Human Rights is almost unique in the evolving history of international human rights. The United States has not ratified the Convention on the Elimination of All Forms of Discrimination Against Women or the Convention on the Rights of the Child, and it has not agreed to the Inter-American Convention on Human Rights, which applies exclusively to the area of Latin America. Consequently, it cannot be criticized by the commission or court in Costa Rica.

When federal officials and the U.S. Senate address the question of ratifying these treaties, they will remember that the United States received a strong rebuke when it filed its first submission on its compliance with the Covenant on Civil and Political Rights.

All the nations that have ratified the ICCPR are expected to report periodically — usually every five to eight years. When the United States is expected to report again, officials will obviously want to rebut some of the charges of the NGOs and, more important, the blunt assessments in the rebuke by the monitors of the Covenant on Civil and Political Rights.

The process is, lamentably, somewhat political. The State Department does not want to publicize the dialogue between it and a generally unknown unit in Geneva which does not have the funds or the desire to make known its findings. In addition, there are no credible reasons the White House or the State Department desires to limit the obligations of the United States to meet only those requirements that are specifically spelled out in federal or state laws or regulations. Moreover, all kinds of political reasons exist for restricting legal requirements on human rights to national and not international obligations.

In addition, the whole process is severely flawed in that every administration will insist that no treaty be self-executing. Consequently, the United States can be criticized by nations abroad because of its apparently adamant refusal to accept any obligations from an international entity which are not already binding on the United States.

Some have suggested that the Constitution should be amended to permit the president to enter into treaties with foreign nations, with only a majority vote required by the Senate. But such a proposal would probably be dead on arrival even though a two-thirds vote is very difficult to obtain.

It is difficult to explain to foreign observers of the American political processes why the United States, the powerful architect and author of the United Nations, is now such a reluctant partner. An oversimplified explanation is the isolationist attitude of Senator Jesse Helms, the Republican chairman of the Senate Foreign Relations Committee. But America's reluctance to enter into treaties and to be judged by commissions and tribunals is deep-seated among Americans and, indeed, may be growing.

The experience the United States has had in ratifying the Covenant on Civil and Political Rights is not likely to induce future administrations to enter into the thicket of international politics and human rights. The political disincentives make active participation by the NGOs indispensable if the United States is, in turn, to participate actively in the development of a world in which the enforcement of internationally recognized human rights is the essential basis of international comity and peace.

Amnesty International, founded in 1961 and now perceived as one of the strongest of the founders of the international human rights movement, has deemed that the "mobilization of shame" is one of its principal purposes. This captivating phrase assumes that nations, like individuals, experience "shame" when its conduct is perceived to be degrading, unworthy, humiliating, in essence, shameful. The feeling of "shame" which citizens have for the conduct of their country can, Amnesty assumes, be "mobilized."

It is difficult to isolate and gather hard empirical evidence of why or how nations become "ashamed" of their conduct. But it has been done—and perhaps will be done more and more frequently. Nations like South Africa, Argentina, and Brazil have created truth and reconciliation commissions. These groups seek to publish all the awful truths about what their governments have done and thereby produce shame and guilt, but also reconciliation. Little is known about the subtle and serious ways by which individuals and nations discover their guilt and make peace by accepting it. But we do know there is "shame" and that its presence can prompt citizens and governments to change their attitudes.

The remedies of the optional protocol and the reporting system set up by the Covenant on Civil and Political Rights were designed to reveal wrongdoing and thereby induce governments to regret their misconduct and feel ashamed.

The process inaugurated by the U.N. Civil Rights Committee is not legal or juridical. It seeks to persuade governments to confess in public that they have made mistakes and violated the law in their failure to live up to the promises they made when they ratified the Covenant on Civil and Political Rights. The response of the U.N. Commission on Human Rights to a nation's report can be a teachable moment for many nations. Criticism of its human rights record has to be a negative event for a small nation seeking to create a reputation as a law-abiding country which could be a valuable ally in banking or business to a wealthier nation.

Private agencies of all kinds collect information about human rights in every country seeking to attract business or investment. If this information can be supplemented by reports from the U.N. Commission on

Human Rights, a nation's reputation as a safe and favorable place can be strengthened. On the other hand, if the commission has disseminated one or more negative reports, a nation can be damaged.

Why should the United States be concerned with this process, which might have a negative impact on struggling nations in Africa or Asia but cannot have an adverse impact on America? The answer to this question is both moral and jurisprudential. The United States in ratifying the U.N. Covenant on Civil and Political Rights made a statement. It declared that it was making solemn promises that it intended to keep. It was in essence entering into a contract with the United Nations and its agencies. The decision to ratify a treaty is not unlike a new state joining the United States. Some years ago Alaska and Hawaii became states; they undertook all the obligations of a state that subscribes to federalism, with all the duties this places on states.

Articles 55 and 56 of the U.N. charter stipulate that nations who join the United Nations not merely promise but "pledge" that they will carry out their duties as members of the United States. The same understanding carries over when a nation ratifies a treaty. That country "pledges" to fulfill its new obligations.

That is what the United States did when it ratified the Covenant on Civil and Political Rights. Even the unfortunate reservations do not cancel out the fact that the White House and the Congress solemnly undertook obligations under international law. Even though there may not be any precise procedures to force compliance, the United States nonetheless made solemn promises to do certain things which otherwise it would not have done. An old and venerated adage in international law is *pacta sunt servanda* — promises must be kept.

The first exchange between the United States and the U.N. Commission on Human Rights did not end in glory for the United States. But the dialogue or debate in which the two entities engaged was the first major exchange the United States, along with 185 other members, was required to have with the commission. A growing body of literature concerns how nations view human rights vis-à-vis the worldview advanced by U.N. officials.

In a generation or two we will know which nations faithfully seek to comply with their obligations under the Covenant on Civil and Political

Rights and which nations evade or avoid their obligations. We will also know which nations have listened to the importunate views of NGOs and have complied with international law.

The United States has many lessons to learn and a long way to go. But at least it has fulfilled its obligations to report. Perhaps it will in the future make available to American citizens their rights under the optional protocol. It may be that eventually the United States will decide that it should listen to and heed the international voice of those who plead and argue for the millions of citizens who are entitled by world law to the rights guaranteed them by the Covenant on Civil and Political Rights.

If America listens to the voice and conscience of other nations, it will be heeding the words in the Declaration of Independence — that we should have "a decent respect for the opinions of mankind."

5

WOMEN'S
WORLDWIDE
PLEA FOR
EQUALITY

On December 18, 1979, the U.N. General Assembly adopted the Convention on the Elimination of All Forms of Discrimination Against Women (also known as the Covenant on Women's Rights or CEDAW). It was clearly a historic occasion. The acceptance of CEDAW may have been one of the most important decisions in world history.

President Carter signed the CEDAW on July 18, 1980, and submitted it to the Senate for ratification. It was in all probability the support and encouragement of the Carter administration that brought about the adoption of the covenant in the United Nations. The treaty entered into force on September 3, 1981.

Subsequently, neither the Reagan nor the Bush administration took any action on the CEDAW. No Senate action occurred until 1993, when sixty-eight senators asked President Clinton to take the steps necessary for ratification. In October 1994, the Senate Foreign Relations Committee voted 13–4 in favor of sending the covenant to the full Senate. But no action has been taken by the Senate since that time.

I testified at the hearings in the Senate in 1994 on behalf of the American Bar Association, which in the 1980s had endorsed the CEDAW. The committee seemed receptive. The witnesses against the covenant seemed to reflect an attitude of isolationism and a deep fear of any additional change in the status of women.

The fears of the opponents of the CEDAW have been met by the four reservations, four understandings, and two declarations offered by the State Department on behalf of the Clinton administration. These ten qualifications have made it clear that the United States will not make any concessions with regard to privacy "except as mandated by the Constitution and laws of the United States." In addition, the United States has refused to accept any obligations under the CEDAW to assign women to military positions which "may require engagement in direct conflict." The United States also has rejected any obligation to use the concept of "comparable worth" in connection with conditions for working women, and to require paid maternity leave. Nor has the United States agreed to give on a cost-free basis health care services related to family planning and pregnancy.

Even though it could be argued that the exceptions carved out by the Clinton administration nullify some of the key provisions of the CEDAW, support for the convention continues to be strong. That support was strengthened after the Equal Rights Amendment obtained the ratification of only thirty-five of the thirty-eight states required. The point was made repeatedly by advocates of women's rights that there must be some form of constitutional protection for the rights of women.

The refusal of the Senate to ratify the CEDAW derives from a wide variety of prejudices, fears, and misconceptions. The concepts set forth in that covenant are not radical or revolutionary. They represent the profound, worldwide awakening by women concerning what has been done to them for centuries. One of the main thrusts of the covenant, which remains in the mainstream of feminist aspirations, is the elimination of all customs and practices originating from the assumption that women are inferior or from stereotyped roles for women. It refers repeatedly to the exclusion of women from participation in government and the vast under-estimation of their contributions. The covenant also asserts, however, that a "change in the traditional role of men as well as the role of women in society and in the family is needed to achieve full equality between men and women."

The overall purpose of the CEDAW is to confer on women worldwide the freedom from discrimination, education, employment, and wages which is guaranteed by federal and state statutes in the United States. It is ambivalent on the need for protective legislation designed to shield women from specific harm that might come to them. But the CEDAW is very clear on the need for affirmative action, which will allow women to enter all those numerous areas of life from which they have been excluded almost from time immemorial.

Article 4 provides as follows:

Adoption . . . of temporary special measures aimed at accelerating de facto equality between men and women shall not be considered discrimination as defined in the present convention, but shall in no way entail as a consequence the maintenance of unequal or separate standards. These measures shall be discontinued when the objectives of equality of opportunity and treatment have been achieved.

This provision echoes a similar measure in the International Convention on the Elimination of Racial Discrimination. That measure entered into force on January 4, 1969, and has been ratified with reservations by the U.S. Senate.

Article 1, 4 of the CERD reads as follows:

Special measures taken for the sole purpose of securing adequate advancement of certain racial or ethnic groups or individuals requiring such protection as may be necessary in order to insure such groups or individuals equal enjoyment or exercise of human rights as fundamental freedoms shall not be deemed racial discrimination.

The only caveat is that "such measures do not as a consequence lead to the maintenance of separate rights for different racial groups." Such measures "shall not be continued after the objectives for which they were taken have been achieved."

These similar provisions in the CEDAW and CERD were conceived to address the situation where, as in India, a caste system had developed which excluded the untouchables from a wide variety of occupations. To correct this situation, "special measures" may be enacted with the proviso that they be eliminated as soon as they are no longer necessary.

In the heated debate over affirmative action as understood in the United States, it should be pointed out that the categories for minorities and women established by prejudice and stereotypes can be phased out with official action or "special measures" to change a pattern or conduct which the government has in essence created or permitted.

Women in America were victimized by a stereotype when a court in Illinois in the late 1800s ruled that women had no right to go to law school or enter the legal profession. The authors of the CEDAW remembered this and the fact that women could not even vote in the United States until 1920 and that some professions are still, at least de facto, closed to women.

The CERD synthesized the legitimate grievances of women worldwide and created a committee of twenty-three members which evaluates the periodic reports of the nations which have promised to implement the directives of the covenant in their own nations.

The accumulated rulings of the U.N. Committee on CEDAW constitute an ever more impressive body of legal judgment on the ways by which governments deny the rights of women. Indeed, in the near future books will bring together the accumulated wisdom of the committee and, even more important, the impact of those judgments on the way the governments of the world treat women.

There has been an astonishing awakening in the past few years to the abuse and degradation imposed on women by men and by many societies. The incidence of spousal abuse has become known as never before. News about the mistreatment of women has exploded around the world. Sophisticated ways of inhibiting or prohibiting the advancement of women have been revealed. The "glass ceiling" is only one of the less subtle ways of reinforcing a stereotype of women as limited in their abilities.

If the U.S. Senate were to ratify the CEDAW, the White House and the State Department would be required to submit periodic reports on America's compliance with the Covenant on Women's Rights. The responses of the committee on America's compliance with the CEDAW would be seen and heard by the world. The exchange between the United States and the U.N. Committee on the Rights of Women would be covered by the press. The United States would finally be required to justify American society's conduct toward women or apologize for its failure to live up to the mandates of the CEDAW.

But the United States is not the only nation in the world that is resisting a change in the status of women. On June 13, 1999, citizens of Switzerland rejected a proposal by a vote of 61–39 that would have granted fourteen weeks of maternity leave at 80 percent of a woman's salary. This sudden action kept Switzerland out of line with European standards. The vote also defied the Constitution of Switzerland, in which the concept of maternity leave was introduced in 1945. It reinforced the image of Switzerland as a chauvinistic stronghold where women did not win the right to vote until 1971. The voters also rejected the parliament of Switzerland — headed by its first female president, Ruth Dreifuss — which in 1998 had agreed on the proposed maternity benefit at a cost of some $330 million per year.

If Switzerland, a highly advanced nation, can reject a relatively basic program for women granting maternity benefits, what can be expected of some less sophisticated nations?

The unanticipated result in Switzerland undoubtedly reveals the dark fears which many men and some women have that the concept of women's rights is being pressed too aggressively and that this development is somehow weakening marriage and the family.

The machinery to carry out the CEDAW is underfunded, inadequately administered, and too feeble to meet the desperate needs women have for legal guidance and assistance. There is no optional protocol. This means that women cannot apply directly to the U.N. committee supervising their legal rights. Nor is there any legal way by which the U.N. Committee on CEDAW can force a nation to comply with its rulings. Sad to say, the half of humanity that is female has no adequate remedy to correct the oppression and discrimination they have experienced for centuries.

The international women's movement, with its international meetings every five years, offers information to the world about the centuries-old grievances of women. But legal avenues open to them are very limited. They can appeal to public opinion with the hope of mobilizing the shame which men and nations increasingly feel for the way societies dominated by men have treated women. But this grief and guilt often seems to be superficial.

Is a worldwide awakening about women's rights taking place? It surely is, but the legal aspirations of the awakening often seem peripheral. The world is still in the process of reconsidering the role assigned to women as mothers and homemakers. Are there ways of accepting and blessing that role while also opening up all the avenues for a larger life for women? That is the cosmic question with which the world is struggling. The emergence of the CEDAW is a symptom and a sign of the globe's rethinking of a very fundamental question.

That rethinking is taking form in the deliberations in the U.N. Committee on CEDAW. It is a tragedy for that group and also for the United States that America does not have a place at the table where twenty-three highly qualified women struggle to understand and articulate ways by which the human family can correct the major mistakes it has made in its treatment of women through the centuries.

The committee that supervises the implementation of the CEDAW tends to concentrate on the rights of women to vote, to hold office, to share equality in all matters with men, and, more and more, to enjoy equal opportunities in business and government. The role of rural women which is provided for in the convention does not seem to attract the same attention.

The frightening persistence of physical abuse of women has prompted the forces of feminism to promulgate a declaration (not a covenant suitable for ratification) lamenting the presence of abuse of women. It is indeed discouraging that as late as December 20, 1993, a world body felt obliged to issue a warning that the physical abuse of women continues and that in some quarters the male abuse of spouses is deemed to be a private offense not punishable by public authority.

On the subject of the elimination of violence against women, the Universal Declaration of Human Rights defines violence as any act that is "likely to result in physical, sexual or psychological harm or suffering to women . . . whether occurring in public or private life." The declaration warns that no country should "invoke any custom, tradition or religious consideration to avoid their obligations to eliminate without delay any policy or practice which assumes the inferiority or superiority of either of the sexes" or is based on "stereotype roles for men and women." Governments are furthermore urged to compile statistics on the prevalence of different forms of violence against women and on the effectiveness of measures implemented to prevent and redress violence against women.

The solemn plea in the U.N. declaration in 1993 put the U.N. General

Assembly at the heart of the struggle against violence aimed at women. It is a reaffirmation — indeed, an expansion — of the widely accepted conviction that violence against women is pervasive, endemic, and a "manifestation of historically unequal power relations between men and women." Violence against women, the declaration asserts, is "one of the crucial social mechanisms by which women are forced into a subordinate position compared with men."

The U.N. declaration on the subject of the elimination of violence against women defines violence as any act that is "likely to result in physical, sexual or psychological harm or suffering to women . . . whether occurring in public or private life." No man can be unaware of the prevalence of wife-battering, marital rape, and the sexual abuse of girls, but the spelling out of the incidence of violence has to be distressing and disturbing.

Assuming that the demands in the declaration against violence are a form of customary international law and thereby binding on governments, is there some hope that centuries-old abuses will be corrected? The basic assumption is that the globalization of the rights of women not to be subjected to violence reminds men everywhere of the shameful aspect of their violence and that the "mobilization of shame" will (at least eventually) have some impact in altering human conduct. Men must first be educated to accept the concept that their conduct in engaging in violence against women derives from their acceptance of the idea that women are inferior. If this stereotype fades away, will violence against women disappear or be sharply diminished?

That is the hope behind the urgent language of the U.N. declaration of December 1993. This statement also reflects and amplifies the strong words on violence against women that were contained in the final declaration of the World Conference on Human Rights in Vienna in June 1993.

Reports of violence against women — especially in the household — come as a shock to most men. Such reports are also appalling to human rights academics and activists. Such conduct, one likes to think, is engaged in only by men out of control or who are vicious and reckless in other areas of their life. But this correlation is not clear, because reports of sex-based domestic and other violence continue to come in from many nations and cultures. Dowry-related violence in India and elsewhere is widespread although it may be diminishing. Sexual harassment is relatively well defined in U.S. law and is presumably being deterred and inhibited, through awareness and enforcement of the law.

The anger and the anguish that instigated the 1993 U.N. declaration against violence are prevalent in the literature about the rights of women and the studies that seek to explain the centuries-old prejudice held by men that women are inferior. One story of the subordination of women by men has been retold in a 1995 study entitled "Human Rights Are Women's Rights," issued by Amnesty International. The last chapter outlines fifteen steps to protect women's human rights. The statement urges government acceptance of recommendations made by the four U.N. world conferences on women.

One of the topics discussed in the Amnesty report is female genital mutilation. An estimated 110 million women suffer serious injuries throughout their lives as a result of female genital mutilation. Approximately 2 million girls are mutilated every year. Female genital mutilation occurs in some twenty countries in Africa, parts of Asia, and the Middle East. Organized opposition to female genital mutilation seems to have surfaced in 1984 at a seminar in Dakar where participants from twenty African countries urged that female genital mutilation be abolished.

The practice has been condemned by the World Medical Association and the World Health Organization. The U.N. World Conference on Human Rights in Vienna in 1993 urged the repeal of existing laws and customs which "cause harm to the girl-child." The World Medical Association, in a statement of condemnation issued in October 1993, stated that irreversible damage is often inflicted on girls who are victimized by female genital mutilation.

But the traditional conceptions or myths continue to be believed and followed. The fear of girls and their families is that men will not marry a girl who has not submitted to female genital mutilation.

The practice seems so cruel and bizarre that its abolition would seemingly be easy and rapid. But it is by no means clear that the practice of female genital mutilation is living on borrowed time.

The actual origin of female genital mutilation can be traced to the Phoenicians and the Egyptians. But the actual purposes of the practice are hard to locate because it was done in secrecy. Mohammed, the prophet of

Islam, did not specifically denounce female genital mutilation. But the more commonly accepted view today seems to hold that the practice is neither required nor authorized by the Muslim religion.

Although it could be argued that a practice with such ancient roots could be tolerated in the name of cultural relativism, this would be difficult to justify in view of the overwhelming and mounting condemnation of female genital mutilation.

The Universal Declaration of Human Rights protects the security of a person, forbids cruel and degrading treatment, and urges protection for mothers and children. The Covenant on Civil and Political Rights and the International Covenant on Economic, Social, and Cultural Rights include similar provisions. The Convention on the Elimination of All Forms of Discrimination Against Women outlaws "practices prejudicial to the health of children."

Section 4.22 of the International Conference on Population and Development states flatly that "governments are urged to prohibit female genital mutilation whenever it exists."

The practice of female genital mutilation is now legally forbidden in Britain, Canada, France, Sweden, Switzerland, and, as of September 19, 1996, the United States. It is now banned in several African countries including Ghana, Guinea, Senegal, and Togo. On the other hand, it is estimated that 90 percent of the girls in Ethiopia, Eritrea, Somalia, and the Sudan (north) are subjected to female genital mutilation.

U.S. immigration law will now routinely grant refugee status to female immigrants if they have a well-founded fear that they or their female children will be subjected to female genital mutilation if they return to their country of origin.

The discussion of female genital mutilation offers a stark example of a practice which seems to be glaringly wrong by any acceptable modern standards. But it cannot be eliminated by any decree from a world body. Its termination can come about only through education, international pressure, and additional condemnations by world medical groups. Because the practice is not carried out by licensed physicians, it cannot be eliminated by prohibiting medical doctors from performing it. But their collaboration with the forty nations that still engage in female genital mutilation could be enormously beneficial.

Information about this topic will be discussed in the periodic reports of the 191 nations that have ratified the Convention on the Rights of the Child. But one has a right to be impatient with the continuation of a practice which the relevant agencies of the United Nations have condemned and which seems difficult to justify under anyone's conception of what is appropriate for children.

Other practices possibly as barbarous as female genital mutilation will almost certainly be discovered as the concept of the rights of women reaches remote places in China and in, for example, the fifteen newly independent nations that were born in 1990 with the collapse of the U.S.S.R.

Among all the horror stories about the degradation of women around the world, the abuse of females in Afghanistan has a special place. In 1996, the Taliban, an extremist military group that claims to follow Islamic theology, took over Kabul, the Afghan capital. The Taliban, which is not recognized by the United Nations, occupied 97 percent of Afghanistan. A special rapporteur for the U.N. Commission on Human Rights reported in September 1999 on the subjugation of women in Afghanistan. The Taliban bans girls from attending school after the age of eight, forbids most women from working outside the home, and severely restricts women's access to medical services by not allowing male physicians to treat them.

The status of women before 1945 was seemingly stable or relatively uniform in most developed countries. In retrospect, however, the status of women before the Charter of the United Nations and its cooperating agencies was in all probability thought to be unfair by many women at that time. The voices and votes of these women have in the past fifty years transformed the legal and global status of women.

The globalization of the rights of women continues to have an impact that is too profound and too long-lasting to evaluate at this time. It is possibly the most radical and revolutionary of all the changes that have occurred in the internationalization of human rights and will bring even deeper changes in the future when the United States ratifies the Convention on the Elimination of All Forms of Discrimination Against Women and joins the global dialogue on the place of women in the twenty-first century.

6

A

GLOBAL

REVOLUTION

FOR

CHILDREN

The authors of the 1945 Charter of the United Nations and the Universal Declaration of Human Rights did not refer specifically to the rights of children. From time immemorial, whatever rights children have had were subordinated to the rights of their parents or guardians. In the crudest statement of the law children "belonged" to their parents. The state was extremely reluctant to interfere with or override the almost sacred rights of parents.

In the twentieth century exceptions have been placed into the law for the delinquent child. But the broad concept of "rights" being inherent in the child was not familiar.

The emergence, therefore, of the U.N. Convention on the Rights of the Child is a breakthrough of enormous consequence. From 1945 until the 1980s virtually no one working in the field of international human rights spoke very much about the rights of those under the age of eighteen. In retrospect at least this is a curious thing because one-third or more of all the human beings in the world at any one time are minors. But the advocates of a global transformation in the way human rights are protected have not had the vision or the courage to internationalize the law regulating families. This law was the most local of all laws. Parents had almost unrestrictable discretion to discipline their children. And local and national governments had the almost total power to dictate what rights if any children should have.

But all those presumably unchangeable principles lost some of their credibility as the United Nations and its affiliated bodies internationalized the scope and enforceability of the basic human rights of all human beings.

The full thrust of the movement to globalize human rights emerged in a dramatic way when nongovernmental organizations persuaded the United Nations to approve the Convention on the Rights of the Child in 1989. The framers of the convention were careful to finesse the question of abortion by speaking only of the human rights of children already born. The drafters of the CRC also steered clear of other contentious questions. But the content and impact of the convention are strong, forthright, and in a sense revolutionary.

The promoters of the Convention on the Rights of the Child probably did not realize that it would attract more signatures in a shorter period of time than any other U.N. convention on human rights. They could not have anticipated that within a decade of approval by the United Nations, 191 nations would ratify it. In 1999, only the United States and Somalia had failed to ratify the CRC. Somalia had an excuse: there was no functional legislative body to act on the covenant.

The failure of the United States to ratify the convention is due to the existence of a handful of individuals and a few radically conservative groups that somehow think that the Convention on the Rights of the Child is anti-family. Even when these individuals are told that the Holy See, surely a pro-family organization, was the fifth nation in the world to ratify the CRC they are not persuaded that the United States should ratify this convention. Even the many reservations that would be added by the U.S. Senate do not placate the opponents of the CRC. They have demonized the treaty and are determined to prevent sixty-seven Senators from approving what they deem to be destructive of the family.

Again, the United States, as in the case of the Convention on the Elimination of All Forms of Discrimination Against Women, is not present at the table at the United Nations where a group of ten experts listen to the reports of 191 nations and prepare constructive ways to improve their treatment of children.

One likes to think that the insistent worldwide emphasis on human rights has improved the status of children throughout the world. But the evidence is mixed.

The 1999 report of UNICEF confirmed the distressing plight of children. Almost a billion people entered the twenty-first century unable to read a book or even sign their names. This means that some 855 million human beings — nearly one-fifth of humanity — are functionally illiterate as the new millennium begins.

In the year 2000, 130 million children had no access to basic education. Girls constituted 73 percent of this number. This lack of schooling for girls raises the rate of births and, hence, infant mortality. This correlation is illustrated in the southern Indian state of Kerala, where literacy is universal. There, the infant mortality rate is the lowest in the developing world. The right to education, central to the Convention on the Rights of the Child, has been heeded. In 1960 fewer than 15 percent of children ages six to eleven in developing nations were enrolled in school. By 1980 primary enrollment had more than doubled in Asia and Latin America. In Africa it had tripled.

But this progress was sharply curtailed in the 1980s. Poor countries, confronted with the interest due on the vast sums they had borrowed from lending entities in the west, allowed spending on education between 1980 and 1987 in Latin America and the Caribbean to decline by almost 40 percent. In sub-Saharan Africa it fell by 75 percent.

The forgiveness of debt for the forty poorest countries recommended by the G-7 in Cologne in 1999 may be helpful to these economically deprived nations. But they will still not be in a position to carry out completely their duties under the Convention on the Rights of the Child. But the remission of the debt that less developed nations accumulated in the 1970s and 1980s is a recognition by the world community that some of the billions borrowed were squandered by dictators or spent on projects for the rich and the well off and that in fairness, the present population should not be required to pay the interest or the capital on those mismanaged debts. The obligations these debtor nations had assumed when they ratified the CRC give present-day rulers a valid reason to ask for forgiveness of the loans so that they can carry out their duties under that convention.

The work of UNICEF and the aspirations of UNESCO continue to change the world's feelings about the rights of children. These sentiments make the task of the U.N. Convention on the Rights of the Child easier and more acceptable to the signatories which must report to the Committee on the Rights of the Child. It is not easy to evaluate the work of the committee, which began in February 1991. The information gathered by this agency and the amazing array of NGOs devoted to the improvement in the lot of children now constitutes an unprecedented resource for those under the age of eighteen.

During its first five years, the Committee on the Rights of the Child examined the records of eighty nations. Even though the committee has not yet attracted popular attention, it is developing a jurisprudence on complicated issues such as the rights of disabled children, teen pregnancy, juvenile delinquency, and corporal punishment. All the forty-one substantive provisions contained in the Convention on the Rights of the Child are being explored.

It is also astonishing to see how the signatory nations continue to include items from the Convention on the Rights of the Child in their constitutions and statutory laws. The court decisions and administrative regulations of many nations are based on the recommendations made in the CRC.

The U.N. machinery to enforce the provisions of the Convention on the Rights of the Child is only ten years old. It is, furthermore, merely a committee with no legally binding jurisdiction. Although its findings cannot be enforced, it serves as a fact-finding entity with respect to the way the signatory nations carry out their solemn promises to protect the internationally recognized rights of children. Theoretically nothing can be more repugnant to the conscience of the world than the violations of the rights of children by nations which have publicly and solemnly agreed to protect those rights.

Perhaps the next step that the United Nations and the world community can take is the protection of the rights of children by the imposition of civil sanctions and fines on the countries that defy their obligations. Such penalties and fines could be used against nations that refuse to carry out their duties under international environmental law or trade regulations.

The recent explosion of concerns over the use of child labor in the manufacturing of consumer items made in Asia and bought in America is an indication of the future direction of the U.N. Committee on the Rights of the Child. The elimination or monitoring of child labor in sweatshops and in the fields is a goal of a wide variety of groups in the developed nations. But it is a problem that is distressingly complex.

On June 15, 1999, President Clinton urged the International Labor Organization in Geneva to adopt a treaty that would bar the most abusive child labor practices. Mr. Clinton made it clear to the 174 member-nations of the ILO that his administration believes in open trade but that labor harmful to children's health, safety, and morals must be eliminated. This policy reinforces the executive order that President Clinton issued in early June 1999 requiring the federal government to buy products only after their producers certify that child labor was not included in their manufacture.

But the difficulties in protecting the rights of children are daunting. The U.N. Committee on the Rights of the Child is at present less than a fact-finding body. It is only an understaffed agency that listens to the presentations of nations which voluntarily comply with their duties under the CRC. But there is really no adversary process, nor does the committee have the resources to follow up in seeking to help various nations in carrying out their mandate under the CRC.

Again, the opportunities for nongovernmental organizations are enormous. Their believability and their voice can quite literally change the world. Advocates for the rights of children, for example, have formed a new agency for children within the structure of the Human Rights Watch. The NGOs dedicated to the rights of children have the advantage that they are not working for unappealing groups like prisoners or aliens or terrorists. But despite all the sentiment that everyone has for innocent children, the task of insisting on the fulfillment of their rights has been blocked by centuries of custom and tradition which held that children can be subordinated to their parents or their governments. The existence of thousands of child soldiers is one barbarous example of that age-old way of thinking.

But unlike the U.N. covenants on economic and political rights, the U.N. machinery to implement the rights of the child at least has been fueled by the instinctive love of children which has always been characteristic of the human race. As a result, while it is easy to think of the globalization of human rights as a utopian and unrealistic dream, it is hard to think that humanity could be entirely impervious to a repeated cry for gentleness to children.

Unfortunately, the record of the United States in its treatment of children is a poor one. The United States leads the developed world in child poverty. In 1979, the poverty rate for children was 14.7 percent; it is currently up to 20.4 percent. The incidence of poverty among children in the United States is four times that of children in western Europe. The number of children in the United States who are reportedly abused has tripled since 1980, to almost 3 million. The number of child murders doubled in the 1980s, and teenage suicide has doubled over the past twenty years. Every day in the United States 110 babies die before their first birthday. A simple analogy: if an airplane with 110 American children crashed every single day, the United States and the world would be in tears.

It is easy to be skeptical of the new energy on behalf of children that has been released by the establishment of the U.N. Committee on the Rights of the Child. This unit seems inadequate to protect the rights of almost 3 billion children in the world.

At the same time, the love of children — with their need for attention and care — is a moral bond that should transcend every local and national barrier.

The concept of the rights of children has now created an important legal mechanism to guarantee the fulfillment of those rights. It is an ancient and noble dream, first put into the world's legal aspirations in 1924 when the League of Nations in its declaration on children's rights stated, "The child that is hungry should be fed; the child that is sick should be helped . . . and the orphaned and the homeless child should be sheltered and succored."

Those moral demands have now been recognized as legally binding on the governments of 191 nations. These countries have made solemn promises and entered into binding contracts to love children by guaranteeing them their rights. The world has obtained an unprecedented level of caring and compassion. The twentieth century was probably the bloodiest and most violent 100 years in human history; perhaps the twenty-first century will be a golden age for children.

7

PERFORMANCE
OF THE
UNITED NATIONS
ON
HUMAN RIGHTS

In addition to the already noted entities within the United Nations devoted to human rights are the committees dedicated to overseeing the compliance to the International Convention on the Elimination of All Forms of Racial Discrimination and the Convention Against Torture and Other Cruel, Inhuman, or Degrading Treatment or Punishment (also known as the Covenant Against Torture).

The United States has ratified both these treaties, but with crippling reservations. On the torture convention, for example, the Senate has accepted qualifications insisted upon by the Bush administration which in essence say that the United States agrees to restrictions on torture only if they do not go beyond existing judicial interpretations in the United States of the Fourth, Fifth, and Fourteenth Amendments.

Although torture has never been an institution, practice, or tradition in America as it is in several countries around the world, the United States looks self-centered and hypocritical when it seeks praise from the international community for ratifying the convention against torture and other cruel, inhuman, or degrading treatment while simultaneously telling the world that it will not change or expand its basic interpretation of the meaning of torture. The fact is that around the world, interpretations of the words "inhuman" and "degrading" named in the Covenant Against Torture do go beyond what American courts have determined is the intent of the "cruel and unusual punishment" forbidden in the Eighth Amendment.

The U.N. Committee on the Elimination of All Forms of Racial Discrimination (CERD) has also issued many rulings on the nature of discrimination that are more advanced than the customary definition in America. In addition, this U.N. committee, which monitors compliance with the CERD, has not directed its attention to the United States. As of late 1999 the State Department had not submitted the report that was due. Clearly the definition of discrimination based on race that the U.N. Committee on CERD has issued is more expansive than are comparable interpretations by U.S. legislatures and courts.

It is easy to criticize the caution and the mired bureaucracy of the U.N. agencies devoted to human rights. That sentiment was prominent at the U.N. World Conference on Human Rights in Vienna in 1993. The cry there, echoing a generation of similar pleas, was for the creation of the office of the U.N. High Commissioner for Human Rights. The model and even the title were taken from the U.N. High Commissioner for Refugees, an effective agency which, despite its limitations, seems to be acting where it is now needed — in Southeast Asia, Rwanda, and Kosovo.

The office of the U.N. High Commissioner on Human Rights was created in 1994 (pursuant to the 1993 World Conference on Human Rights) and is headed by Mary Robinson, the former president of Ireland. Her mandate is daunting: coordinate and intensify all U.N. efforts to improve and enhance human rights. The long-held dream of having a "czar" for human rights has been realized. But the decentralized and fragmented agencies on human rights established by the United Nations over the past fifty-five years cannot easily be integrated into a unified system.

Underlying the resistance is the seemingly ineradicable idea of national sovereignty. It would be nice to be able to think that the radical self-centeredness of individual nations has been downsized in the past fifty years. But this is not clear or at least provable.

The fact is that the victors in World War II retained their sovereignty in a basically crude way by insisting on their veto power in the U.N. Security Council. This would be tantamount to the U.S. Senate declaring that 5 of the 100 senators have the power to veto any development or vote that they disapprove. This veto power allowed — and, perhaps, helped create — the forty-five-year struggle between the United States and the U.S.S.R. If neither of these giants had the veto power, a majority of the members of the United Nations could have used all their diplomatic and even military strength to prevent the Soviet Union from invading eastern Europe and the United States from sending military forces to Vietnam.

Can the efforts of the United Nations to promote and protect those human rights guaranteed in the 1945 Charter of the United Nations and the covenants on human rights be increased as long as the veto power remains in the charter? The fact that the veto power has rarely been exercised since the collapse of Communism in 1990 is a sign of hope that the former superpowers, while they may disagree on some basic world issues, are not opponents on the question of human rights.

It should also be noted that the moral concepts underlying the protection of human rights may take time — even generations — to become embedded in the souls of governments and people around the world. The Magna Carta, it could be argued, bore fruit in the legal institutions of England and America only after hundreds of years had passed. Generations of slaves suffered and died before European nations and the United States came to the conclusion that slavery was a degrading affront to the inherent dignity of persons of color.

In evaluating the effectiveness of the United Nations on international human rights, close attention should be paid to the enormous contributions of U.N. agencies like the Food and Agriculture Organization, the World Health Organization, UNICEF, UNESCO, and the U.N. Development Fund. These agencies have quite literally transformed the world. No prior world agencies, except possibly the International Labor Organization, rival their achievements. These units, it should be pointed out, are devoted to the fulfillment of the economic rights guaranteed in the Universal Declaration of Human Rights and in the International Covenant on Economic, Social, and Cultural Rights.

These agencies have actually done extraordinarily well, considering that the population of the earth since 1945 has increased roughly from 3 billion to 6 billion.

At the Vienna World Conference on Human Rights in 1993, the issue that permeated every topic was the changes that are needed in the United Nations. The issue is complex beyond imagination. United Nations watchers who have followed this sprawling agency in the years 1948 to 1990 apparently found themselves incapable after 1990 of recommending the essential elements of a change in the U.N. structure. The Vienna meeting was not exactly devoted to that intractable topic, but the issue could not be avoided.

The Vienna conference ended without an articulated consensus on the reform of the United Nations. It did conclude that the United Nations' legacy on human rights transcends the concept of "cultural relativism." Secretary of State Warren Christopher said: "We respect the religious, social and cultural characteristics that make each country unique. But we cannot let cultural relativism become the last refuge of repression." The World Conference on Human Rights in 1993 made it clear that the end of the Cold War would not be an occasion for any group of nations to use their own long-standing practices to become, as Christopher put it, "the last refuge of repression." Child slavery or bondage and female infanticide, for example, must go the way of foot-binding in China.

What, then, are the primordial tasks facing the United Nations with regard to the promotion and protection of human rights? One is tempted to settle on massive education. If people everywhere could see and hear internationally recognized economic and political human rights exalted on CNN, on the World Wide Web, and in all the rapidly emerging avenues of communicating ideas, could there be a worldwide acceptance of those basic rights which for almost sixty years have been proclaimed as the patrimony of the human race?

No one can accurately predict what moral ideas will take hold at a particular time. This depends on the presence or absence of leadership. It also depends on the attitude of the new colonialists — the dominant industries of developed nations as they "descend" on nations like Angola, where the political scene is chaotic.

Could there be an alliance between the newer nations and the economic Goliaths of developed nations? The international mergers of the largest industrial corporations in the west and in Japan may bring an infusion of economic power to countries in Asia and Africa, which in turn could bring about a new colonialism even more savage and repressive than the worst examples of colonialism which Europe inflicted on nations in Africa and Asia.

The dream of the United Nations, as updated in the final declaration of human rights in Vienna in 1993, is that the proclamation of human rights as redefined and reasserted in 1993 will be able to direct the new economic invasions of underdeveloped countries so that the 2 or more billion people in those nations will simultaneously enjoy the benefits of capitalism and the blessings of democracy.

Although the United States — specifically, the Clinton administration — led the way in preparing for and staging the Vienna World Conference on Human Rights in 1993, the real movers were the thousands of delegates from the NGOs. These groups, stifled by the forty years of an east-west impasse, saw a way to revivify the human rights promises that had been so central to the plans underlying the very concept of the United Nations. NGOs representing the disabled, children, indigenous peoples, the tortured, and prisoners of conscience electrified the scene in Vienna. One delegate representing the disabled praised the Americans With Disabilities Act, signed by George Bush, as the best and most promising of all the laws in the world enacted to assist the mentally or physically challenged. A representative of an Asian group of battered and tortured women told me that a presidential commission on which I served to indemnify the 120,000 Japanese interned in World War II had written a report which is the model for a plan to obtain reparation for the 200,000 women forcibly taken by Japan from Korea to serve Japanese soldiers at war throughout the Pacific. She felt that the sum of $20,000 given by the U.S. government to each surviving Japanese internee was a fine model for the Korean women whose lives had been ruined by the Japanese kidnappings.

The Vienna conference sought to revive the United Nations after its long twilight in the shadow of the east-west Cold War. In the final statement, the delegates recognized that the United Nations had undergone what in essence is a rebirth, echoing that profound conviction by the pledge of 161 countries to return with vigor and enthusiasm to the original devotion to international human rights embodied in the U.N. charter, the Universal Declaration of Human Rights, and the score of covenants on human rights.

Unfortunately, the United States remains the country that neglects and defies the vision of the United Nations and the final declaration in Vienna. In addition to committing the unforgivable act of partially paralyzing the United Nations by not paying its dues, the United States failed to approve the International Criminal Court in June 1998 in Rome, has not returned to UNESCO, has declined to sign the world agreement on banning land mines, and continues to refuse to collaborate with the agreements on the law of the sea.

Is there some fatal flaw in the American character when it comes to operating as only one of 191 nations in the United Nations? Is the United States an actor in an ongoing Greek tragedy of monumental proportions? Will the United States ever return to the role of moral leadership it assumed during the first few years of the existence of the United Nations? Or is the United States irreversibly entrenched in a posture of isolationism and self-centeredness?

Everyone talks about globalization as inevitable, good for American business, and the next step somehow in the manifest destiny of America.

The discontent of the Congress and the country with America's record on human rights caused the Congress in 1976 to put into statutory law several measures to force the government to fulfill the promises it made on human rights. We now turn to that defining development in the foreign policy of the United States when the Congress acted along with President Ford in 1976.

Part II

THE
UNITED STATES
AND
HUMAN RIGHTS

8

THE UNITED STATES
INTERVENES ON BEHALF
OF INTERNATIONAL
HUMAN RIGHTS

When it came out in Senate hearings in the early 1970s that the
United States had intervened in Chile and helped to bring General Augusto Pinochet to power over the popularly elected Salvador Allende,
there was anger and fury in the country. The United States justified its
conduct by asserting that because Allende, a professor, was a Marxist the
United States had no choice. The rhetoric flowed that the Communists
had planned to take over the southern cone of Latin America and that
Argentina would be the next victim.

Many members of the U.S. Congress felt embarrassed that the United
States in its struggle to stop Soviet aggression ended up arming dictators
because they were enemies of our enemy. The pattern was familiar in
America's defense of South Korea, Nicaragua's Somoza, and similar anti-
Communist officials.

But the Nixon administration's part in helping General Pinochet
somehow triggered a revolt. Congressman Don Fraser, the Democrat
from Minnesota, was the chairman of the relevant subcommittee of the
House Foreign Affairs Committee. He began a long series of hearings on
the question of how the United States was carrying out its solemn pledge
made in its ratification of the 1945 Charter of the United Nations to
protect human rights. Congressman Fraser conducted up to a hundred
hearings and heard the exiles and representatives of dozens of nations

where human rights were not protected by either the United States or the United Nations.

I followed those hearings closely. I met some of the witnesses — exiles from dozens of countries like Burma, Chile, China, and the "captive nations" of eastern Europe.

Eventually Congressman Fraser prepared a bill which would remind the United States of its duties under the U.N. charter to protect and promote human rights. The actual words of the U.N. charter, and especially the pledge to advance human rights contained in Articles 55 and 56, are quoted in the preamble of the Fraser Bill. The thrust of the bill was to prevent the United States from giving aid, military or civilian, to those nations engaged in a pattern or practice of denying internationally recognized human rights. The practice must be persistent and carried out not by terrorist groups within a country but by the government itself. The State Department was designated as the agency to compile an annual report on the state of human rights in every nation that received aid from the United States. That requirement was later extended to every nation, whether or not they are the direct recipients of aid from the United States.

The first version of the Fraser Bill was vetoed by President Ford. He followed the advice of Secretary of State Henry Kissinger, who felt that the standards set by the Congress would be too mechanistic and too inflexible to be a part of the efforts of the State Department and the Department of Defense in their mission to carry out America's policy of containing Communism.

The veto was not overridden, but a second bill with some modifications was signed into law by President Ford. One of the better features of the original Fraser Bill provided for the creation of a bipartisan commission on human rights outside the State Department that, as through the highly regarded U.S. Commission on Civil Rights, would hold hearings and publish periodic reports on the state of human rights around the world. This amendment was unfortunately defeated on the floor largely by Republicans, many of whom opposed the underlying bill.

No attempt has been initiated to restore the nonpartisan commission on human rights defeated on the House floor. This way of collecting information on human rights and communicating it would have been more professional and much preferred to the present arrangement. Political and partisan positions affect the objectivity of the annual report issued by the State Department. Information in the report is gathered by U.S. ambassadors around the world aided in larger countries by their human rights officers. The reports have become less political during the twenty years of their existence. But a report issued by an agency with a reputation for objectivity would more accurately reflect the obligation the United States assumed when it agreed in Article 56 of the U.N. charter: that it would advance and enhance the human rights noted in Article 55. It should be noted that those rights are broad and inclusive. No distinction is made between economic and political rights.

Article 55 provides that all signatory nations shall promote

(a) higher standards of living, full employment and conditions of economic and social practice and development; (b) the solutions of international economic, social, health, and related problems; and international cultural and education cooperation; and (c) universal respect for and observance of human rights and fundamental freedoms for all without distinction as to race, sex, language or religion.

The Fraser Bill—which became Section 502b of the Foreign Assistance Act—begins with these words:

The United States shall, in accordance with its international obligations as set forth in the charter of the United Nations and in keeping with the constitutional heritage and traditions of the United States, promote and encourage increased respect for human rights and fundamental freedoms throughout the world without distinction as to race, sex, language or religion. Accordingly, a principal goal of the foreign policy of the United States shall be to promote increased observance of internationally recognized human rights by all countries.

The bill goes on to state that "no security assistance may be provided to any country the government of which engages in a consistent pattern of gross violations of internationally recognized human rights." It should be noted that a government must engage in a "consistent" pattern. In addition, the violations must be "gross." The president does, however, have some discretion in that he can certify that "extraordinary circumstances" exist that warrant an exception to the policy.

The basic rationale of the Fraser initiative is explained in the bill by saying that the United States should "avoid identification . . . with governments which deny to their people internationally recognized human rights and fundamental freedoms, in violation of international law or in contravention of the policy of the United States."

This policy is modified by another portion of a separate law which stipulates that the U.S. government "in connection with its voice and vote" in the international development banks must advance the humanitarian purposes and the protection for human rights implicit in the U.N. charter.

These laws have led to a cutoff of aid in fewer than ten instances— mostly in Latin America. The policy was executed by Congress itself with a specific cutoff of all aid to Chile after General Pinochet seized power. Most of the worst offenders of human rights during the years of the Cold War did not, of course, receive any U.S. aid and hence did not constitute a problem.

For a generation, there has been a great debate over the advisability, feasibility, and wisdom of Section 502b. The objectives of the measure are so laudable that hardly anyone is calling for its repeal. But U.S. ambassadors in countries with problematic human rights records (like Malaysia) are troubled about their role in collecting information on violations of human rights. Their participation in this role does not endear them to the host government.

Some of the situations on which the ambassador and his or her staff are required to report are deeply political. The most serious cases involve alleged torture, disappearances, restrictions on the press and radio, and denial of rights such as free elections. In instances like these, the facts are often disputed. Local government can always dispute the allegations of wrongdoing. Should the U.S. embassy be in a bitter dispute between contending political factions?

In the ideal scenario, some fact-finding entity related to the United Nations should be the mediator or judge. But as we have seen, the U.N. Commission on Human Rights is far less engaged in this area than would be ideal. The nongovernmental agencies, especially Amnesty International, are engaged in collecting information for their own annual reports on human rights. No ambassador would feel comfortable in contradicting findings by Amnesty International, knowing that its reputation for accuracy and credibility is very high.

The State Department report card every February now numbers over 2,000 pages. It complies with several congressional demands that the volume include all relevant information on topics such as the rights of women, the number of children who work, and the freedom of labor unions. The reports are, increasingly, the work of a professional staff in the office of the assistant secretary of state for human rights.

The annual report on human rights financed by the U.S. government is unique in the world. No other nation has even attempted to compile such a comprehensive document. Does the report alienate the governments whose human rights records are criticized? Does it ingratiate the United States with other nations?

At the very least, the report is an annual announcement that the United States is committed to the promotion of human rights. But it almost inevitably raises questions everywhere about the presumptions of America, gathering the facts and delivering the report, to the whole world.

If Japan put out an annual "shame sheet" on the United States and all the other nations of the world, it would be embarrassing for the United States and many others. All the criticized countries would challenge Japan's right to evaluate them.

The fact that nations do not openly criticize the United States for its involvement in the human rights conditions of other nations is a silent concession that the United States is deemed the world's principal leader in advancing human rights.

That is the image which politicians and some diplomats seek to project. To some extent, it is accurate. In the 1970s the Congress passed a bill named after Senator Henry Jackson (the Democrat from Washington) and Representative Charles Vanik (the Democrat from Ohio) which sought to expedite the release of Soviet Jews. Several thousand were able to migrate to Israel or to the United States. But there was and is criticism that there were better ways of accomplishing the release of some of the 3 million Jews in the Soviet Union whose religious liberty had been restricted by the Kremlin since at least 1917.

It is ironic indeed that the United States — the country which insisted on being the home of the United Nations and a nation considered the principal protector of that body—has in part abandoned its own creation on human rights by the construction of an American agency to do the work which originally the United Nations was slated to do. But the State Department's work of monitoring human rights, however valuable, cannot possibly match that which the United Nations is chartered to do. The United States disseminates its annual assessment on all the nations of the earth but does not offer consultation and guidance. Although the State Department has one remedy available to punish countries with truly egregious human rights conditions—the cutoff of funds—that remedy is seldom employed.

The enactment of Section 502b was no doubt a milestone in America's pilgrimage to carry out its pledge to comply with Article 56 of the U.N. charter. But it is an incomplete, unilateral, awkward, and problematic way of seeking to effectuate the purposes and aims of the United Nations' unprecedented efforts to focus on the fulfillment of human rights as one of the central missions of this world agency.

The new human rights program set forth in Section 502b did not become an issue in the presidential campaign in 1976. But candidate Jimmy Carter stressed human rights and promised in essence to make human rights the "soul of his foreign policy." Although Carter may have received some political support from human rights activists, there was almost no political controversy during the campaign over the Fraser-initiated novel role for the United States in advancing human rights.

But the establishment of the Bureau of Democracy, Human Rights, and Labor (previously called the Bureau of Human Rights and Humanitarian Affairs) by the State Department during the Reagan years and President Carter's appointment of Patricia Derian as its first head led to battles between the Pentagon, the State Department, and its regional bureaus. The warfare over the place of human rights in America's foreign policy waged between 1977 and 1981 has not been documented in any thorough academic way. The keepers of some of the solemn traditions of the State Department felt assaulted by the intervention of Congress. They had been trained to operate on the principle that America's interests, not its ideals, should be the predominant criterion in carrying out America's foreign policy.

In the Carter administration the highest officials spoke repeatedly and insistently that America's ideals as well as its interests should both be present in the way the United States reacts to other nations. The objectives of Section 502b were taken seriously and sometimes literally. The United States rebuked the military government of Argentina which reigned from 1976 to 1983. The threat of termination of aid to Brazil angered the ruling generals in that country. But few such threats were leveled at nations where the United States had important business or military alliances.

In the four years of the Carter administration the stress on human rights became accepted—at least on the surface. Yet, militant anti-Communists felt strongly that the policy was unfair to some U.S. allies who might have been weak on human rights but were strong in keeping the Soviets out of their area of the world.

The principal objections to the human rights program of the Carter administration were not clearly defined. The critics of the new program had to admit that Section 502b gives a great deal of discretion and flexibility to the president and to the State Department. The law does not say explicitly that the United States must sacrifice some of its important interests to avoid compromising its ideals. The law was intended to insist on a strong emphasis on human rights — but without flat command or inflexible criteria.

The speeches and rhetoric of President Carter on human rights certainly raised the decibels on that topic around the world. It gave hope and inspiration to countless dissidents and to the untold millions who longed to be free from the bondage of military dictatorships or economic penury. Indeed, it may be that the Carter administration caused the idea of human rights to enter the political and moral coinage of the nation and to some extent of the world. The concept of human rights had been everywhere since the United Nations and its agency began talking about it in the 1940s and 1950s. But seemingly overnight in the 1970s and 1980s, the United States and all the developed countries were talking about their duty to make human rights an active part of their foreign policy.

The resistance to an active role in international human rights by the United States surged as the Reagan administration took over in 1981. The Reagan White House apparently decided it was not possible to simply abolish the office of the assistant secretary of state for human rights.

Instead, it tried to do just that by indirect means: it appointed Ernest Lefever to the position of assistant secretary of state for human rights even though Lefever, the holder of a doctorate in divinity from Yale, had on several occasions opposed the very creation and perpetuation of the position of assistant secretary of state for human rights.

I recall chatting with Lefever in February 1981 in the office designated for the human rights official at the State Department. He fully expected to be confirmed by the Senate and to sit for at least four years in the chair he occupied when I and a group of human rights academics questioned him. Lefever was strong on prepossessions but short on answers to the nagging question of why he wanted the job that he said should not exist.

To the amazement of almost everyone, scores of nongovernmental organizations appeared at the Senate hearing on Lefever's appointment. Sitting in the cavernous Senate room during those hearings, I and every other participant was astonished at the number and vigor of those opposing Lefever's appointment. The new and untested NGOs dedicated to human rights seemed to discover one another and their collective strength when they gathered and lobbied against the appointment of a man who, as far as they could discern, was an enemy of any program by the United States that sought to advance human rights.

Patricia Derian had made her position into a bully pulpit for victims all over the world. The rejection of Lefever's appointment by the Republican-controlled U.S. Senate Foreign Relations Committee stunned almost everyone. To vote down a nominee for a minor position in the State Department was a rebuke to the recently elected popular President Reagan. It was also an explosive announcement that the forces behind the human rights movement had arrived in Washington and that their idealistic appeal to global standards of human decency would not fade away.

For several months the Reagan White House seemed to be in shock. No one had been appointed to the position on human rights created by the Fraser Bill and the Carter White House. Activists in the human rights movement, elated and exuberant over their victory in the Lefever matter, did not vigorously urge the appointment of another because they feared that in a second hearing they might not be able to prevail in the Republican Senate.

After months of silence and inaction, the Reagan White House appointed Elliott Abrams as assistant secretary of state for human rights. He was confirmed after making the implementation of human rights an important objective of the Reagan administration—but with the understanding that the principal objective would be to protest the intimidation of citizens in the "captive nations" of eastern Europe, in Cuba, and, of course, in China.

Abrams was confirmed because he and his colleagues had devised a plausible, if seriously curtailed, role for the office on human rights. The human rights arm of the State Department pounded away at the loss of political liberties in lands controlled by the Communists. At its annual event on December 10, Human Rights Day, the accent was always on escapees from the Soviet Union or Cuba but seldom if ever on the problems of the victims of dictatorships in Nicaragua, El Salvador, or Chile. The heroes on December 10, the day when the Universal Declaration of Human Rights was ratified in Paris in 1948, almost always supported the anti-Communist theme of Assistant Secretary of State Elliott Abrams.

But even the strong anti-Communist theme of the Reagan administration could not drown out the cries for human rights in Haiti, South Africa, and elsewhere. Under the pressure of public opinion, the Reagan administration quietly shifted to a position that embraced the violation of human rights of all kinds—whether by Communists or authoritarian regimes. The Reagan administration finally persuaded the U.S. Senate to ratify the Covenant on Genocide—which had been pending in the Senate for some forty years.

In the second Reagan administration, the fifty-year struggle of the international community against apartheid in South Africa finally reached crisis proportions. President Reagan warned everybody that he would veto tougher economic sanctions against South Africa. Despite that threat, Congress enacted Draconian sanctions against South Africa—prohibiting, in essence, U.S. banks and corporations from doing business there. To the astonishment of everyone, both the House and the Senate overrode the White House veto by the necessary two-thirds vote. It was the African-American and civil rights community in the United States that made this a decisive issue. One could probably argue that it was the international human rights movement that finally prevailed in the abolition of apartheid. And it was the boycott by the United States that prompted Pretoria to release Nelson Mandela and move toward multi-party democratic elections.

It is plausible that the negative attitude or hostility of the Reagan administration toward the promotion of human rights deepened the idealism and determination of those in the human rights movement. New NGOs were formed. The Human Rights Watch split into units to monitor conditions in Latin America, Asia, Europe, and Africa. The Lawyers Committee for Human Rights, founded in 1979, flourished. And Amnesty International, established in 1961 by a lawyer in London, continued to be the senior "guardian angel" of human rights everywhere.

At the bicentennial of Georgetown University in 1989, I chaired a series of symposia on every aspect of international human rights. The variety and vigor of the initiatives by NGOs was dazzling.

The Bush administration, like its predecessor, did not want to be aggressively proactive in its defense of human rights. The assistant secretary of human rights ambassador was Richard Schifter, whom the Reagan administration had appointed to succeed Elliott Abrams. Speaking at the Georgetown University bicentennial conference, Schifter was correct and careful, but not in any way crusading. Many of the participants were disappointed; their concept of the office of human rights at the State Department clearly differed from that of the Reagan and the Bush administrations.

Although the twelve years of the Reagan-Bush administrations did not advance human rights as many of the supporters of the Fraser bill had intended or hoped, the institutionalization of international human rights as an important component of America's foreign policy did progress. The annual reports of the State Department contained rebukes to most non-democratic nations. NGOs, Human Rights Watch, and the Lawyers Committee for Human Rights issued annual critiques of the errors and inadequacies of these reports. The Lawyers Committee for Human Rights prepared a quadrennial report which offered constructive suggestions to the incoming president on an ever wider range of issues involving human rights. This report included recommendations on topics related to international trade, refugees, the covenants on human rights, and improvements in the way the U.S. State Department should handle issues related directly to human rights.

Proactive NGOs found the Reagan and Bush administrations seriously inadequate or even inexcusably negligent in the way they failed to promote human rights.

In fairness, those with views differing from the militant approach of groups like the Human Rights Watch are not necessarily less sensitive to human rights. The U.S. State Department, in their view, should not be compelled by Congress to "correct" or "scold" other nations. Their view of statecraft, diplomacy, and separation of powers results in a different position. Like Secretary of State Henry Kissinger in the Ford administration, they do not think that the Congress should dictate that human rights should be a crucial or paramount part of U.S. foreign policy. This body feels that the nation should weigh and balance many factors in the formulation of its foreign policy. The Congress theoretically agrees with this approach; Section 502b does not make human rights the only — or even the most crucial — factor in the making of foreign policy.

But the point of view of Kissinger and the many professionals and diplomats who agree with it has been defeated. It has succumbed to the ever-present desire of Americans to be fighting some kind of crusade for democracy, a better world, or global peace. The convictions expressed in the Declaration of Independence seem to be inherent in the psyche of Americans. Those dreams and aspirations played a significant part in America's participation in World War I and World War II as well as its support of the Cold War against the U.S.S.R. from 1948 to 1990.

Much of America's distinctive desire to protect and fight for human freedom has been the soul of the new protection offered to international human rights by the enactment of Section 502b.

The passion to enforce and expand human rights prompted President Clinton to appoint John Shattuck to the position of assistant secretary of state for human rights. Shattuck had been the director of the American Civil Liberties Union in Washington for ten years, and then became vice president and general counsel at Harvard University. He was active there in Amnesty International and was clearly identified as an enthusiast for human rights. More than any previous holder of this position, Shattuck sought to expand its role within the boundaries of the law.

Like all his predecessors, Shattuck had to take into consideration the views and interests of the White House, the Pentagon, and other relevant agencies in the formulation of what the United States should say and do about, for example, the state of human rights in China. In addition, he and his professional staff had to be sensitive to efforts being made by other branches of government in seeking to improve human rights in specific cases or in nations moving toward democracy. The mere mention of a problem in a particular nation could alienate the leaders of that country and cause them to regress on human rights initiatives.

Some day the voluminous files of the human rights office of the State Department will be opened so that humanity can see how and why the United States remained firm or became conciliatory toward abuses in a country whose leaders were sincerely moving toward compliance with their duties under the U.N. charter.

Shattuck was obligated to prepare the first American report on its compliance with the U.N. International Covenant on Civil and Political Rights. The Clinton administration had added some qualifications, understandings, and declarations that Shattuck almost certainly would oppose. But the mere filing of that report was a new milestone in America's obedience to its obligations under international law.

During Secretary Shattuck's term from 1993 to 1998 the bureau became more institutionalized and professionalized. It also acquired a new name from Congress: the Department for Democracy, Human Rights and Labor. When Shattuck was appointed as the Ambassador to the Czech Republic his position was taken by Harold Hongju Koh, a professor of human rights law at Yale who is of South Korean ancestry. The confirmation of Koh was surprisingly easy and quick. Perhaps the Republican Senate had been informed about the sincere work of Professor Koh on behalf of exiled Cubans.

Secretary Koh had some tough human rights issues facing him early in his administration. The Dayton Accords, the struggle over Kosovo, the proposed International Criminal Court all involved intricate problems at least indirectly related to the issues assigned by the Congress to the Bureau of Democracy, Human Rights, and Labor.

Koh made it clear as soon as he had been confirmed by the Senate that he, like his immediate predecessor, would reach out to nongovernmental organizations. The number, strength, and influence of the NGOs increased almost unbelievably during the Clinton administration. These organizations had been heartened by their impact at the World Conference on Human Rights in Vienna in 1993. Indeed, those who do not want the influence of the Bureau for Democracy, Human Rights and Labor to expand must be fearful of the power of the human rights lobby in Washington and in the country. These groups regularly caucus with other units and can orchestrate thousands of e-mails to the Congress and the White House. The bureau is now such a familiar part of the Washington landscape that almost everyone assumes it is a permanent part of the State Department. But even the most cursory review of this agency shows that it is an anomaly and that its role could possibly be carried out more effectively if it were part of a nonpartisan commission not inhibited by its obligation to work in harmony with the State Department, which must naturally be in political alignment with the elected officials in the White House.

The Congress that created the Bureau for Democracy, Human Rights and Labor in 1976 realized that it was fashioning an anomaly. But Congress was angry that the United States was not carrying out its promises made pursuant to the U.N. charter. The United States in 1976 had not ratified the major human rights treaties and, in addition, had polarized the world's nations according to their friendship or enmity with the Soviet Union.

Congressman Don Fraser, the prime architect of America's modern human rights policy, conducted extensive hearings on human rights and reviewed all options to the Congress. If the impeachment of President Nixon and the tumult over the Vietnam War had not been on the agenda of Congress during that period, it is conceivable that a different approach to the enforcement of international human rights might have emerged. But probably not. Beginning with the polarization of the east and the west, the invasion of eastern Europe in 1948, and the fall of Peking in 1949 to the Communists, the United States became locked into a mindset that the containment of Communism was the only objective of America's foreign policy. That objective overshadowed everything else. But the detestation of Communism was not enough to prompt the United States to invade the "captive nations" of armed Communist China or to even land in Cuba. There were a number of contradictions and incoherencies in America's approach to the u.s.s.r. and its satellites. It could be argued that containment was a policy which basically was an expansion of America's endorsement of those human rights which were made inviolable in the U.N. charter.

The members of Congress in 1976 realized all this, but they were ashamed of what their country was doing to attract authoritarian nations to join the struggle against totalitarian countries. The United States helped to create the nonaligned countries through its adamant desire to turn all nations outside the Communist sphere into the enemies of Marxism. This one myopic determination had, in the minds of a majority of Congress members, led the United States to abandon its solemn pledge in Articles 55 and 56 of the U.N. charter to work for political and economic human rights for all persons.

The months-long struggle to establish new laws protecting and promoting international human rights may well have caused an echo in Europe. The birth of the nebulous concept of detente occurred as the Congress was ending the war in Vietnam and thinking out its strategy on penalizing nations that neglected their duties under world law to observe international human rights. In the chanceries of Europe in the early 1970s a haphazard process, later called Helsinki, began to emerge. At dozens of meetings of low- and middle-level diplomats a document developed listing the rights European countries wanted their sister nations to observe. Political, economic, and cultural rights were thrown into three so-called baskets. In some cases, no one knew who had suggested these rights; they simply ended up in the 35,000-word final document signed by President Ford and the leaders of thirty-four other countries in Helsinki on August 1, 1975. Ford's coming to Helsinki on behalf of human rights was a strategy devised or at least allowed by Secretary of State Henry Kissinger. The dramatic ceremony in which the u.s.s.r. and all the satellite nations except Albania signed the document on human rights agreed to by all the European nations, Canada, and the United States was probably the greatest triumph for human rights since the U.N. General Assembly agreed to the Universal Declaration of Human Rights in 1948. Indeed, the Helsinki Accords reaffirmed most of the pledges of the Universal Declaration of Human Rights.

President Ford and Secretary Kissinger might have wanted only to deter the Congress from placing a new burden related to human rights on the State Department. But they probably strengthened the resolve of the majority in Congress to make certain that the State Department carried out the bold promises which the United States had re-ratified in Helsinki.

I happened to be in Moscow on a human rights mission on the days immediately following Moscow's dramatic signing of the Helsinki Accords. To the amazement of almost everyone, the total text of the Helsinki document was carried in the newspapers *Pravda* and *Izvestia*. My guide and translator, Anatoly Sharansky, and one of my hosts, Dr. Andre Sakharov, were amazed but jubilant. (I recall using one of the Helsinki promises in a specific way. The Accords say categorically that if a person is denied the right to leave a nation, he may not be charged a fee for a second application. I cited that clause to a sullen clerk at the Obir (immigration office). He waived the second fee!

The surge in the use of the Helsinki Accords in all the Iron Curtain countries was one of the principal reasons for the solidarity movement in Poland and comparable developments all over eastern and central Europe. This document was one of the many reasons why over 500,000 Soviets were able to immigrate to Israel.

It seems clear, therefore, that the human rights content of the U.N. charter and all its progeny came to flower in the United States and in Europe in the mid-1970s.

At a meeting of the Helsinki nations in November 1980 in Madrid, in which I participated, it seemed evident that a new era for human rights was being born. Members of the U.S. Congress like myself posed tough questions to the Soviets about specific prisoners or victims. But the smaller nations of Europe, including the Holy See, were grateful for the Helsinki process because finally they had a forum in which to raise questions about individual refugees or property taken in an east European nation or promises that had been broken concerning long festering issues of religious freedom.

The Soviets were aware in 1980 that pursuant to congressional action the State Department was now publishing an annual report on the misdeeds related to human rights in the Soviet Union and its "captive nations." The Kremlin wanted and needed trade with the United States. Soviet leaders feared the consequences of a few negative words or paragraphs in the annual report card on human rights of the State Department.

Without the protests of nongovernmental agencies in 1981 over the appointment of Ernest Lefever, the Bureau of Democracy, Human Rights, and Labor could have been eviscerated and almost extinguished. But the bureau had received such impetus and support during the Carter administration that its opponents could not destroy it or even de-fang it.

The idea, the concept, the dream of guaranteeing basic human rights to every person on the planet has entered into the human psyche and into international law. The way in which this happened was not neat or carefully planned or thoughtfully carried out. The human rights revolution occurred because certain ideas at certain times become irresistible — like the abolition of slavery or the granting of the right to vote to women.

We could go further and assert that the new support for human rights in the Helsinki Accords made the collapse of the Communist system inevitable.

The value and the beauty of the idea of a worldwide set of human rights accepted by everyone is a concept which, almost like the gospel, suddenly becomes appealing to groups or nations for reasons that are not entirely predictable or explainable. Those who advance the value of the gospel ordinarily assume that it is the grace of God which inspires believers to embrace the truths in the Bible. The proponents of international human rights do not have a superhuman source to which to appeal, but they can rely upon the firm words of the Preamble of the U.N. charter. Here all nations "reaffirm faith in fundamental human rights, in the dignity and worth of the human person, in the equal rights of men and women and of nations large and small." The term "dignity" may not be theological or metaphysical, but it is a strong, firm, clear, persuasive concept.

Theorists can speculate as to whether the secular concept of "dignity" can persuade nations to sacrifice some economic or historic gain in order to enlarge the scope of the human rights claimed by another nation, possibly even a traditional rival.

It is easy to rename "dignity" as "the rule of law" or "the democratic process," but are these ideas potentially more likely to induce a nation to comply with an intangible moral ideal which requires self-sacrifice?

It was the deep-seated self-interest of all nations — sometimes exalted to the concept of sovereignty — that led the authors of the U.N. charter to require the nations ratifying it to take on a legally binding obligation to live up to the pledges and promises therein. These nations were required for the first time in history to apply to the U.N. Security Council for permission to make war on another country. But there is no built-in mechanism in the U.N. charter to punish nations that are egregious violators of the human rights which they have agreed to safeguard. Nations which ratify the covenants on human rights are required to give an accounting of their compliance, but there are no juridical penalties for the offenders — even the worst of them.

If the development of the United Nations as an institution had not been radically and unexpectedly interrupted by the Cold War between 1948 and 1990, the idea of the inviolability of human rights even by sovereign nations might well have been at the center of a stunningly new international order.

9

THE
UNITED STATES
WALKS OUT ON THE
INTERNATIONAL
CRIMINAL COURT

The U.S. Congress was creative and persistent in establishing the machinery by which the State Department sits in judgment on the records on human rights of every member in the United Nations. That process improved during the Clinton administration.

But the Clinton White House will not be remembered as a friend of human rights; in July 1998 it declined to sign the documents of the International Criminal Court (ICC). The reasons for that decision were set forth by Ambassador at Large David J. Scheffer, who led the U.S. delegation to the Rome conference. Scheffer's ten-page exposition in the *American Journal of International Law* in January 1999 does not satisfy many persons who had been hoping for over fifty years for the establishment of a permanent Nuremberg.

Ambassador Scheffer described the six occasions on which President Clinton had endorsed the ICC prior to the diplomatic conference in Rome in June–July 1998, a meeting attended by 160 nations, 33 intergovernmental organizations, and a coalition of 236 nongovernmental organizations. The United States disappointed this impressive group when after the voice vote of 120 in favor, 7 against, and 21 abstentions, the United States elected to indicate publicly that it had voted against the statute. France, the United Kingdom, and the Russian federation supported the statute.

As often in the area of human rights, the United States voted on the basis of shortsighted reasons contrary to its obligations under world law and the expectations which the whole of humanity had for a country that, more than any other, could have put international human rights on the world agenda.

The ICC is an old and controversial entity. The United States voted against its formation after World War I. The concept of such a body received a moderate amount of attention in the years up to the establishment of the Nuremberg tribunal. According to the vast literature on the Nuremberg and Tokyo trials, the great weakness of that noble experiment was the obvious fact that it was a tribunal set up by the victors over the vanquished.

After the Nuremberg trials, Europe and especially the United States lost interest in the trials of war criminals. The hope or the illusion grew that there would never be a need for another Nuremberg. The scholars of international law probed all of the different options facing a court that seeks to develop a just process to indict, try, and punish the world's worse malefactors. The problems are baffling. Should there be an equivalent of a world's attorney general? Should the proposed tribunal be tied in with the Security Council, and, if so, should the five nations that now have the veto power be able to kill the indictment of leaders of a nation that is accused of crimes against humanity?

The questions persist. Any acceptable accommodation between the interests of the rich and powerful nations and the poor and undemocratic countries may end up in the form of a tribunal which is (or appears to be) controlled by countries that will seek the status quo if that is better for their trade routes and their economic progress.

The American Bar Association formed a task force to address these sticky issues. As a member of that task force, I gained a detailed perspective on the complexity of the problems that must be resolved before a truly independent tribunal can be born—a court that can require the leaders of sovereign nations to defend themselves against charges that they have committed or condoned crimes which for at least fifty years humanity has deemed to be inexcusable.

But the fact that 120 sovereign nations—having reviewed the matter for many years and having discussed it in Rome for seven weeks—

voted to establish the ICC means that there is substantial consensus on the topic.

Many students of the evolution of the ICC feel that its mission has been watered down in regrettable ways. The working text submitted to the Rome conference contained 116 articles, some of which were complicated with many options. The final statute is composed of a Preamble with 128 articles and 13 parts.

Possibly the most important principle is that of complementarity — that is, that the ICC may assume jurisdiction only when national legal systems are unable or unwilling to exercise jurisdiction. The ICC is clearly intended not to replace local courts but to operate only when there is no expectation that local or national courts will bring serious wrongdoers to justice.

The statute furthermore deals only with the most serious crimes that are of concern to the international community as a whole. Consequently, drug trafficking and terrorism are not included unless they somehow reach the level of crimes against humanity. The most serious crimes indictable by the ICC must be "core" offenses that are punishable as violations of customary international law.

Article 12 of the statute seems to weaken if not undermine the whole process. This provision requires the consent by the state of the nationality of the accused. The United States insisted on the inclusion of this restriction, which in the eyes of many could turn the court into a permanent invalid. The United States went further and cited the possible exclusion of Article 12 as the central reason for its opposing the entire statute. This position is apparently based on the Pentagon's fear that its military personnel could be arrested and tried for alleged crimes in nations where by treaty the United States is required to send soldiers.

The statute is weak in other ways. The traditional sovereignty of nations has scarcely been curbed by the ICC. The court can exercise its jurisdiction only if the state on whose territory the conduct in question occurred or if the state of nationality of the accused has accepted the court's jurisdiction. Iraq, consequently, is not touchable. It voted against the statute and is unlikely to join the ICC as long as Saddam Hussein is in power.

The enforceability of the Rome statute raises further questions. Article

86 imposes on state parties an obligation to "cooperate fully with the court." But the court will itself have no practical means to enforce its orders and decisions. The tribunal, moreover, is stymied in additional ways because the prosecutor does not have the authority to conduct investigations independently of national authorities. It seems disappointingly clear, therefore, that recalcitrant governments have many opportunities to defeat the letter and the spirit of the International Criminal Court.

But one positive development in the Rome statute is the explicit inclusion of crimes of sexual assault as crimes against humanity. Among the acts that can now be considered crimes against humanity and war crimes are "rape, sexual slavery, enforced prostitution, forced pregnancy, and forced sterilization or any other form of sexual violence of comparable gravity" (Article 7). The inclusion of war crimes committed in civil wars is a realistic development because most conflicts in the modern world take place within the borders of a single state.

The ICC provides for the presumption of innocence, the right to avoid self-incrimination, a prosecutor's burden of proving guilt beyond a reasonable doubt, the right of the accused to remain silent and to be questioned in the presence of counsel. No jury trial, however, is contemplated.

Jurists and academics will be debating for years on what happened in Rome and why an apparent strong consensus among nations ended up with a statute which has such serious flaws. The United States will be blamed for some of the deterioration. The fact is that the United States ends up as the only major nation in the world unwilling to contribute to the internationalization of the prosecution of offenses deemed crimes against humanity.

The United States has not ratified the U.N. covenants on economic rights, the rights of women, and the rights of the child. It has not accepted the Inter-American Convention on Human Rights (also known as the American Convention on Human Rights) or the Treaty on the Law of the Sea. Now it has boycotted the International Criminal Court. Is there something in the American psyche which favors isolationism and fears some globalization of our jurisprudence and our courts?

Clearly, the flat rejection of the ICC is unusually strong in reaction to a widely held fear of Senator Jesse Helms, the chairman of the Senate Foreign Relations Committee. The White House was inhibited, as well as the Pentagon, when Senator Helms proclaimed that the ICC would be "dead on arrival." There were other political and prudential reasons the White House and especially the Defense Department did not want to tangle with the Republican Congress over the ICC. The administration needs opportunities for collaboration and cooperation on a large number of other matters.

Ambassador David Scheffer justified the decisions the United States made in Rome in his January 1998 article in the *American Journal of International Law,* which is ultimately a lawyer's brief defending what his client requested him to do. In its most revealing sentence, he states:

> It is simply and logically untenable to expose the largest deployed military force in the world, stationed across the globe to help maintain international peace and security and to defend allies and friends, to the jurisdiction of a criminal court the United States government had not yet joined and whose authority over U.S. citizens the United States does not yet recognize. (p. 18)

The clear implication is that the Pentagon made the final decision not to sign the Rome treaty. Ambassador Scheffer concludes his remarks by stating that the "political will remains within the Clinton administration to support a treaty that is firmly and realistically constituted" (p. 21).

But the presence of American troops across the world will presumably remain. Must the proposed court give them immunity? If American military personnel engage in offenses which allegedly are crimes against humanity or crimes of war, should they not be treated like soldiers from Indonesia in East Timor? Or are American military personnel asking to be treated with special consideration?

Ambassador Scheffer concludes with the assertion that the "problems concerning the Rome treaty are solvable" (p. 21). But little has been forthcoming from the Clinton administration as to how these problems are "solvable."

The countless lawyers, human rights activists, and surviving participants in the Nuremberg process who worked for years to develop the International Criminal Court are deeply disappointed — even stunned — that the United States, the foremost proponent of the Nuremberg court and the principal architect of the ad hoc tribunal to try the perpetrators of the wars in the former Yugoslavia and in Rwanda, walked away from the creation of the ICC.

What is particularly troubling and, indeed, offensive is that no individual, no agency or group in the Clinton administration announced its responsibility for the ultimate awesome decision. The administration clearly had profound concerns, as did the thousands of advisors and participants who have been involved in the development of the ICC over the past two generations.

But who engaged in the legal or political decision-making that visibly angered the delegates from 160 nations and 236 nongovernmental organizations? The decision was not made by a public vote of the Joint Chiefs of Staff at the Pentagon or by the White House Cabinet.

Furthermore if the problems related to the ICC are "solvable," what are the White House and the Department of Defense going to do to expedite their resolution?

The process of putting the ICC into operation will go forward, but its probable success has certainly been curtailed by America's walkout. There is also the suspicion that some highly placed military officials at the Pentagon are lobbying America's allies to slow or stop the process of ratification.

The United States will continue to insist that the legal questions and the juridical process are very complicated and that the United States must be cautious and careful. No one denies that. Lawyers working on the ICC for the past several years have explored all the knotty problems and have weighed a thousand hypotheticals. But weighty decisions have to be made before any court is established; the issues involved in the establishment of the first worldwide court on human rights are complicated almost beyond comprehension.

But the impression one obtains concerning the explanation of America's walkout is that the United States has decided that while the court is a wonderful idea, it cannot be supported because it might adversely affect some American service personnel. What is brushed aside is the fact that the ICC is going to have an impact on every nation that joins and even those nations that do not. When the U.S. Constitution took effect in the United States, every single state lost some of their rights by the preemption given to Congress by the Constitution or by Congress passing laws under its constitutional right to legislate on matters affecting interstate commerce.

The ICC will have effects. The process is carefully constructed so that no nation will ever be required to accept the jurisdiction of the ICC if that nation in good faith investigates the conduct of one of its nationals charged with serious wrongdoing.

The implication of the negative vote in Rome is that the United States fears some nations will bring false charges against American personnel because these individuals have aroused suspicion or hatred within the country where they happen to reside at the moment.

Such an attitude or an assumption will almost certainly be annoying to most other nations that, following the end of the most violent century in human history, cast their votes for the world's first criminal court.

A thorough presentation of all the issues involved in the formation of the ICC was provided following the publication of Ambassador Scheffer's article in the January 1999 issue of the *American Journal of International Law*. This wonderful summary was written by Darryl Robinson, a high-level diplomat from Canada who was a member of the Canadian delegation to the Rome conference. The twenty-five-page article explores each of the major issues related to jurisdiction, potential punishment, and probable future problems with the ICC.

The rejection by the United States of the ICC still stuns activists and academics in the international human rights movement. They have been virtually forced to impute the defeat to the Pentagon and not to the White House or Secretary of State Madeleine Albright. Anger at the decision seems out of place because honest public officials sincerely devoted to human rights made the call.

The issue really involves the role of the United States in international affairs. In his journal article, Ambassador Scheffer assumes that the role of the United States must remain exactly as it is. Anything that endangers the worldwide presence of American soldiers is bad for the universe.

A great deal of ignorance or arrogance — or both — is inherent in that position. The American soldiers the Pentagon insists must be immune from the jurisdiction of the ICC were placed there during the Cold War to shore up active or potential allies of the United States in its stance against the "evil empire." Why these military personnel now remain in these faraway places is a question crying out for review. Perhaps in the not-too-distant future many or most of them will be withdrawn, as they were in West Germany. Will the ICC then be less objectionable?

The four Geneva treaties on the rules of war agreed to after World War II in 1949 are binding on U.S. military officials. The Pentagon used these treaties when it tried Lt. William Calley for alleged violations of the rules of war in the massacre at My Lai in Vietnam.

Why, then, is the United States so afraid of the International Criminal Court using these same rules — along with the Nuremberg principles — in cases when persons engaged in international or civil war are charged with crimes against humanity?

The decision of the Clinton administration in Rome not to support the ICC was particularly disappointing because it had worked so diligently and successfully to launch the tribunal for the former Yugoslavia. Key observers theorize that the 1993 court for the former Yugoslavia would facilitate the acceptance of the International Criminal Court. It may have for the vast majority of nations. But not for the United States.

10

GRADING THE
STATE DEPARTMENT'S
REPORTS ON HUMAN
RIGHTS

It seems clear that the record of the United States on international human rights has been uneven, uncertain, and unpredictable. The moral aspirations of the United States for the world have often been laudable. But the country has been haunted by hubris, imperialism, delusions of grandeur, and just plain pride.

Yet, the United States has been consistent and persistent in its desires to enhance the ideals of democracy here and abroad. Those aspirations are spelled out in the annual report on human rights issued by the State Department pursuant to the directive of Congress. For almost twenty years the United States has annually published reports on human rights which now accumulate to some 20,000 pages. It is an astonishing achievement that has undoubtedly had enormous if unmeasurable impact on nations which for dozens of reasons want to be in the good graces of the United States.

The preface to each of the annual reports reviews the anxieties and aspirations of the U.S. government in the area of human rights. Clearly the State Department has turned around completely from the era when John Foster Dulles in one of his acts as secretary of state removed Eleanor Roosevelt from the U.N. Commission on Human Rights and claimed that the United States "would not become a party to any human rights treaty approval by the United Nations." All of Dulles's successors up to

Henry Kissinger regarded human rights as a hindrance to the pursuit of great power politics.

The State Department report on human rights for 1998 is over 2,000 pages long, including detailed accounts about every country from Angola to Zimbabwe. There does not yet exist a generally accepted formula by which to judge a nation on human rights — as there is for other criteria such as literacy, infant mortality rates, or the average age at death. But a litmus test for human rights is surely around the corner. When that becomes available nations will pay attention because corporations in developed countries are far less likely to invest in nations with human rights problems than in areas where democracy is thriving.

The facts in the annual State Department report on human rights, therefore, have consequences. What that report says can easily determine the future of a country. Take, for example, the report on Tanzania for the year 1998. The State Department reported "pervasive corruption" that had a "broad impact on human rights." There also existed, the State Department noted, "arbitrary arrest and detention" and a nation where "mob justice remains severe and widespread."

This report details the conditions of every country with respect to political and other extrajudicial killing, disappearances, torture, arbitrary arrest, denial of fair trial, the state of freedom of speech and press, freedom of religion, the right of citizens to change their government, and discrimination based on race, sex, religion, disability, and social status. Children's and workers' rights are also included.

The profile of most underdeveloped or recently decolonized countries under all these criteria leaves only a few with high grades. As one reads the very detailed reports written by American observers in struggling countries, the question repeatedly arises as to the fairness of it all. Take the fifteen pages in small print on Togo. The country they describe is not a very attractive place. One constantly wonders whether a harsh assessment would be written if the human rights criteria used in judging Togo were applied to the United States. But the State Department report does want to be fair and just. Although its five pages on Australia, for example, are necessarily positive about the highly developed democratic institutions in that country, they are blunt — even harsh — concerning the indigenous people of that country. They are imprisoned at twenty-one times the rate of nonindigenous people. The government of Australia, in the view of the human rights report, has not responded to a series of recommendations made by a 1991 royal commission.

Have such criticisms helped the indigenous people of Australia to remedy their condition? The answer of the State Department and Congress, which authorized the process of annual reports, is certainly yes. This is a way to carry out the "mobilization of shame."

Does the exposure of the neglect of its indigenous population help the government in Australia? Again, the answer has to be affirmative. This kind of exposure puts international pressure on Australia to accelerate its efforts to provide equality for the descendants of those living in Australia long before the Europeans came to colonize that vast land.

The systematic reporting of the deficiencies of all the nations of the earth is salutary in another way. The nongovernmental organizations devoted to the rights of women, the disabled, or the indigenous have a new source of information which — because that information comes from the U.S. government — is an authoritative way to demonstrate that a particular nation is violating international human rights law.

The annual report also serves as a way of reiterating world law. The first page of the report for 1998 noted that Article 21 of the Universal Declaration of Human Rights provides that "the will of the people shall be the basis of the authority of government . . . expressed in periodic and genuine elections." This gave the State Department the opportunity to boast that the U.S. government spends over $1 billion each year to defend democracies under attack. This expenditure was justified as not only "right" but also necessary, because the security of the United States as a nation "depends upon the expansion of democracy worldwide."

It is noteworthy that the State Department report includes "open and competitive economic structures" as an integral part of the respect for human rights which international law now requires. But this theme of "open and competitive" structures is muted in the State Department assessments. One could argue cogently that economic and political rights go together and that the advent of human rights depends on a healthy economy and a vigorous democratic government. That theme is suggested by State Department reports, but Congress has not mandated that the department collect and disseminate data on the state of free enterprise in individual nations. Actually, an evaluation on topics such as the tax structure for corporations and the state of antitrust law on certain economic enterprises would be helpful and meaningful to everyone. It would also illustrate the State Department's traditional position that the strength of a nation's democratic structures must include information on the freedom of operation granted to corporations. The report also includes information on the status of unions that is incomplete without data on the state of management. This would be particularly relevant for nations like the fifteen countries that since 1990 have been able to disaffiliate from the U.S.S.R.

The symbiosis between economic and political rights was noted in the final resolution of the 1993 World Conference on Human Rights in Vienna in these words: "While development facilitates the enjoyment of human rights, the lack of development may not be invoked to justify the abridgement of internationally recognized human rights."

The State Department report for 1997 stressed the interconnection between economic and political rights in this statement: "It is now well established that the ultimate economic crisis — famine and mass starvation — is not occurring . . . in those countries whose rulers bear the consequences of their decisions, whose people participate in their own government, and in which information freely circulates." The authors of the 1997 report realized that "the global movement for human rights is one of the most extraordinary political developments in modern history." But they felt constrained to recognize the slowness of progress, concluding that "the greatest works of the human spirit take a long time to come into being, and they must be constantly nurtured less they collapse, with horrific results" and that "the evolving global network of laws and institutions protecting and promoting human rights has taken a long time, but its roots lie deep in the hopes, aspirations and beliefs in human dignity of all cultures and societies."

The authors of the State Department's annual report on human rights must certainly know that their words and their accusations produce resentment, some of which might lead to long-term alienation and even violence. In 1999, a significant number of U.S. embassies felt so threatened by extremists that they closed for a period and asked Congress for vast sums of money in order to enhance security.

There is possibly no way to persuade the world's nations that the United States, lonely at the top, is really their friend and benefactor. Secretary of State Madeleine Albright called the United States "the indispensable nation." She meant it in a benign sense. But many nations want to resist the domination of one powerful country; they resent the United States for proclaiming its high political ideals and its devotion to human rights while poor countries are experiencing chronic malnutrition, AIDS epidemics, and persistent high unemployment rates. Poor countries will always resent rich countries. But today the United States simultaneously flaunts its wealth and proclaims its devotion to human rights by publicizing each year 2,000 pages of denunciations of the human rights conditions in most if not all nondemocratic poor countries in the world.

No one has publicly urged that Congress modify the law so that the United States is no longer perceived as a hypocrite that conceals its own failures on human rights but denounces similar failures in other countries.

The disparity of America's record on human rights and its blunt and sometimes brutal condemnations of countries in Latin America is especially glaring because the United States has never ratified the Inter-American Convention on Human Rights (also known as the American Convention on Human Rights). President Carter signed the treaty, but the U.S. Senate has never expressed an interest in joining in the partnership, which brings together the nations of Latin America and the Caribbean. If the United States did ratify the convention it would be a party to the Inter-American Commission and Court on Human Rights, based in San José, Costa Rica. The United States would, of course, also be subject to the jurisdiction of the commission and the court and thus could be sued by individuals and nations alleging that the United States or an entity directed or controlled by the United States had engaged in conduct in violation of the Inter-American Convention on Human Rights.

It is consequently a bit incongruous for the United States to cite the nations of Latin America for their failure to comply with internationally recognized human rights while abstaining from the elaborate process set up to offer indemnification to the people of North and South America.

The U.S. government is also open to the charge that in its reports on countries like El Salvador and Nicaragua, it is not being candid about the fact that massive U.S. involvement in these nations in the 1980s substantially altered the political structure of these countries. The Reagan administration spent over $3 billion to defeat allegedly Communist rebels in El Salvador and put in place a group closely identified with the fourteen dominant families and the strong military that has dominated El Salvador's history for generations.

There was hardly a mention of that turbulent story—in which 75,000 persons lost their lives—in the State Department Report on Human Rights in El Salvador for 1998. The report was careful and cautious, and it could easily be criticized and corrected by observers familiar with the tragedies that befell El Salvador during the twelve-year war in which the United States financed one side. The report made its own assumptions. It praised El Salvador's "market-based, mixed economy" and the "privatization and free-market reforms," although it conceded that "about 48 percent of the population lives below the poverty level."

The State Department's report was fact-filled and touched on all the topics required by Congress. But close observers of the tragedies that have occurred in El Salvador since Archbishop Oscar Romero was assassinated in March 1980 are skeptical of the report. Is the State Department required to pretend that U.S. intervention in the 1980s did not happen or did not radically change what would have happened if it had not taken up warfare against the Farabundo Marti National Liberation front (FMLN)?

We should be grateful to the staff of the U.S. Embassy in San Salvador for their comprehensive collection of facts and their meticulous reporting of them. But are there assumptions that conceal or minimize what the United States did to the poor country of El Salvador? Is the human rights report ultimately a way for the United States to exalt the U.N. human rights agenda while pretending that it is carrying out its duties to protect and promote human rights?

There is something artificial, pretentious, and hypocritical about the way in which the U.S. government through the State Department sits in judgment every year on the state of human rights in El Salvador.

The same could be said about Nicaragua. The report did not refer to the massive U.S. intervention in which it organized and deployed the

"Contras." The report said only that the civil war ended in June 1990 with the mobilization of the Nicaraguan Contras. It did concede, though, that because of a "weak judiciary" most of the "human rights abuses cited by the Tripartite Commission in well-documented reports remains unpunished."

The report on Nicaragua for 1998 reveals that the prison population rose in 1998 to 5,570, up from 3,946 in 1997. Caloric intake for the prisoners remained at 750 to 800 a day, well below the 1,800 calories per day recommended by the United Nations. The U.S. report also notes that one-third of all prisoners are jailed for six months or more without trial.

The report on Nicaragua reveals once again the tendency of the State Department to overrely on the existence of a democratically elected government. The document opens by rejoicing in the elections of President Arnoldo Aleman in 1996 in a "free and fair election." American diplomats and elected officials regularly boast that now all the nations of Latin America except Cuba have a popularly elected government. But one must raise the question whether this new phenomenon has been used to downplay or obscure the fact that massive denials of human rights continue after a fair election. In some instances the poor have not been allowed to organize or participate in open elections where voters have a meaningful choice.

Although the State Department report on every country is probably open to criticism, the existence of a conflict of interest between the U.S. government and the nations in question needs to be explored. This is why the work of the nongovernmental organizations criticizing the department reports in the 1980s were so valuable. If the United States has had direct or indirect ideological or economic links with a nation, it is understandable that the drafters of the report on such a nation would tend to mute the bad news and magnify the good news.

The ideological basis of the Cold War years is no longer reflected in the human rights report, except for North Korea and, of course, China. I have read and dissected every report on China since the first one appeared in 1978. The 1998 report contained harsh accusations. The human rights record "deteriorated sharply . . . with a crackdown against organized political dissent." The government, it was charged, blocked the Voice of

America broadcast, was restrictive of the press, and sought to infringe on the freedom of religion.

The charges were not new. They have horrified the world for decades. There is no suggestion that the State Department report mitigated or exaggerated the accusations against China. The issue is what the United States should do that it is not now doing to improve the status of human rights in China.

The record on this issue is extensive and contentious. Everyone wants to curb the abuses in China. For several years the United States imposed restrictions on China by denying them so-called Most Favored Nation status; this meant that the ordinary trade privileges given to America's friends and allies have not been extended to China.

In the 1990s, Congress and the White House had lengthy debates about removing the Most Favored Nation status from China. The Tiananmen massacre and the unrelenting repression of religion in China and its policy on abortion have been central to that debate. The support that China gave to the Khmer Rouge in Cambodia also played a part in the extended debate.

Members of Congress representing farm states favored the granting of the Most Favored Nation status of China lest U.S. farmers lose an opportunity to sell massive amounts of grain to that country. On the other side, the persons who want to punish China for its persistent adherence to Communism push aggressively for economic sanctions.

China has in effect now been granted the right to ship most of its exports to the United States without paying tariffs. The threat that this right could be terminated is, theoretically, an incentive to China to honor human rights. But that threat does not seem to be working.

The detente now granted to China does not really resolve the basic policy question posed by Section 502b. That law, enacted in 1976, says flatly that the United States should not extend benefits to those nations that practice gross violations of human rights. China surely falls into that category — possibly more than any other nation.

But the policy has been quietly adopted that it is better to trade with China with the hope that more frequent and better relations with that country, which counts for one-fifth to one-fourth of all humanity, will in the long run be more advantageous to the advancement of human rights than a policy of isolating and humiliating that vast country.

The best policy to follow varies with each nation and with each situation. In 1976 Congress decided that the United States must have a policy on this matter. The State Department has tried to carry out that policy. But there are intractable problems. If the U.S. government is too adamant, it might end up with more Cubas. If it is too lenient, it might be accused of being unfaithful to the objectives of Section 502b and, even worse, of being "soft" on carrying out America's basic foreign policy role as guardian of all the human rights which 160 nations re-ratified as precious and inviolable in 1993 at the Vienna conference.

In the war to protect human rights there are no quick victories or even easy problems. Crafty and evil political leaders, when combined with a poorly educated citizenry, can mislead and abuse people for a considerable period of years. Individuals in this situation can claim or reclaim their rights only if they are encouraged and supported by outside forces. Even when this support is forthcoming, it cannot succeed unless there is some deep feeling among the citizens that no government is valid without the consent of the governed.

While the State Department feels itself bound to pursue only the specific topics mandated by Congress, it does interpret the idea of human rights in a broad sense. As a result it is involved in working to bring about a satisfactory resolution of a long-hidden controversy which arose in 1997 concerning Swiss and other banks not returning money or other valuables to the descendants of Jews killed by the Nazis. The State Department report for 1998 remarks that "history's greatest genocide was almost certainly also its largest organized robbery."

In 1998, the State Department and the U.S. Holocaust Memorial Museum co-sponsored a conference in Washington attended by forty-four governments and thirteen nongovernmental organizations. The conference helped bring about the enactment of restitution laws in several European nations. The Holocaust, the report notes, more than any other event brought about the human rights movement; it is therefore necessary to move forward while the past is still a living memory.

Obviously, the promotion of elections is one of the core duties of the State Department Bureau of Human Rights. In its report it quotes the statement of Freedom House (a nongovernmental organization based in New York and Washington, devoted to the enhancement and implementation of human rights around the world) that at the end of 1998 there were 117 electoral democracies constituting 55 percent of the world's population. The number of democracies has almost doubled in the past ten years.

The State Department report also pays a good deal of attention to a new mandate on religious freedom given to it in 1997 by Congress. The directive was to place religious freedom squarely in the mainstream of U.S. foreign policy. A special representative for international religious freedom was appointed pursuant to the bill signed by President Clinton in October 1998. This measure gives the president and the State Department the right and the duty to take suitable steps to deter infringements on religious freedom around the world.

When this measure was moving through Congress, certain dissenters felt that it had been the creation of the religious right and that it exalted religious freedom over other comparably valuable human rights. It remains to be seen how the new emphasis on religious liberty will play out.

The United States speaks and acts about human rights in a wide range of forums. To some extent the government has moved to a position where, as President Carter used to say, human rights is the "soul of America's foreign policy." The unprecedented emphasis on the rights of women has certainly been heard around the world. The denunciation of female genital mutilation has helped to force a rethinking of that hitherto seldom discussed problem. The accent on the rights of millions of child workers has added a new voice to the worldwide debate on that issue. Most people still do not know that, according to the International Labor Organization, as many as 250 million children under the age of fifteen are employed full- or part-time around the world.

The report on human rights that appeared early in 1999 on the record of 1998 is deeply impressive. But, alas, probably the most critical issue on human rights in that year—the International Criminal Commission—is hardly mentioned. In June 1998 the Clinton administration voted no on the ICC in Rome. If the decision on that matter had been given to the human rights experts at the State Department, the outcome almost certainly would have been different. History books may well conclude that the abandonment of the commission by the United States was the worst mistake made by any government in the world in 1998.

The philosophical premises underlying the annual reports of the State Department are relatively clear. They reflect the 1945 Charter of the United Nations, the Universal Declaration of Human Rights, and the laws enacted by the U.S. Congress. The principles become clearer and more compelling each year. Adherence to the core moral principles that support international human rights becomes more unquestioned every year. The real problem is how to make that enforceable. The State Department cannot effectively command officials in distant lands to use their authority to enforce international human rights. Proponents of international human rights can only propose the nature and value of human rights and hope that their intrinsic value will be found attractive enough to ensure their acceptance and enforcement.

Even the mighty government of the United States must resort to the "mobilization of shame." Ultimately this is the moral power which, more than laws or economic sanctions, will induce nations to follow the less traveled road that leads to democracy and equality.

11

THE
UNITED STATES
PUTS THE
WORLD'S TORTURERS
ON TRIAL

On March 22, 1992, the United States became the first country in the world to enact legislation offering the victims of torture the right to sue their oppressors for civil damages. Under the Tort Victim Protection Act (TVPA) victims of torture now have a federal cause of action in the U.S. courts against their torturers who acted under cover of law.

The process by which this unique law came into existence began with the 1980 decision *Filartiga v. Peña Irala*, in which Judge Irving Kaufman stated that "official torture is now prohibited by the law of nations." As a result, the judge held that Dolly Filartiga could sue and recover damages from the official who tortured and killed her brother Joelito in Paraguay. The case for the plaintiff, argued creatively by lawyers from the Center for Constitutional Rights, was strengthened by the affirmative support offered by the Justice Department of the Carter administration. The decision of the Second Circuit Court of Appeals in New York eventually led to a ruling that awarded the victims a total of $10 million in compensatory and punitive damages.

The *Filartiga* decision and its progeny were obviously influenced by the adoption on December 18, 1979, of the Torture Convention by the U.N. General Assembly. Similarly, the *Filartiga* result was one of the many reasons the U.S. Senate ratified the Torture Convention on October 27, 1990, and passed the TVPA in 1992.

Judge Kaufman's opinion reminds Americans that the framers of the U.S. Constitution knew about international law and favored its inclusion in the law of the United States. The Constitution itself grants Congress the authority to "define and punish . . . offenses against the law of nations."

The power granted to Congress by the Constitution with respect to international law is the basic reason the very first Congress enacted the Alien Tort Claims Act (ATCA). The act provided that "the district courts should have original jurisdiction of any civil tort action by an alien . . . committed *in violation of the law of nations* or a treaty of the United States" [emphasis supplied]. For reasons that remain obscure, the ATCA had rarely been used until it appeared in the Filartiga decision. But U.S. courts have made it clear that international law is a part of America's legal heritage.

In 1900 the Supreme Court in *Paquete Habava* made it clear that "international law is part of our law and must be ascertained and administered by the courts of justice of appropriate jurisdiction." As a result, the Supreme Court ruled against the United States, which had captured two Spanish fishing vessels off the coast of Cuba during the Spanish-American War. The United States was not a party to any treaty or written international agreement specifying that ordinary fishing vessels were exempt from capture as a prize of war. Despite that fact, the Supreme Court ruled that the United States had violated international law as established through history. The Court determined that the capture of the vessels was unlawful and ordered the proceeds of the sale returned to the claimants with damages and costs.

The Supreme Court in *Paquete Habava* also specifically acknowledged the validity of customary international law. The words of the Court are striking: "Where there is no treaty, and no controlling executive or legislative act or judicial decision resort must be had to the customs and usages of civilized nations; and, . . . of these, to the works of jurists and commentators, who by years of labor, research and experience, have made themselves peculiarly well acquainted with the subjects of which they treat."

American jurists continue to be uneasy about utilizing norms that derive from customary international law. This resistance has been addressed by the efforts of the American Law Institute to define and clarify the precise nature of customary international law. The restatement (3rd) on the foreign relations law of the United States, a generally accepted guide to international law as applicable to the United States, names in Section 702 the following seven offenses which have achieved the status of customary international law: genocide, slavery or slave trade, murdering or causing the disappearance of individuals, torture or other cruel or inhuman or degrading treatment or punishment, prolonged arbitrary detention, systematic racial discrimination, and a consistent pattern of gross violations of internationally recognized human rights.

The list in the restatement is not meant to be exhaustive. The notes of the reporter concede that even in 1986 when the restatement was being finalized after years of discussion and debate, systematic religious discrimination, the right to own and not be arbitrarily deprived of property, and gender discrimination were already principles of customary international law or were on the verge of achieving that status.

This view was echoed in 1991 in the book *International Law in Theory and Practice,* by Oscar Schacter. He opines that the right to basic subsistence, the right to public assistance in matters of health, welfare, and basic education, and the rights of women to full equality have all gained the acceptance required to become customary international law.

The ambiguities of the content of customary international law led the Congress to codify the results of *Filartiga* and similar decisions.

When I testified before the U.S. Senate and the House on behalf of the Torture Victim Protection Act for the American Bar Association, I recognized that the issue was arcane and that it had little political appeal to the members of Congress. But the 1789 Alien Tort statute was being litigated and its ambiguities needed to be clarified by Congress.

The proposed Torture Victim Protection Act offered clarity. A ten-year statute of limitations was added to the law, which would include citizens and aliens. There really was little resistance in the Congress because all that was being attempted was the modification of law passed by the very first Congress. In addition, no immunity is granted to a foreign torturer on the basis that he or she was only following the orders of a superior. But American officials are not covered in the bill; no action can be brought against any American authority acting in his or her official capacity in the

United States or abroad. A further qualification of the law requires that all plaintiffs exhaust their remedies abroad before they can ask for relief in an American court under the Torture Victim Protection Act.

The TVPA includes "extra judicial killing" as a cause of action in addition to torture. The definition of "extra judicial killing" is taken from Article 3 of the Geneva Convention of 1949 — long since accepted by the United States. The definition of torture in the TVPA tracks the language of the Torture Convention. Under that treaty the torture must intentionally inflict "severe pain or suffering . . . whether physical or mental" in order to obtain a confession, punishment, intimidation, or coercions. The language includes mental torture as a justifiable cause of action. Other examples include intense psychological pressure, sensory deprivation, and the use of hallucinatory drugs.

My involvement in the enactment of the Tort Victim Protection Act was personalized by a meeting with a victim of torture when I was on a human rights mission in Chile just before the fall of General Pinochet. Marcella was fifteen years old when she became involved in a Catholic movement of young people. The group she headed was not political but was a unit to study Catholic social teaching. Almost inevitably the Catholic movement, which took positions on human rights, was perceived by the government to be anti-Pinochet. Marcella was questioned and tortured by the authorities, who wanted information on her colleagues. In order to intimidate Marcella and discourage her associates the government branded Marcella with a crucifix on her forehead.

A church-related clinic giving Marcella medical and psychological assistance brought her to my human rights group in Santiago. With long black hair and a frightened demeanor Marcella was reluctant to say anything. She was filled with guilt over her feeling that, under pressure and torture, she had revealed information about the other members of her Catholic group. She was also dreading her probable return to the process of torture, during which she would be required to either commit perjury or confess to alleged crimes against the dictatorship.

Marcella would now have a judicial process available to her in the United States. Would torture decrease around the world if Marcella and every victim of torture had available the remedies under the TVPA? The answer is not clear. But the remedy for the victims of torture in the TVPA is creative, constructive, and exciting.

Torture is a dark, insidious, and clandestine practice that has an astonishing presence in the world. In its annual report for 1999, Amnesty International states that the incidence of torture has increased. In 1998, 55 percent of all nations indulged in torture and other comparable abuses. In 1999, the figure rose to 66 percent.

It should be noted that the U.N. Convention Against Torture and Other Cruel, Inhuman, or Degrading Treatment or Punishment calls for no exceptions. Any exception, however useful to law enforcement, would undercut the purpose of the treaty and render it subject to uncontrollable exceptions. This means that a government may not torture someone even if such a procedure could lead to, for example, the knowledge of the identity of a kidnapper of a child. According to international law, torture for any reason is now forbidden.

The Torture Victim Protection Act did not override the Alien Tort statute of 1789. The TVPA authorizes relief only for torture and extrajudicial killing. For other wrongs the Alien Tort statute may be used.

There is a further restriction on the use of the TVPA. Visiting heads of state are immune from lawsuits under this American law. But former heads of state, like Pinochet of Chile, could conceivably be subject to suits under the TVPA. The Foreign Sovereign Immunity Act (FSIA) of 1976, however, may in some cases grant immunity to foreign visitors who were once public officials in their own nations.

An ever lengthening series of decisions based on *Filartiga* show more and more clearly that international law is becoming a source of authority for plaintiffs who seek indemnification for wrongs done to them in another country which are now compensable because they violate the law of nations.

A list of some of the cases based on the *Filartiga* decision is impressive — even though in most of the cases the petitioners have not been able to recover actual money against offending presidents or dictators. But future remedies may be forthcoming. It is noteworthy that for many years there were no remedies at law for the victims of the Holocaust whose gold or jewelry was deposited in banks in Switzerland or elsewhere. But now some settlement has been agreed to between banks in Switzerland and depositors in the United States, Germany, and elsewhere.

It is not clear that these victims could have recovered if the *Filartiga* decision had come down in 1948 instead of 1980. But surely there should have been some lawful remedy for those whose assets had been tortiously seized during the Nazi era. It could be demonstrated that the theft and/ or embezzlement of the assets of the victims of Hitler were or should have been violations of international law.

In 1988, several citizens of Argentina successfully sued former General Carlos Suarez-Mason for human rights violations committed during the war years — 1976 to 1983. In 1995, a group of Guatemalan plaintiffs in Massachusetts were awarded a judgment for $47 million against General Hector Gramajo. In 1996, three women who were tortured in Ethiopia sued the perpetrators in Atlanta, Georgia. The judge awarded the plaintiffs a total of $1.5 million for torturous and arbitrary detention. The mother of a man killed in a massacre in East Timor successfully sued an Indonesian general living in Boston.

The enactment of the Torture Victim Protection Act of 1992 has not brought all the relief that many of its advocates had hoped for. But it is still a very significant piece of legislation because it is the first statute ever enacted by a country which allows aliens and its own citizens to attempt to obtain damages for violations committed in a distant land if they are contrary to international law.

The potential consequences of the TVPA are immense. As the case law and the jurisprudence engendered by the act develop, foreign leaders may hesitate to enter the United States because they could be sued for having violated international law when they were in power. The detention in England of former president of Chile Pinochet is one example of what can happen.

The impact of the *Filartiga* decision and its progeny should not be overinterpreted. The potential of this law is limited by the long tradition of deference among nations. That deference was synthesized in the 1976 law passed by Congress, the Foreign Sovereign Immunities Act. This law, which cleared Congress without difficulty, was requested by the State Department as a way of promulgating a clear statement to the world as to what the United States could or would do when a lawsuit is brought against a foreign leader in a U.S. court. The FSIA may seem to restrict the rights of plaintiffs in America to sue a foreign leader, but this is not inconsistent with the Torture Victim Protection Act. The *Filartiga* law allows victims in the United States to sue former public officials in order to acquire restitution for wrongs done in an official capacity that were a violation of world law.

Will other nations follow the progressive example of the United States and let victims sue in their courts for violations of international law committed by their political leaders in another country? As of yet, we have no concrete example. But many nations follow the legal developments in the United States and sometimes emulate them.

If most nations adopted the purposes of the TVPA, would it make an important difference in the availability of remedies for the infringement of human rights? It could, but the statute should be broadened so that it embraces not only torture but other egregious violations of international law. The various adaptations of the TVPA should also include provisions for extradition and for the collection of penalties and reparations.

The International Criminal Court is intended to implement some features of the TVPA. The ICC would take care of the indictment, trial, conviction, and punishment of the world's worst offenders. In turn, the TVPA would provide for civil penalties and compensatory damages for those who have been convicted by the ICC.

Are these scenarios too idealistic, unrealistic, and utopian? Many will think so. But the incredibly rapid movement of the globalization of commerce, communication, and democratic institutions means that almost inevitably the moral and legal principles that established the nature of international law will be accepted at the local level. That means that individuals like Dolly Filartiga will be able to obtain a remedy for the disasters that befall them.

The globalization of the law of personal injury by public officials could be closer than it now appears. The universal standards fixed by the International Labor Organization, the World Health Organization, and the new World Trade Organization will be a model for the architects of a world plan to inhibit and deter the violations of the ever enlarging group of human rights which are the legacy of all members of the human race.

The challenge underlying the struggle of American courts concerning how and when they should use international law as a source of their decisions is complex and profound. Most state judges do not want to give their opponents or critics an opportunity to challenge them on the grounds that they relied on some international document as the equivalent of sound American law. There is enormous resistance to the use of legal norms that have not been passed by Congress and signed by the president. But the fact is that American law does not always adequately extend the new protections for privacy, for example, available under international law.

If one reads the constitutions accepted by many nations in the world, it is evident that they have protections not available in the U.S. Constitution. The constitution of South Africa, for example, is the first constitution to contain guarantees against discrimination toward gays and lesbians. The constitution of Canada expresses more clearly and guarantees more expressly some of the rights not explicitly recognized in America's constitutional heritage. Some of the new constitutions have explicit guarantees for the rights of women and children not available in any constitution, federal or state, in America.

Despite the shortcomings in the constitutional protections in the United States, the courts and citizens share a profound reluctance to assert new rights not now contained in the Constitution of the United States or of the fifty states.

That is why the Torture Victim Protection Act might have surprising results. It depends on international law, but its enforcement does not require a judge to reach out to some world norm not set forth explicitly in the relevant statute.

The statute is very restrictive because it requires the defendant to be present in the United States in a manner that makes possible the services of process. This is clearly a warning to any former public official who could be subject to the act if he enters the United States. The ancient principle that the defendant must be physically present or at least reachable by legal process derives ultimately from the protections of national sovereignty. Theoretically, if a person violates international or world law he should be penalized where he is found. If the nation where the crime was committed will not try him for a violation of law that binds all nations, that country should at least be required to extradite the suspect to another nation.

This is a new jurisprudence that governs the world when a person is chargeable with a serious crime. Can this logic be extended to those who under world law have a right to damages in a civil case? That would be the next logical step if nations really desire to compensate those who have been hurt through torture or other offenses against the law of nations.

With the enactment of the Torture Victim Protection Act, the United States took a step that is unprecedented in the history of the international human rights movement. The TVPA is a timid beginning by the United States — the prime architect of the United Nations and the principal cheerleader for its efforts to promote and protect human rights. The act can be enlarged by the Congress and expanded by the courts. It is one of those laws which, like the Civil Rights Act of 1964, has the potential to transform a nation and a world.

Part III

HUMAN RIGHTS
TRANSFORM THE
WORLD

12

REGIONAL

TRIBUNALS

FOR HUMAN

RIGHTS

Events moved at lightning speed after the end of World War II in 1945. The inhabitants of Europe were stunned to learn that at least 6 million Jews had been murdered and that neither Europe nor the United States had spoken out and tried to save the Jews soon after it became clear that Hitler was determined to carry out his plan to eliminate the Jewish community. Years later the silence of the United States concerning the Jews was documented in a searing book, *The Abandonment of the Jews,* by David Wyman (Norton, 1984).

The establishment in 1953 of two separate entities, the European Convention on Human Rights (also known as the European convention) and the European Court on Human Rights, suggested the people of Europe felt shame and guilt soon after the war. Reportedly at the suggestion of Winston Churchill, all the nations of western Europe created a human rights tribunal which convened in 1953 in Strasbourg.

The history of this convention and court brings not a little glory to the nations that established it. The founding of this transnational entity is also due in part to the terror of Europeans as they saw the fall to the Kremlin of the countries of eastern and central Europe. The U.S.S.R., an ally of the United States and the United Kingdom and their partners in founding the United Nations, became the occupier of large areas of Europe after helping the allies defeat Germany's occupation of these very nations.

The preamble to the Commission and Court on Human Rights makes it clear that the victors wanted to make certain that if there ever was a dictator again in Europe, all the citizens in every country would have a place to register their protests. Such a right was theoretically granted to everyone in the world with the creation of the U.N. Commission on Human Rights. But the framers of the court in Strasbourg intended that the people living in a relatively homogeneous area with a common culture would have complaints about civil rights and civil liberties that might be too complicated and sophisticated for a worldwide commission serving the 3 billion human beings then on the planet.

The nations that formed what was probably the first transnational tribunal on human rights in the history of the human race were cautious. They made individuals prove that they had exhausted their remedies in their own country and that they could really prove a violation of one or more of the guarantees spelled out in the new European Convention on Human Rights.

Scores of pages of casuistry concerning the differing jurisdictions of the commission and the court hindered the progress of the Strasbourg tribunal. The structure of the entity in Strasbourg was greatly simplified in 1997 when the convention was folded into the court and straightforward, streamlined procedures were adopted.

It is a delight to be in England and talk to the lawyers who regularly apply to litigate in Strasbourg. England, without a written constitution and without a modernized system of judicial review, has been affected by the court in Strasbourg more than any other country. Every new decision releasing a prisoner or curbing corporal punishment of children incites again the perennial debate about the protection of civil liberties in Great Britain. That age-old quarrel has not yet been resolved, but the presence and the decisions of the court in Strasbourg have prolonged and intensified the debate.

The ever mounting number of decisions emanating from Strasbourg form a highly developed system of jurisprudence. A book entitled *Leading Cases of the European Court of Human Rights* (Gaunt, 1997), edited by R. A. Lawson and H. G. Schermers, illustrates the sweep and scope of the rapidly emerging law of human rights in Europe.

In addition, the mere existence of a complaint pending at Strasbourg frequently prompts action by a nation to change the practice complained of. Spontaneous actions by governments before actual litigation and rulings have, for example, removed the ban on Jesuits in Norway, have allowed women to vote in certain places in Switzerland, and have modified procedures against criminals. This type of reform in response to the threat of a lawsuit is now accelerating in the new nations in eastern Europe which have accepted the jurisdiction of the European Court on Human Rights.

It is significant that in 1995 the court held that the European convention "cannot be interpreted solely in accordance with the intentions of their authors as expressed more than 40 years . . . at a time when a minority of the present contracting parties adopted the convention."

There are, however, serious problems with the European court. Its docket tends to be crowded, the opinions of the majority and the dissent are sometimes prolix, and some nations comply reluctantly if at all with the decrees of Strasbourg.

But the European Court on Human Rights is without doubt the most comprehensive and efficient regional court on human rights in the world. It may be a bit premature to try to assess its overall impact on Europe and the world, but studies may be forthcoming on this topic in the relatively near future.

One of the most important features of the European Court on Human Rights is the fact that in about one-half of the states' parties the convention enjoys the status of domestic law. In these countries the convention may be invoked as law in the national courts. In these courts the Strasbourg tribunal creates rights directly enforceable by individuals. In other countries where the convention is not directly binding, courts can and do look to the European convention and the decisions interpreting it.

One of the most important changes brought about by the Strasbourg tribunal was its decision to overturn the British Parliament and the House of Lords in their decision to require the *London Times* to withhold information at the demand of the government. That ruling brought freedom of speech to England and arguably brought the country into line with the interpretations of the first amendment by the U.S. Supreme Court.

The European court has also broadened the rights of gays and lesbians, increased respect for privacy, and enhanced the rights of minorities to use their native language. The court has not yet resolved the claims of certain religious groups like the Jehovah's Witnesses nor has it taken on the question of state-sponsored religious traditions like the presence of a certain number of unelected Anglican bishops sitting in the House of Lords in London.

A conversation I had in 1999 with high officials of the European court gave me hope and confidence that the court will increasingly live up to its expectations and will continue to issue opinions that concretize and clarify the noble aspirations placed in the European Convention on Human Rights, the basic document interpreted by the European Commission and Court on Human Rights. The court will reflect the resolve of millions of people on one of the most highly developed continents in the world as they see that basic rights of their own citizens have been denied and that victims have had no place to complain.

In 1999, forty-one nations including Russia belonged to the European court. There were 9,000 applications in 1999, including 300 cases from Russia.

As one views the rapidly enlarging corpus of the decisions of the European Court on Human Rights it becomes clear that the Strasbourg tribunal is the principal constitutional court of western Europe for civil liberties. Most rights guaranteed in the convention have now been interpreted by the European Court on Human Rights. The rich case law that exists may well have a profound impact in eastern Europe as the citizens of newly liberated nations litigate in the court.

The power of the U.S. Supreme Court was not appreciated at the outset of the American republic. Even after the court clearly asserted its power to invalidate an act of Congress in *Madison v. Marbury* in 1803, the potential of the high court had not been fully recognized until many decades later. The same may be true of the European Court on Human Rights. The convention it interprets and applies is in some ways more comprehensive than the U.S. Constitution. In addition, unlike the United States, the leaders of European nations may ask for advisory opinions.

The impact of the court in Strasbourg on European entities has become increasingly clear. The court of justice of the European Common Market looks to the human rights court for fundamental principles to integrate with the legal framework of the European Community.

Similarly, the European Social Charter, which entered into force in

1965, borrows from the jurisprudence of the European Court on Human Rights in its endeavors to protect economic and social rights.

The presence of the European Social Charter, with its mission to enforce the economic guarantees of the U.N. covenants and the Universal Declaration of Human Rights, is one of the reasons the decisions of the European Court on Human Rights seem to some to concentrate on political issues that could be perceived as marginal to the vast constitutional framework present in post–World War II Europe. The conception does not minimize the monumental task of the court but only points up that the nations of Europe over the past fifty years have developed an astonishing number of interlocking entities devoted to the promotion and enforcement of that vast array of political and economic rights that came into existence as a result of the unspeakable tragedies of World War II and the foundation of the United Nations.

It should be noted that even in the highly developed machinery in Europe to enforce human rights, there is a separation of political and economic rights. Theoretically they may still be treated as equal, but they are construed and enforced by different legal bodies. Economic and social rights do not receive the same degree of constitutional protection as do civil and political rights.

Any assessment of the effectiveness of the European Court on Human Rights would be premature at this point. Its mission has hardly begun, and it is a work in progress. It is now more ready to operate than ever, having streamlined its procedures by absorbing the work of the commission into the jurisdiction of the court.

Hundreds of cases are on the docket from Poland, the Czech Republic, Hungary, and Romania. The stream of cases will overshadow what the court in Strasbourg has already achieved. These accomplishments should be remembered. No member-nation, furthermore, has ever defied a binding decision. Rulings of the court have prompted Britain and France to change their laws on telephone tapping, Germany to give non-German-speaking defendants the right to an interpreter, Austria to abolish a state monopoly on cable and satellite television, and Britain to revise its military court martial process.

It is true that the European Court on Human Rights operates on a continent where human rights are already widely respected. Nonetheless, the court at Strasbourg continues to demonstrate that the rule of law has a steady, possibly increasing appeal to nations and to individuals.

People everywhere look at the 523 volumes of decisions of the U.S. Supreme Court with awe. They recognize that Americans are people of the book.

Institutions are based on the acceptance of the law as interpreted and proclaimed by the nation's highest tribunal as the binding norm on all, whether they agree or disagree.

The European Court on Human Rights will continue to grow into that stature. It confronts an enormous challenge because Russia and seventeen other former Communist countries have now ratified the European Convention on Human Rights. The task of speaking truth to power has seldom had such a challenge.

THE INTER-AMERICAN COMMISSION AND COURT ON HUMAN RIGHTS

The attraction to human rights that surged in Europe after World War II came almost simultaneously to the thirty-two nations that formed the Organization of American States (OAS). In 1948, that focus motivated the formation of the American Convention on Human Rights — a few months before the adoption of the Universal Declaration of Human Rights on December 10, 1948.

The establishment of the Inter-American Convention on Human Rights was created in 1959 and gradually developed into the Inter-American Commission and Court on Human Rights located in Costa Rica. Its history has not been as productive or successful as the European Court on Human Rights, but it is nonetheless a very significant and promising vehicle for the advancement of international human rights.

The American convention guarantees some two dozen broad categories of civil and political rights. They track the Universal Declaration of Human Rights and the European convention. But the American convention includes a longer list of those rights which are not negotiable even in emergency situations.

Unlike the European arrangements, the American convention permits nations to file complaints against another nation if both are willing. The convention also allows all individuals to bring grievances. In Europe, nations must agree in a separate protocol to allow their citizens to file. In addition, any group of persons and some nongovernmental organizations may also become plaintiffs in Costa Rica.

Although these practices seem commonplace, it must be noted how extraordinary they are. For centuries no individual could sue the king, much less complain about the king to a tribunal outside his kingdom! In Europe and Latin America the immunity of governmental leaders from prosecution for violations of international law has now been abrogated. The right of every person to have a day in court has been elevated far beyond what was even imagined in the world prior to World War II and the Holocaust.

The nations of Latin America have yielded some of their sovereignty in agreeing to the convention, but states' rights have to some extent been maintained. Article 17 of the OAS charter provides that each state has the right to develop its cultural, political, and economic life freely and naturally. In this development, the states "shall respect the rights of the individual and the principles of universal morality."

The essential difference between these European and inter-American systems is that in the latter, the outcomes of proceedings are not necessarily legally binding decisions. This is so because very few cases reach the court where a result would be binding; the conclusions and recommendations of the commission are not legally obligatory.

This arrangement is perhaps understandable because the history of Latin America since World War II has been characterized by military dictatorships, violent repression of political opposition, and judiciaries that are not independent. As a result, the work of the tribunal in San José has been concerned with the gross violations of human rights related to formal disappearances, killings, torture, and arbitrary detention of political opponents.

Although the United States is a member of the OAS, it has never ratified the American convention. President Carter signed it in 1979 and urged the Senate to ratify it. But there has never been any serious chance that such a ratification would be possible — even with stringent reservations. The possibility of citizens from Latin American countries and citizens of the United States bringing action against the United States in a tribunal in Central America is a scenario that has never gained much acceptance among lawmakers in America. The detention of Pinochet in England has deepened the fears of American citizens against submitting to the jurisdiction of any court in Latin America or elsewhere.

Because the United States has always been juridically detached from the adjudications of human rights in Latin America, it is hard to get Americans interested — much less involved — in the commission or court. Unfortunately, the literature on the Inter-American Commission and Court on Human Rights is filled with legalistic jargon about jurisdiction, the exhaustion of remedies, and the endless difficulties in enforcing the rulings of that body.

An excellent collection of essays entitled *The Inter-American System of Human Rights* (Clarendon Press, 1998), edited by David J. Harris and Stephen Livingstone, is a comprehensive description of the difficulties and dilemmas of those who desire to make the Inter-American system of human rights more effective. The fourteen essayists are perplexed and discouraged by the ongoing, massive assault on human rights that plagues so many nations in Latin America.

Scores of questions must be resolved before the human rights court in Costa Rica can be as effective as the tribunal in Strasbourg. The central one may be whether the United States will be present or absent. If the United States ever ratified the treaty and made its citizens subject to the commission and the court, it is possible that actions for and against the United States could dominate that body in San José. Lawsuits against what the United States did in the 1980s in El Salvador and Nicaragua could be numerous. Complaints against the United States for its conduct under NAFTA are conceivable. Actions to claim damages for America's conduct in Panama, Grenada, and elsewhere are likely to be brought.

There are challenges beyond count for the Inter-American Commission and Court. One of them is the presence of 400 indigenous groups in the Americas — comprising more than 30 million people — roughly 10 percent of the population of the continent. The problems of the 4 million indigenous peoples in Guatemala is a situation well known in the United States.

A draft declaration on the rights of the indigenous has long been a project of the Organization of American States. Its implementation will not be simple or easy. It is not clear whether nations that agree to the protection of the human rights of their citizens understand that they have signed up to rectify the grievances of those groups living in large numbers in the Americas before Spain and Portugal came to conquer their ancestral lands.

Another knotty problem relates to amnesties granted by governments to officials in previous governments. The U.N. Commission on Human Rights has been inundated with petitions from victims alleging that laws giving amnesty to assailants have violated their rights to judicial protection.

One dramatic case of invalidation of an amnesty granted by a government is El Salvador. Following the murder of six Jesuit priests in that country on November 16, 1989, it became clear to all parties that neither the revolutionaries (the Farabundo Marti National Liberation front, or FMLN) nor the authoritarian government had the capacity to win militarily. Both sides asked the United Nations to negotiate a settlement. In July 1990 the parties signed an agreement which included a U.N. verification mission to oversee the human rights situation. The following year the parties agreed to the establishment of an international truth commission. That group released its report on March 15, 1993, charging senior military officers and government officials with serious wrongdoing.

President Alfredo Cristiani promptly granted a general amnesty. The Salvadoran legislative assembly passed a law that granted a "full, absolute and unconditional amnesty" to all who since January 1, 1993, had participated in political or common crimes.

The Commission on Human Rights, in its strongest response to any amnesty measure, condemned El Salvador's amnesty as incompatible with its obligations under international law. The commission insisted that El Salvador could not undermine the recommendations of the Truth Commission or erase the rights of its citizens to the guarantees under the American convention, which El Salvador had ratified. In its annual report in 1994 the commission recommended that the government in El Salvador repeal the amnesty law and punish those responsible for violating the basic rights of persons who deserve compensation.

The situation in Guatemala concerning amnesty is even more anguishing than that in El Salvador. The thirty-six-year-old civil war in Guatemala ended in comprehensive peace accords in 1996. The amnesty question, which was intentionally omitted from the final peace accords, was resolved ambiguously by the legislature in December 1996. The law enhancing national reconciliation states that amnesty does not apply to genocide, torture, forced disappearances, or acts not clearly related to a war effort. The legality of amnesties in the Americas is a question on which military and police officials have passionate views. Commissions in Argentina, Brazil, and Chile have been designed to bring about both revelations and reconciliation. Whether that has happened cannot be discerned for some time. In the interim the Commission on Human Rights will continue to search for black letter law that will spell out the duties of nations on the rights of victims. The commission has been rebuffed in its attempts to compel the nations of Latin America to fulfill their duties to their citizens before they forgive the crimes of their generals.

The Inter-American Convention on Human Rights practice of publishing country reports may be one of its most useful customs. It is not done with the regularity of the U.S. State Department, which reports every February on every nation. The commission has developed a practice of filing a report on a nation that has critical problems or where, as in the case of the new government in Nicaragua in 1980, it is asked to do so. The commission also includes relevant items in its annual report on the state of human rights in specific countries.

In addition to making periodic reports, the commission can send human rights observers to countries that need help in their efforts to becoming democracies. The commission sent observers to Argentina when a dictator took over that country in 1976. It seemed to be commonly agreed that observers who speak the same language and who share the culture of the same continent may well receive a better reception and be more effective than would visitors from foreign cultures.

Although the many efforts and several achievements of the human rights teams of the commission have not been fully documented, this function and role of the commission may be one of the most important functions assigned to it.

In one sense, the achievements of the commission and court over some twenty years have been truly remarkable. They can take some credit for the fact that all nations in Latin America except Cuba are now democracies. The continent has been transformed. The principles of human rights have, at least by implication, triumphed in the return to civilian governments in Argentina, Chile, and Brazil. Central America has also been transfigured by democratic structures.

On the other hand, the commission and court have been a part-time voice on a continent which with its resources, traditions, and culture should be doing more about the tremendous problem than it is.

Questions abound. Has the presence of a regional agency to enforce international human rights diminished the role and the importance of the U.N. Commission on Human Rights and the several U.N. units that monitor compliance with the U.N. covenants on human rights? The 1945 Charter of the United Nations neither authorizes nor forbids regional groups from supplementing its work on human rights. But if the U.N. General Assembly and Security Council were in fact fulfilling all their obligations to work on behalf of human rights under the charter and the authority of the Universal Declaration of Human Rights, would regional commissions and courts be necessary?

These questions may seem academic and remote. But the intensity of convictions and feelings about the internationalization of human rights suggests that there is more universal commitment to human rights than ever before. The desire to persuade and force nations to live up to their commitments under international law is a moral force of unprecedented magnitude.

Is this new moral consensus being fragmented by the present arrangements involving a haphazard plan for regional enforcement of human rights? No one can really say. At least it is clear that NGOs are working heroically in Europe and Latin America to stop the most egregious abuses and to develop the most promising programs.

If the global concern for international human rights continues to intensify, it may be that Latin America could in a generation become a model for the acceptance and enforcement of human rights. When the intellectual and political leaders of a country or a continent believe in and adhere to the standards included in the International Bill of Rights, dramatic transformations of public morality can occur.

The newly decolonized nations of Africa were in the 1960s under-standably obsessed with apartheid in South Africa. That awful system dominated their politics and their revolutions. They longed for liberation so single-mindedly that their aspirations colored every thought about international human rights.

One would think that Africa would rally with great enthusiasm to a regime in which internationally recognized human rights would be avail-able. But the International Bill of Rights was perceived to be a product of the European or western or, even worse, colonial powers which had done so much to destroy African culture.

An African movement for human rights did result in the establishment of legal machinery to bring the African peoples the guarantees of human rights. The African Charter on Human and Peoples' Rights was adopted in 1981 and entered into force in October 1986. This commission, inaug-urated in November 1987, meets twice a year and concluded its twenty-second meeting in 1997. Made up of eleven experts, the commission has struggled to combat multiple political crises in Africa. A comprehensive report of the twenty-first and twenty-second meetings of the commission in Mauritania was published in the November 30, 1998, issue of *Human Rights Law Journal.*

The African charter is different from the European and American con-ventions in that it protects both civil and political rights as well as eco-nomic, social, and cultural rights. It is, moreover, specifically devoted to the preservation of the "virtues of African historical tradition and the values of African civilization." The stress is also on "peoples' rights"— which in essence is the right to development.

The African charter asserts strongly that "civil and political rights can-not be disassociated from economic, social, and cultural rights in their concept as well as universality." The charter goes further, insisting that "the satisfaction of economic, social and cultural rights is a guarantee for the enjoyment of civil and political rights."

The African charter does not stress the western concept of the su-premacy of individual rights. Article 17(c) declares, "The promotion and protection of morals and traditional values recognized by the community shall be the duty of the state." Article 18 affirms the concept that "the state shall have the duty to assist the family which is the custodian of morals and traditional values recognized by the community."

The preservation of African values is central to the African charter. Article 29(7) imposes the duty "to preserve and strengthen the practice of African cultural values." As a result of this deference to African values, the charter does not provide for a court. Rather than using a judicial proceeding, disputes about human rights are to be settled by negotiation and conciliation. The absence of a court is probably unthinkable to the authorities who govern the human rights process in Europe and Latin America.

Under the African charter nations can bring complaints against other nations, but individuals can qualify only if they can bring evidence of a series of serious violations of peoples' rights.

The usual remedies for petitioners in human rights cases are not readily present in the entity created by the Organization of African Unity (OAU). Its only real sanction — publicity — can be limited by the assembly which is an essentially political body which may not always be willing to publicize violations of human rights.

At the twenty-second meeting of the African commission the participants lamented the lack of political will and compliance with its decisions on the part of its members. But the nongovernmental organizations were present and active. They raised concerns about slavery in Africa, child labor, and women's rights. Other problems were legion — in Nigeria, Kenya, Sierra Leone, Gambia, and Malawi. The International Commission of Jurists, an influential NGO in Geneva was present; the commission expressed its gratitude to the ICJ and to other NGOs for their partnership.

A reading of the tenth annual report of the commission — released in June 1997 — makes clear that the vast problems of human rights in Africa's fifty-two nations are far too complicated to be handled by the understaffed and underfunded African Charter on Human and Peoples' Rights. The question arises again as to why the United Nations and its agencies on human rights are so inactive in Africa. Indeed, the frailty of the African commission has tended to confirm the conclusion of many if not most human rights experts that Africa is the most neglected of all the continents and that this area of the world may well need enforcement of international human rights more than any other continent on the planet.

Regional tribunals for human rights will almost certainly continue and be strengthened. The long-standing desire for a human rights court for Asia may not be fulfilled soon. Would it even be conceivable that a court on human rights for China, India, and the rest of the east could function? Sad to say, this vast area — including some 2 or 3 billion human beings — can look to no agency except the U.N. Commission on Human Rights.

Must one reluctantly conclude that brave proclamations of human rights in the 1940s and 1950s brought few results in Africa? The rights in the International Bill of Rights may have become customary international law, but who can or will enforce them?

The possibility of having a human rights tribunal in Asia is an intriguing thought, but its prospects seem dubious. First, the term "Asia" is a western construct. It presumably includes China, India, Indonesia, and a dozen other less populous nations. Unlike Europe, these countries have few cultural or even geographical links.

In addition, at the Vienna World Conference on Human Rights in 1993, China protested that human rights are the invention of the west — a sentiment deeply held by influential Chinese diplomats. I recall spending three hours with twelve high-level Chinese government officials in Washington in 1996; they seemed adamant in their conviction that the United States had no right to impose allegedly western ideals of human rights on China.

India is, of course, very sensitive to human rights. Its constitution calls for a sort of affirmative action for those classes long deemed to be the "untouchables."

Human rights issues in Malaysia and Indonesia are complicated by the presence of Islamic groups, some of which aspire to make Islamic law, or Shari'ah, more controlling.

A commission on human rights in Asia or in parts of Asia should logically be the next step in the evolution of internationally recognized human rights. But the leadership or the resources to bring about such a supranational commission do not seem to be present at this time in the global human rights movement.

Could it be that the enforcement of internationally recognized human rights has actually declined since the world took up the business of making them a part of world law? Should the human family look for other ways to convey the rich treasures of its newly minted legacy? If the United States changed its attitude and became a proactive enforcer of human rights, would the world be changed? It could be, but men are not angels and crime, cruelty, and corruption will continue in government as well as in private life.

People with religious faith can have some assurance that sometimes sinners change and public officials cease to abuse their power. The U.N. documents on human rights urge such a conversion, but for secular reasons. These documents urge everyone to remember that each person has inherent dignity, possesses a conscience, and is our "brother" or "sister." When combined, the moral and philosophical content of the legal articles on human rights adds up to a moral and metaphysical teaching. This teaching is a distillation of the best thought through the ages. It embraces Asian wisdom, western teaching, and the moral precepts of the Judeo-Christian tradition. Would it be more effective if it openly embraced theistic teaching? Would the documents on which the whole human rights movement is based be more compelling if they embraced more explicitly the concept that God is the creator of humanity and ultimately the author of the moral and spiritual truths that are the basis of all international covenants on human rights?

No one can say for certain. But the nontheistic approach adopted by the authors and architects of the human rights movement is now the lynchpin of the world, the moral code which furnishes the spirituality by which the human family can avoid war and violence and bestow on everyone the basic human dignity they deserve.

THE

RIGHT

TO

FOOD

The framers of the documents that created the human rights movement made it clear that the right to food is fundamental. The Universal Declaration of Human Rights states, "Everyone has the right to a standard of living adequate for the health and well being of himself and his family, including food, clothing, housing, medical care and necessary social services." Article 11 of the International Covenant on Economic, Social, and Cultural Rights recognizes both a right to adequate food and the right of everyone to be free from hunger.

Signatory nations commit themselves to "take appropriate steps to insure the realization" of these rights both "individually and through international cooperation." The commitments are quite specific. Nations pledge themselves to "improve methods of production, conservation and distribution of food making full use of technical and scientific knowledge, by disseminating knowledge of the principles of nutrition and by developing or reforming agrarian systems in such a way as to achieve the most efficient development and utilization of natural resources." Economic rights, then, are not merely aspirations but definite legal commitments made by nations to their subjects and to all around the world.

A right that has become a part of customary international law empowers people. Rights are sources of power. The right to food bestowed by customary international law on every person on the planet means that people can demand action to secure their entitlements. The Food and Agriculture Organization and similar groups have performed miracles in multiplying the availability of food. The sad fact is that the fundamental right above all human rights — the right to food — has not been given the attention it deserves as a part of international law. Philip Alston, one of the world's top experts on human rights, puts it this way: "It is paradoxical, but hardly surprising, that the right to food has been endorsed more often and with greater unanimity and urgency than most other human rights while at the same time being violated more comprehensively and systematically than probably any other right."

What a shocking observation. A human right which is more compelling than most and which is more easily fulfilled than most is "violated more comprehensively and systematically than probably any other right."

The thought keeps recurring — if the international human rights movement cannot secure the primitive, fundamental right to food, then why hope that the movement can obtain the realization of other less compelling human rights?

There is no totally satisfying response to that question. The human rights movement struggles and stumbles in the face of appalling ignorance, apathy, and resistance. The only certainty is that the abuse of human rights will almost certainly increase if there are no renewed protests or more humane and humanitarian laws.

Neglect of the right to food is particularly unforgivable because today, for the first time in human history, famines can be anticipated and their effects eliminated. There is enough food for 6 billion mouths. Chronic malnutrition of some 800 million individuals and the needless deaths each day of 35,000 children are preventable. These are also offenses against international law — more clearly than any other violation of the political and economic rights guaranteed by the human race in newly emerging world law.

Constructive anger within Congress brought about the enactment of Section 502(b) in 1976, which in turn encouraged the United States to take a proactive role in defending human rights in the world. This effort led to a resolution concerning the right to food by Congress, initiated by Bread for the World Institute and other nongovernmental agencies. The resolution had been aimed at the World Conference on Hunger, which was being conducted at that time in Rome.

Congress declared:

It is the sense of Congress that:
The United States reaffirms the right of every person in this country and throughout the world to food and a nutritionally adequate diet; and

The need to combat hunger shall be a fundamental point of reference in the formulation and implementation of United States policy in all areas which bear on hunger including international trade, monetary arrangements, and foreign assistance.

In response to demands from Congress, Secretary of State Henry Kissinger vowed that within a decade no child would go to bed hungry. His pledge echoed what President Kennedy said in 1961 when he declared that the 1960s would see a man on the moon and the phasing out of hunger among children.

So the question recurs: Why has the world community refused or neglected to make possible the fulfillment of the most basic of all human rights — the right to food?

There is some hope that the world scene can change so that the right to food becomes exercisable for the 1.3 billion people who live in absolute poverty — with incomes of less than a dollar a day. There is hope also for the 841 million people — almost one in seven on the planet — who are chronically malnourished. That hope derives from the death of the Cold War and the new market-oriented global economy. That economy, however, cuts in different directions. It creates great wealth for a few, and provides benefits for many, while increasing hunger and insecurity for many others.

Because the globalization of the market economy seems inevitable the countless nongovernmental agencies devoted to the alleviation and elimination of hunger must work within that framework. With that in mind the Bread for the World Institute in 1998 issued its eighth annual report on the state of world hunger. The document contains a wealth of information and exhortation. But it also makes it clear that while there has been an organized world effort to eliminate polio and other dread diseases there seems to be no one organized world movement to eliminate hunger. In fact, there is now a lull in the cries of anguish heard around the world to end hunger. The new assumption — or delusion — is that the emerging global marketplace will create a new middle class in poor countries and that somehow their wealth will trickle down. This new rationalization — or evasion — is a silent premise of conservatives and libertarians who are not asking the United States to increase its foreign aid — even to alleviate hunger.

As a result academics and activists involved in human rights who have been working for some forty years to persuade the U.S. Congress to assume a leadership role in phasing out hunger have a new and difficult barrier facing them. They are told in essence that "the magic of the marketplace" will bring food to the hungry. Any governmental interference with the "magic" will only impede the efficiency of the process by which capitalism allegedly will bring prosperity to the countries it enters.

There is, of course, some truth in this contention. But if the process is not directed and controlled, it can deny the needs and the right to food of whole populations. It is understandable that there is fierce resistance and resentment toward multinational corporations who want to establish factories or farms in underdeveloped countries.

Look at recent events in Brazil. That country is one of the major foreign investment targets in the developing world. But 32 million Brazilians are poor, and 25 million face hunger. The gap between the rich and the poor is the highest in the world, with the top 20 percent earning thirty-two times the income of the poorest 20 percent.

In Latin America I have listened to the reactions of residents who see what U.S. companies do to their countries. In one nation, for example, a huge corporation from the United States acquired 10,000 acres of formerly fertile farmland to grow orchids. Each evening, air-conditioned jets fly the flowers to the United States where on the following evening they will be worn by high school seniors at their prom in Peoria. Peasants pick the flowers but they see little of the substantial profits. In addition, a substantial number of people in that area go hungry.

The authors of the Covenant on Economic, Social, and Cultural Rights anticipated this situation and required the officials of each signatory nation to report at regular intervals to the committee that supervises compliance with the covenant. Each country must record in some detail how they are carrying out their pledge to bring the economic rights that are now a part of customary international law to the citizens of their country.

The book *The United Nations and Human Rights,* by Philip Alston, reveals some of the difficulties of accomplishing this daunting task. One of them is, of course, the fact that government officials are not able to control or even direct the economic development of their nation. Capitalistic enterprises enter and in essence are in control. Their primary purpose is not to develop energy sources in the country or to eradicate disease but to maximize profits for the stockholders of the corporation who reside in Europe or America. Public officials can tell the officials of foreign corporations that they are required to work for the fulfillment of the economic rights of their citizens. But little will happen. Many multinational corporations would respond simply by assuming or asserting that the forces of the marketplace will bring about economic justice in the country in which they have chosen to locate.

The leaders of the United Nations and related agencies in the 1950s and 1960s could see these problems coming with the massive decolonization of some 100 nations. They created the World Bank, the International Monetary Fund, and similar organizations. It is evident to everyone that the mission and mode of operation of all these agencies have to be rethought. But in the interim the world must be reminded of the unspeakable conditions that persist despite the presence of standards on human rights. No one can or should say that these standards are unenforceable. But the human right to economic equality is sometimes more difficult to enforce than political rights.

It is a truism that vast economic inequalities in developing nations bring discontent and breed dictatorships and terrorism. On the other hand, the presence of economic opportunities helps develop the adoption of democratic institutions.

There has been some progress. From 1970 to 1992 the number of people afflicted with hunger fell from 918 million to 841 million. The 1996 World Food Summit, organized by the Food and Agricultural Organization, declared that the present situation is unacceptable and pledged concerted international action to reduce the number of hungry people by half before the year 2015.

But most figures on world malnutrition are bleak — especially for children. In India 21 percent of the overall population was chronically malnourished in 1990 to 1992 but 53 percent of preschool children were underweight in 1996. Undernourishment often adversely affects children's physical and mental development.

Hunger has increased in some countries since 1970 — especially in Africa. The proportion of the population that is hungry has jumped 13 percent over the past 25 years; the absolute number of hungry Africans has more than doubled in that period. The Food and Agricultural Organization has predicted that unless recent trends change 265 million Africans will suffer from hunger in the year 2010.

But some poor countries do much better. The proportion of hungry people in China fell from 45 percent in 1969 to 1971 to 16 percent in 1990 to 1992. Despite this unusual progress some 189 million Chinese remain chronically malnourished.

Of the roughly 40,000 transnational corporations in existence, 200 account for 29 percent of global economic activity. They, more than anyone, point to trade liberalization, free markets, and private investment as the keys to solving the problem of food security.

In the next twenty-five years the world's population will grow from 6 billion to 8 billion, with more than 90 percent of that growth occurring in developing countries.

It is clear, therefore, that merely stressing the internationally recognized right to food may be an oversimplified norm to use as the most important criterion. Other human rights are intertwined along with the flexible norms set forth for nations in the U.N. Covenant on Economic, Social, and Cultural Rights.

All these problems were in play at the 1996 World Food Summit in Rome. The world scene had changed radically since the 1976 world conference also held in Rome. The summit plan of action set forth a sensible blueprint, but the passion and political will present in 1976 were not visible. It was disappointing when the Clinton administration claimed that the language in the final statement does not create an enforceable international obligation. Apparently the United States feared litigation, its own inadequate food supplies, and demands for more foreign aid.

Some 1,300 nongovernmental agencies sought to strengthen the summit plan for action at the Rome conference. They stressed "food sovereignty" and the right of each nation to maintain and develop its own capacity to produce its basic food.

In all the literature on the right to food, the persistent and pervasive theme is the need of a "political will" to alleviate hunger and starvation. The concept of "political will" is not as clear-cut as it seems. No "political will" is seemingly necessary to maintain the status quo. But it is essential — yes, indispensable — in order to change things. The assumption also is that "political will" is something that does not necessarily benefit the political actor but is something suggested by idealistic forces which have finally reached the convictions or the conscience of the political officials involved.

Massive resistance to segregation created in President Johnson the "political will" to fight to pass the Civil Rights law in 1964. Vehement opposition to the war in Vietnam impelled Congress to de-fund the war and President Nixon to acquiesce in that decision.

What kind of a worldwide movement is needed to create the "political will" to implement the right to food?

One way surely is to remind nations of their solemn pledge to carry out their commitments under the several U.N. documents that guarantee the right to food. Unfortunately the United States has never ratified the Covenant on Economic, Social, and Cultural Rights.

The other major way is to intensify the efforts of the nongovernmental agencies to insist on compliance with the right to food. The NGOs include CARE, Bread for the World, Oxfam America, Freedom From Hunger, and many more. Public agencies include UNICEF and the U.N. Development Program (UNDP).

The right to food is virtually inseparable from all the other economic and political rights which are the patrimony of all those who belong to the United Nations and are part of the human family. But the right to food is so central and crucial that its dimensions deserve very special attention. The dream of abolishing hunger is a centuries-old hope of the human race. It is not impossible that that dream can become a reality in the twenty-first century.

When President Carter was in the White House, he appointed a presidential commission on world hunger chaired by Sol Linowitz. The comprehensive report of the commission recommended that the U.S. government "make the elimination of hunger the primary focus of its relationships with the developing countries." In its report, the commission documented evidence for its conclusion that "it would be possible to eliminate the worst aspects of hunger and malnutrition by the year 2000."

The position was never adopted by the United States. Consequently, it is not now possible to predict with confidence when hunger will be phased out.

The position of the Commission on the Right to Food is an eloquent exhortation:

Whether one speaks of human rights or basic human needs, the right to food is the most basic of all. Unless that right is first fulfilled, the protection of other human rights becomes a mockery for those who must spend all their energy merely to maintain life itself. The correct moral and ethical position on hunger is beyond debate. The world's major religions and philosophical systems share two universal values: respect for human dignity and a sense of social justice. Hunger is the ultimate affront to both.

14

DOES THE
DEATH PENALTY
VIOLATE CUSTOMARY
INTERNATIONAL
LAW?

Could the death penalty be the next thing forbidden by customary international law because that source of prohibited conduct brought about the demise of slavery and piracy? The answer increasingly seems to be in the affirmative. But it is still not entirely clear that capital punishment is living on borrowed time.

The visceral feelings which a majority of people have concerning the death penalty are not rooted entirely in reason or wisdom. They cross the spectrum from sheer vindictiveness to a deep conviction that violence may never be used for any purpose, however commendable.

The thought of the inevitability of death makes cowards of us all. It is hardly possible that anyone who is not mentally limited could conclude that he or she deserves death for mistakes or sins committed. The imposition of the death sentence somehow does not seem congruous or reasonable — at least when it applies to ourselves.

It is difficult to construct a rational case for that position. That human instinct to abhor cruelty found its first mention in Anglo-American law in the English Bill of Rights in 1689. It declared that "cruel and inhuman treatment or punishment" would not be allowed.

How could the death penalty *not* be "cruel and inhuman"? That is the question which today's international human rights movement must resolve.

During the nineteenth and twentieth centuries the norm forbidding "cruel and inhuman treatment or punishment" filtered into domestic institutions throughout the world. Despite some minor differences in the wording, the essential message is the same: cruel, unusual, inhuman, and degrading treatment or punishment violates customary international law.

Physical torture is presumably worse than cruel, inhuman, or degrading treatment or punishment. Torture is clearly outlawed by the Covenant on Torture, which most of the nations of the world, including the United States, have ratified.

In 1948 the authors of the Universal Declaration of Human Rights had to face the fact that the death penalty had been imposed by the Nuremberg and Tokyo tribunals on war criminals. In addition, the vast majority of nations employed the death penalty. It was proposed that the death penalty be noted specifically in the Universal Declaration of Human Rights as an exception to the right to life. Eleanor Roosevelt and René Cassin, the European jurist who was the principal author of the Universal Declaration of Human Rights, rejected the idea that the declaration should contain a reference to capital punishment as an exception to the right to life. Mrs. Roosevelt, who chaired the drafting committee, cited the movement under way in many countries to abolish the death penalty.

A half century later their clairvoyance must be acknowledged. That admission has allowed customary international law to develop so that today the elimination of the death penalty is more possible than ever before.

The European Convention on Human Rights, adopted two years after the Universal Declaration of Human Rights, recognized the right to life "save in the execution of a sentence of a court following his conviction of a crime for which this penalty is provided by law." But this provision was almost immediately anachronistic. In the early 1970s the Council of Europe began work on a protocol to the convention which was adopted in 1983 by which the death penalty in peacetime is abolished. In 1989, the European Court on Human Rights noted that capital punishment had been de facto abolished in Europe.

In 1976, the International Covenant on Civil and Political Rights entered into force. Article 6 of that covenant includes the death penalty as an exception to the right to life, but it lists detailed safeguards. The death penalty may be imposed only for the "most serious crimes" and with elaborate and rigorous procedural rules. Pregnant women and those under the age of eighteen are spared. Article 6, furthermore, points to the abolition of the death penalty as a human rights objective and implies that nations that have already abolished the death penalty may not reinstate it. An additional protocol adopted in 1989 proclaimed that the death penalty was abolished in Europe in time of peace and war. Many European states have signed this protocol, making the death penalty nonexistent in Europe.

The Inter-American Convention on Human Rights (also known as the American Convention on Human Rights), which entered into force in 1978, replicates the European doctrine. It forbids any nation that has abolished the death penalty to revive it. Because of this treaty and several other factors in world opinion, the death penalty has in effect been abolished in Latin America.

The African Charter of Human and Peoples' Rights, which entered into force in 1986, makes no mention of capital punishment as an exception or limitation on the right to life. Yet, the continent of Africa appears to be moving to abolish the death penalty. The countries in Africa were certainly influenced by the unanimous decision of the Supreme Court of South Africa in 1995 that declared the death penalty to be inconsistent with South Africa's new constitution.

The Arab Charter of Human Rights, adopted September 15, 1994, is somewhat different. Articles 10, 11, and 12 recognize the legitimacy of the death penalty in the case of "serious violators of general law," but it is excluded in cases involving political crimes, those under the age of eighteen, and pregnant or nursing mothers. Some Islamic nations have defended the use of the death penalty in the name of obedience to Islamic law and to strictures of the Shari'ah, which is a collection or code of laws binding those who follow the Koran.

Scholars seem to differ in their interpretation of the clarity or the binding quality of Islamic law with respect to the death penalty. Theoretically it is a question of vital importance because the forty predominantly

Muslim nations contain some 1 billion people. If the Koran and other sources of Islamic doctrine were construed as allowing or even requiring the death penalty in certain cases, this would clearly be a strong argument contrary to that of those scholars who want to reach a careful judgment as to whether customary international law now forbids the death penalty.

But the Islamic nations appear to be ambivalent on the death penalty. Those who resist the concept that the Koran is a binding source of civil law downplay the allegedly divine revelation that capital punishment is authorized by the Koran. In addition, the Islamic nations that signed the final document of the Vienna World Conference on Human Rights in 1993 agreed to re-ratify the treaties which at least clearly imply that the death penalty violates the ban on cruel and inhuman treatment and punishment.

The classic weakness of the international human rights law lies, of course, in its means of implementation. But increasingly, international human rights law is being applied in domestic courts. Courts in South Africa, Canada, Tanzania, Zimbabwe, and the United Kingdom have found international law to be helpful in the interpretation of the ban on cruel, inhuman, or degrading punishment. Several international organizations have also been skeptical of the death penalty. The United Nations leads the list. In 1968, the U.N. Commission on Human Rights initiated a resolution calling for a moratorium on the death penalty. The U.N. General Assembly agreed to this resolution with minor amendments. The vote was 94–0, with 3 abstentions. In 1972, the U.N. General Assembly passed a resolution endorsing "the desirability of abolishing the punishment in all countries."

But strong opposition to the abolition of the death penalty emerged at the U.N. Congress on Crime Prevention and Control. Meeting in Caracas in 1980, the congress drafted a resolution calling for the eventual abolition of the death penalty. The resolution was met with opposition and was withdrawn. When that same congress convened in 1990, the idea of a moratorium failed to obtain the necessary two-thirds vote.

In 1994, a resolution of the U.N. General Assembly called for a moratorium on the death penalty. It originated in a newly formed nongovernmental organization named "Hands Off Cain — the International League for Abolishing the Death Penalty." Even though the resolution had forty-nine co-sponsors, it failed to pass on a procedural gambit.

In 1997, the U.N. Commission on Human Rights passed a resolution calling for a moratorium on the death penalty. The vote was 27–11, with 14 abstentions.

The "abolitionists" are happy to see that all the nations that created the war crimes tribunal for those involved in the war in the former Yugoslavia and in Rwanda agreed to forgo capital punishment. The opponents of the death penalty also approved of the ban on the death penalty in the charter of the International Criminal Commission.

The abolitionists note that all 190 nations that have ratified the Convention on the Rights of the Child (the United States and Somalia are the only nonratifiers) have done so without a reservation to Article 37(a), which bans the death penalty for offenders who were under age eighteen at the time of the crime. In 1997, China abolished the death penalty for those under age eighteen.

Since 1990, some nineteen people in six nations are known to have been executed for crimes committed when they were under the age of eighteen. Ten of the nineteen were in the United States. In contrast, 3,670 people were on death row as of April 1, 2000; of these, 69 were juveniles who had committed crimes when they were sixteen or seventeen years old.

The worldwide picture of the use of the death penalty reveals that ninety-nine nations have abolished the punishment, whereas ninety-four retain the death penalty. This means that over 50 percent of all countries have now abolished the death penalty in law or in practice.

In 1998, at least 1,625 prisoners were reported to have been executed in 37 countries. A small number of countries accounted for most of the executions. There were, according to Amnesty International, 1,065 executions in China, over 100 in the Democratic Republic of Congo, 68 in the United States, and 66 in Iran. These four nations accounted for 80 percent of all executions. Amnesty International also received reports of hundreds of executions in Iraq but was unable to confirm most of these.

One of the most significant victories for the abolitionists occurred in 1999, when President Boris Yeltsin all but abolished capital punishment, commuting to life in prison the sentence of the last Russian prisoner on death row. Yeltsin, who had permitted the execution of 163 prisoners during his terms in office, placed a moratorium on executions in 1996 after Russia joined the Council of Europe, which bans capital punishment in peacetime. Although Yeltsin had agreed to halt any more executions, they remain legal because the parliament has been unwilling to repeal the law.

Moves to reinstitute the death penalty after it has been abolished are usually unsuccessful. Since 1985, only four abolitionist countries have reinstated the death penalty. One, Nepal, has since abolished the death penalty again. Canada and England have refused to reinstitute capital punishment even when conservative governments have come to power and urged a return to the death penalty.

To abolitionists, arguments justifying the death penalty are easy to refute. A U.N. study done in 1988 and updated in 1996 shows that crime does not increase when the death penalty is abolished. In Canada the homicide rate per 100,000 fell from a peak of 3.09 in 1975, the year before the abolition of the death penalty, to 2.41 in 1980 and has remained steady since that time. In 1993, the homicide rate was 2.19 per 100,000 people, 27 percent lower than in 1975.

The abolitionists also stress the risk of executing the innocent. A 1987 study showed that 350 persons convicted of capital crimes between 1900 and 1985 were innocent of the crimes charged, while 23 were actually executed. A report of the House Judiciary Committee in 1993 listed 48 condemned men who had been freed from death row since 1972.

The racial disparity among individuals on death row is well known. Attempts to prove that the selection of those charged with the death penalty is a process infected with racism have not been successful, as was manifest in the *McClesky* decision of the U.S. Supreme Court. That ruling made clear that the Court would not take up the sociological or statistical evidence indicating that race had played a part in the selection or prosecution of persons accused of committing a capital offense.

New efforts to seek to prevent the execution of mentally retarded or emotionally unstable individuals are also well known. In the decision *Thompson v. Oklahoma* in 1988 a plurality of the Supreme Court concluded that a death sentence for an offender who is fifteen years old at the time of his crime constituted cruel and unusual punishment under the Eighth Amendment. Justice Stevens, writing for the majority, cited views of the international community in reasoning that the death penalty would "offend civilized standards of decency." He cited decisions from western European countries as well as the Soviet Union that prohibit juvenile executions. In addition he cited the three treaties ratified or signed by the United States which explicitly prohibit juvenile death penalties. In dissent, Justice Scalia argued that international standards should never be imposed according to the U.S. Constitution. This latter view became the law of the country the following year when in *Stanford v. Kentucky* Justice Scalia in essence rejected the relevance of international law and the practices of other countries in construing the Eighth Amendment.

In 1958, the U.S. Supreme Court confirmed that the Court is entitled to look at the "evolving standards of decency that mark the progress of a maturing society" as a norm for its decisions. Judges in America are torn between the black letter law set forth in the opinion of Justice Scalia and the flexible standard of following the "evolving standards of decency." It is very clear that American judges are anxious to discover clearly defined rules that are clear rather than grope for the "evolving standards of decency." The U.S. Supreme Court in its 5–4 ruling in the *Stanford* decision tipped the scales to a norm that would preclude the use of international principles not set forth clearly in U.S. statutory law.

If the death penalty is eventually curtailed or even eliminated in the United States, will that happen because of international customary law, public opinion, or a reexamination of the concepts behind cruel, inhuman, or degrading treatment? For some — perhaps for many — the idea of detaining persons on death row for months and years, depriving them of their lives, fulfills and exceeds every standard contained in the ban on "cruel, inhuman, degrading" treatment or punishment. Even the retentionists are inclined to admit that all five current methods of execution — hanging, electrocution, shooting, lethal gas, and poisonous injection — have to be seen as cruel or inhuman or degrading. Those words are not novel in American jurisprudence. They appeared in 1689 in the English Bill of Rights. It could be hoped — indeed, expected — that over a period of 300 years the evolving standards of decency would bar ways of treating human beings which in 1689 were allowed. Anglo-American law has elevated the standards so that all forms of torture, disembowelment, amputation, and similar offenses are forbidden.

The retentionists question who decides on the "evolving standards of decency." If one nation in its legislature or courts refuses to accept or adopt a higher level, can the citizens of the nation insist that the courts be responsive to customary international law and insist that their countries are obliged to follow that form of law?

How soon will customary international law be clear and precise enough for U.S. courts to use it as a source of authority for decisions on the death penalty which do not exist in American law?

The Restatement of the Foreign Relations Law of the United States is the authoritative source for what laws are binding on U.S. courts. The latest edition, issued in 1987 by the American Law Institute, contains the black letter law which U.S. courts must follow. But the aspirations of the world community or the "emerging" norms are not codified in the restatement.

Opinions of many nations support the abolitionists' arguments. Compelling reasons are set forth in the opinion of the Supreme Court of South Africa in June 1995, which abolished the death penalty. If opinions of foreign courts are increasingly negative on the legality of the death penalty, can or should the U.S. courts follow the test and standards for the legality of capital punishment as they emerge from the courts and legislatures around the world? Not all jurists agree on the answer to this inquiry. Judges should not be excessively activist but they are nonetheless required, as the U.S. Constitution itself sets forth, to follow the law of nations.

When will the condemnations of the death penalty by the U.N. General Assembly, the committees that monitor the U.N. covenants, and comparable bodies add up to a norm which U.S. courts can use to settle disputes about the definition of concepts like cruel, inhuman, and degrading?

When will American judges take notice of the remarkable evolution of consensus of religious opinions in the United States and elsewhere against the death penalty? The Catholic Church has made the most visible and dramatic movement toward a condemnation of the death penalty. All the documents of the Second Vatican Council did not specifically disallow the death penalty but a remarkable unanimity against capital punishment has emerged in the past few years. Indeed, virtually all religious groups in the United States share in the unanimous condemnation of the death penalty which has appeared in Catholic thought. No one would say that courts should follow the opinion of one or all of the churches, but courts must employ some criteria to discern what are the "evolving standards of decency" in a democracy.

One way by which public officials in the United States could be induced to drop the death penalty is by accepting the *Soering* decision of the European Court of Human Rights. Hans Soering, a native of Germany, killed the parents of his girlfriend in Virginia. He escaped to Europe, where he fought the extradition sought by the Commonwealth of Virginia in the European Court of Human Rights in Strasbourg. It was clear that Virginia intended to execute Soering for first-degree murder. Soering's creative lawyers argued that the prospect of long years on death row in Virginia constituted a violation of international law because the experience would be cruel, inhuman, and degrading. The court spelled out with eloquence the dreadful wait and the other humiliations which Soering would be required to undergo in some seven years or more of appeals.

The officials of Virginia finally conceded and agreed to imprison Soering for life. Virginia made no admissions that the death penalty violated customary international law, but its conduct in essence admitted that.

How did the United States get itself into the trap in which it now finds itself in the struggle over the death penalty? Unlike all the major nations of the world except China, the United States keeps some 3,500 people on death row and will in due course execute most of them. Can it escape from the trap if the Supreme Court reverses its 1976 decision, which in essence said that the states could resume executions? Some kind of a mania or fixation took hold of the United States after that decision in 1976. No U.S. president since that time has taken any moral or political leadership against the death penalty. Indeed, the federal government itself enacted laws authorizing up to fifty grounds for capital punishment. Some of the twelve states without the death penalty, like New York, have restored it. A strong coalition of nongovernmental organizations lobbied vigorously at the state and federal levels, but to no avail. The Catholic bishops were energized by the vigorous opposition to the death penalty at the highest levels of the church in Rome.

In 1996, the American Bar Association voted for a moratorium on the death penalty. This surprising ruling—from an organization of 400,000 lawyers deemed to be conservative — will have an enormous impact over a period of years.

The best recent scholarly book on international law and the death penalty is *The Death Penalty as Cruel Treatment and Torture: Capital Punishment Challenged in the World's Courts,* by William A. Schavas (Northeastern University Press, 1996). The conclusions of this Canadian academic are cautious and carefully measured. He marshals evidence that the international ban on torture and cruelty may eventually grow into elimination of the death penalty. A thorough review of Schavas's flawless scholarship suggests that if the death penalty is to be ended, it will be done not by legal arguments or subtle interpretations of customary international law but by a sense of horror concerning the death penalty by the people of the world. This horror is shared and expanded by the NGOs of the world, and has been dramatized by the book entitled *Dead Man Walking,* by Sister Helen Prejean. That book portrayed the feeling in the last line of Dostoyevsky's novel *The Idiot:* "You can't treat a man like that."

Dostoyevsky's full statement explains why the death penalty is cruel, inhuman, and degrading:

"To kill for murder is an immeasurably greater evil than the crime itself. . . . Here all . . . last hope, which makes it ten times easier to die, is taken away for certain; here you have been sentenced to death, and the whole terrible agony lies in the fact that you will most certainly not escape, and there is no agony greater than that. Take a soldier and put him in front of a cannon in battle and fire at him and he will still hope, but read the same soldier his death sentence for certain, and he will go mad or burst out crying. Who says that human nature is capable of bearing this without madness? Why this cruel, hideous, unnecessary, and useless mockery? . . . It was of agony like this and of such horror that Christ spoke. No, you can't treat a man like that!"

15

THE

HUMAN RIGHTS

OF PRISONERS

It would be logical to think that the architects of the human rights movement had paid attention very early to the human rights of prisoners. Surely, hardly anyone is more vulnerable than a human being who has been deprived of his or her basic and fundamental right of freedom.

But the human rights movement cannot say that it has achieved great things for prisoners. In 1955, the United Nations adopted the Standard Minimum Rules for the Treatment of Prisoners. It was not a convention or even a declaration. Nations were not asked to ratify it as they had been for most of the documents issued by the United Nations with regard to political, economic, and social rights.

In 1988, the U.N. General Assembly issued a document entitled "Body of Principles for the Protection of All Persons Under Any Form of Detention or Imprisonment." The message sounded stern and insisted that any person under any form of detention or imprisonment should be treated "in a humane manner and with respect to the inherent dignity of the human person."

However, the U.N. document was simply a statement of thirty-nine principles that did not require member-nations to sign or ratify it.

In 1990, the United Nations issued another document entitled "Basic Principles for the Treatment of Prisoners." It advanced previous statements in that it urged the "abolition of solitary confinement as a punishment." It also recommended that favorable conditions "shall be created for the reintegration of the ex-prisoner into society under the best possible conditions."

Someday soon we may well be stating that prison inmates were the orphans in the worldwide human rights movement. To be sure, during the fifty years of the human rights movement some improvements have been made in prison life, but there has also been a decline in the quality of life and availability of opportunities in prisons during that period. One of the amazing facts in American life is that virtually no one knows anything about prisons. Wardens and jailers keep it that way. They have aggressively and systematically kept out the press and the public. In *Saxbe v. Washington Post*, prison officials won their case against the newspaper in the U.S. Supreme Court in 1974. The case was brought when prison officials kept the *Washington Post* from entering a jail where some high-level public officials in the Watergate scandal were locked up.

This state of events is even more amazing in view of the fact that the prison population in the United States has almost tripled from 1980 to 1999 — up to 1.8 million inmates — larger than any prison population in any nation on earth.

I experienced the isolation of prison life when, as a member of a subcommittee of the House Judiciary Committee with supervisory power of federal prisoners, I visited scores of prisons in every part of the country. Even in the 1970s federal prisons were overcrowded and had far too few programs to rehabilitate the inmates or to prepare them for employment when they were released.

It is, of course, easy to criticize penal officials without recognizing that many of them have to manage individuals who have committed very serious crimes and who have a history of engaging in violence.

In the 1970s federal prisons had the stated duty of seeking to rehabilitate the inmates, but that goal faded in the 1980s. Parole was abolished. Sentences became longer, and the rule of three strikes and you're out was invented.

In the 1980s and 1990s a certain amount of revenge entered into the American attitude toward criminals. It was exploited by elected officials who sought to gain attention and praise by demonstrating how "tough" they could be on law enforcement — especially toward those who sell narcotics, participate in gangs, and steal cars.

The "war on drugs," which became a mantra for politicians, led to unfortunate, unintended consequences such as the imprisonment of hundreds of thousands of persons who had not engaged in any violent conduct or even in activities that brought harm to third persons.

In 1980, I participated in a conference in Caracas of penal officials from all over the world. This group, which had met every fifth year since the adoption of the Standard Minimum Rules in 1955, was perplexed and upset because while the human rights movement was gaining momentum everywhere with respect to its concern for political and economic rights, the entire human rights movement was paying little attention to the rights of prisoners.

Some eight years after the Caracas meeting, Human Rights Watch started the prison project. This NGO published reports on prisons in a score of countries including the United States. The reports are commendable and still appear. But it cannot be said that the international human rights movement has stirred up the interest in human rights for prisoners as it has for the rights of women, children, and the disabled, for example.

The neglect of prisoners by the human rights movement has not been planned or deliberate. The Convention on Civil and Political Rights, which entered into force on March 23, 1976, provided in Article 10 that "all persons deprived of their liberty shall be treated with humanity and with respect for the inherent dignity of the human person." The same article insisted that accused persons be kept apart from convicted persons and that juveniles be segregated from adults. Article 10 also made it clear that "the penitentiary shall furnish treatment of prisoners the essential aim of which shall be their reformation and social rehabilitation."

The statement is forthright — the essential aim of the institution shall be "reformation and social rehabilitation." The assumption is that this transformation is possible in a "penitentiary." The word "penitentiary" goes back to the Quaker origin of the reform of the prison system in America in the nineteenth century in Pennsylvania.

The objective of "social rehabilitation" has apparently disappeared in the contemporary jurisprudence of prisons. Yet the idea of rehabilitation was very much alive in the minds of the penal officials who gathered in Caracas in 1980. They admitted with sadness that they often did not have the resources to carry out the rehabilitation they desired, but the dominant philosophy was that incarceration is a means to a doable end and not merely for punitive purposes.

But the officials from poor nations at the Caracas conference had to admit that they were not getting the support from the United Nations which they needed to carry out the objectives that very entity had continued to endorse. This was admitted in 1993 in a report entitled "Human Rights Watch Global Report on Prisons." That document noted the concern for the human rights of prisoners in the Universal Declaration of Human Rights and in the International Covenant on Civil and Political Rights, as well as the Standard Minimum Rules. The Human Rights Watch document conceded that these "have been largely unsuccessful in improving the conditions under which prisoners live."

The human rights movement does, of course, pay more attention to political prisoners. Indeed the NGOs in the United States engage in monitoring the destiny of those who are detained for their ideological views. If these unlucky individuals are lawyers or journalists, they are more likely to obtain the attention of the international human rights community.

Amnesty International has a highly developed approach for spotting the incarceration of political prisoners and seeking to liberate them. I was very impressed at the efficacy of Amnesty International when I was on a human rights mission in Chile just before Pinochet was ousted. A medical doctor was jailed hundreds of miles from Santiago because he had correctly accused the government of employing torture. With pressure from Amnesty International, ambassadors of more than fifty countries pressured the government in Chile to release the physician. He was home within forty-eight hours.

But the human rights movement does not have the same aptitude for paying attention to prisoners who have lost their liberty because of their alleged wrongdoing. Even in South Africa after it abolished apartheid, the human rights groups of the world did not give vigorous attention to the conditions in the jails which held thousands of persons who were incarcerated partially because of their political opposition to the all-white government.

In summer 1995, I visited prisons and lectured to public officials about the international human rights of prisoners in South Africa. The human rights activists in that country understandably had many urgent priorities aside from the rights of prisoners. And, indeed, it seems true almost everywhere that the living conditions and human rights of prisoners have always seemed to be trumped by other concerns.

In the vast explosion of reports and literature on human rights, the amount of material on prisoners is relatively small. And even in reports that do address the topic of human rights and prisoners, there is little questioning of the basic assumptions of what government thinks they are doing when they take people convicted of a crime and force them to wear prison garb, live in a cell, and lose virtually every semblance of privacy.

Experts in the international human rights movement seem to leave their concerns at the door of the prison. All the norms for human rights and conduct center on what is cruel, inhuman, and degrading. How are these norms applied to the dozens of humiliations that prison guards impose on inmates?

The Standard Minimum Rules and other documents of the United Nations on the rights of those detained for any reason unfortunately function at a level of generality that does not seem to give prisoners or their attorneys anything specific to use. At least eight states in the United States have adopted the rules, but it is not certain that inmates in these states enjoy a higher level of respect for their internationally recognized human rights.

There are some provisions with "bite" in the Standard Minimum Rules. These relate to the right to be treated with dignity and respect, the right to confidentiality with one's attorney, and the right to a reasonable level of health care. But the U.N. document does not get into the harder questions of the essential fairness of, for example, taking a man away from his wife and two children for a crime related to drugs; the whole complicated question of what is condign punishment is not adequately addressed by any U.N. document that relates to crime and punishment.

One of the most helpful documents monitoring the history of human rights of prisoners is the addition to the U.S. State Department annual report on human rights. This document now by congressional mandate includes information on the state of prisons in each of the nations surveyed. In the report issued in April 1999 for the year 1998, the report on El Salvador contained three paragraphs about jails in that country. In 1998, prisons remained overcrowded, with the number of inmates at 28 percent over the designed maximum capacity; there were 7,147 men in seventeen prisons and 398 women in two facilities designed for 180 women. Gang violence — especially in the three oldest facilities — seems to be endemic in the prisons of El Salvador — as elsewhere. At least 10 deaths had occurred in the prisons as a result of violence.

A reading of the State Department reports and the extensive documents from Human Rights Watch and Amnesty International raises the basic question: Is the incarceration of prisoners — except in rare cases of persons who are dangerous — humane, effective, outdated, or just vindictive?

A book by Vivien Stern entitled *A Sin Against the Future: Imprisonment in the World* (Northeastern University Press, 1998) is an excellent summary of the history of the idea of prisons and how they are functioning today. The author clearly calls for reform, asserting that imprisonment no longer fits modern society. In many cases imprisonment "gives rise to more problems than it solves." Every prison, moreover, is a place "in which profound abuses of human rights can be carried out under the reasoning justification that this is needed to protect the public."

Stern highlights the trend in the United States with its massive number of prisoners — an example, incidentally, that appears to be attracting attention in Europe, where the minimal use of prisons has been the norm.

Stern points out forcefully that prisons do not heal or transform inmates. She concludes that after "a spell in prison the young man involved in petty crime has become a person who rejects society's values as society has rejected him" (p. 338).

The author, a British academic, makes out a powerful case for the thesis that prisons are "a sin against the future" in the same category as "polluting the environment and using up the natural resources of the globe."

Can the international human rights movement have an impact on the vast and brutal systems of prisons in the former Soviet republics, the new countries of Africa, the struggling democracies in Latin America, and the "penitentiaries" in the United States? Clearly, the academics and activists in the NGOs devoted to that objective have been working diligently with little if any recognition or reward.

It is indeed ironic that the United States, which has escalated its use of prisons beyond anyone's prediction fifteen years ago, has through its

State Department reports become the compiler of one of the most comprehensive sources of information about the state of the world's prisons.

A handful of groups in New York — especially the American Civil Liberties Union — lobby and litigate to improve the human rights of prisoners in the United States. They are confronted with almost insurmountable obstacles. One result of this work is the fact that over one-half of state prison systems are under court orders to improve the facilities or services of the nation's prisoners.

Although there have been some opportunities to take their cases to the European Court of Human Rights in Strasbourg, one must conclude that prisoners have not benefited from the international human rights movement in the way that they deserve. Prisoners under international human rights law may not be deprived of internationally recognized human rights unless such a deprivation is required by the very condition of being imprisoned. Inmates, furthermore, should not be deprived of due process by their jailers. They are already punished enough by the removal of their liberty; they cannot be further prohibited at the whim of prison guards, who have almost total control over the lives of inmates.

The depth of the desire to punish prisoners in the United States is appalling. The deprivations and humiliations inflicted in prison continue in several states where even former felons may never vote in any state election. The contempt extended to prisoners by their superiors reflects and deepens the profound feelings of alienation which the public has for prisoners. Racism is also involved, because over 50 percent of prisoners in the United States are African-Americans, although only 12 percent of the general population is black.

Compassion for prisoners is one of the virtues which Christ emphasized. Visiting those in prison is exalted in the gospels as a high virtue. It is in essence an integral part of the entire Judeo-Christian tradition. It could be argued that prison policy in the United States makes that virtue almost impossible to carry out. Prisons are erected in areas totally segregated from the communities in which they reside; this is accomplished by high walls, severe restrictions on the number of visitors, and the implicit statement that prisoners must be locked up and segregated from society because they are dangerous.

It does seem quixotic to suggest that inmates would benefit by sharing in a community beyond the walls of a prison and that this could be a very effective way to begin the reintegration of prisoners into the community to which they will inevitably be returned.

I have spoken through the years to and with prison officials. They have a difficult task, but almost automatically they tend to adopt a policy of hostility toward inmates. The guards are placed in an awkward role. They are in all probability given copies of the rules set forth by the United Nations to protect the human rights of prisoners, yet they know that these rules have no legal binding power in America's courts and that the prisoners probably have no knowledge of the existence of such rules.

Persons involved in prison reform are now deeply discouraged at the prevailing simplistic attitudes which seem to be in ascendancy at the moment.

It could be that the international human rights movement has some moral and legal principles which might inject rationality into the American obsession with the idea that more prisons and longer sentences are the solution to crime.

The ban on cruel, inhuman, and degrading treatment and punishment is one of the cornerstones of the human rights movement. If this compelling and elevating doctrine were seriously applied to the work of prisons, a global transformation could result.

16

HUMAN RIGHTS
DEPEND ON AN
INDEPENDENT
JUDICIARY

The concept that the judge in any human rights case should be independent and impartial has always been so axiomatic that in the history of the international human rights movement there has never been any great debate about it.

The issue was seemingly settled in 1948, when Article 10 of the Universal Declaration of Human Rights proclaimed: "Everyone is entitled in full equality to a fair and public hearing by a competent, independent and impartial tribunal in the determination . . . of any charge against him."

The International Covenant on Civil and Political Rights in Article 14(1) repeats the idea that everyone's entitlement is to "a fair and public hearing by a competent, independent and impartial tribunal."

Likewise Article 8(1) of the American Convention on Human Rights insists that "every person has a right to a hearing . . . by a competent, independent and impartial tribunal." The European Convention on Human Rights also guarantees "a fair and public hearing . . . by an independent and impartial tribunal by law."

The value and importance of an independent judge are dramatically preserved in the four 1949 Geneva conventions. The 153 contracting parties to this compact, including the United States, have the right in a public emergency situation to suspend fair trial guarantees. But in Article 3 the passing of sentences and carrying out of executions cannot be done except by a regularly constituted court previously established by law.

Article 3 is not subject to derogation under any circumstances. It seems clear that jurists can argue that insisting on a regularly constituted court even in situations involving conflict should be regarded as a peremptory norm of international law.

The European Court on Human Rights and the Inter-American Commission on Human Rights have stressed the indispensability of an independent tribunal. The latter has conducted on-site investigations and has issued public reports deploring the absence of an independent judge — even in situations where a state of siege exists.

The idea and the centrality of the independence of the bench are so self-evident that one could hope there would be no sustained controversy over it. But the desire of despots to control the situation and the determination of even democratically elected governments to be completely in charge are foreign to the concept of an "independent" person or entity that makes the crucial decisions.

The idea of a judge who is "independent" and "impartial" can be seen as idealistic and even unrealistic. The Code of Judicial Conduct adopted by the American Bar Association in 1990 stresses the idea of the independence of the judge and the need to avoid all impropriety. Indeed, the code, unlike the 1983 Model Rules governing attorneys, retains and enforces the ban on even the "appearance of impropriety."

But it is still difficult to comprehend how one person can rise above all the prejudices and prepossessions that every human being inherits or develops. Justice Benjamin Cardozo said it well in his book *The Nature of the Judicial Process* (Yale University Press, 1921): "There is in each of us a stream of tendency, whether you choose to call it philosophy or not, which gives coherence and direction to thought and action. Judges cannot escape that current any more than other mortals. All their lives, forces which they do not recognize and cannot name, have been tugging at them — inherited instinct, traditional beliefs, acquired convictions; and the resultant is an outlook on life, a conception of social needs. . . . In this mental background every problem finds its setting. We may try to see things as objectively as we please. None the less, we can never see them with any eyes except our own" (pp. 12–13).

The very idea of an independent tribunal is of course foreign to the concept of majority control and to the idea that legislatures and the executive branches of government make the ultimate decisions. Judicial review is the twin of the idea that there are certain human rights which no legislature or executive branch of a government can deny. All the international and regional groups that have promulgated codes or manifestos of human rights have assumed that, even under the best of circumstances, they are not self-enforcing. The human rights that are created and guaranteed should theoretically be readily available to the persons in whom these rights inhere and who are entitled to claim them because of their inherent dignity.

But history repeats the need for a moral force to exist that thrives on moral principles and that can force the elected branches of government to carry out the promises their governments have made. No nation is being forced by a judge to do something contrary to what the elected officials or the people desire at the moment. A tribunal simply reminds a government that it has made solemn promises to carry out the mandates of a covenant on human rights, a contract which the nation has made with the international community.

It is obvious that the judge who is required to enforce such contracts can understandably be tempted to defer to the leaders whose wishes the judge must reject or at least postpone. The history of the world is filled with the sad story of judges who caved or compromised in order to retain their positions. In the dark years of Argentina from 1976 to 1983 when the military controlled the government, there were not a few judges who ruled in such a way that they retained their jobs rather than follow what was clearly required by international human rights law.

It is for all these reasons that the international human rights community has stressed and cherished the independence of the judiciary. Since 1978 the International Commission of Jurists has issued reports on the state of judicial independence throughout the world. The commission's creation, the Center for the Independence of Judges and Lawyers Code of Judicial Conduct, defines as carefully as possible the profound cluster of ideas and ideals underlining the independence of the bench and the bar. The purpose of the center is to mobilize support for judges who are being harassed or intimidated or even persecuted for their professional work in upholding the principles of the rule of law.

An ever wider group of nongovernmental organizations assists the

International Commission of Jurists. The International Bar Association in 1981, along with other legal entities, prepared a document in Siracusa, Italy, on the independence of the bench. Thirty-two principles in this document were designed to produce a properly functioning independent judiciary everywhere. They have been discussed throughout the world. There are no substantial differences on the overall purposes of the document. But difficult political questions remain, such as how judges are to be appointed and for how long.

The Siracusa Manifesto does, however, contain in Article 2 a definition on which there is a broad consensus:

Independence of the judiciary means (1) that every judge is free to decide matters before him in accordance with his assessment of the facts and his understanding of the law without any improper influence, inducements or pressures, direct or indirect, from any quarter or for any reasons, and (2) that the judiciary is independent of the executive and legislature, and has jurisdiction, directly or by way of review, over all issues of a judicial nature.

It is questionable whether military courts of certain kinds can fulfill this definition. For generations most nations have created courts to serve exclusively military service personnel — with possibly a few exceptions. The independence of the persons who make the decisions in military courts raises thorny issues. This is especially true when martial law is declared — as in Pakistan in the 1980s where the rulings of military courts were immunized from judicial review.

The same thing happened in December 1980 in El Salvador, when the government created a military court to authorize procedures by which a civilian could remain incommunicado for 195 days. Courts of this nature constitute a major departure from the basic principles of judicial independence.

Actions that compromise the independence of lawyers are engaged in by governments who are unable or unwilling to follow the decisions of their judges. Governments seldom abolish bar associations, as was done when the government of Syria in 1980 dissolved the Damascus and Syrian bar associations for their standards opposing the prolonged emergency, arbitrary arrest, and torture of political prisoners.

Governments have tried similar tactics against lawyers in South Africa, Latin America, and especially countries where the government can appeal to the presence or threat of terrorism as a reason the defense bar should be silenced or immobilized.

The literature on the independence of the bench and the bar is extensive and growing. It is grounded in the idea of a rule of law which is rather easily knowable and which presupposes or posits the existence of international human rights which are binding on all the countries who are members of the United Nations. Enforcement of basic human rights is legally required of these countries even if they have not ratified the U.N. covenants on human rights.

The independence of the bench was one of the central ideas advanced in the Declaration of Independence and the U.S. Constitution. The Declaration of Independence enumerates a "long train of abuses," which includes the efforts of the British Crown to remove judges from their positions. Article 3 of the Constitution made the independence of judges the cornerstone of the new American government. Judges were appointed for life by the president with the consent of the Senate, and could be removed only for committing "bribery, treason or other high crimes or misdemeanors." These standards are so high that fewer than thirty federal judges have ever been impeached and removed from office by the House and the Senate.

The endemic resistance of elected officials to unelected judges surfaced early in American history when during the outbursts of Jacksonian democracy, many states outside of New England adopted the practice of electing judges. Some thirty-eight states now follow that system. The implications for the rule of law and the independence of the judiciary will continue to be debated. But the continued survival of this form of judicial review offers very relevant evidence of the worldwide tensions between the elected and the unelected officials of government.

The struggle for an independent judiciary has intensified as the international human rights movement has become more universal. The 1999 yearbook for the Center for the Independence of Judges and Lawyers listed some of the incredible attacks on judges as, for example, in Colombia, where 122 judges and jurists were murdered between 1979 and 1995.

The yearbook also noted the several international declarations promoting the independence of the judiciary. These include the U.N. General Assembly's adoption in 1985 of a set of principles on the independence of the judiciary. The United Nations has also appointed a special rapporteur who has carried out investigations and conducted missions in countries where attacks on judges have been egregious.

The academics and the activists in the international human rights movement will understandably carry forward the mobilization of shame, propaganda for the sanctity of human rights, and appeals for the rule of law. But hidden in the undertow in the struggle for human rights are subtle and silent currents through which government can undermine compliance with international human rights standards by eroding the independence of the courts. This can be done by appointing timid rather than courageous jurors or by selecting persons known to be so politically ambitious that they would be likely to make decisions based on the wishes and whims of the appointing authorities.

The thorny issue of the independence of judges clearly cannot be separated from any aspect of the human rights movement. It may be that the universal acceptance of specific human rights as international law may eventually make it difficult if not impossible for any judge anywhere, for example, to deny freedom of the press or to allow torture.

Education, in other words, is the key to a more universal acceptance of human rights. That is why the Vienna declaration in 1993 strongly urged worldwide education about the nature and universality of human rights.

The very idea of judicial independence assumes that many nations will resist the reach of the newly proclaimed internationally recognized moral and legal values which nations have agreed to accept and follow. In due course, some supranational tribunal will be established to enforce the new world standards. In the interim, judges at the national and local levels have the duty of insisting that the governments that have appointed them comply with norms set forth by the international community.

The achievement of this daunting task will require the appointment or election of judges who are competent and courageous. They can rise to this level only if they are independent and impartial.

IS FREEDOM OF RELIGION THE MOST FUNDAMENTAL OF ALL HUMAN RIGHTS?

In writing codes and commentary about the nature of human rights all around the world, one would think that religion — as the source of the moral and spiritual values underlying the vast majority of human rights — would be referred to more than most sources of human rights. But in the fifty years of the international human rights movement, religion has not attained the level of importance that some secular ideals such as the freedom of speech have reached.

All observers and participants in the human rights movement would concede that both religious and secular activists have contributed to the development of democracy and the fulfillment of human rights. But there has been a persistent and understandable feeling over the past fifty years that religious institutions have had a checkered record of defining and legitimating the human rights of the children of God. The advocates of international human rights cannot forget that religious bodies for centuries followed the maxim that "Error has rights." The fact that the Catholic church in Vatican II in 1965 solemnly renounced this doctrine does not convince the human rights activists that religion is now the full partner of those vast official and nongovernmental organizations that have made the observance of human rights the centerpiece of a new world in which 191 nations follow the Universal Declaration of Human Rights as their national and foreign policy.

But the record of government with regard to religious freedom and other human rights has also been traumatic. The practice of many governments before 1948 and the adoption of the Universal Declaration suggests that human rights require protection from both government and religion.

Consequently, for years there has been a truce, a partnership, and a symbiosis between governments and religions with respect to the new regime in which all nations have, for the first time in history, pledged to comply with standards of human rights that are defined by the international community.

The secular advocates of human rights know that would-be friends in the religious community sometimes feel required to follow absolutes which those without religious faith do not share. Martin Luther exemplified this characteristic when in 1521 he published the words: "Dare I Stand I Can Do No Other."

This sense of being compelled by a divine intervention and driven by an irreversible demand of conscience seems antithetical to the sense of needing to accommodate to differing views — a sense which epitomizes the flexibility of those who seek to adopt universal values for the present situation. Justice Learned Hand captured this sense in his observation that "the spirit of liberty is the spirit that is not too sure it is right."

The framers of the Constitution created a situation where citizens of fundamentally different views could co-exist in peace with the separation of powers and even the right to amend the Constitution. Religious bodies, with their adherence to certain unchangeable truths, are not likely to be prepared to be flexible on certain issues. Indeed, some observers of the human rights movement claim that human rights cannot ultimately succeed unless humanity accepts and adheres to some suprahuman set of values which will assist the advocates of human rights in their struggle to resist and defeat the vigorous and vociferous defenders of nationalistic policies which defy the command of the international human rights movement. The partisans of a theological point of view do not claim that they are superior to humanists; they simply assert that persons driven by what they concede to be a call from an eternal lawgiver are more likely to be stalwart defenders of human rights than are those whose call or persuasion derives from some secular, rationalistic, or humanitarian motivation.

The sense of persons of faith that they are needed in the world struggle against barbarism is supported by what the monstrous totalitarian systems perpetuated in the twentieth century—whether those systems be Fascist, Nazi, Communist, or Maoist.

The claim of people of faith was expressed by John Paul II when he said that religious rights are the "cornerstone of all other rights."

This is the dualism which has been the underlying and often unspoken theme in the way the human rights community has treated religion.

The U.N. charter postponed the formulation of a specific bill of rights but did say that respect for "human rights and fundamental freedoms" is incompatible with any discrimination as to "race, sex, language or religion."

The Universal Declaration of Human Rights reaffirmed this in several places. Article 1 teaches that all human beings are "endowed with reason and cognizance and should act towards one another in a spirit of brotherhood." Article 18 says, "Everyone has the right to freedom of thought, conscience and religion; this right includes freedom to change his religion or belief, and freedom to live alone or in community with others and in public or private, to manifest his religion or belief in teaching, practice, worship or observance."

It is most significant that the 1993 Vienna declaration from the World Conference on Human Rights reaffirmed these sentiments. Paragraph 22 urges that all governments "take all appropriate measures to counter intolerant and related violence based on religion and belief . . . including the desecrating of religious sites, recognizing that every individual has the right to freedom of thought, conscience, expression and religion." The Vienna declaration went on to invite "all states to put into practice the provisions of the Declaration on the Elimination of all Forms of Intolerance and of Discrimination Based on Religion or Belief." The declaration gained added force by the unusual and possibly unprecedented statement that "human rights and fundamental freedoms are the birthright of all human beings; their protection and promotion is the *first* responsibility of governments" [emphasis added].

Despite the inclusion of rights based on religion in all the essential international documents on human rights, the fact is that there is no convention on religious human rights—but only a declaration issued in 1981. The history of how this happened has been traced in the book

Freedom of Religion or Belief (Kluwer, 1996), by Bahiyyih G. Tahzib. We will return to this topic.

Article 18 of the Universal Declaration makes it clear that any individual has the right to hold a "belief" instead of a "religion." There is therefore no preference in favor of believers over nonbelievers.

The Universal Declaration was adopted by a vote of forty-eight nations in favor, none against, and eight abstentions. Saudi Arabia, South Africa, and six Eastern European nations abstained from voting. All Muslim states other than Saudi Arabia voted in favor of the declaration. It seems clear, consequently, that the portions of the Universal Declaration related to religion are customary international law if not *jus cogens*.

In the early 1950s the United Nations began its efforts to formulate what ultimately became the International Covenant on Civil and Political Rights. Article 21 of this instrument includes the following protection, which does not exist in the Universal Declaration: "Any advocacy for religious hatred that constitutes incitement to discrimination, hostility or violence shall be prohibited by law." In addition, Article 24 provides that special protection shall be given to children without discrimination on account of religion.

The International Covenant on Economic, Social and Cultural Rights also supports religious freedom. Article 13 is designed to guarantee the religious freedom of parents. Article 13 proposes that parents have the right to "ensure the religious and moral education of their children in conformity with their own convictions."

Other U.N. covenants protect the right to religious freedom. Article 5 of the International Convention on the Elimination of All Forms of Racial Discrimination, which was put into force in 1965, guarantees the right to freedom of thought, conscience, and religion. The 1989 Convention on the Rights of the Child reiterates the ample protection for religious rights in other covenants. The 1990 International Convention on the Protection of the Rights of All Migrant Workers and Their Families reaffirms the provisions relating to freedom of religion or beliefs present in preexisting conventions.

The International Labor Organization has been replicating the emphasis on religious freedom found in U.N. documents. In the seventy-five years of its existence, the ILO has adopted more than 170 covenants. Since

World War II, fifteen of these ILO conventions have included provisions pertaining to freedom of religion and belief.

In 1960 following the submission by a U.N. rapporteur on religion several groups around the world felt the need for the United Nations to take a stronger position on religious freedom. A draft declaration was drawn up in 1960. Manifestations of religious intolerance had been present and across the globe. Antisemitic incidents were occurring in Europe and in the western hemisphere. The U.N. General Assembly condemned all manifestations of racial and religious hatred as violations of the U.N. charter and the Universal Declaration of Human Rights. In 1962 the U.N. General Assembly adopted a resolution calling on all members to take all necessary steps to adopt legislation to combat prejudice and intolerance. The United Nations also called for a draft convention on religious intolerance. Some nations favored the idea of a convention on religious intolerance rather than a mere declaration; a convention, unlike the declaration, would have binding power. But other observers saw great difficulties in crafting a convention on religion which would be enforceable.

Debate within the United Nations on a convention or a declaration on religious freedom went on for several years. In November 1981, the United Nations finally adopted the Declaration on the Elimination of All Forms of Intolerance and of Discrimination Based on Religion or Belief. Its paragraph preamble and its eight substantive articles are a triumph for its authors, who persisted for years in the drafting of a document on a topic which is sensitive and difficult.

The Islamic states succeeded in deleting the provision that a person has the right to change his or her religious belief. This, however, was weakened if not nullified by Article 8, which provides that nothing in the declaration concerning religious intolerance restricts or detracts from the portion of the Universal Declaration of Human Rights that specifically safeguards the right to change one's religion.

Iraq entered a collective reservation on behalf of the Organization of the Islamic Conference rejecting any provisions which would be contrary to Islamic law (Shari'ah) or to any law based on Islamic principles.

The 1981 declaration is not a convention, nor does it have a supervisory mechanism. It does not participate directly in the monitoring of the several treaty bodies within the U.N. human rights systems. But it is normative rather than exhortatory. It has, furthermore, been implemented by a series of rapporteurs who in nine reports between 1981 and 1995 pinpointed the places in the world where manifestations of religious intolerance were clear.

The question of a possibility or the need for a legally binding international instrument on freedom of religion or belief has not yet been resolved. Nongovernmental organizations continue to discuss this issue, which seems less urgent in view of the fact that at least four of the seven U.N. monitoring committees do handle petitions based on a denial of religious freedom. Controversies related to conscientious objectors, discrimination against specific religious denominations, and eligibility for public services for members of a particular religion have been some of the issues touched upon by the U.N. Commission on Human Rights, which monitors compliance with the International Covenant on Civil and Political Rights. Blasphemies, incitement to religious intolerance, compulsory religion in public schools, and the closing of places of worship are other topics touched upon by the commission.

The apparent absence of a consensus to create a legally binding mechanism within the United Nations to penalize violations of religious freedoms is clearly disappointing to many observers, whether they are religious or not. They observe the persecution of persons of faith in China, the religious controversies in India and Pakistan, and the interreligious conflicts in dozens of countries. Cannot the United Nations and its agencies do more to protect the religious beliefs and actions of millions of believers?

Material gathered by Tahzig relates to the questions and comments on reports submitted to the U.N. Commission on Human Rights, which monitors all the nations which have ratified the International Covenant on Civil and Political Rights. The commission has no specific juridical control over these countries, but it is required to raise questions and offer recommendations. Its comments on the performance of nations with regard to Article 18 are, Tahzig feels, "cautious." In the first years of the commission's existence, several cases arrived through the use of the optional protocol. Some fourteen questions about religious liberty went to the committee — eight of them on conscientious objection to war. The commission was restrictive and gave little relief to the petitioners.

The U.N. Commission on Human Rights told Costa Rica that it could not give the National Episcopal Conference of that country the power to bar Catholics from teaching religion in the public schools. The commission ruled that in Denmark, parents should not be required to obtain special permission for their children to exempt themselves from religious instruction; required religious instruction violates Article 18.

The U.N. commission interpreted Article 18 to encompass freedom of theistic, nontheistic, and atheistic beliefs. The 1981 Declaration on Religion supports that conclusion. Nevertheless, the rulings of the United Nations over the past twenty years have not conveyed the impression that the human rights watchdogs at the United Nations are aggressively broadening the parameters of religious freedom. But the relatively unknown decisions of the U.N. committees supervising the implementation of the various international covenants may be more forward-looking than they now appear. At least it is significant that for the first time in history there are units within the United Nations which observe conduct deemed to be restrictive of religious human rights and speak about it. It also seems clear that the 1981 declaration against intolerance has implications which in due course may have consequences not foreseeable at this time.

Over the past fifty years religious groups have increasingly embraced and expanded their devotion to human rights. It is fair to say that all the religions of the earth have in truly unique ways helped the dearth and growth of the international human rights movement.

Faith-based groups have wondered whether in past years they should have been proactive in seeking to obtain better juridical machinery for human rights from the United Nations. Perhaps church-based entities everywhere should have clarified their positions on human rights and annunciated them in dramatic ways.

RELIGIOUS GROUPS AND HUMAN RIGHTS

When one looks back in history, the claims of religious institutions and the claims of human rights advocates do not always reflect glory on either group. It is a consolation to be able to realize that those positions have been altered during the fifty years of the human rights revolution. The staunchest secularist has to recognize that most religious bodies have abandoned their disdain for the secularist and have embraced human rights as a direct derivative of the religious faith which they cherish. Indeed, history may reflect favorably on what religious groups have done for human rights in the decades since the formation of the United Nations. Both religion and secularism have made contributions to the human rights movement. Both have learned to rely on each other and to drop the traditional attitudes that they have competing claims. The rapprochement of secular human rights activists with traditional religious groups was dramatically realized when clerics and theologians in Vatican II and at the Episcopal conferences at Medellín and Puebla in Latin America joined in the rebirth of international human rights throughout the world.

At the same time, not all keen observers of the human rights scene think that an appeal to human rights can be simultaneously secular and religious. Louis Henkin, an emeritus professor at Columbia University and the dean of human rights experts, opines: "For our time one has to justify human rights by some contemporary universal version of natural law, whether religious or secular, by appeal to a common moral condition of human dignity." This is the sentiment of the late Catholic philosopher Jacques Maritain. When he read the charter of the United Nations he welcomed it as the embodiment of a sort of "secular faith."

On the other hand, Professor Max Stackhouse of Princeton Theological Seminary argues persuasively that "certain theological principles are indispensable to sustaining the idea of human rights." He argues that "some theological — that is some God-given and normative — insights bind all humanity together."

Stackhouse points forcefully to dreadful situations that arise when nations become "disconnected from their reasonable good." Movements that have repudiated theology, he continued, have become "the greatest violation of human rights." He points to Papa Doc in Haiti, Pol Pot in Cambodia, Marcos in the Philippines, Mao in China, and Stalin in the Soviet Union.

Does the theology of human rights matter to the revolution on human rights that started in San Francisco when the U.N. charter was adopted? By every objective norm the position of the church with regard to the evolution of human rights has to be relevant.

Robert Traer's important book, *Faith in Human Rights: The Force in Religious Tradition for a Global Struggle* (Georgetown University Press, 1991), is helpful, encouraging, and even inspiring in its examination of what has happened since 1945 among the world's great religions. In essence, religions have gone back to their roots and discovered that they are in agreement with most of the principles set forth in the U.N. documents that are foundational in the human rights revolution.

Traer, a Protestant clergyman and a lawyer, boldly proclaims that "Human rights are at the center of the global moral language that is being justified, elaborated and advocated by members of different religious traditions and cultures" (p. 10). The consensus which Traer discovered among Catholics, liberals, and conservative Protestants, as well as Christian groups around the world, is quite remarkable. Traer asserts that "faith in human rights cuts across the Christian community, uniting those that are divided by other issues of doctrine and practice" (p. 91). He concludes that "for many Christians today, human rights are as clear as God's creative and redemptive presence and as compelling as life itself. Human rights are at the heart of what they believe to be their common faith" (p. 92).

The Jewish legacy is even more supportive of human rights than are Christian traditions. Although the term "human rights" did not appear in the Bible and was invented rather recently, the entire Jewish culture can be described as one that derives directly from the sacred rights of every person. Central to Jewish and Christian belief is the certainty that every person is created as an "image of God."

THE MUSLIM APPROACH TO HUMAN RIGHTS

The attitude of the twenty-two Arab nations and the entire Islamic world concerning human rights is obviously of paramount concern to everyone involved in the struggle to promote the human rights which have been internationalized and globalized over the past five decades.

The basic beliefs of the Muslim world on human rights continue to be the subject of intense interest and extensive scholarship. When the U.N. General Assembly in 1948 approved the Universal Declaration of Human Rights, the government of Saudi Arabia abstained on the ground that the declaration did not recognize rights to be the gift of God and in addition violated the Koran by asserting the right to change one's religion. But the Muslim foreign minister of Pakistan defended his country's support for the declaration on the ground that the Koran permits one to believe or disbelieve.

The issue continues to be debated in the Islamic world. It is intertwined with the deep animosity which many in countries like Indonesia have toward the nation that colonized them. Some people in the postcolonial world feel that the European nations corrupted them, weakened their Muslim faith, and sought to impose western concepts of individualized rights not in harmony with the Muslin background of their countries.

The Muslim countries have ratified the human rights treaties and in large numbers approved the final declaration of the 1993 World Conference on Human Rights in Vienna.

It is not feasible to generalize about what the Islamic world thinks about international human rights. Each nation and each region is grappling with new problems such as the sudden massive shift to urban living in the past twenty years. In addition, there is the invasion of western popular culture and the promulgation by some countries of newly developed Islamic rules, some of which have dubious or debatable authority. All this is complicated by officials using Islamization in ways that serve their political goals.

The 1979 Constitution of the Islamic Republic of Iran adds confusion to an assessment of what the Islamic world thinks of human rights. That revolutionary constitution limits freedom of the press, the right of association, and human and cultural rights "according to Islamic standards."

All this may seem contradictory to a seminar on human rights which was organized in 1980 by the International Commission of Jurists, the University of Kuwait, and the Union of Arab Lawyers. The sixty-five participants affirmed that "Islam was the first to recognize human rights almost fourteen centuries ago." The statement continued by noting that Islam through the centuries set up guarantees and safeguards "that have only recently been incorporated in universal declarations of human rights."

In 1986, a group of Arab experts and the Arab Union of Lawyers, with a claimed membership of 100,000, reaffirmed their "faith in the principles

in the charter of the United Nations and the International Bill of Rights."
But they also affirmed an "Islamic interpretation of human rights that
they feel is best suited to the particular needs of the modern Arab world."

There are, however, voices and authorities in the Islamic world that are
less supportive of human rights. The reality is that it is virtually impossible to be certain how the nations in which over 1 billion Muslims reside
are reacting to the challenges of the human rights movement. But it is
clear that there is firm support in the Islamic world for international
human rights. There are no major contradictions between the basic truths
contained in the human rights documents and the core teachings of Islamic culture. Some observers may have problems with that generaliza-
tion because of the restrictions the Islamic world places on the rights
of women and some non-Islamic religions. Recognizing once again the
great turmoil and the astonishing changes occurring in the world of Islam, it does seems clear that the momentum in those nations is toward
democracy, freedom of speech, and fair elections.

It still is true that the Arab states are the least liberal corner of the
globe. But Algeria and Egypt have granted amnesties to prisoners. Even
Sudan, crippled by an interminable civil war, appears to be improving.
Aging despots may be replaced by rulers who have listened to the steady
drumbeat urging equality for women, freedom of the press, and suffrage
for all citizens.

ASIA AND HUMAN RIGHTS

The lands of Asia with a Hindu or Buddhist background do not speak
or think in terms of human rights. But the ideology underlying the notion
of human rights is not incompatible with the centuries-old perspective of
Chinese and Asian culture. We forget that China was one of the original
sponsors of the United Nations and that it is still one of the five countries
with veto power in the Security Council.

It is, however, hard to understand why China continues to be so harsh
on human rights. Its record on respecting religious freedom is especially
deplorable. Why did Beijing react so savagely in 1999 to the religious
group Falun Gong? This group, drawing on a prayerful tradition of Bud-

dhism and Taoism, is neither subversive nor sinister. In the eyes of the Chinese rulers, the cult constituted a challenge to their power that had to be crushed. If the entities charged with defending international human rights had been operating effectively, could swift reaction have prevented China from challenging this sect? The official suppression of Falun Gong cannot be justified by any religious tradition in China, because religious groups would clearly preach tolerance and gentleness.

U Thant, a Burmese Buddhist who served as secretary general of the United Nations (1962–1971), almost certainly reflected the Asian view of human rights. He urged: "We must all foster and encourage a climate of opinion in which human rights can flourish. We must be alive to any encroachment upon the rights and freedom of an individual. And, above all, we must practice tolerance and respect the rights and freedoms of others."

At the heart of the guarantees given to religious beliefs in all the U.N. documents is the unquestioned assumption that all individuals have the right to follow their conscience because that is their duty. The assumption is never questioned. Everyone is entitled to act "in accordance with the dictates of his own conscience" — as the Helsinki and other proclamations put it.

The major premise underlying all the U.N. provisions on religious freedom — the supremacy of conscience — also lies at the heart of the Christian religion; Martin Luther and Cardinal Newman proclaim it in almost identical phrasing. Its abiding presence in all the documents internationalizing the sovereignty of conscience has unfortunately not been adequately analyzed. This is true even in the magisterial two-volume *Religious Human Rights in Global Perspectives,* issued in 1996 by the Law and Religion Program at Emory University.

The question raised at the Vienna World Conference on Human Rights in 1993 concerning the universality of human rights did not directly attack the centrality of conscience as enshrined in international documents on human rights. The complaint, rather, focused on the alleged western orientation of the rights proclaimed in the U.N. documents.

There appears to be, then, a truth that brooks no opposition and needs no explanation: each person has the right to follow his or her conscience.

The inviolability of conscience follows as an unquestioned corollary from the basic concept affirmed in all the U.N. documents—that dignity and equality are inherent in all human beings.

At the end of the discussion on the presence and relative effectiveness of the religious and secular advocates of human rights, one would like to avoid the question and urge the participants in the struggle for human rights to battle on—whatever their ultimate motivation may be. At the same time, some human rights activists who are religious wonder whether humanists, with their nonreligious orientation, have the same depth of conviction and perseverance in the battle for human rights as those who see Christ himself in each victim and are thereby motivated to the core of their being. Although such musings may be unfair to those who identify themselves as individuals without religious faith, the onslaught of the enemies of human rights are so intense and unrelenting that surely one must need some kind of deep and abiding faith in order to persevere in the cause.

The question, however complicated and unanswerable, is nonetheless important. Among secular and religious human rights activists, there exist deep differences in the approach to certain human rights. Ideally, these differences should be discussed kindly, but at times they seem nonnegotiable. This is why suspicions in both camps continue to exist, and why many people of faith—especially Catholics—are absent from the vast and growing armies who battle for improvement in human rights.

That absence is a profound abdication of militant advocacy by Catholic officials in the human rights revolution. The real question, and a troubling one, is why Catholics are significantly underrepresented among the lawyers, publicists, and workers who launched and continue the mission of the nongovernmental organizations devoted to human rights.

As the human rights movement develops, will persons of faith enter in significant numbers and will the churches make more contributions in resources and personnel? At the high official levels of the church, the endorsements and applause for human rights continue. But if America's 62 million Catholics and 100 million mainline Protestants, along with the millions of Evangelicals, the Jewish community, and all believers, really joined and participated, the difference would be dramatic.

Even if the miracle of enlightenment and grace occurred, would there be more respect for human rights in China, Africa, and elsewhere? No one can predict with much accuracy. But mass movements depend on a nearly universal consensus on some basic issues — a consensus so profound and pervasive that it simply changes the culture and the way a nation thinks and acts.

The religious bodies in the United States theoretically possess the moral and spiritual power to mobilize themselves and change the way America thinks of its role in the human rights revolution. Catholics are especially well equipped to influence the way the United States thinks about human rights. They've inherited a rich legacy from Vatican II, from the struggles of the church for human rights in Latin America, and from the compelling cry of the gospel that everyone love one another as a brother or sister.

Religion has been a formidable force throughout the fifty years of the human rights movement. Although no one should try to assess the comparative influence of secular or religious persons or institutions within that movement, the force of religion can only be described as a sleeping giant.

Another "sleeping giant" is the Declaration on Religious Freedom issued by Vatican II in 1965. For the first time in the history of the Catholic church the 2,500 bishops gathered in Rome affirmed that it is a violation of the "sacred rights of the person and the family of nations when forces are brought to bear in any way in order to destroy or repress religion."

The declaration clearly tracks the statements on the free exercise of religion which were approved in the basic documents that are the foundation of the human rights movement. The Vatican Council notes that "religious freedom has already been declared to be a civil right in most constitutions and, it is solemnly recognized in international documents." This the Vatican Council "greets with joy."

The Vatican document on religious freedom is strong. Consider these words: "In spreading religious faith and in introducing religious practices, everyone ought at all times to refrain from any manner of action which might seem to carry a hint of coercion or a kind of persuasion that would be dishonorable or unworthy, especially when dealing with poor or uneducated people." The statement bans "any form of action" which has a "hint of coercion." Such an action is a "violation of the rights of others."

The Vatican pronouncement echoed what the U.N. documents say in several ways. The Vatican asserts that "the protection and promotion of the inviolable rights of man rank among the essential duties of government." The statement of the Holy See even uses the very words of the United Nations: "the protection and promotion" of human rights.

The Vatican statement goes beyond the language of the articles of the human rights movement when it asserts that "the usages of society are to be the usage of freedom in their full range. These require that the freedom of man be respected as far as possible, and curtailed only when and insofar as necessary."

The Declaration of Religious Freedom continues to amaze the world. For centuries the Catholic church had held that if a nation is Catholic, it has some duty to prefer Catholics over non-Catholics and even to penalize those who are not believers. The history of the church's intolerance and even persecution is shameful.

The document of the Vatican in repudiating the church's long history speaks of the development of doctrine as an inherent part of the growth and sanctification of the church. The architects of the human rights movement in the past fifty years refer to a secular counterpart to the development of doctrine, called the internationalization of human rights. It is the outgrowth of the dismay of humankind at the Holocaust and the slaughters of World War II.

The parallel paths followed by the Catholic church and the human rights movement form a remarkable example of how in this age of instant communication there can be a profound interaction between institutions and movements.

Could the world regress, allowing the savage interreligious wars that have darkened history? Can the bold defense of religion which is so strong in the human rights movement and the unprecedented proclamations on behalf of religious freedom in Vatican II combine to banish the persecution of religion in dustbin of history? It has not happened yet in China, the Sudan, or North Korea. But it is plausible to think that the abolition of intolerance and persecution based on religious differences may be on the horizon.

Only the declaration, not a convention or treaty, addresses the free exercise of religion in the U.N. community. But the extraordinarily wide-spread respect for religious freedom and the pledge by virtually all the Christian churches and synagogues in the world to repudiate intolerance based on religion may signal the advent of an era when discrimination based on religion can go the way of slavery and piracy.

18

DO AMNESTY
AND RECONCILIATION
BRING JUSTICE?

One of the most important criteria for judging the effectiveness of a law is the manner in which it gives some type of compensation to the victims. Laws exist to punish and to deter. An element of both the punishment and the deterrence is the way the victim is treated.

The laws of many states have provisions that give monetary compensation to the victims of crime. These arrangements are not very satisfactory. The compensation is usually small, and there are no punitive damages.

At the international level, the system of giving restitution to the victims of violations of human rights is just struggling to be born. In South Africa, El Salvador, and Chile, courts and commissions are struggling to find a formula which punishes violators of human rights, deters other possible violators, and rewards victims.

The laws of every state have provisions to compensate those who have suffered unjustly by the misdeeds of others. Multiple concepts are involved: restitution, indemnification, reparations, damages, compensation, redress, rehabilitation, and reimbursement. Indeed, it seems clear that one of the major, primordial functions of the law is to return the victims of an unjust act to their previous condition.

It is clear that the framers of the intellectual human rights law intended that victims must be indemnified. The International Covenant on Civil and Political Rights in Article 9(5) and the European Convention on Human Rights in Article 5(5) referred to an "enforceable right to compensation." Similarly, the Convention Against Torture and other Cruel,

Inhuman, or Degrading Treatment or Punishment contains in Article 14(1), a measure that provides for the victims to receive redress and "an enforceable right to fair and adequate compensation" along with "means for as full a rehabilitation as possible."

The American Convention on Human Rights speaks of "compensatory damages" (Article 68), saying that "fair compensation [should] be paid to the injured party" (Article 63(i)). The African charter (Article 21(2)) guarantees the "right to an adequate compensation." The Convention on the Elimination of All Forms of Racial Discrimination appeals in Article 6 to the right to seek "just and adequate reparations or satisfaction for any damage suffered." The International Labor Organization's Convention on Indigenous Peoples refers to "fair compensation for damages" (Article 16(4)) and to full compensation "for any loss or injury" (Article 16(5)). The Convention on the Rights of the Child in Article 39 requires all nations to take all appropriate measures to "promote physical and psychological recovery."

In 1985 the U.N. General Assembly spelled out the nature of indemnification in the Declaration of Basic Principles of Justice for Victims of Crime and Abuses of Power. This declaration insists that "victims are entitled to prompt redress for the harm that they have suffered" and that offenders should "pay fair restitution to victims, their families and dependents." If such reimbursement is not available from the offender, "states should endeavor to provide financial compensation."

The four Geneva conventions of 1949 sternly provide that no contracting party shall be allowed to absolve itself from any liability incurred by itself for grave breaches, including willfully causing great suffering or serious injury.

The Geneva treaties and other documents respecting international human rights make it clear that governments have a duty to offer compensation if private persons are allowed to engage in conduct which violates internationally recognized human rights.

International juridical bodies such as the U.N. Commission on Human Rights and the Inter-American Court of Human Rights have developed a substantial body of case law in which they have defined the obligations which offending states are required to carry out. The European Court of Human Rights has awarded "just compensation" (Article 50 of the convention) in well over 100 cases. The Inter-American Court has ruled in fewer cases but the principle of the requirement of indemnification is becoming more clearly defined with each case. Punitive damages have not usually been awarded.

Reparations are, of course, not an entirely new issue. In the aftermath of World War II the new government of Germany was required to pay substantial reparations to the survivors of the Holocaust in Israel or elsewhere. In 1965, the German Federal Compensation Law became the most complete and systematic example of compensation given by any nation to the victims of its predecessor government. The overall assessment of this law is positive, but it did not reach all the victims of Nazi violence because they left Germany or were stateless or could not document their injuries.

One example of how the United States observed its duty under international law to compensate the victims of its own wrongdoing was the $20,000 indemnification it awarded to every surviving person of Japanese ancestry who was confined in camps during World War II. I served on a presidential commission that heard days of testimony from survivors and experts on the internment of up to three years of some 120,000 Japanese, half of them citizens. This action was ordered by President Roosevelt, paid for by Congress, and validated by a divided decision of the U.S. Supreme Court. After four years and a report of a presidential commission on which the late Justice Arthur Goldberg served, Congress and the president concurred in the judgment of this commission that the detention of the Japanese was not necessary and was a violation of the Constitution. The figure of $20,000 was arrived at as a result of estimates and accommodation. The amount of indemnification awarded some 75,000 survivors totaled around $1.2 billion.

In view of all these precedents why is it that the basic requirement of reparation is not receiving the attention and enforcement it deserves? This is without doubt one of the most difficult questions that confronts the international human rights movement. All around the world the victims are clearly identifiable, yet there is no precise pattern of compensation or damages.

The prospect, moreover, for adequate and systematic compensation is bleak. For example, aside from the possibility of the international criminal court entering into this field, there is little hope that malefactors in Cambodia who murdered countless thousands will be apprehended or punished. Aside from the special international tribunals set up for the former Yugoslavia and Rwanda, will the victims of Stalin's madness or China's cultural revolution ever receive a hearing or indemnification? Can the countless innocent victims of dictators and despots expect that somehow, sometime the advocates and apostles of international human rights will reward them with some compensation, however inadequate?

The questions seem overwhelming and the answers romantically unrealistic. But certain concepts and developments in international law may bring about a system of reparations for all victims analogous to the legal mechanism that made reparations to the victims of Nazi brutality.

One sign of such a development is occurring in South Africa where the Commission on Peace and Reconciliation is through its philosophy and conclusions changing the way the world thinks and acts about a government that had for a long period of time denied the basics of equality, fairness, and decency. It must be pointed out, however, that South Africa is unique. Its concept of apartheid was indefensible and had been condemned by the United Nations each year since 1945. The International Court of Justice (or the World Court) ruled that apartheid clearly violated international law. Most nations, including eventually the United States, imposed economic sanctions on South Africa. Consequently when the government in Pretoria conceded that apartheid was wrong and allowed an election the world was convinced that the all-white government of South Africa had committed many offenses which were indefensible and that some type of compensation was due.

Even the formation of the Commission on Peace and Reconciliation was creative and constructive. Headed by Archbishop Desmond Tutu, it tried to formulate a solution through which the new international human rights law could become operational. The overall philosophy of international human rights adopted by the commission has intrigued the world and has engaged the international human rights community in discussions without end. Should a government that succeeds a corrupt predecessor allow the worst malefactors in that government to escape punishment if they "confess" in public? Would this really bring about reconciliation? The establishment of the Commission on Truth and Reconciliation on July 19,

1995, has changed the entire course of thinking and action by persons involved in the international human rights movement.

Once again, the South African government is different from almost any other in the world. The 10 percent of white people who had controlled the country for generations are charged with the most serious misconduct. In a sense, all of them are guilty because they were complicit in perpetuating a system which for generations denied basic human rights to some 30 million persons of African ancestry.

The members of the African National Committee (ANC) were also guilty because for decades they participated in a series of lawless attacks on white leaders and followers. If all white people are charged with human rights violations, should the same charges be leveled at the ANC?

Is it possible or just sensible to try to punish most of the 4 million white people in South Africa? In the summer of 1995 I lectured and consulted for many weeks in South Africa. The nation — at least the blacks — were jubilant at their recent liberation. The idea of significant reconciliation was discussed everywhere. It is obviously a profoundly Christian idea, but in South Africa it was also a concept filled with utilitarian and pragmatic considerations. The country needed its white bankers and entrepreneurs; South Africa needs to be perceived as a stable country if new businesses are to be attracted. A threat to try to penalize almost every white South African would have prompted a mass migration. It could also have inhibited the nonwhite population so that a permanent anti-white class warfare would have been initiated.

For all these reasons, South Africa agreed to the creation of the Commission on Truth and Reconciliation in the 1990s. Countless assessments have been made through the years of that process. The transcripts of the hearings and conclusions of the commission are constructive. Indeed, they are awesome, challenging, and, yes, bewildering. Was this the way to try to bring some type of resolution and reconciliation to a tormented country? Frederik de Klerk, the former president and co-winner of the Nobel Peace Prize with Nelson Mandela, declined to apologize meaningfully for apartheid. He would not admit that the system he and his father had implemented was evil. It was, he conceded, a mistake because it did not work but apartheid was, he insisted, meant to benefit the interests of all South Africans.

One of the most thoughtful books on South Africa is *Between Vengeance and Forgiveness* (Beacon Press, 1998), by Martha Minow of Harvard Law School. It explores the unfathomable concept of how a society comes together after decades of deep hostility between racial groups. Many will conclude that for South Africa there was no other solution except that of allowing all sides to confess their misdeeds and thereby acquire some type of reconciliation. But others will side with the survivors of Steve Biko, the black activist who was tortured and killed by government forces. His family filed a lawsuit challenging the very existence of the Commission on Truth and Reconciliation. They claimed that the amnesty provision violated the rights of survivors to seek redress for the murders of their loved ones. The new constitutional court of South Africa rejected the claim. The justices felt that the Geneva conventions allow the government to grant amnesty in return for the truth.

The trading of a truthful confession for amnesty is, of course, the difference in the South African process. No blanket forgiveness is granted to torturers or pirates. They are required to confess their sins in public in order to receive public forgiveness.

This process in South Africa is further complicated by the use of the idea of "healing." This is a concept that is very unfamiliar in the legal language underpinning prosecution. Many psychologists and jurists feel that after a society has been polarized, there is a need for the public and the courts to promote a form of reconciliation which can be "healing." Even if "healing" is occurring in South Africa, this can hardly be satisfactory to the family of Steve Biko; they know the names of those who helped kill their son, but these individuals will go free if they confess at a hearing of the Truth and Reconciliation Commission.

What *is* the path between vengeance and forgiveness? Many years must pass before a verdict on the history of South Africa is determined. I have talked with black students in South Africa. They want to move ahead in the careers now open to them. But they are also quick to express deep anger and resentment at the former government which did such awful things to their parents and grandparents. That valid resentment may emerge in unpredictable ways. These young people — now able to go to college, to vote, and to think about participating in public affairs — dare not suggest that their "masters" have excluded them from reaping the fabulous profits enjoyed by the white majority from the gold and diamond industries. In fact, these young blacks feel strongly that they and their predecessors have been deprived of the basic education and skills required simply to obtain a decent job. The term "reconciliation" sounds peaceful and reasonable, but how do you reconcile a history in which you and everyone you know have been cheated, defeated, and dehumanized? What do you do to obtain the human rights stolen from you?

South Africa has employed a combination of techniques available in international law to balance the desire for a peaceful resolution to an awful problem. It has used the power to grant amnesty in exchange for the revelation of truth—an experiment with noble aspirations and, to date, many successes. But will it be a model applicable to future situations where a country tries to expose the truth of what dictators have done without bringing about a violent uprising or a form of anarchy where the rule of law is set aside in the name of effecting redress?

Should the idea of massive reparations—demanded of Germany, for example—be repudiated in South Africa? A nation like Germany, devastated in 1945, was able to make reparations without hindering its remarkable economic recovery. Suppose that the world community requires individuals who have benefited from the labors of those held captive by apartheid to give the downtrodden indemnification and a share of the enormous riches they helped to create?

Is it too late to initiate such a system of reparations? A comparable proposed program of giving restitution to every African American whose ancestors were slaves has never been contemplated, much less accepted, by any significant number of African American scholars or activists. Ideas along this line were proposed in the reconstruction period after the Civil War, but the majority of the white population, North and South, did not believe the program worthy of consideration.

It is clear that all the mandates to give restitution to victims outlined at the beginning of this chapter have seldom been implemented. But the plan to render justice for past wrongdoing is an essential part of the international human rights movement. When human rights have been violated, a debt is created on the part of a nation. That country should not be allowed to cancel its debt by offering amnesty—even if the amnesty requires some truth-telling.

Some consensus about the connection between the denial of human rights and the need for reconciliation is emerging. It is not yet clear on the international scene. But it is increasingly apparent that international law now requires prosecution of especially atrocious crimes. In a comprehensive article on this and related points, Professor Diane F. Orentlichter of American University Law School brought forth a persuasive argument for this new reality in international law. Writing in the *Yale Law Review* in 1991, Orentlichter argued that a successful government cannot act in accordance with international law and grant wholesale immunity to atrocious crimes committed by a previous government. This is a departure from the traditional approach of international human rights law.

How does amnesty fit into this new reality? An amnesty for the former rulers of a country could arguably violate the spirit if not the letter of recent international human rights law. It could bring about a culture of impunity which would encourage other political leaders to engage in violations of international human rights.

Latin American countries with newly elected democracies have granted amnesties but have been rebuked by the Inter-American Commission on Human Rights. For example, after six Jesuits and their housekeeper and her minor daughter were murdered on November 16, 1989, by agents of the state, the government granted amnesty to the murderers and to many others. Many felt that this was a sensible way to bring to a close the grim events outlined by a U.N. commission set up in El Salvador. There were those who were opposed to granting any amnesty until the real authorities behind the slaughter of the Jesuits were discovered. In the extensive literature on this event, the term "intellectual authors of the killings" seemed to take on a meaning of its own. It was obviously the government at its highest levels that had ordered the killings, which had been carried out by lower-level soldiers. The parties opposed to the attempts to cover up the case against the intellectual authors of the killings successfully persuaded the commission to rule that El Salvador had no right to grant amnesty because this is in contravention to the Inter-American Convention on Human Rights, which allows everyone to obtain a remedy for the violation of their rights.

Similar rulings have raised basic doubts about the amnesties granted by the legislatures in Argentina, Chile, and elsewhere. Some resolution of this complicated clash between national and international law may eventually be discovered in the resolution of the legal proceedings in Spain and England over General Augusto Pinochet. The families of victims who "disappeared" during the regime of Pinochet in Chile want information about their loved ones. The Chilean Supreme Court has raised basic questions about the amnesty laws, which have largely protected officers from prosecution. But the families of the 3,000 missing persons are not likely to be silenced.

The cries of the loved ones of the victims of human rights abuses can be heard everywhere. The families of the 1 million Cambodians killed in the Maoist regime want trials. They decry a culture which knows that dastardly crimes have been committed but watches the perpetrators go unpunished because of rampant bribery and political influence. Pol Pot, the head of the homicidal Cambodian regime, died in April 1998. It has been over twenty years since the Khmer Rouge was toppled from power in Cambodia. Discussions between officers in Phnom Penh and the United Nations about the possibility of a trial have ended in roadblocks. Democratic administrations who have succeeded regimes in which international human rights were abused are likely to theorize that if Cambodia can continue to postpone or delay trials, other governments will follow suit.

In the 1980s and 1990s, dozens of countries moved from dictatorships to democracies. The new leaders, with the possible exception of those in South Africa, fully intended to ignore their predecessors and move on to create open democracies that observed human rights. But there is now a strong international demand to hold violators of human rights to a new and ever stricter standard of accountability. The proponents of a higher standard are not an organized phalanx of militants with national or international offices. They are, among others, the citizens who lost their children in Buenos Aires, the victims of Pinochet in Chile, and the lawyers who are suing to make the murderers of the Jesuits in El Salvador accountable for their crimes.

Voices everywhere in the world echo the age-old truth that there should be no right without a remedy. These voices were present in the 1993 United Nations World Conference on Human Rights in Vienna. The final statement of the Vienna declaration recommended that "states should abrogate legislation leading to impunity for those responsible for grave violations of human rights such as torture" (II, 60).

But the process of inducing nations to try their own subjects — some of whom are their former rulers — has met with resistance. It is this resistance that led the international community to create new transnational commissions and tribunals to protect human rights. Now those international tribunals have to cope with the practice of national leaders granting amnesty to political leaders who have disgraced their nations by engaging in "ethnic cleansing" or other crimes against humanity. Even if the International Criminal Commission continues to develop and become functional, individual nations will still be authorized and even encouraged to establish courts for the prosecution of their own alleged violations of international human rights.

The tide against amnesty for political figures is strong. The Chilean Supreme Court concluded that the statute of limitations should not apply to kidnappings, because concealment of these crimes continues, making them subject to indictment and prosecution. Journalists estimated that some 3,000 people had disappeared during the Pinochet regime. The subsequent regime of President Patrice Alwyn (1991 to 1994) was able to demonstrate adequate proof that at least 1,102 persons were missing. In 1991, the Inter-American Commission on Human Rights ruled that amnesty laws are not compatible with the 1969 American Convention on Human Rights. In 1996, nongovernmental organizations fought for the exclusion of all crimes against humanity from an amnesty law in Guatemala.

Amnesties or multiple pardons are sometimes the best solution for a country that finds itself divided by factions seeking revenge or forgiveness. Virtually every national constitution has some provision allowing the chief executive to pardon criminals. Should some new international mechanism be put in place by which an international entity can set aside a decree of amnesty?

Applied to the United States, this proposal produces astonishing implications. Imagine the appropriate international body decreeing that the amnesty or pardon of former President Nixon by President Ford must be set aside. The theory would be that the pardon was a violation of the rights of those citizens who should know more about Watergate and the persons who victimized them. If this sounds impossible, then the setting aside of the amnesty decree for the murders of the six Jesuits in El Salvador sounds just as implausible to those people in El Salvador who want to "bury" everything concerning the wars in the 1990s. They do not want to remember that this war resulted in the deaths of 75,000 people, and that it produced vast numbers of refugees in and out of the country.

The intense grip which nations and patriots have on their own people is a result of centuries of political indoctrination and sincere cultural attachment. Those sentiments have been radically altered in the past fifty years — by the idea of international human rights and scores of other forces. The moves toward democratic elections and the observance of the rule of law have transformed the way citizens view their government. But intense and bitter rivalries within nations continue and even have grown more dangerous. Internationalization of the world and the globalization of human rights have doubtlessly had an irreversible impact on the options for national action.

International pressure for relief and reparation from unjust regimes has just begun. It is one of the most recent impulses in the movement for international human rights. Its impact is not yet very visible, but the widespread interest in the results of the South African Commission on Peace and Reconciliation will have an enormous influence — especially on the fifty nations of Africa.

Accountability is a priority issue in South Africa and in every country that has ousted or is in the process of getting rid of a dictator. If rulers knew that they would be held accountable for any substantial violation of international human rights law, they would, theoretically, be more law-abiding. Their aides would also be more restrained because they would know that they, too, would be held accountable.

How can accountability be inculcated in public officials? The newly established series of international guidelines could be efficacious, but their weak enforcement is the problem. Even if their enforcement is not as effective as would be desired, the fact is that some rulers — Marcos, Pol Pot, Idi Amin, Pinochet, for example — have abused their powers by not heeding the new standards of international human rights.

Curtailing the power of leaders like these individuals while they are still in power is the quintessential purpose of the United Nations. This organization was established so that a Hitler could never rise to power again. But if this goal is to be achieved, the egregious abuses of human rights must be made known and stopped. The elaborate U.N. monitoring missions and the increasing revelations of nations defying human rights are testimony to the twin, co-equal purposes of the United Nations: to stop war and enforce human rights.

Defining and guaranteeing the rights of the victims of leaders who have defied the human rights mission of the United Nations is one of the most important and solemn tasks of that body. The exaltation of human rights emerged in dramatic ways in the 1990s. Its transformation into a global moral force is, ideally, about to happen.

CONTEMPORARY

DEVELOPMENTS IN

HUMAN RIGHTS

The development of the law related to internationally recognized human rights has been uneven, sporadic, and unpredictable. Developments seem to be dependent on political movements, unexpected leadership in unusual places, or outbursts of anger and indefensible injustices.

THE WORLD AFTER PINOCHET

One such development occurred in the detention in England of General Augusto Pinochet, the dictator-president of Chile for eighteen years, whose regime began with his coup in 1973. Pinochet was charged by a prosecutor in Spain with violations of international law for government-sponsored torture in Chile. Violence led to the death of some 3,000 persons, at least 1,000 of whom disappeared without a trace.

The saga of Pinochet is particularly moving to me because in the mid-1980s I was a member of a human rights mission that traveled to Chile under the auspices of the International League for Human Rights. Chile ratified the Torture Convention and thus made a commitment to cease this unspeakable practice. Its commitment to end torture was one of the reasons Pinochet was indicted in Spain and detained in England. He and his nation had engaged in a practice which is now a crime against world law and is thus punishable in any nation where the offender is apprehended. Torture is thus a crime like piracy, which is now punishable within any nation where the pirate or slave trader is apprehended.

Whatever the ultimate outcome of the Pinochet case, it has altered world law. It has made clear that those who torture or engage in any other offenses forbidden by world law can be tried in any nation to which they travel. Will leaders who allowed atrocities in Cambodia or war crimes in Vietnam be fearful of leaving the United States?

International law is highly developed concerning nations' immunity from alleged crimes and diplomatic protection for national leaders. These issues had been unaddressed for decades, in a world where national sovereignty was sacrosanct and where nations were not accountable in any international forum for their violations of human rights. But that era is in the process of fading away. Nations and their leaders can be charged by other countries with violations of those human rights guaranteed by international law.

The ancient concept of humanitarian intervention by one nation on another in order to protect human rights needs to be rethought. The 1945 Charter of the United Nations theoretically terminated the permission to nations to engage in humanitarian intervention in order to stop abuse of human rights. The U.N. charter made it clear that no nation could make war on another country without approval by the U.N. Security Council. That arrangement has not always functioned as it was intended. Does that mean that a nation may intervene in another country to stop a massive violation of human rights? The answer is not clear, but as the preciousness of human rights is acknowledged more widely, nations or groups of nations will want to intervene in order to protect human rights.

The desire to protect international human rights was one of the many reasons NATO was extended and enlarged — even though its target, the Soviet bloc, had collapsed. But the world is still groping to discover some regional or global mechanism through which to protest the violation of those human rights acknowledged by every country and by the international order.

If the inviolability granted human rights in the U.N. charter, the Universal Declaration of Human Rights, and all the covenants were respected would there be any need for military intervention? It is not easy to predict whether legal and juridical measures will preclude the need for military force. But if there is a need for armed force, it should be centralized and controlled by the United Nations. That is the purpose of the peacekeeping forces of the United Nations — whose number has greatly increased since the end of the Cold War. America's lack of participation in these efforts has not helped the establishment of those useful ways to reestablish peace and restore human rights.

The method by which Pinochet was detained is by no means the ideal way of apprehending tyrants. A permanent investigatory body within the international criminal court — a sort of world attorney general — would be more effective, efficient, and predictable. But regardless of the final outcome of the Pinochet affair, international law has proved that it can respond positively to an unanticipated earthquake.

THE WORLD'S REFUGEES

The vast world of refugees has also developed in truly spectacular ways. The establishment of the U.N. High Commissioner on Refugees (UNHCR) in the first days of the United Nations is an accomplishment for which neither the United Nations nor the world community has received thanks. The problems of the 18 million refugees and the millions of internally displaced persons confound the mind and the heart. To be sure, there have always been refugees. But now, all nations have agreed that they will not send back a refugee who has a "well-founded fear of persecution."

In 1980, the House Judiciary Committee, of which I was a member, accepted world law on refugees and pledged the United States to follow international law and grant asylum to those who feared persecution in their country of origin. Neither the U.S. Congress nor the White House has consistently followed the implications of that pledge. But America by almost any standard must be categorized as generous in the number of immigrants and refugees it has welcomed over the past generation. In recent years the United States has probably granted residence and eventually citizenship to more persons than the rest of the world combined.

But a flood of refugees in unprecedented numbers is predictable in the United States. The absence of a functioning government in Somalia has prompted thousands of its citizens to go anyplace where they will be admitted. Other nations in Africa are experiencing the same exodus. Is it possible that countless others will move out of their countries in order to feed their children? Millions may leave their native countries—like the Vietnamese boat people, the Cubans who have fled to Miami, or Mexicans who have crossed the Rio Grande. Under international law they have a right to leave their country if they have a "well-founded fear of persecution." Should they have an equivalent right to migrate if their homeland cannot or will not give them food, medicine, and education for their children? Political rights are not superior to economic rights. All human rights are equal and indivisible.

No one at the international level—certainly not those in charge of resettling refugees—wants to consider the legal status of economic refugees. But everyone must admit that millions are being deprived of their basic economic rights. These rights are guaranteed them by world law. At the same time there is a solid consensus around the world that arrangements should be created so that most people can remain in their country of origin. Any move to another country with a different language and culture is almost always traumatic. But the experts in resettling refugees recognize more and more that millions of people, after seeing a world of freedom and plenty on television and through an ever increasing number of other media sources, will ask importunately for a better life. They will also increasingly be aware that international law guarantees them and their families the basic rights to decent housing, food, education, and medicine.

As one contemplates the predictable massive migration of hungry people, it is obvious that it behooves the prosperous nations to plan for an onslaught. The United States experienced this in a small way when thousands fled Haiti in boats bound for Florida after a military coup that deposed the democratically elected president Aristide. The U.S. government, through the Coast Guard, intercepted thousands of these refugees in international waters and returned them to Haiti. The Supreme Court held by a vote of 8–1 that international law does not impose any obligation on the United States to allow these refugees to reach the coast of Florida. The decision was legally and technically correct, but the attempted migration highlighted the pent-up anger and frustration of peoples around the world who are desperate to claim the political and economic rights promised them by their own countries and by the family of nations.

For fifty-five years the UNHCR has been virtually a model agency in the achievement of an almost impossible task. It has cared for the downtrodden and the exiles of the earth. It has carried out and enlarged international law. The heroic efforts of the commission and its noble vision of the world community struck me some time ago when I visited refugee camps in Vietnam and southeastern Asia. I cannot help but wonder whether similar camps will be necessary on a vast scale if hundreds of families leave their own countries in a desperate search for food.

The world finally agreed in 1966 to separate the U.N. political and economic covenants; each entered into force in 1976. They confer political and economic rights on the vast majority of the human race. In the near future the men, women, and children of the world will be demanding that the promises made to them be fulfilled.

THE MORAL DUTY TO PROVIDE
RESTITUTION FOR INJURY

The legal obligation to offer restitution for injury is as old as the Code of Hammurabi, the first formal set of laws in history. But this duty has been applied to nations only recently. Germany, for example, was required to offer reparations to the survivors of the 6 million people killed by the Nazis.

There are some indications that governments are recognizing or being forced to recognize that they owe indemnification to those whose rights they have violated. Various forms of such restitution are being considered in South Africa, Argentina, Chile, El Salvador, and several other countries.

Massive reparations to African Americans in the United States have occasionally been proposed. One of the most recent proposals is made in a book by Randall Robinson, an African American attorney, in his book *The Debt—What America Owes to Blacks* (Dutton/Plume, 1999). But indifference or even resistance to the idea of reparation to African Americans is predictable. The concept of affirmative action is, of course, a form of reparation because it is intended to compensate blacks for the discrimination they have suffered since the first African slaves were brought to Virginia in the early 1600s.

Affirmative action is permitted and indeed required in international law in the Convention on the Elimination of Racial Discrimination and the Convention on the Elimination of Discrimination Against Women. The call for restitution, reparation, or indemnification is implicit in the law of all countries. The United States accepted that concept when it awarded $20,000 to each person of Japanese ancestry who was interned during World War II. A commission in Oklahoma has urged reparations for the victims of a race riot in Tulsa in the 1920s. Two hundred thousand women from Korea were taken by the Japanese before and during World War II to serve Japanese soldiers all over the Pacific. Some of these victims and their survivors are making demands for reparations from the government of Japan.

American soldiers were harmed by exposure to Agent Orange in Vietnam. They successfully sued the U.S. government and the manufacturer of the defoliant for serious medical conditions caused by the chemical. Should the U.S. government similarly give restitution to the Vietnamese who were also hurt by that chemical?

If the United States admits some day that its war in Vietnam was not authorized by the United Nations or by international law, should the United States indemnify the survivors of the 2 million Vietnamese killed in that war by the American military?

The basic moral law of every society asserts that a government which wrongly injures its own citizens must make them whole insofar as this is possible. The new world order brought about by the United Nations reaffirms that obligation, although the ways to fulfill it need clarification.

Could the cry for restitution be a part of the emerging consensus that treaties and covenants are contracts between nations and that they should be enforced just as contracts between individuals can be executed by court order?

Individuals often come to a realization that they have harmed another person. Sometimes that realization comes years after the injury was inflicted. In increasing numbers, corporations are being required to make amends for products sold that were later found to be harmful. A rising number of nongovernmental organizations are now calling upon international law to remind nations of the harm that they have inflicted. The next step will be a widespread consensus that the offending governments are expected and required under the international law of human rights to make reparations to those who have been hurt.

There is strong resistance to the broad-based conviction that governments should pay money to those who have been hurt. Remnants of the old theory that the king can do no harm remain embedded in the laws of the world. There is also the myth that malingerers and troublemakers will make unfounded and exorbitant demands on the government.

But entrenched in the moral consensus everywhere is the deepening conviction that the governments should be honest with their own people, admit their mistakes, apologize to their victims, and make financial amends. Most governments, however, still try to evade and avoid any obligation to give reparation. But the emerging law of human rights will ever more insistently provide that every right must have a remedy. That powerful moral command will increasingly put moral and legal pressure on governments to ask for forgiveness for their sins and to offer relief to their victims.

Other aspirations to enforce human rights will be burgeoning—often in unpredictable ways and in unexpected places. These efforts may not necessarily be tied to any global legal initiative. Demands for justice and equality heard around the world derive from and depend on the ever more insistent cries for human rights made by the world's nongovernmental organizations and activists.

But even the most ardent supporters of human rights have to wonder whether the world would be suddenly free of tyranny if the mandates and aspirations of the 1993 Vienna Declaration on Human Rights were followed. History has been changed—even dominated—by tyrants and murderers like Stalin, Hitler, and Mao. Can laws protecting equality and demanding human rights prevent dictators from defying the decrees of world law?

For the past fifty-five years the world has for the first time proclaimed its faith in a rule of law grounded in a respect for the basic political and economic rights asserted in the Charter of the United Nations and in all its derivative covenants on human rights.

This giant experiment is in a sense another version of what the framers of the U.S. Constitution sought to do. Even the Bill of Rights, added in

1791, could not bring justice to Americans of African ancestry until 1954, when the Supreme Court decided *Brown v. Board of Education*. This disappointing record has occurred despite the fact that the U.S. Constitution — unlike the United Nations — had provided for judicial review to correct the failings of the legislative and executive branches of government.

The Code of Hammurabi, 2,500 years before Christ, declared that the purpose of law is to protect the powerless from the powerful. That is still one of the fundamental purposes of law — including the recently formulated international law.

20

THE FUTURE OF
INTERNATIONAL
HUMAN RIGHTS

Respect for others is one of the oldest moral ideas in civilization. The second commandment demands that everyone "love" their neighbor like themselves. Indeed, the love we are required to give to others must be equivalent to the love we have for ourselves and for God — as required in the First Commandment.

Injury to any child of God is wrong — indeed, it is a sacrilege.

Put in secular terms, this theory means that every individual possesses a dignity and is endowed with human rights that cannot be violated. Theoretically those who believe in a creator should be the strongest defenders of human rights. But both believers and nonbelievers are content to prescind from religious convictions when they talk about human rights. Religion has too often been used to transgress the human rights of those who are deemed to be heretics or dissidents. Religious people have, to be sure, sometimes been in the vanguard of those battling for human rights. But it is easy to think of the occasions in history when religious zealots or fanatics have trampled upon human rights in the name of a divine good.

Therefore, despite the historical similarity between the Second Commandment and the United Nations covenants on human rights, there is a worldwide consensus that the struggle for such rights is based on a nontheistic approach. Even raising this question places the focus on the problematic status of certain Muslim nations where the primacy of the Shari'ah, the basic Muslim code of law, is asserted in their adherence to the covenants on human rights. Petitioners on human rights are acutely aware of the problems in some of the nations where Muslims live. The complexity of the social and political scene in those countries is immense. In predominantly Muslim nations once colonized by European powers there resides a deep and intense feeling that the western colonial powers have destroyed some precious Islamic values and that these nations, now liberated from the west, should restore these values. Despite this deep but not unanimous feeling, Islamic countries have generally ratified the United Nations covenants on human rights. Some nations have, to be sure, insisted that the law of Shari'ah should take precedence over some of the values incorporated in the International Bill of Rights. But Islamic countries have sometimes supported the freedom of the press, the free exercise of religion, and the ever more strict, key demands of the covenants on economic and political rights. A crucial question remains for many observers: Will the Islamic countries continue to be faithful to their pledge to uphold the human rights standard in the United Nations documents?

The largest question about the future of human rights centers, of course, on China. Will this nation with 1.2 billion people—one-fifth of the global village—embrace freedom of the press, religious liberty, and the right to marry and have children without governmental interference? The horrors of China's cultural revolution still arouse the most profound anxieties about the fundamental stability of China and its adherence to the standards to which China agreed in its acceptance of the Vienna Declaration on Human Rights in 1993. It is reassuring to remember that China was one of the founders of the United Nations, is a permanent member of the U.N. Security Council, and has ratified some of the human rights covenants. But the impenetrability of China arouses the deepest anxiety among those who hope that the priority of human rights can constitute a new basis for international morality.

The fragmentation of Africa also raises the severest doubts among those who hope that the International Bill of Rights can unify the world in guaranteeing a uniform level of dignity and respect for all human beings. The horrors of Rwanda, the chaos of Zaire, and the political fragility of Nigeria are not encouraging signs that Africa is approaching an acceptable level of compliance with the standards set by the world's lawmakers over the past fifty years.

It seems self-evident that the future of human rights in the world depends upon what transpires in China and Africa. It is also clear that the United States more than any other country will shape the future of the amazing developments in international human rights that have occurred since the end of World War II. The enlightened leadership of the United States that was so dramatically effective in the late 1940s faded into twilight in the 1950s and has been sporadic since that time. The leadership of President Carter in human rights faltered during the Reagan and Bush years. It was revived to some extent during the Clinton administration, although the demise of the U.S.S.R. altered the entire history and future of international human rights.

It can be argued that the Clinton administration did not take advantage of the spectacular opportunity offered by the collapse of the Soviet bloc. Clearly, a whole new foreign policy was called for with the end of the Cold War. The foreign policy of the United States was no longer dictated by the necessity to be friendly toward less-than-democratic nations simply because they were the enemies of our enemy, the Soviet Union. But the United States in many instances did not move toward an entirely new approach. It did, however, make significant sacrifices to return Haiti to a democratic government, collaborate with others to maintain democracy in Kosovo, and use its good offices to bring democracy to Northern Ireland.

Will history look back at the United States and conclude that it squandered many opportunities in the 1990s when unprecedented occasions to advance human rights presented themselves in the nations of eastern Europe and in the other fifteen nations that separated from the former U.S.S.R.?

The United States remained firm in its policy of being prepared for war — a war that almost always resembled a conflict with the threat of nuclear weapons. Similarly, it continued to sell arms and military equipment to almost any nation — absorbing the world trade in arms previously conducted by the Soviet Union.

The United States was active in bringing together 170 nations for the 1993 World Conference on Human Rights in Vienna. It was clear then and is even clearer now that the United States has the moral and political clout to transform the nations of the earth into a world where international human rights is the coin of the realm and the starting point and centerpiece of all discussions about the future of international peace.

Still, a streak of isolationism runs deep through the United States. Surrounded by two oceans, it has never been invaded. The philosophy that prompted the U.S. Senate to refuse membership in the League of Nations is still alive. It reemerges when Congress refuses to pay its dues to the United Nations and when it fails to become a partner in the International Criminal Commission.

It is difficult to predict how enthusiastic the United States will be toward the monitoring and enforcement of international human rights. The resistance Americans routinely demonstrate to supporting world standards on the environment is echoed in its resistance to the imposition of world standards in areas such as the rights of women and the status of refugees.

At the same time, lying deep within the American soul is the desire to provide leadership and moral ideals. The United States has done that, at least in limited ways, in the field of nuclear arms control. Is there some outside event or series of events which could galvanize America's leaders to be as bold in the arena of international human rights as it was in the late 1940s?

One possible response to that question is reflected in the attitudes of the several nongovernmental organizations devoted to international human rights. The moral power of groups like Amnesty International, Human Rights Watch, and the Lawyers Committee for Human Rights is considerable. Fully engaged in the mobilization of shame, they are relentless, persuasive, and pervasive. Could they, in alliance with a broad base of NGOs, change America's policy so that the United States would become an ardent friend of international human rights around the globe? This is not impossible. Leaders and supporters of human rights were among the abolitionists who finally obtained the Emancipation Proclamation, the suffragettes who in 1920 obtained the vote for women, and those who caused the U.S. Congress to de-fund the war in Vietnam.

The level of anger of the abolitionists, the suffragettes, and the anti-war militants was high — extremely high. Could the indignation of international human rights activists rise to the level of a compelling force in American politics? It could. Yet, the worldwide violation of international human rights is not as dramatic or compelling as are daily affronts to justice and equality on American soil. But amazing things can happen when even a small group of activists come together to protest injustice. The potential is even greater when international law clearly bans the conduct in question.

The human race has been struggling for centuries to stop injustice and to offer reparations to its victims. There is no one pattern or force that prompts nations to be just. Sometimes it is the voice of the victims that accomplishes such a feat, but more often it is the conscience and moral outrage of nonvictims. Traditionally, they more than any others have championed the rights of those who have been victimized.

Solon, the ancient Athenian jurist, summed up this truth in words that have a striking relevance: "Justice will not come until those who are not hurt feel just as indignant as those who are."

APPENDIX:

VIENNA DECLARATION AND PROGRAMME OF
ACTION ADOPTED AT THE WORLD CONFERENCE
ON HUMAN RIGHTS, 25 JUNE 1993

The World Conference on Human Rights,
Considering that the promotion and protection of human rights is a
matter of priority for the international community, and that the Conference affords a unique opportunity to carry out a comprehensive analysis of the international human rights system and of the machinery for the
protection of human rights, in order to enhance and thus promote a fuller
observance of those rights, in a just and balanced manner,

Recognizing and affirming that all human rights derive from the dignity
and worth inherent in the human person, and that the human person is
the central subject of human rights and fundamental freedoms, and consequently should be the principal beneficiary and should participate actively in the realization of these rights and freedoms,

Reaffirming their commitment to the purposes and principles contained in the Charter of the United Nations and the Universal Declaration of Human Rights,

Reaffirming the commitment contained in Article 56 of the Charter of
the United Nations to take joint and separate action, placing proper
emphasis on developing effective international cooperation for the realization of the purposes set out in Article 55, including universal respect
for, and observance of, human rights and fundamental freedoms for all,

Emphasizing the responsibilities of all States, in conformity with the
Charter of the United Nations, to develop and encourage respect for

human rights and fundamental freedoms for all, without distinction as to race, sex, language or religion,

Recalling the Preamble to the Charter of the United Nations, in particular the determination to reaffirm faith in fundamental human rights, in the dignity and worth of the human person, and in the equal rights of men and women and of nations large and small,

Recalling also the determination expressed in the Preamble of the Charter of the United Nations to save succeeding generations from the scourge of war, to establish conditions under which justice and respect for obligations arising from treaties and other sources of international law can be maintained, to promote social progress and better standards of life in larger freedom, to practice tolerance and good neighbourliness, and to employ international machinery for the promotion of the economic and social advancement of all peoples,

Emphasizing that the Universal Declaration of Human Rights, which constitutes a common standard of achievement for all peoples and all nations, is the source of inspiration and has been the basis for the United Nations in making advances in standard setting as contained in the existing international human rights instruments, in particular the International Covenant on Civil and Political Rights and the International Covenant on Economic, Social and Cultural Rights,

Considering the major changes taking place on the international scene and the aspirations of all the peoples for an international order based on the principles enshrined in the Charter of the United Nations, including promoting and encouraging respect for human rights and fundamental freedoms for all and respect for the principle of equal rights and self-determination of peoples, peace, democracy, justice, equality, rule of law, pluralism, development, better standards of living and solidarity,

Deeply concerned by various forms of discrimination and violence, to which women continue to be exposed all over the world,

Recognizing that the activities of the United Nations in the field of human rights should be rationalized and enhanced in order to strengthen the United Nations machinery in this field and to further the objectives of universal respect for observance of international human rights standards,

Having taken into account the Declarations adopted by the three regional meetings at Tunis, San José and Bangkok and the contributions made by Governments, and bearing in mind the suggestions made by intergovernmental and non-governmental organizations, as well as the studies prepared by independent experts during the preparatory process leading to the World Conference on Human Rights,

Welcoming the International Year of the World's Indigenous People 1993 as a reaffirmation of the commitment of the international community to ensure their enjoyment of all human rights and fundamental freedoms and to respect the value and diversity of their cultures and identities,

Recognizing also that the international community should devise ways and means to remove the current obstacles and meet challenges to the full realization of all human rights and to prevent the continuation of human rights violations resulting thereof throughout the world,

Invoking the spirit of our age and the realities of our time which call upon the peoples of the world and all States Members of the United Nations to rededicate themselves to the global task of promoting and protecting all human rights and fundamental freedoms so as to secure full and universal enjoyment of these rights,

Determined to take new steps forward in the commitment of the international community with a view to achieving substantial progress in human rights endeavours by an increased and sustained effort of international cooperation and solidarity,

Solemnly adopts the Vienna Declaration and Programme of Action.

I

1. The World Conference on Human Rights reaffirms the solemn commitment of all States to fulfil their obligations to promote universal respect for, and observance and protection of, all human rights and fundamental freedoms for all in accordance with the Charter of the United Nations, other instruments relating to human rights, and international law. The universal nature of these rights and freedoms is beyond question.

In this framework, enhancement of international cooperation in the field of human rights is essential for the full achievement of the purposes of the United Nations.

Human rights and fundamental freedoms are the birthright of all human beings; their protection and promotion is the first responsibility of Governments.

2. All peoples have the right of self-determination. By virtue of that right they freely determine their political status, and freely pursue their economic, social and cultural development.

Taking into account the particular situation of peoples under colonial or other forms of alien domination or foreign occupation, the World Conference on Human Rights recognizes the right of peoples to take any legitimate action, in accordance with the Charter of the United Nations, to realize their inalienable right of self-determination. The World Conference on Human Rights considers the denial of the right of self-determination as a violation of human rights and underlines the importance of the effective realization of this right.

In accordance with the Declaration on Principles of International Law concerning Friendly Relations and Cooperation Among States in accordance with the Charter of the United Nations, this shall not be construed as authorizing or encouraging any action which would dismember or impair, totally or in part, the territorial integrity or political unity of sovereign and independent States conducting themselves in compliance with the principle of equal rights and self-determination of peoples and thus possessed of a Government representing the whole people belonging to the territory without distinction of any kind.

3. Effective international measures to guarantee and monitor the implementation of human rights standards should be taken in respect of people under foreign occupation, and effective legal protection against the violation of their human rights should be provided, in accordance with human rights norms and international law, particularly the Geneva Convention relative to the Protection of Civilian Persons in Time of War, of 14 August 1949, and other applicable norms of humanitarian law.

4. The promotion and protection of all human rights and fundamental freedoms must be considered as a priority objective of the United Nations in accordance with its purposes and principles, in particular the purpose of international cooperation. In the framework of these purposes and principles, the promotion and protection of all human rights is a legitimate concern of the international community. The organs and specialized

agencies related to human rights should therefore further enhance the coordination of their activities based on the consistent and objective application of international human rights instruments.

5. All human rights are universal, indivisible and interdependent and interrelated. The international community must treat human rights globally in a fair and equal manner, on the same footing, and with the same emphasis. While the significance of national and regional particularities and various historical, cultural and religious backgrounds must be borne in mind, it is the duty of States, regardless of their political, economic and cultural systems, to promote and protect all human rights and fundamental freedoms.

6. The efforts of the United Nations system towards the universal respect for, and observance of, human rights and fundamental freedoms for all, contribute to the stability and well-being necessary for peaceful and friendly relations among nations, and to improved conditions for peace and security as well as social and economic development, in conformity with the Charter of the United Nations.

7. The processes of promoting and protecting human rights should be conducted in conformity with the purposes and principles of the Charter of the United Nations, and international law.

8. Democracy, development and respect for human rights and fundamental freedoms are interdependent and mutually reinforcing. Democracy is based on the freely expressed will of the people to determine their own political, economic, social and cultural systems and their full participation in all aspects of their lives. In the context of the above, the promotion and protection of human rights and fundamental freedoms at the national and international levels should be universal and conducted without conditions attached. The international community should support the strengthening and promoting of democracy, development and respect for human rights and fundamental freedoms in the entire world.

9. The World Conference on Human Rights reaffirms that least developed countries committed to the process of democratization and economic reforms, many of which are in Africa, should be supported by the international community in order to succeed in their transition to democracy and economic development.

10. The World Conference on Human Rights reaffirms the right to

development, as established in the Declaration on the Right to Development, as a universal and inalienable right and an integral part of fundamental human rights.

As stated in the Declaration on the Right to Development, the human person is the central subject of development.

While development facilitates the enjoyment of all human rights, the lack of development may not be invoked to justify the abridgement of internationally recognized human rights.

States should cooperate with each other in ensuring development and eliminating obstacles to development. The international community should promote an effective international cooperation for the realization of the right to development and the elimination of obstacles to development.

Lasting progress towards the implementation of the right to development requires effective development policies at the national level, as well as equitable economic relations and a favourable economic environment at the international level.

11. The right to development should be fulfilled so as to meet equitably the developmental and environmental needs of present and future generations. The World Conference on Human Rights recognizes that illicit dumping of toxic and dangerous substances and waste potentially constitutes a serious threat to the human rights to life and health of everyone.

Consequently, the World Conference on Human Rights calls on all States to adopt and vigorously implement existing conventions relating to the dumping of toxic and dangerous products and waste and to cooperate in the prevention of illicit dumping.

Everyone has the right to enjoy the benefits of scientific progress and its applications. The World Conference on Human Rights notes that certain advances, notably in the biomedical and life sciences as well as in information technology, may have potentially adverse consequences for the integrity, dignity and human rights of the individual, and calls for international cooperation to ensure that human rights and dignity are fully respected in this area of universal concern.

12. The World Conference on Human Rights calls upon the international community to make all efforts to help alleviate the external debt

burden of developing countries, in order to supplement the efforts of the Governments of such countries to attain the full realization of the economic, social and cultural rights of their people.

13. There is a need for States and international organizations, in cooperation with non-governmental organizations, to create favourable conditions at the national, regional and international levels to ensure the full and effective enjoyment of human rights. States should eliminate all violations of human rights and their causes, as well as obstacles to the enjoyment of these rights.

14. The existence of widespread extreme poverty inhibits the full and effective enjoyment of human rights; its immediate alleviation and eventual elimination must remain a high priority for the international community.

15. Respect for human rights and for fundamental freedoms without distinction of any kind is a fundamental rule of international human rights law. The speedy and comprehensive elimination of all forms of racism and racial discrimination, xenophobia and related intolerance is a priority task for the international community. Governments should take effective measures to prevent and combat them. Groups, institutions, intergovernmental and non-governmental organizations and individuals are urged to intensify their efforts in cooperating and coordinating their activities against these evils.

16. The World Conference on Human Rights welcomes the progress made in dismantling apartheid and calls upon the international community and the United Nations system to assist in this process.

The World Conference on Human Rights also deplores the continuing acts of violence aimed at undermining the quest for a peaceful dismantling of apartheid.

17. The acts, methods and practices of terrorism in all its forms and manifestations as well as linkage in some countries to drug trafficking are activities aimed at the destruction of human rights, fundamental freedoms and democracy, threatening territorial integrity, security of States and destabilizing legitimately constituted Governments. The international community should take the necessary steps to enhance cooperation to prevent and combat terrorism.

18. The human rights of women and of the girl-child are an inalienable,

integral and indivisible part of universal human rights. The full and equal participation of women in political, civil, economic, social and cultural life, at the national, regional and international levels, and the eradication of all forms of discrimination on grounds of sex are priority objectives of the international community.

Gender-based violence and all forms of sexual harassment and exploitation, including those resulting from cultural prejudice and international trafficking, are incompatible with the dignity and worth of the human person, and must be eliminated. This can be achieved by legal measures and through national action and international cooperation in such fields as economic and social development, education, safe maternity and health care, and social support.

The human rights of women should form an integral part of the United Nations human rights activities, including the promotion of all human rights instruments relating to women.

The World Conference on Human Rights urges Governments, institutions, intergovernmental and non-governmental organizations to intensify their efforts for the protection and promotion of human rights of women and the girl-child.

19. Considering the importance of the promotion and protection of the rights of persons belonging to minorities and the contribution of such promotion and protection to the political and social stability of the States in which such persons live,

The World Conference on Human Rights reaffirms the obligation of States to ensure that persons belonging to minorities may exercise fully and effectively all human rights and fundamental freedoms without any discrimination and in full equality before the law in accordance with the Declaration on the Rights of Persons Belonging to National or Ethnic, Religious and Linguistic Minorities.

The persons belonging to minorities have the right to enjoy their own culture, to profess and practise their own religion and to use their own language in private and in public, freely and without interference or any form of discrimination.

20. The World Conference on Human Rights recognizes the inherent dignity and the unique contribution of indigenous people to the development and plurality of society and strongly reaffirms the commitment of

the international community to their economic, social and cultural well-being and their enjoyment of the fruits of sustainable development. States should ensure the full and free participation of indigenous people in all aspects of society, in particular in matters of concern to them. Considering the importance of the promotion and protection of the rights of indigenous people, and the contribution of such promotion and protection to the political and social stability of the States in which such people live, States should, in accordance with international law, take concerted positive steps to ensure respect for all human rights and fundamental freedoms of indigenous people, on the basis of equality and non-discrimination, and recognize the value and diversity of their distinct identities, cultures and social organization.

21. The World Conference on Human Rights, welcoming the early ratification of the Convention on the Rights of the Child by a large number of States and noting the recognition of the human rights of children in the World Declaration on the Survival, Protection and Development of Children and Plan of Action adopted by the World Summit for Children, urges universal ratification of the Convention by 1995 and its effective implementation by States parties through the adoption of all the necessary legislative, administrative and other measures and the allocation to the maximum extent of the available resources. In all actions concerning children, non-discrimination and the best interest of the child should be primary considerations and the views of the child given due weight. National and international mechanisms and programmes should be strengthened for the defence and protection of children, in particular, the girl-child, abandoned children, street children, economically and sexually exploited children, including through child pornography, child prostitution or sale of organs, children victims of diseases, including acquired immunodeficiency syndrome, refugee and displaced children, children in detention, children in armed conflict, as well as children victims of famine and drought and other emergencies. International cooperation and solidarity should be promoted to support the implementation of the Convention and the rights of the child should be a priority in the United Nations system-wide action on human rights.

The World Conference on Human Rights also stresses that the child for the full and harmonious development of his or her personality should grow up in a family environment which accordingly merits broader protection.

22. Special attention needs to be paid to ensuring non-discrimination, and the equal enjoyment of all human rights and fundamental freedoms by disabled persons, including their active participation in all aspects of society.

23. The World Conference on Human Rights reaffirms that everyone, without distinction of any kind, is entitled to the right to seek and to enjoy in other countries asylum from persecution, as well as the right to return to one's own country. In this respect it stresses the importance of the Universal Declaration of Human Rights, the 1951 Convention relating to the Status of Refugees, its 1967 Protocol and regional instruments. It expresses its appreciation to States that continue to admit and host large numbers of refugees in their territories, and to the Office of the United Nations High Commissioner for Refugees for its dedication to its task. It also expresses its appreciation to the United Nations Relief and Works Agency for Palestine Refugees in the Near East.

The World Conference on Human Rights recognizes that gross violations of human rights, including in armed conflicts, are among the multiple and complex factors leading to displacement of people.

The World Conference on Human Rights recognizes that, in view of the complexities of the global refugee crisis and in accordance with the Charter of the United Nations, relevant international instruments and international solidarity and in the spirit of burden-sharing, a comprehensive approach by the international community is needed in coordination and cooperation with the countries concerned and relevant organizations, bearing in mind the mandate of the United Nations High Commissioner for Refugees. This should include the development of strategies to address the root causes and effects of movements of refugees and other displaced persons, the strengthening of emergency preparedness and response mechanisms, the provision of effective protection and assistance, bearing in mind the special needs of women and children, as well as the achievement of durable solutions, primarily through the preferred solution of dignified and safe voluntary repatriation, including solutions such as those adopted by the international refugee conferences. The World

Conference on Human Rights underlines the responsibilities of States, particularly as they relate to the countries of origin.

In the light of the comprehensive approach, the World Conference on Human Rights emphasizes the importance of giving special attention including through intergovernmental and humanitarian organizations and finding lasting solutions to questions related to internally displaced persons including their voluntary and safe return and rehabilitation.

In accordance with the Charter of the United Nations and the principles of humanitarian law, the World Conference on Human Rights further emphasizes the importance of and the need for humanitarian assistance to victims of all natural and man-made disasters.

24. Great importance must be given to the promotion and protection of the human rights of persons belonging to groups which have been rendered vulnerable, including migrant workers, the elimination of all forms of discrimination against them, and the strengthening and more effective implementation of existing human rights instruments. States have an obligation to create and maintain adequate measures at the national level, in particular in the fields of education, health and social support, for the promotion and protection of the rights of persons in vulnerable sectors of their populations and to ensure the participation of those among them who are interested in finding a solution to their own problems.

25. The World Conference on Human Rights affirms that extreme poverty and social exclusion constitute a violation of human dignity and that urgent steps are necessary to achieve better knowledge of extreme poverty and its causes, including those related to the problem of development, in order to promote the human rights of the poorest, and to put an end to extreme poverty and social exclusion and to promote the enjoyment of the fruits of social progress. It is essential for States to foster participation by the poorest people in the decision-making process by the community in which they live, the promotion of human rights and efforts to combat extreme poverty.

26. The World Conference on Human Rights welcomes the progress made in the codification of human rights instruments, which is a dynamic and evolving process, and urges the universal ratification of human rights

treaties. All States are encouraged to accede to these international instruments; all States are encouraged to avoid, as far as possible, the resort to reservations.

27. Every State should provide an effective framework of remedies to redress human rights grievances or violations. The administration of justice, including law enforcement and prosecutorial agencies and, especially, an independent judiciary and legal profession in full conformity with applicable standards contained in international human rights instruments, are essential to the full and non-discriminatory realization of human rights and indispensable to the processes of democracy and sustainable development. In this context, institutions concerned with the administration of justice should be properly funded, and an increased level of both technical and financial assistance should be provided by the international community. It is incumbent upon the United Nations to make use of special programmes of advisory services on a priority basis for the achievement of a strong and independent administration of justice.

28. The World Conference on Human Rights expresses its dismay at massive violations of human rights especially in the form of genocide, "ethnic cleansing" and systematic rape of women in war situations, creating mass exodus of refugees and displaced persons. While strongly condemning such abhorrent practices it reiterates the call that perpetrators of such crimes be punished and such practices immediately stopped.

29. The World Conference on Human Rights expresses grave concern about continuing human rights violations in all parts of the world in disregard of standards as contained in international human rights instruments and international humanitarian law and about the lack of sufficient and effective remedies for the victims.

The World Conference on Human Rights is deeply concerned about violations of human rights during armed conflicts, affecting the civilian population, especially women, children, the elderly and the disabled. The Conference therefore calls upon States and all parties to armed conflicts strictly to observe international humanitarian law, as set forth in the Geneva Conventions of 1949 and other rules and principles of international law, as well as minimum standards for protection of human rights, as laid down in international conventions.

The World Conference on Human Rights reaffirms the right of the victims to be assisted by humanitarian organizations, as set forth in the Geneva Conventions of 1949 and other relevant instruments of international humanitarian law, and calls for the safe and timely access for such assistance.

30. The World Conference on Human Rights also expresses its dismay and condemnation that gross and systematic violations and situations that constitute serious obstacles to the full enjoyment of all human rights continue to occur in different parts of the world. Such violations and obstacles include, as well as torture and cruel, inhuman and degrading treatment or punishment, summary and arbitrary executions, disappearances, arbitrary detentions, all forms of racism, racial discrimination and apartheid, foreign occupation and alien domination, xenophobia, poverty, hunger and other denials of economic, social and cultural rights, religious intolerance, terrorism, discrimination against women and lack of the rule of law.

31. The World Conference on Human Rights calls upon States to refrain from any unilateral measure not in accordance with international law and the Charter of the United Nations that creates obstacles to trade relations among States and impedes the full realization of the human rights set forth in the Universal Declaration of Human Rights and international human rights instruments, in particular the rights of everyone to a standard of living adequate for their health and well-being, including food and medical care, housing and the necessary social services. The World Conference on Human Rights affirms that food should not be used as a tool for political pressure.

32. The World Conference on Human Rights reaffirms the importance of ensuring the universality, objectivity and non-selectivity of the consideration of human rights issues.

33. The World Conference on Human Rights reaffirms that States are duty-bound, as stipulated in the Universal Declaration of Human Rights and the International Covenant on Economic, Social and Cultural Rights and in other international human rights instruments, to ensure that education is aimed at strengthening the respect of human rights and fundamental freedoms. The World Conference on Human Rights emphasizes the importance of incorporating the subject of human rights education programmes and calls upon States to do so. Education should promote

understanding, tolerance, peace and friendly relations between the nations and all racial or religious groups and encourage the development of United Nations activities in pursuance of these objectives. Therefore, education on human rights and the dissemination of proper information, both theoretical and practical, play an important role in the promotion and respect of human rights with regard to all individuals without distinction of any kind such as race, sex, language or religion, and this should be integrated in the education policies at the national as well as international levels. The World Conference on Human Rights notes that resource constraints and institutional inadequacies may impede the immediate realization of these objectives.

34. Increased efforts should be made to assist countries which so request to create the conditions whereby each individual can enjoy universal human rights and fundamental freedoms. Governments, the United Nations system as well as other multilateral organizations are urged to increase considerably the resources allocated to programmes aiming at the establishment and strengthening of national legislation, national institutions and related infrastructures which uphold the rule of law and democracy, electoral assistance, human rights awareness through training, teaching and education, popular participation and civil society.

The programmes of advisory services and technical cooperation under the Centre for Human Rights should be strengthened as well as made more efficient and transparent and thus become a major contribution to improving respect for human rights. States are called upon to increase their contributions to these programmes, both through promoting a larger allocation from the United Nations regular budget, and through voluntary contributions.

35. The full and effective implementation of United Nations activities to promote and protect human rights must reflect the high importance accorded to human rights by the Charter of the United Nations and the demands of the United Nations human rights activities, as mandated by Member States. To this end, United Nations human rights activities should be provided with increased resources.

36. The World Conference on Human Rights reaffirms the important and constructive role played by national institutions for the promotion and protection of human rights, in particular in their advisory capacity to

the competent authorities, their role in remedying human rights violations, in the dissemination of human rights information, and education in human rights.

The World Conference on Human Rights encourages the establishment and strengthening of national institutions, having regard to the "Principles relating to the status of national institutions" and recognizing that it is the right of each State to choose the framework which is best suited to its particular needs at the national level.

37. Regional arrangements play a fundamental role in promoting and protecting human rights. They should reinforce universal human rights standards, as contained in international human rights instruments, and their protection. The World Conference on Human Rights endorses efforts under way to strengthen these arrangements and to increase their effectiveness, while at the same time stressing the importance of cooperation with the United Nations human rights activities.

The World Conference on Human Rights reiterates the need to consider the possibility of establishing regional and subregional arrangements for the promotion and protection of human rights where they do not already exist.

38. The World Conference on Human Rights recognizes the important role of non-governmental organizations in the promotion of all human rights and in humanitarian activities at national, regional and international levels. The World Conference on Human Rights appreciates their contribution to increasing public awareness of human rights issues, to the conduct of education, training and research in this field, and to the promotion and protection of all human rights and fundamental freedoms. While recognizing that the primary responsibility for standard-setting lies with States, the conference also appreciates the contribution of non-governmental organizations to this process. In this respect, the World Conference on Human Rights emphasizes the importance of continued dialogue and cooperation between Governments and non-governmental organizations. Non-governmental organizations and their members genuinely involved in the field of human rights should enjoy the rights and freedoms recognized in the Universal Declaration of Human Rights, and the protection of the national law. These rights and freedoms may not be exercised contrary to the purposes and principles of the

United Nations. Non-governmental organizations should be free to carry out their human rights activities, without interference, within the framework of national law and the Universal Declaration of Human Rights.

39. Underlining the importance of objective, responsible and impartial information about human rights and humanitarian issues, the World Conference on Human Rights encourages the increased involvement of the media, for whom freedom and protection should be guaranteed within the framework of national law.

II

A. INCREASED COORDINATION ON HUMAN RIGHTS WITHIN THE UNITED NATIONS SYSTEM

1. The World Conference on Human Rights recommends increased coordination in support of human rights and fundamental freedoms within the United Nations system. To this end, the World Conference on Human Rights urges all United Nations organs, bodies and the specialized agencies whose activities deal with human rights to cooperate in order to strengthen, rationalize and streamline their activities, taking into account the need to avoid unnecessary duplication. The World Conference on Human Rights also recommends to the Secretary-General that high-level officials of relevant United Nations bodies and specialized agencies at their annual meeting, besides coordinating their activities, also assess the impact of their strategies and policies on the enjoyment of all human rights.

2. Furthermore, the World Conference on Human Rights calls on regional organizations and prominent international and regional finance and development institutions to assess also the impact of their policies and programmes on the enjoyment of human rights.

3. The World Conference on Human Rights recognizes that relevant specialized agencies and bodies and institutions of the United Nations system as well as other relevant intergovernmental organizations whose activities deal with human rights play a vital role in the formulation, promotion and implementation of human rights standards, within their

respective mandates, and should take into account the outcome of the World Conference on Human Rights within their fields of competence.

4. The World Conference on Human Rights strongly recommends that a concerted effort be made to encourage and facilitate the ratification of and accession or succession to international human rights treaties and protocols adopted within the framework of the United Nations system with the aim of universal acceptance. The Secretary-General, in consultation with treaty bodies, should consider opening a dialogue with States not having acceded to these human rights treaties, in order to identify obstacles and to seek ways of overcoming them.

5. The World Conference on Human Rights encourages States to consider limiting the extent of any reservations they lodge to international human rights instruments, formulate any reservations as precisely and narrowly as possible, ensure that none is incompatible with the object and purpose of the relevant treaty and regularly review any reservations with a view to withdrawing them.

6. The World Conference on Human Rights, recognizing the need to maintain consistency with the high quality of existing international standards and to avoid proliferation of human rights instruments, reaffirms the guidelines relating to the elaboration of new international instruments contained in General Assembly resolution 41 / 120 of 4 December 1986 and calls on the United Nations human rights bodies, when considering the elaboration of new international standards, to keep those guidelines in mind, to consult with human rights treaty bodies on the necessity for drafting new standards and to request the Secretariat to carry out technical reviews of proposed new instruments.

7. The World Conference on Human Rights recommends that human rights officers be assigned if and when necessary to regional offices of the United Nations Organization with the purpose of disseminating information and offering training and other technical assistance in the field of human rights upon the request of concerned Member States. Human rights training for international civil servants who are assigned to work relating to human rights should be organized.

8. The World Conference on Human Rights welcomes the convening of emergency sessions of the Commission on Human Rights as a positive

initiative and that other ways of responding to acute violations of human rights be considered by the relevant organs of the United Nations system.

Resources

9. The World Conference on Human Rights, concerned by the growing disparity between the activities of the Centre for Human Rights and the human, financial and other resources available to carry them out, and bearing in mind the resources needed for other important United Nations programmes, requests the Secretary-General and the General Assembly to take immediate steps to increase substantially the resources for the human rights programme from within the existing and future regular budgets of the United Nations, and to take urgent steps to seek increased extrabudgetary resources.

10. Within this framework, an increased proportion of the regular budget should be allocated directly to the Centre for Human Rights to cover its costs and all other costs borne by the Centre for Human Rights, including those related to the United Nations human rights bodies. Voluntary funding of the Centre's technical cooperation activities should reinforce this enhanced budget; the World Conference on Human Rights calls for generous contributions to the existing trust funds.

11. The World Conference on Human Rights requests the Secretary-General and the General Assembly to provide sufficient human, financial and other resources to the Centre for Human Rights to enable it effectively, efficiently and expeditiously to carry out its activities.

12. The World Conference on Human Rights, noting the need to ensure that human and financial resources are available to carry out the human rights activities, as mandated by intergovernmental bodies, urges the Secretary-General, in accordance with Article 101 of the Charter of the United Nations, and Member States to adopt a coherent approach aimed at securing that resources commensurate to the increased mandates are allocated to the Secretariat. The World Conference on Human Rights invites the Secretary-General to consider whether adjustments to procedures in the programme budget cycle would be necessary or helpful to ensure the timely and effective implementation of human rights activities as mandated by Member States.

13. The World Conference on Human Rights stresses the importance of strengthening the United Nations Centre for Human Rights.

14. The Centre for Human Rights should play an important role in coordinating system-wide attention for human rights. The focal role of the Centre can best be realized if it is enabled to cooperate fully with other United Nations bodies and organs. The coordinating role of the Centre for Human Rights also implies that the office of the Centre for Human Rights in New York is strengthened.

15. The Centre for Human Rights should be assured adequate means for the system of thematic and country rapporteurs, experts, working groups and treaty bodies. Follow-up on recommendations should become a priority matter for consideration by the Commission on Human Rights.

16. The Centre for Human Rights should assume a larger role in the promotion of human rights. This role could be given shape through cooperation with Member States and by an enhanced programme of advisory services and technical assistance. The existing voluntary funds will have to be expanded substantially for these purposes and should be managed in a more efficient and coordinated way. All activities should follow strict and transparent project management rules and regular programme and project evaluations should be held periodically. To this end, the results of such evaluation exercises and other relevant information should be made available regularly. The Centre should, in particular, organize at least once a year information meetings open to all Member States and organizations directly involved in these projects and programmes.

Adaptation and strengthening of the United Nations machinery for human rights, including the question of the establishment of a United Nations High Commissioner for Human Rights

17. The World Conference on Human Rights recognizes the necessity for a continuing adaptation of the United Nations human rights machinery to the current and future needs in the promotion and protection

of human rights, as reflected in the present Declaration and within the framework of a balanced and sustainable development for all people. In particular, the United Nations human rights organs should improve their coordination, efficiency and effectiveness.

18. The World Conference on Human Rights recommends to the General Assembly that when examining the report of the Conference at its forty-eighth session, it begin, as a matter of priority, consideration of the question of the establishment of a High Commissioner for Human Rights for the promotion and protection of all human rights.

B. EQUALITY, DIGNITY AND TOLERANCE

1. RACISM, RACIAL DISCRIMINATION, XENOPHOBIA
AND OTHER FORMS OF INTOLERANCE

19. The World Conference on Human Rights considers the elimination of racism and racial discrimination, in particular in their institutionalized forms such as apartheid or resulting from doctrines of racial superiority or exclusivity or contemporary forms and manifestations of racism, as a primary objective for the international community and a worldwide promotion programme in the field of human rights. United Nations organs and agencies should strengthen their efforts to implement such a programme of action related to the third decade to combat racism and racial discrimination as well as subsequent mandates to the same end. The World Conference on Human Rights strongly appeals to the international community to contribute generously to the Trust Fund for the Programme for the Decade for Action to Combat Racism and Racial Discrimination.

20. The World Conference on Human Rights urges all Governments to take immediate measures and to develop strong policies to prevent and combat all forms and manifestations of racism, xenophobia or related intolerance, where necessary by enactment of appropriate legislation, including penal measures, and by the establishment of national institutions to combat such phenomena.

21. The World Conference on Human Rights welcomes the decision of the Commission on Human Rights to appoint a Special Rapporteur

on contemporary forms of racism, racial discrimination, xenophobia and related intolerance. The World Conference on Human Rights also appeals to all States parties to the International Convention on the Elimination of All Forms of Racial Discrimination to consider making the declaration under article 14 of the Convention.

22. The World Conference on Human Rights calls upon all Governments to take all appropriate measures in compliance with their international obligations and with due regard to their respective legal systems to counter intolerance and related violence based on religion or belief, including practices of discrimination against women and including the desecration of religious sites, recognizing that every individual has the right to freedom of thought, conscience, expression and religion. The Conference also invites all States to put into practice the provisions of the Declaration on the Elimination of All Forms of Intolerance and of Discrimination Based on Religion or Belief.

23. The World Conference on Human Rights stresses that all persons who perpetrate or authorize criminal acts associated with ethnic cleansing are individually responsible and accountable for such human rights violations, and that the international community should exert every effort to bring those legally responsible for such violations to justice.

24. The World Conference on Human Rights calls on all States to take immediate measures, individually and collectively, to combat the practice of ethnic cleansing to bring it quickly to an end. Victims of the abhorrent practice of ethnic cleansing are entitled to appropriate and effective remedies.

2. PERSONS BELONGING TO NATIONAL OR ETHNIC, RELIGIOUS AND LINGUISTIC MINORITIES

25. The World Conference on Human Rights calls on the Commission on Human Rights to examine ways and means to promote and protect effectively the rights of persons belonging to minorities as set out in the Declaration on the Rights of Persons belonging to National or Ethnic, Religious and Linguistic Minorities. In this context, the World Conference on Human Rights calls upon the Centre for Human Rights to provide, at the request of Governments concerned and as part of its

programme of advisory services and technical assistance, qualified expertise on minority issues and human rights, as well as on the prevention and resolution of disputes, to assist in existing or potential situations involving minorities.

26. The World Conference on Human Rights urges States and the international community to promote and protect the rights of persons belonging to national or ethnic, religious and linguistic minorities in accordance with the Declaration on the Rights of Persons belonging to National or Ethnic, Religious and Linguistic Minorities.

27. Measures to be taken, where appropriate, should include facilitation of their full participation in all aspects of the political, economic, social, religious and cultural life of society and in the economic progress and development in their country.

Indigenous people

28. The World Conference on Human Rights calls on the Working Group on Indigenous Populations of the Sub-Commission on Prevention of Discrimination and Protection of Minorities to complete the drafting of a declaration on the rights of indigenous people at its eleventh session.

29. The World Conference on Human Rights recommends that the Commission on Human Rights consider the renewal and updating of the mandate of the Working Group on Indigenous Populations upon completion of the drafting of a declaration on the rights of indigenous people.

30. The World Conference on Human Rights also recommends that advisory services and technical assistance programmes within the United Nations system respond positively to requests by States for assistance which would be of direct benefit to indigenous people. The World Conference on Human Rights further recommends that adequate human and financial resources be made available to the Centre for Human Rights within the overall framework of strengthening the Centre's activities as envisaged by this document.

31. The World Conference on Human Rights urges States to ensure the full and free participation of indigenous people in all aspects of society, in particular in matters of concern to them.

32. The World Conference on Human Rights recommends that the

General Assembly proclaim an international decade of the world's indigenous people, to begin from January 1994, including action-orientated programmes, to be decided upon in partnership with indigenous people. An appropriate voluntary trust fund should be set up for this purpose. In the framework of such a decade, the establishment of a permanent forum for indigenous people in the United Nations system should be considered.

Migrant workers

33. The World Conference on Human Rights urges all States to guarantee the protection of the human rights of all migrant workers and their families.

34. The World Conference on Human Rights considers that the creation of conditions to foster greater harmony and tolerance between migrant workers and the rest of the society of the State in which they reside is of particular importance.

35. The World Conference on Human Rights invites States to consider the possibility of signing and ratifying, at the earliest possible time, the International Convention on the Rights of All Migrant Workers and Members of Their Families.

3. THE EQUAL STATUS AND HUMAN RIGHTS OF WOMEN

36. The World Conference on Human Rights urges the full and equal enjoyment by women of all human rights and that this be a priority for Governments and for the United Nations. The World Conference on Human Rights also underlines the importance of the integration and full participation of women as both agents and beneficiaries in the development process, and reiterates the objectives established on global action for women towards sustainable and equitable development set forth in the Rio Declaration on Environment and Development and chapter 24 of Agenda 21, adopted by the United Nations Conference on Environment and Development (Rio de Janeiro, Brazil, 3–14 June 1992).

37. The equal status of women and the human rights of women should be integrated into the mainstream of United Nations system-wide activity. These issues should be regularly and systematically addressed throughout

relevant United Nations bodies and mechanisms. In particular, steps should be taken to increase cooperation and promote further integration of objectives and goals between the Commission on the Status of Women, the Commission on Human Rights, the Committee for the Elimination of Discrimination against Women, the United Nations Development Fund for Women, the United Nations Development Programme and other United Nations agencies. In this context, cooperation and coordination should be strengthened between the Centre for Human Rights and the Division for the Advancement of Women.

38. In particular, the World Conference on Human Rights stresses the importance of working towards the elimination of violence against women in public and private life, the elimination of all forms of sexual harassment, exploitation and trafficking in women, the elimination of gender bias in the administration of justice and the eradication of any conflicts which may arise between the rights of women and the harmful effects of certain traditional or customary practices, cultural prejudices and religious extremism. The World Conference on Human Rights calls upon the General Assembly to adopt the draft declaration on violence against women and urges States to combat violence against women in accordance with its provisions. Violations of the human rights of women in situations of armed conflict are violations of the fundamental principles of international human rights and humanitarian law. All violations of this kind, including in particular murder, systematic rape, sexual slavery, and forced pregnancy, require a particularly effective response.

39. The World Conference on Human Rights urges the eradication of all forms of discrimination against women, both hidden and overt. The United Nations should encourage the goal of universal ratification by all States of the Convention on the Elimination of All Forms of Discrimination against Women by the year 2000. Ways and means of addressing the particularly large number of reservations to the Convention should be encouraged. *Inter alia,* the Committee on the Elimination of Discrimination against Women should continue its review of reservations to the Convention. States are urged to withdraw reservations that are contrary to the object and purpose of the Convention or which are otherwise incompatible with international treaty law.

40. Treaty monitoring bodies should disseminate necessary informa-

tion to enable women to make more effective use of existing implementation procedures in their pursuits of full and equal enjoyment of human rights and non-discrimination. New procedures should also be adopted to strengthen implementation of the commitment to women's equality and the human rights of women. The Commission on the Status of Women and the Committee on the Elimination of Discrimination against Women should quickly examine the possibility of introducing the right of petition through the preparation of an optional protocol to the Convention on the Elimination of All Forms of Discrimination against Women. The World Conference on Human Rights welcomes the decision of the Commission on Human Rights to consider the appointment of a special rapporteur on violence against women at its fiftieth session.

41. The World Conference on Human Rights recognizes the importance of the enjoyment by women of the highest standard of physical and mental health throughout their life span. In the context of the World Conference on Women and the Convention on the Elimination of All Forms of Discrimination against Women, as well as the Proclamation of Tehran of 1968, the World Conference on Human Rights reaffirms, on the basis of equality between women and men, a woman's right to accessible and adequate health care and the widest range of family planning services, as well as equal access to education at all levels.

42. Treaty monitoring bodies should include the status of women and the human rights of women in their deliberations and findings, making use of gender-specific data. States should be encouraged to supply information on the situation of women *de jure* and de facto in their reports to treaty monitoring bodies. The World Conference on Human Rights notes with satisfaction that the Commission on Human Rights adopted at its forty-ninth session resolution 1993/46 of 8 March 1993 stating that rapporteurs and working groups in the field of human rights should also be encouraged to do so. Steps should also be taken by the Division for the Advancement of Women in cooperation with other United Nations bodies, specifically the Centre for Human Rights, to ensure that the human rights activities of the United Nations regularly address violations of women's human rights, including gender-specific abuses. Training for United Nations human rights and humanitarian relief personnel to assist them to recognize and deal with human rights abuses particular

to women and to carry out their work without gender bias should be encouraged.

43. The World Conference on Human Rights urges Governments and regional and international organizations to facilitate the access of women to decision-making posts and their greater participation in the decision-making process. It encourages further steps within the United Nations Secretariat to appoint and promote women staff members in accordance with the Charter of the United Nations, and encourages other principal and subsidiary organs of the United Nations to guarantee the participation of women under conditions of equality.

44. The World Conference on Human Rights welcomes the World Conference on Women to be held in Beijing in 1995 and urges that human rights of women should play an important role in its deliberations, in accordance with the priority themes of the World Conference on Women of equality, development and peace.

4. THE RIGHTS OF THE CHILD

45. The World Conference on Human Rights reiterates the principle of "First Call for Children" and, in this respect, underlines the importance of major national and international efforts, especially those of the United Nations Children's Fund, for promoting respect for the rights of the child to survival, protection, development and participation.

46. Measures should be taken to achieve universal ratification of the Convention on the Rights of the Child by 1995 and the universal signing of the World Declaration on the Survival, Protection and Development of Children and Plan of Action adopted by the World Summit for Children, as well as their effective implementation. The World Conference on Human Rights urges States to withdraw reservations to the Convention on the Rights of the Child contrary to the object and purpose of the Convention or otherwise contrary to international treaty law.

47. The World Conference on Human Rights urges all nations to undertake measures to the maximum extent of their available resources, with the support of international cooperation, to achieve the goals in the World Summit Plan of Action. The Conference calls on States to integrate the Convention on the Rights of the Child into their national action

plans. By means of these national action plans and through international efforts, particular priority should be placed on reducing infant and maternal mortality rates, reducing malnutrition and illiteracy rates and providing access to safe drinking water and to basic education. Whenever so called for, national plans of action should be devised to combat devastating emergencies resulting from natural disasters and armed conflicts and the equally grave problem of children in extreme poverty.

48. The World Conference on Human Rights urges all States, with the support of international cooperation, to address the acute problem of children under especially difficult circumstances. Exploitation and abuse of children should be actively combated, including by addressing their root causes. Effective measures are required against female infanticide, harmful child labour, sale of children and organs, child prostitution, child pornography, as well as other forms of sexual abuse.

49. The World Conference on Human Rights supports all measures by the United Nations and its specialized agencies to ensure the effective protection and promotion of human rights of the girl child. The World Conference on Human Rights urges States to repeal existing laws and regulations and remove customs and practices which discriminate against and cause harm to the girl child.

50. The World Conference on Human Rights strongly supports the proposal that the Secretary-General initiate a study into means of improving the protection of children in armed conflicts. Humanitarian norms should be implemented and measures taken in order to protect and facilitate assistance to children in war zones. Measures should include protection for children against indiscriminate use of all weapons of war, especially anti-personnel mines. The need for aftercare and rehabilitation of children traumatized by war must be addressed urgently. The Conference calls on the Committee on the Rights of the Child to study the question of raising the minimum age of recruitment into armed forces.

51. The World Conference on Human Rights recommends that matters relating to human rights and the situation of children be regularly reviewed and monitored by all relevant organs and mechanisms of the United Nations system and by the supervisory bodies of the specialized agencies in accordance with their mandates.

52. The World Conference on Human Rights recognizes the important

role played by non-governmental organizations in the effective implementation of all human rights instruments and, in particular, the Convention on the Rights of the Child.

53. The World Conference on Human Rights recommends that the Committee on the Rights of the Child, with the assistance of the Centre for Human Rights, be enabled expeditiously and effectively to meet its mandate, especially in view of the unprecedented extent of ratification and subsequent submission of country reports.

5. FREEDOM FROM TORTURE

54. The World Conference of Human Rights welcomes the ratification by many Member States of the Convention against Torture and Other Cruel, Inhuman or Degrading Treatment or Punishment and encourages its speedy ratification by all other Member States.

55. The World Conference on Human Rights emphasizes that one of the most atrocious violations against human dignity is the act of torture, the result of which destroys the dignity and impairs the capability of victims to continue their lives and their activities.

56. The World Conference on Human Rights reaffirms that under human rights law and international humanitarian law, freedom from torture is a right which must be protected under all circumstances, including in times of internal or international disturbance or armed conflicts.

57. The World Conference on Human Rights therefore urges all States to put an immediate end to the practice of torture and eradicate this evil forever through full implementation of the Universal Declaration of Human Rights as well as the relevant conventions and, where necessary, strengthening of existing mechanisms. The World Conference on Human Rights calls on all States to cooperate fully with the Special Rapporteur on the question of torture in the fulfilment of his mandate.

58. Special attention should be given to ensure universal respect for, and effective implementation of, the Principles of Medical Ethics relevant to the Role of Health Personnel, particularly Physicians, in the Protection of Prisoners and Detainees against Torture and other Cruel, Inhuman or Degrading Treatment or Punishment adopted by the General Assembly of the United Nations.

59. The World Conference on Human Rights stresses the importance of further concrete action within the framework of the United Nations with the view to providing assistance to victims of torture and ensure more effective remedies for their physical, psychological and social rehabilitation. Providing the necessary resources for this purpose should be given high priority, *inter alia,* by additional contributions to the United Nations Voluntary Fund for the Victims of Torture.

60. States should abrogate legislation leading to impunity for those responsible for grave violations of human rights such as torture and prosecute such violations, thereby providing a firm basis for the rule of law.

61. The World Conference on Human Rights reaffirms that efforts to eradicate torture should, first and foremost, be concentrated on prevention and, therefore, calls for the early adoption of an optional protocol to the Convention against Torture and Other Cruel, Inhuman and Degrading Treatment or Punishment, which is intended to establish a preventive system of regular visits to places of detention.

Enforced disappearances

62. The World Conference on Human Rights, welcoming the adoption by the General Assembly of the Declaration on the Protection of All Persons from Enforced Disappearance, calls upon all States to take effective legislative, administrative, judicial or other measures to prevent, terminate and punish acts of enforced disappearances. The World Conference on Human Rights reaffirms that it is the duty of all States, under any circumstances, to make investigations whenever there is reason to believe that an enforced disappearance has taken place on a territory under their jurisdiction and, if allegations are confirmed, to prosecute its perpetrators.

6. THE RIGHTS OF THE DISABLED PERSON

63. The World Conference on Human Rights reaffirms that all human rights and fundamental freedoms are universal and thus unreservedly include persons with disabilities. Every person is born equal and has the same rights to life and welfare, education and work, living independently and active participation in all aspects of society. Any direct discrimination or other negative discriminatory treatment of a disabled person is

therefore a violation of his or her rights. The World Conference on Human Rights calls on Governments, where necessary, to adopt or adjust legislation to assure access to these and other rights for disabled persons.

64. The place of disabled persons is everywhere. Persons with disabilities should be guaranteed equal opportunity through the elimination of all socially determined barriers, be they physical, financial, social or psychological, which exclude or restrict full participation in society.

65. Recalling the World Programme of Action concerning Disabled Persons, adopted by the General Assembly at its thirty-seventh session, the World Conference on Human Rights calls upon the General Assembly and the Economic and Social Council to adopt the draft standard rules on the equalization of opportunities for persons with disabilities, at their meetings in 1993.

C. COOPERATION, DEVELOPMENT AND STRENGTHENING OF HUMAN RIGHTS

66. The World Conference on Human Rights recommends that priority be given to national and international action to promote democracy, development and human rights.

67. Special emphasis should be given to measures to assist in the strengthening and building of institutions relating to human rights, strengthening of a pluralistic civil society and the protection of groups which have been rendered vulnerable. In this context, assistance provided upon the request of Governments for the conduct of free and fair elections, including assistance in the human rights aspects of elections and public information about elections, is of particular importance. Equally important is the assistance to be given to the strengthening of the rule of law, the promotion of freedom of expression and the administration of justice, and to the real and effective participation of the people in the decision-making processes.

68. The World Conference on Human Rights stresses the need for the implementation of strengthened advisory services and technical assistance activities by the Centre for Human Rights. The Centre should make available to States upon request assistance on specific human rights issues, including the preparation of reports under human rights treaties as well as

for the implementation of coherent and comprehensive plans of action for the promotion and protection of human rights. Strengthening the institutions of human rights and democracy, the legal protection of human rights, training of officials and others, broad-based education and public information aimed at promoting respect for human rights should all be available as components of these programmes.

69. The World Conference on Human Rights strongly recommends that a comprehensive programme be established within the United Nations in order to help States in the task of building and strengthening adequate national structures which have a direct impact on the overall observance of human rights and the maintenance of the rule of law. Such a programme, to be coordinated by the Centre for Human Rights, should be able to provide, upon the request of the interested Government, technical and financial assistance to national projects in reforming penal and correctional establishments, education and training of lawyers, judges and security forces in human rights, and any other sphere of activity relevant to the good functioning of the rule of law. That programme should make available to States assistance for the implementation of plans of action for the promotion and protection of human rights.

70. The World Conference on Human Rights requests the Secretary-General of the United Nations to submit proposals to the United Nations General Assembly, containing alternatives for the establishment, structure, operational modalities and funding of the proposed programme.

71. The World Conference on Human Rights recommends that each State consider the desirability of drawing up a national action plan identifying steps whereby that State would improve the promotion and protection of human rights.

72. The World Conference on Human Rights reaffirms that the universal and inalienable right to development, as established in the Declaration on the Right to Development, must be implemented and realized. In this context, the World Conference on Human Rights welcomes the appointment by the Commission on Human Rights of a thematic working group on the right to development and urges that the Working Group, in consultation and cooperation with other organs and agencies of the United Nations system, promptly formulate, for early consideration by the United Nations General Assembly, comprehensive and effective

measures to eliminate obstacles to the implementation and realization of the Declaration on the Right to Development and recommending ways and means towards the realization of the right to development by all States.

73. The World Conference on Human Rights recommends that non-governmental and other grass-roots organizations active in development and/or human rights should be enabled to play a major role on the national and international levels in the debate, activities and implementation relating to the right to development and, in cooperation with Governments, in all relevant aspects of development cooperation.

74. The World Conference on Human Rights appeals to Governments, competent agencies and institutions to increase considerably the resources devoted to building well-functioning legal systems able to protect human rights, and to national institutions working in this area. Actors in the field of development cooperation should bear in mind the mutually reinforcing interrelationship between development, democracy and human rights. Cooperation should be based on dialogue and transparency. The World Conference on Human Rights also calls for the establishment of comprehensive programmes, including resource banks of information and personnel with expertise relating to the strengthening of the rule of law and of democratic institutions.

75. The World Conference on Human Rights encourages the Commission on Human Rights, in cooperation with the Committee on Economic, Social and Cultural Rights, to continue the examination of optional protocols to the International Covenant on Economic, Social and Cultural Rights.

76. The World Conference on Human Rights recommends that more resources be made available for the strengthening or the establishment of regional arrangements for the promotion and protection of human rights under the programmes of advisory services and technical assistance of the Centre for Human Rights. States are encouraged to request assistance for such purposes as regional and subregional workshops, seminars and information exchanges designed to strengthen regional arrangements for the promotion and protection of human rights in accord with universal human rights standards as contained in international human rights instruments.

77. The World Conference on Human Rights supports all measures by the United Nations and its relevant specialized agencies to ensure the effective promotion and protection of trade union rights, as stipulated in the International Covenant on Economic, Social and Cultural Rights and other relevant international instruments. It calls on all States to abide fully by their obligations in this regard contained in international instruments.

D. HUMAN RIGHTS EDUCATION

78. The World Conference on Human Rights considers human rights education, training and public information essential for the promotion and achievement of stable and harmonious relations among communities and for fostering mutual understanding, tolerance and peace.

79. States should strive to eradicate illiteracy and should direct education towards the full development of the human personality and to the strengthening of respect for human rights and fundamental freedoms. The World Conference on Human Rights calls on all States and institutions to include human rights, humanitarian law, democracy and rule of law as subjects in the curricula of all learning institutions in formal and non-formal settings.

80. Human rights education should include peace, democracy, development and social justice, as set forth in international and regional human rights instruments, in order to achieve common understanding and awareness with a view to strengthening universal commitment to human rights.

81. Taking into account the World Plan of Action on Education for Human Rights and Democracy, adopted in March 1993 by the International Congress on Education for Human Rights and Democracy of the United Nations Educational, Scientific and Cultural Organization, and other human rights instruments, the World Conference on Human Rights recommends that States develop specific programmes and strategies for ensuring the widest human rights education and the dissemination of public information, taking particular account of the human rights needs of women.

82. Governments, with the assistance of intergovernmental organizations, national institutions and non-governmental organizations, should

promote an increased awareness of human rights and mutual tolerance. The World Conference on Human Rights underlines the importance of strengthening the World Public Information Campaign for Human Rights carried out by the United Nations. They should initiate and support education in human rights and undertake effective dissemination of public information in this field. The advisory services and technical assistance programmes of the United Nations system should be able to respond immediately to requests from States for educational and training activities in the field of human rights as well as for special education concerning standards as contained in international human rights instruments and in humanitarian law and their application to special groups such as military forces, law enforcement personnel, policy and the health profession. The proclamation of a United Nations decade for human rights education in order to promote, encourage and focus these educational activities should be considered.

E. IMPLEMENTATION AND MONITORING METHODS

83. The World Conference on Human Rights urges Governments to incorporate standards as contained in international human rights instruments in domestic legislation and to strengthen national structures, institutions and organs of society which play a role in promoting and safeguarding human rights.

84. The World Conference on Human Rights recommends the strengthening of United Nations activities and programmes to meet requests for assistance by States which want to establish or strengthen their own national institutions for the promotion and protection of human rights.

85. The World Conference on Human Rights also encourages the strengthening of cooperation between national institutions for the promotion and protection of human rights, particularly through exchanges of information and experience, as well as cooperation with regional organizations and the United Nations.

86. The World Conference on Human Rights strongly recommends in this regard that representatives of national institutions for the promotion

and protection of human rights convene periodic meetings under the auspices of the Centre for Human Rights to examine ways and means of improving their mechanisms and sharing experiences.

87. The World Conference on Human Rights recommends to the human rights treaty bodies, to the meetings of chairpersons of the treaty bodies and to the meetings of States parties that they continue to take steps aimed at coordinating the multiple reporting requirements and guidelines for preparing State reports under the respective human rights conventions and study the suggestion that the submission of one overall report on treaty obligations undertaken by each State would make these procedures more effective and increase their impact.

88. The World Conference on Human Rights recommends that the States parties to international human rights instruments, the General Assembly and the Economic and Social Council should consider studying the existing human rights treaty bodies and the various thematic mechanisms and procedures with a view to promoting greater efficiency and effectiveness through better coordination of the various bodies, mechanisms and procedures, taking into account the need to avoid unnecessary duplication and overlapping of their mandates and tasks.

89. The World Conference on Human Rights recommends continued work on the improvement of the functioning, including the monitoring tasks, of the treaty bodies, taking into account multiple proposals made in this respect, in particular those made by the treaty bodies themselves and by the meetings of the chairpersons of the treaty bodies. The comprehensive national approach taken by the Committee on the Rights of the Child should also be encouraged.

90. The World Conference on Human Rights recommends that States parties to human rights treaties consider accepting all the available optional communication procedures.

91. The World Conference on Human Rights views with concern the issue of impunity of perpetrators of human rights violations, and supports the efforts of the Commission on Human Rights and the Sub-Commission on Prevention of Discrimination and Protection of Minorities to examine all aspects of the issue.

92. The World Conference on Human Rights recommends that the

Commission on Human Rights examine the possibility for better implementation of existing human rights instruments at the international and regional levels and encourages the International Law Commission to continue its work on an international criminal court.

93. The World Conference on Human Rights appeals to States which have not yet done so to accede to the Geneva Conventions of 12 August 1949 and the Protocols thereto, and to take all appropriate national measures, including legislative ones, for their full implementation.

94. The World Conference on Human Rights recommends the speedy completion and adoption of the draft declaration on the right and responsibility of individuals, groups and organs of society to promote and protect universally recognized human rights and fundamental freedoms.

95. The World Conference on Human Rights underlines the importance of preserving and strengthening the system of special procedures, rapporteurs, representatives, experts and working groups of the Commission on Human Rights and the Sub-Commission on the Prevention of Discrimination and Protection of Minorities, in order to enable them to carry out their mandates in all countries throughout the world, providing them with the necessary human and financial resources. The procedures and mechanisms should be enabled to harmonize and rationalize their work through periodic meetings. All States are asked to cooperate fully with these procedures and mechanisms.

96. The World Conference on Human Rights recommends that the United Nations assume a more active role in the promotion and protection of human rights in ensuring full respect for international humanitarian law in all situations of armed conflict, in accordance with the purposes and principles of the Charter of the United Nations.

97. The World Conference on Human Rights, recognizing the important role of human rights components in specific arrangements concerning some peace-keeping operations by the United Nations, recommends that the Secretary-General take into account the reporting, experience and capabilities of the Centre for Human Rights and human rights mechanisms, in conformity with the Charter of the United Nations.

98. To strengthen the enjoyment of economic, social and cultural rights, additional approaches should be examined, such as a system of indicators to measure progress in the realization of the rights set forth in

the International Covenant on Economic, Social and Cultural Rights. There must be a concerted effort to ensure recognition of economic, social and cultural rights at the national, regional and international levels.

F. FOLLOW-UP TO THE WORLD CONFERENCE ON HUMAN RIGHTS

99. The World Conference on Human Rights recommends that the General Assembly, the Commission on Human Rights and other organs and agencies of the United Nations system related to human rights consider ways and means for the full implementation, without delay, of the recommendations contained in the present Declaration, including the possibility of proclaiming a United Nations decade for human rights. The World Conference on Human Rights further recommends that the Commission on Human Rights annually review the progress towards this end.

100. The World Conference on Human Rights requests the Secretary-General of the United Nations to invite on the occasion of the fiftieth anniversary of the Universal Declaration of Human Rights all States, all organs and agencies of the United Nations system related to human rights, to report to him on the progress made in the implementation of the present Declaration and to submit a report to the General Assembly at its fifty-third session, through the Commission on Human Rights and the Economic and Social Council. Likewise, regional and, as appropriate, national human rights institutions, as well as non-governmental organizations, may present their views to the Secretary-General on the progress made in the implementation of the present Declaration. Special attention should be paid to assessing the progress towards the goal of universal ratification of international human rights treaties and protocols adopted within the framework of the United Nations system.

SOURCES OF
INFORMATION ON
INTERNATIONAL
HUMAN RIGHTS

The proliferation of reports and literature on international human rights has been so immense that one hesitates to point to any one source as being more important than another. The fact is that the cascading information about human rights forms a seamless web. All human rights are universal, interrelated, and indivisible. Some of the most important information on human rights can be found in the following ten sources:

1. When Congress in 1976 mandated the U.S. Department of State to issue an annual report on the state of human rights around the world, the initial annual review was small, hesitant, and incomplete. But the report for 1999 runs to some 2,000 pages in two volumes. It is comprehensive and covers virtually every major aspect of the struggle for human rights in 191 nations. Leaders and followers in the scores of nations that are less than fully free use the annual State Department country reports on human rights practices as their guide. As a result, the United States has set the bar for compliance with internationally recognized human rights standards.

Those who want to learn about the status of human rights anywhere in the world could profitably begin with the current annual *U.S. Department of State's Country Reports on Human Rights Practices*.

2. Any biases or inaccuracies that may exist in the State Department's reports on human rights do not exist in the annual reports on human

rights issued by Amnesty International and Human Rights Watch. These candid documents can be supplemented by the copious reports issued by the Lawyers Committee for Human Rights and the International League for Human Rights. A more academic approach can be found in the twenty volumes of the *Human Rights Quarterly* and in a dozen law reviews devoted to a discussion of international human rights.

3. The amazing but little-known work of the United Nations on human rights is reported in a magisterial work edited by Philip Alston, *The United Nations and Human Rights: A Critical Appraisal* (Oxford University Press, 1995). Here are essays by several experts on the work of the United Nations Commission on Human Rights and the several U.N. committees that monitor compliance with the covenants on human rights. For several years, committees at the United Nations have been assessing the compliance of nations on treaties related to race, torture, and the rights of women and children. The backup material of these several committees constitutes a gold mine for those who desire to learn how highly developed nations and less developed countries try to carry out their commitments to the covenants on human rights that they have ratified.

4. One of the least known but very important nongovernmental organizations is Article 19, based in London. It keeps the world's mind on compliance with Article 19 of the Universal Declaration of Human Rights, which guarantees freedom of the press. Article 19 issues authoritative material on the status of freedom of expression and the press around the world. It is probably no exaggeration to say that freedom of the press is the matrix and the guarantor of all human rights.

5. It is evident that the right to religious freedom is central to everyone who cherishes human rights. The right to worship according to one's conscience is central to every declaration on human rights. For complicated reasons, no covenant on religious freedom has emerged from the United Nations. But declarations and resolutions do exist that are morally binding on nations.

The present status of religious freedom in the world is expressed in a very important work. The main title of the twin volumes on the legal and religious perspectives on human rights is *Religious Human Rights in Global Perspective* (Scholars Press and Kluwer Academie, 1996). The two volumes were produced by an ongoing project of the Carter Center and Emory University.

6. The final statement of the 1993 U.N. World Conference on Human Rights in Vienna makes it clear that economic and political rights are equal and indivisible. But economic rights have always been deemed — at least by the United States — to be less important, or at least less enforceable, than political rights. This "heresy" has been refuted in an excellent book entitled *Basic Rights: Subsistence, Affluence, and U.S. Foreign Policy,* second edition, by Henry Shue (Princeton University Press, 1996). This outstanding explanation of the right to food and basic subsistence has made clear that the nations by ratifying the 1945 Charter of the United Nations and the Universal Declaration of Human Rights along with similar treaties have solemnly pledged to guarantee the right of every individual to adequate nutrition and basic economic equality.

7. On one issue, international law seems to be evolving into a consensus that the death penalty violates customary international law. The classic — even definitive — study on this issue is entitled *The Death Penalty as Cruel Treatment and Torture,* by William A. Schabas, a Canadian academic (Northeastern University Press, 1996).

Schabas is careful and cautious but demonstrates how international law can evolve from the growth of a moral consensus among nations.

A related volume is *The Killing State: Capital Punishment in Law, Politics and Culture,* edited by Austin Sarat (Oxford University Press, 1998).

8. Literature and court rulings on the rights of women have appeared in abundance everywhere in the recent past. It is hard to think of any area of human rights where the development of legal and moral doctrine has been more spectacular. There are a score of legal periodicals on gender and the law, while feminist nongovernmental organizations can claim an escalating influence. Most instructive are the rulings and advisories of the U.N. committee that monitors compliance with the U.N. Convention on the Elimination of All Forms of Discrimination Against Women.

9. The rapid acceptance of the U.N. Covenant on the Rights of the Child illustrates the sensitivity of the conscience of nations to the rights of its most vulnerable citizens. The recent application of the moral principle of equality to children has produced watchdog agencies with increasing

influence. The moral indignation they are proclaiming today may well become the binding law of tomorrow.

10. The philosophical basis of human rights may be the most important aspect of the human rights movement. Many participants in the human rights revolution tend to feel that the presence and preciousness of human rights is a truth that is self-evident.

One thoughtful presentation of the philosophy underlying human rights appeared in a 1983 issue of *Daedalus* (a quarterly published by the American Academy of Arts and Sciences). It discusses the philosophical and religious background of human rights. NOMOS XXIII, the yearbook for the American Society for Political and Legal Philosophy, titled *Human Rights* (New York University Press, 1981), also pays a good deal of thoughtful attention to the future of rights.

INDEX

NO SAVING GRACE

ALSO BY ZACHARY KLEIN

Still Among the Living
Two Way Toll

NO
SAVING
GRACE

A MATT JACOB MYSTERY

ZACHARY KLEIN

FAWCETT COLUMBINE • NEW YORK

A Fawcett Columbine Book
Published by Ballantine Books

Copyright © 1993 by Zachary Klein

Library of Congress Cataloging-in-Publication Data

Klein, Zachary, 1948–
    No saving grace: a Matt Jacob novel / Zachary Klein—1st ed.
        p.   cm.
    ISBN 0-449-90733-3
    1. Jacob, Matt (Fictitious character)—Fiction.   2. Private
investigators—Israel—Fiction.   3. Hate crimes—Israel—Fiction.
I.   Title.
PS3561.L3768N6   1993
813'.54—dc20   93-35929
                                                                                    CIP

Text Design by Debbie Glasserman

Manufactured in the United States of America
First Edition: January 1994
10 9 8 7 6 5 4 3 2 1

To Susan. Always a source of strength and reason. And more so during turbulent times.

ACKNOWLEDGMENTS

Many thanks to the usual crew of likely suspects, this time adding Barbara, Marc, and Leona Nevler, my new editor and publisher, to the cabal. A special nod to Lee Goldberg and Eric Loeb — both were rock solid when it counted.

And, as always, thank you, Eve.

NO SAVING GRACE

CHAPTER 1

When the telephone screams at four A.M., you can make book it ain't the State waking you into an instant million. I wide-eyed the shadow-mottled ceiling and thought hard about letting my 1940s black bakelite model cry itself back to sleep. But bad news always gets through the door so I shoved my hand toward the receiver and grabbed hold.

"I'm glad you didn't use my last check for an answering machine." The joke was forced, Simon's voice tight with fatigue.

"You don't pay enough. Damn, Simon, the only time you're supposed to see four in the morning is when you party on through."

"Believe me, this is no party," he muttered. "What's with you, Matt? Why aren't you yelling at me? You sound awake, almost chipper. Julius bring you a batch of uppers?"

I glanced at the bedside table and realized I had fallen asleep *before* I'd smoked the usual lullaby pipe. "You didn't call to practice stand-up," I snapped, suddenly annoyed. "Who died?"

"Reb Dov."

I had a momentary vision of birds falling from the sky. "Who? What are you talking about?"

"Rabbi Dov Horowitz. It was a prime-time murder. Turn on your television."

I took another look at my full pipe. "I don't want to turn on the television. I want to go back to sleep."

"Matt-man, I just got back from Cop Central. Come over and I'll explain, but goddamnit, don't do any drugs. I gotta have you alert."

His urgency was unusual. Since Simon and I reconnected, he'd been my major source of work, which meant I worked regularly but never really urgently. When Simon originally bought me my PI ticket, he was teamed with his father-in-law Alex on the briefcase-and-Bimmer side of the legal fence. In those days I did his corporate research inside libraries. After Alex's death, Simon's practice evolved and my work became a little more interesting. Now he chewed on some of those same companies, especially the ones that inflicted serious hurt on their neighbors and workers. When Simon got involved, poisoned people pocketed serious green in trade for their shortened lives. And I pocketed mine for doing interviews, research, and legwork. Sometimes it felt like blood money, but I enjoyed collecting the Suit's donations.

I squinted toward the clock which still read the wrong time for my kind of corporate head-hunting. "You want me to come to the office *now?*" I knew he wasn't inviting me to his home. We'd moved on together, but Fran, Simon's wife, still had trouble with me. That was all right, I still had trouble with me too.

"Since when do you do homicide?" I joked.

"When I have to," he said guardedly after a moment's hesitation. "Look, I don't want to kibitz. I've been working all fucking night, and the sooner you get here the sooner I'll be able to leave."

I had regretted my homicide remark right after I'd said it but, before I could promise to show, the line went belly up. I slipped the heavy black receiver back into its cradle, stretched across the bed, and plucked the pipe from the ashtray.

I fired up on the way to the kitchen where I fixed half espresso, half French. The coffeepot perked despite the unrea-

sonable hour. I dressed, found the remote lurking under the couch, located my cigarettes, and marveled at my energy. It was hours before dawn and I was charged, *smoking, mon.* Then I yawned watching the gray tendrils from both the cigarette and pipe float upward, interlocking over the brown glass ashtray. No doubt about the smoking.

I fished the electronic ocean until I hooked the news: bearded Jews wearing calf-length black coats, fur-trimmed upturned hats and flowing earlocks running panic-stricken in every direction. Cries of disbelief and wails of keening prayers accompanied their frantic movements. The news director let the tape roll without voice-over or explanation. Four-thirty in the morning was television art time.

I jacked up the anguish and retreated to the kitchen. The coffee was ready and so, mercifully, was the announcer. The leader of an ultra-Orthodox sect had been shot and killed by a member of an anti-Semitic gang called the White Avengers. He shot the Rabbi while the congregation danced in the street during their *Simchas Torah* celebration. I initially guessed that Simon had been retained by the gang, but the late night commentator kept talking. One of the dancing Rabbis had demanded an immediate "eye-for-an-eye," dropping the anti-Semite with a bullet to the chest. That left Simon with the Rabbi.

Which made more sense. Hard to see my friend losing sleep over a New Age Nazi. The TV announcer promised an in-depth background report on the Jewish sect and its neighboring Irish community following a dog food commercial. I slapped at the remote. I wasn't hungry and didn't own a dog.

I dumped the ashes from my pipe, smoked another cigarette, and looked at my sorry reflection in the kitchen window. I belonged in bed. What the hell was Simon doing working a criminal case? Worse. What the hell was I doing up?

CHAPTER 2

During shut-down time, Simon's office was an easy walk through the city's underlife. By now junkies were home nodding happily in their cribs if they had scored, sniffling and sweating miserably if they hadn't. Hookers, grifters, and pretty boys dragged tired cheeks away from the Boylston Arch oblivious to anyone but themselves. A tall, pockmarked cracker in a cowboy hat and imitation zebra boots smiled menacingly and herded three of his girls into the all-night deli. I hesitated, saw another two doxies flop inside a candy-apple Mustang, and listened to its engine's roar—the only musical accompaniment to the night's chilly grim tableaux. I tried to guess which suburb the two women called home; almost nobody wants to live in the city.

Simon's office was the top floor of a commercial building near Copley Square. He could gaze down from his double windows and watch well-heeled, blow-dried pedestrians stride eagerly to their next score. Or, he could focus on the old dirtballs who shacked on the steps of the main library. Just enough distance to comfortably view his life or contemplate his ancestry.

Simon and I had become friends while mutually suffering the First Wife Blues. We had known each other through remarriages: his successful and continuing; mine golden with an ab-

rupt and terrible conclusion — my wife Chana and my daughter Becky slaughtered in a senseless car crash.

Simon and I had known each other through despair, hatred, therapy, rebirth, and betrayal. Still, the early years had been our friendship's best — the only real opportunity to play on the same side of a crumbling '60s street. Since then, our relationship had been colored by Simon's intense upwardly mobile escape from his family's alcoholic past. My folks worked the other side of the bar so I never had his ambition.

I opened the burnished cherry door somehow expecting to see Sadie, thrown when I found the secretary's room deserted and dark. "Simon?" I called, fighting a sudden shiver of anxiety.

"Back here," he answered from the rear office. "I should have left it open."

The door swung open and there he stood, hair disheveled, arms akimbo, reading glasses pushed high on his head. Rumpleman, loose in the middle of sleek, high profile modern. His eyes matched his clothes and both needed ironing.

"It took you long enough. Get in okay?" he asked. "I left the downstairs unlocked."

"You know me too well. I never said I'd show."

He looked at me glumly. "We *both* know each other too well. Come sit down and I'll fill you in."

I followed him through his office door into wall to ceiling Roche Bobois, broken only by a framed Phillie's scorecard signed by Richie Allen. The scorecard hung at eye level along-side the cherry étagère. I pulled the closest thing to four legs over near Richie's signature.

Simon went to his desk then swiveled in his leather seat. "Do you sit there just to annoy me?" he asked, nodding at the score-card. "I don't need you to underline the past. I see it well enough from here."

I stared over his shoulder at the numberless wall clock. "You didn't drag me out of bed for a deep and real. What's going on?"

The telephone interrupted before he answered. Simon pushed

a button and the room suddenly filled with the tinny speaker drone of an insistent reporter asking about the night's double death. By the time the conversation ended I'd had my briefing. The only surprise was the reporter's focus on the ongoing confrontations between the congregation and the nearby hate gang. Maybe I should have suffered the dog food commercial.

Simon had just buttoned off when the phone rang again with another reporter and I was dosed with a second helping of the same two shootings.

"Shut it down, Boss," I demanded once he'd finished.

He shrugged and flipped a switch. "This has been going on since I got here."

"Why?"

"There's a lot of eyes looking at this one and the State won't talk. For the past couple years, there has been nothing but trouble between the Hasidim and this particular hate gang. Swastikas, chasings, broken windows, beatings. Don't you read the papers?"

"Sports, gossip, arts and entertainment. The Eternals."

"Well, sport, this is another eternal. Only now two people are dead — the head Rabbi of the Hasidic community and a bigshot member of the gang. The ultimate escalation."

"And you have the killer Hasid for a client?"

"Don't joke around. He's a Rabbi."

"I understand why the dogs" — I pointed toward the phone — "are barking, but what's got you so wired? Your client defends himself and protects the rest of his people. Someone will throw a testimonial dinner."

"I'm telling you, Matt, this isn't funny!" Simon rubbed his hand across his eyes. "When I got Downtown, Assistant District Attorney O'Neil was already there. This guy doesn't normally work the graveyard shift."

"Had to be there to get his name in the morning edition?"

"Not this guy. Everyone is worried about the neighborhood blowing up like Brooklyn."

"Come on, Simon, this isn't New York. Did he spell his name for the press?"

Simon shook his head. "I'm telling you it's not that way. O'Neil is their shut-down, clean-up guy. He rolls his sleeves when the State wants quiet. I don't like it."

"What's your client's name?"

"Yonah Saperstein. Reb Yonah."

"I never met a Jew named Reb."

"Don't be an asshole. It's a term Hasidim use for their Rabbis. The Rabbi who was shot was called Reb Dov or 'The Rebbe.' "

"What's your Reb charged with?"

"They're still dicking with it. No one wants to act 'precipitously.' "

"Maybe the hard working O'Neil didn't want the weight."

"Maybe. But right now there are too damn many 'maybes,' " he grunted while he rummaged inside a large desk drawer.

"What do you want with me?" I asked.

He looked up with his bleary, baggy eyes. "What do you think I want? I want you to investigate. We're going to proceed as if they intend to charge Reb Yonah with something serious. I want everything I can get on the dirty Jew-hating putz and all his friends." His voice grew harsh. "I want to know about every illegal, immoral, or ugly thing Sean Kelly ever did or *thought* about doing. I want to know about each and every time he uttered the word 'Jew.' I want to know everything about the cocksucker and every one of the White Avengers . . ."

"What are they avenging? We won the war with the Indians."

He didn't throw change onto the stage, didn't even smile. Simon just wasn't gonna loosen up.

"I don't know much about them. From what I read they are a variation on the Zionist/Commies/Blacks/Eastern seaboard conspiracy mongers." He smiled grimly. "We're not talking about chart-busting IQs."

I tried to follow his mood. "Chest-beaters or serious nasty?"

"I don't really know what they are. That's what I want you to

find out." His voice rose with his temper. "I want to know about every time those fucking neo-Nazis farted near a Jew."

I looked at the different angles in the room's sleek modernity, looked around again, then asked, "Simon, what's really going on?"

His head jerked. "What do you mean?"

"You Doberman lawyers like O'Neil. This time you tiptoe away. Then you call me here and circle the wagons. What is this bullshit?"

His eyes dropped. "You're still worrying about my lying to you. No matter how much time goes by . . ."

For a brief instant I saw the dead bodies that had created the chasm between us but I quickly pushed the image from my head. Hell, Simon was still among the living. And so was I. "This has nothing to do with Alex."

He studied my face to see if I was lying. I didn't know myself so I figured he couldn't tell either.

"I can't just slash and burn through this case," he finally groused. "You don't understand the pressure. Every Jewish organization is looking at me through a magnifying glass. The case *should* be a lock, but right now the D.A. wants to keep the situation 'fluid.' That's the word. I have to be careful not to push too soon."

In other words, if he fucked up, his career would pay. "I have trouble seeing you on the short end of this stick, Simon."

He stared at me with very hard eyes. "Look, two people are dead and the State has the right to charge my client for one of those deaths. We can debate all day but I just don't know what they plan to do. Your job is to provide me usable background. That's all you have to worry about. I'll take care of the O'Neils." He bent over his open desk drawer and came up with another tight smile and a cupped fist. "Here, have some coke. I want you to start digging today but if you go back to sleep . . ."

"Back off, Bwahna. You don't have to bribe me with sugar to keep me awake."

Simon stared at me. "You don't want to get high?"

I grew annoyed and stubborn. "Maybe I don't like coke sweats early in the morning."

Simon raised his hand. "Don't get pissed, I wasn't trying to bribe you. I'm just not used to you turning down dope." He shrugged. "Anyhow the stuff is too clean to make you sweat."

"Well, if you never saw me say no before, there's no reason to break new ground now." I grinned with a junkie's change of heart, leaned across the desk, and whisked the tiny glass bottle out of his hand. "What's on the end of it?" I asked, staring at a small chamber attached to the bottle's black plastic cover.

"It measures toots." Simon reached for the bottle, turned it upside down, then up again. "Here. Just put it under your nose and snort."

I did as he said. Then I did it again. Twice. I reluctantly flipped the bottle back, lit a cigarette, and watched Simon's ambivalence before he helped himself to a single snort. I pushed my chair away from the desk and tilted it against the wall. The coke was strong and smooth. Simon hadn't lied, there would be very little speed rush. "Does anyone have tapes?"

"Tapes?"

"Videos of the Jewish party. Maybe someone caught the shootings?"

"No," he said. "I asked."

"You asked the cable news channel?"

"Yes."

"You *have* been busy," I said impressed. "Individual camcorders?"

"I haven't checked, but I'd guess not. Most of the people outside were Hasidim."

"Jews buy video equipment."

"Hasidim don't like having their pictures taken."

"How do you know?"

"I'm Jewish."

"So am I but I didn't know it."

He averted his eyes and shuffled the papers on his desk.

"Simon, stop lawyering me. Why the hell did you get involved with this?"

He met my eyes with a defiant look. "I'm doing a favor for my Rabbi."

My chair dropped down onto its front legs. "Your *Rabbi*? What are you doing with a Rabbi? A Hasidic Rabbi? This Reb Yonah?" I couldn't keep the amazement out of my voice.

Simon's wary face relaxed into a wry smile. "Not Reb Yonah. No Hasidic Rabbi. During the last couple of years Fran and I have gotten involved with a Reform Temple. Our Rabbi is famous for his ecumenicism and often serves as a mediator between the larger Jewish community and the secular world. The Hasidim called him and he called me."

"The Rabbi calls and you jump? And you wake me?"

A look of anger flashed across his face. "It's not just the Rabbi. Anti-Semitism has spread like AIDS during the past ten years. It's one thing to paint hate on a wall, but what's been going on is different. Once again Jews are under siege and if there is a way to turn this incident against us . . ."

He relaxed his fist. "That's why the Hasidim called Sheinfeld and Sheinfeld called me." His chin pointed forward. "You know enough history to know when Jews defend themselves it always gets turned around. Look at Israel!"

I was taken back and uncomfortable with his lecture. "Every time I look at Israel I see them with South Africa and Korea."

"That's what I mean," he retorted. "Pin the blame on the victim. Exactly what will happen with this case if I'm not careful."

I didn't know why, but my chest was tight with echoes of abandonment. "What are you doing involved with a Temple? Was this Fran's idea?"

His anger was gone and he was back fidgeting with his papers. "No, I had to convince her. I just got tired of having nothing to believe in." Simon lifted his head and stuck out his jaw. "Aren't you?"

I don't think it had to do with my lack of belief or even the hour of the day, but suddenly, despite the cocaine, I was *very* tired. More tired than I'd been since he'd pulled me out of bed. So tired that I stood up, reached across the desk, and palmed his little glass bottle. I was tired enough to know it was time to leave.

CHAPTER 3

The sound of slamming delivery truck doors slapped at my ears the moment I walked onto the street. While I was in Simon's office early morning light had replaced the sky's pre-dawn gray: October's brittle beacon for the city's first shift.

I hadn't walked very far before realizing the cocaine had eliminated my hunger. Simon's ploy had been a good one; I was also no longer tired. I decided against the apartment but headed home for my car. Maybe I'd think of somewhere to go when I got there.

Simon's assignment seemed straightforward: interview the Hasids, interview the punks. But his religious conversion, however sugar-coated, continued to feel uncomfortably complicated. This wasn't one of his political "joins," but something from the heart. At the very least, it was a new wrinkle on an old friend's middle age. His conversion recalled a time when almost everyone I knew returned to school for a graduate degree. As if, in unison, their alternative lifestyle had grown obsolete. I'd never been as political as my friends, nor as straight, so I just stayed put and felt abandoned. I was feeling some of that now and wondered whether it was Simon's decision that disturbed me, or his parting question? *Was* I tired of having nothing to believe in?

I kept my eyes on the street scene while I walked past clumps of wage-earners huddled around the urban oases—subshops and newsstands. There is something seismic about a metropolitan area just before showtime; an urban potpourri of ambiguous feelings steaming into the cold daylight. People leaned into the fall chill with grim determination or weary resignation. Too many days doing the same damn thing. *Some* people, though, actually had a bounce to their step. The ones who couldn't re-member yesterday.

My fist uncurled to grasp the car door handle and I felt a fierce desire to roll down the windows and cut a radio-blasting swathe through town. To hell with propriety, the new case, or Si-mon's middle age.

To hell with my middle age.

I let the keys dangle, kept the windows rolled, and lit a joint hoping to ratchet down. I inhaled and thought about throwing the little glass bottle out the window. But I knew better. By nightfall I'd be back crawling around in the street.

Two cigarettes later I pulled my head out of a minor midlife crisis, no longer needing to teen-race through the city. I felt a lit-tle more like myself, though still reluctant to spend the day alone. I stayed with my decision to work, but didn't want to meet with the Avengers until after I'd met with the Hasids.

And meeting the Hasids meant introducing myself to Rabbi Sheinfeld. Simon's Rabbi would be my first step on the stairway to Hasidic heaven. I'd received the Temple's address along with a warning to park my personality before I went calling. Simon didn't want me to leave a bad impression. He was more than a little worried I'd be hostile in a House of the Lord.

My anxiety flared as I approached the massive limestone building. I'd always been aware of the Temple's presence, but never before noticed the amount of high-priced, tax-free real es-tate it consumed. The frontage faced the main thoroughfare of the city's adjoining suburb—a town proud of its schools and its ability to hold the line against Black immigration. When I

turned onto the bordering side street I saw, for the first time, a driveway sign offering substantial parking to the Temple's worshippers. I stretched the invitation and turned in anyway. I didn't think God towed.

I was relieved when Rabbi Sheinfeld pointedly pulled an ashtray from his desk. "I generally don't allow anyone to smoke in my office but sometimes it's impolitic to make a fuss."

I didn't think this was one of those times so felt doubly grateful as I lit up.

"They aren't very good for you, as I'm sure you know," Rabbi Sheinfeld said with a friendly nod.

"I'm not a just-say-no kind of guy," I acknowledged after a tension-releasing drag. "Who were the people we passed on our way to your office?"

"The Temple's fundraising group. The more heinous the anti-Semitism, the harder they work. These days Israel needs as much support as possible."

I wasn't sure why. "I suppose," I said noncommittally.

The Rabbi looked at me carefully, leaned back in his executive maroon leather chair, and changed the subject. "This has been an extraordinary twenty-four hours." He pointed to the telephone. "If my secretary weren't holding calls we wouldn't have a moment to talk. Organizations, Hasidim, members of my own congregation . . . ," he said shaking his head. "I had to nap right here in the Temple."

"News travels fast."

"Instantaneously. Reb Dov's brutal murder has shocked the entire Jewish world." Sheinfeld pulled a pair of tortoiseshell half-glasses from his suit's breast pocket, perched them on his nose, and peered. "Simon suggested I might find you . . . ," he groped for a moment, "distant from your heritage."

"Depends on your definition of heritage. Some people think I'm too much like what came before. When did you speak to Simon?"

"Before coming downstairs to greet you. I'm afraid I woke him up. Again."

"I'm sure he didn't mind. He's pretty upset himself."

"You seem surprised. You're Jewish, aren't you upset?"

I wasn't going to tell him that the measure of my Jewishness had been tossed into a hospital's foreskin container a couple of minutes after my birth. "I never like unnecessary death."

"Of course. But doesn't it horrify you when it's the result of violent anti-Semitism? Perhaps you think it paranoia, but when something like this happens it elicits terrible memories. I grew up during the Second World War. Although none of my immediate family died in concentration camps, we had relatives." He hesitated then added, "All Jews had relatives."

He waited for me to agree but I couldn't. There had been no talk of losing family in my house. There had been no talk of Jewish. Hell, there had been no family. Of course, I only lived there for twelve years. Maybe the subject came up after I'd gone.

"Rabbi, I don't know whether I had relatives in concentration camps or not. It doesn't really matter. Simon asked me to investigate the White Avengers and their relationship with the Hasids. I intend to do a thorough job. I hoped you might make a few calls to some of them, letting them know who I am."

"Absolutely. Simon was surprised you arrived here so quickly."

I smiled. "Tell you the truth, I don't think Rabbi Yonah has much to worry about, but I understand the pressure everyone is under. The Rabbi who died was an important religious figure, wasn't he?"

"Murdered," Sheinfeld corrected. "Yes, extremely important. He was the spiritual teacher of the Hasidim throughout New England. More than that really. At the time Reb Dov became *Rosh Yeshiva*, the Rebbe, the Hasidim were a small community, isolated and practically irrelevant to the rest of the Jewish world." Sheinfeld smiled wryly. "It would be an exaggeration to suggest that Reb Dov marched them into the twentieth century, but the Yeshiva expanded under his humanitarian leadership.

Reb Dov brought a warmth and joy to religion. He created an atmosphere that reduced the distance between the Hasidim and the rest of the Jewish community."

He grimaced. "Perhaps you know how difficult it is to get the three major factions of our religion to agree on anything." Genuine remorse sliced through Sheinfeld's polish. "Reb Dov's ability to command this wide-ranging respect is one of the bitter ironies. Over the years the Yeshiva drew larger and larger crowds for their *Simchas Torah* celebration. By necessity they were forced to dance outside." Rabbi Sheinfeld shrugged. "In truth, the Rebbe relished the large participation."

"One of the ironies?"

"Well, Mr. Jacob, in a perverse way it is quite ironic that the bastards chose him to kill."

"Perverse?"

"Reb Dov was a gentle man. He demanded non-violence from his followers regardless of the provocation." A grave look clouded his face. "I'm sorry to say, his approach is not universally shared. A growing number of Jews are enraged with the rising tide of anti-Semitic incidents. The Rebbe deplored violence, but his death, especially if something . . . *unexpected* happens to Reb Yonah, will add ammunition to those calling for a preemptive defense."

"Preemptive defense? Sounds like something left over from Vietnam. What do you mean 'if something unexpected should occur' to Reb Yonah?"

"If Reb Yonah were to be engaged in a long legal wrangle, the militants among us will have an opportunity and platform to promote their views. Especially among the Hasidim. I believe in the old admonition to 'choose our enemies carefully for one day we will come to resemble them.' Unfortunately, there are people already rattling sabers. Reb Dov's death is a bitter pill and there are those who simply won't swallow it."

He nodded absently, still caught in his concern. "It's a tricky situation. Last night's horror didn't occur in a vacuum. The

number and magnitude of incidents against the Jewish people throughout the world have steadily increased."

The glasses were off again and his lean tennis body edged forward. "The Hasidim have absorbed the brunt of the trouble." He shook his head. "I suppose they most resemble an anti-Semite's picture of a Jew." He paused as a quick smile flew across his face. "I'm sorry, Mr. Jacob. I don't think you asked for a sermon."

"Matt, Rabbi. This is helpful. It gives me a context to work from. I don't have any experience with Hasids, and I'm somewhat apprehensive about interviewing them."

Rabbi Sheinfeld nodded sympathetically but when he spoke his voice had an edge. "I'm happy to make a few calls but understand, the Hasidim use me when they need to, but otherwise have nothing to do with me or my Reform Temple."

"Why is that?"

"In their eyes I represent someone who separates Jews from their religion. Many Hasidim believe you are either Orthodox or you are not a Jew. There is no in-between."

"You don't sound entirely comfortable with the situation."

"To be the object of scorn is unpleasant. It also represents an intolerance I find disturbing."

"But you help them when they need it?"

"They are my brothers, Mr. Jacob . . . Matt. And, as I said, Reb Dov was different. A man with enough breadth and insight to respect all people."

"All people or all Jews?"

Sheinfeld stood. "Do you always bring that chip with you, or is it reserved for religion?"

"I'm leery of fanatics, that's all."

Sheinfeld sat back down and pulled the telephone closer. "I don't think you mean it when you say 'that's all.' "

I thought of my discomfort with Simon's relationship to the Temple. "There's been an awful lot of innocent blood spilled in God's name." I paused then shrugged. "Besides, like I said, the

thought of interviewing Hasids is intimidating. I've never seen one up close."

He appreciated my admission. "Don't be alarmed, they don't have horns."

"I hope you meant that as a joke?"

Sheinfeld raised his eyebrow. "I didn't, but it's not bad."

CHAPTER 4

I gave up trying to sleep and settled for *The Spy Who Came in from the Cold*, Fritos, marijuana, and diet Coke. I was just getting couch-comfortable when the telephone rang. I automatically began my neurotic do-I-or-don't-I, but was too damn tired for the debate.

"I just spoke to Rabbi Sheinfeld." Simon's sleep-thick voice barked over the wire. "He thought you were pretty interesting."

" 'We are all interesting in the eyes of the Lord.' Or is that 'sinners'?"

"I was certain you'd have the phone off the hook. Instead, you're up and running your mouth. I'm not sure which is worse."

"Me asleep? When there are Rabbis to question? God to investigate?"

Simon grew suspicious. "Have you been burying your nose in the rest of that sugar? Shit, Matt, I can't have you on a binge and crash routine. This case is important to me."

"What the hell are you complaining about? You gave me the coke."

"I gave you a toot, Matt. *You* walked off with the bottle."

"Always a lawyer, aren't you?"

"Not always. Now. Do I have to get Lou to baby-sit?"

Lou was my dead wife's father who had recently moved into the building from Chicago after *his* wife, Martha, died. Though both our names were on the six-flats' title, Lou was the real owner. After the accident he bought the original building and hired me to manage it. He wanted to give me something to do while I theoretically pulled my life back together. Since that time, Lou had bought the building next door and I'd stopped superintending. These days he talked about adding to the empire. As far as me getting it together, well, theories are, sometimes, just theories. And reality had me forgetting about Simon's little glass bottle. Now that was a surprise.

"Don't get your hopes up, Bwahna," I growled. "Lou knows better than to take that gig. Anyway, I'm not fucked up; some of us don't sleep real good during the day."

"Some of us don't speak English real good either."

"But I understand it well enough to know I don't belong pulling on earlocks. What are you dragging me into? I was there when Sheinfeld made the calls. Hasids prefer to speak in *Yiddish!*"

"Look, I'm not really concerned about the drugs, you have a fucking hollow head," Simon said, oblivious to my remark. "It's your attitude that has me worried."

"Say what?"

"Your attitude," he repeated. "I know it pisses you off that I'm involved with a Temple. But I want you to keep that separate. This case is important for a lot of reasons. If you keep your nose to the highway and away from the coke, I'll be better off."

I lifted my Diet Coke can, sniffed loudly, and released a deep sigh.

"I heard that, smartass. Try to pay attention, will you? I know you have to speak with the Hasidim to get started—but that's it. Your job is Sean Kelly and the White Avengers. You work the Hasidim once then be done with them, *capiche?*"

"*Capiche* my hindquarter. I don't need you to tell me how to work. And I don't need you looking up my nose; I told you this morning I'd get the job done."

"A minute ago . . ." he started.

"A minute ago I was complaining about doing business with Hasids who don't want to speak English. Next I'll complain about white supremacists who *can't* speak it. I'm an equal opportunity complainer. Now put it down, will you?" I couldn't clamp my irritation over his patronizing attitude; although he acted like this whenever we worked a case that stressed him, this was much worse than usual.

Simon stayed quiet on the other end of the line until he had coughed up more of the wake-up from his throat. "Well, I don't think the crap about religion is part of your general whining, but I didn't call to argue." He paused. "Look, Matt, I'm uptight about what you think."

"About the case?"

"About the Jewish thing."

"My Jewish thing?"

"Mine."

Whatever taste I had for a fight evaporated. "Come on, Simon, I understand you want something to believe in. Hell," I lied, "I don't have any problem with that. For you. I just don't want anything with a capital letter for me." I neglected to add that when I *had* things to believe in, they usually broke my heart.

"But that's my trip," I finished. "What you do for a spiritual life is your business."

He grunted his agreement. "So what did you think of Sheinfeld?" he asked.

"He made time to see me and let the Hasids know I was going to interview them. What was I supposed to think?"

"Lighten up, Matt. I just want to know whether you liked him. Since you know about my . . ."

"It's one thing to know, Simon," I interrupted, "another to hear about it every time we talk. Let's leave the music to the angels." I sounded harsher than I felt. Maybe.

"What happened to Mr. Tolerance?"

Before I had a retort, his tone changed. "Enough about this shit, let's talk case," he said, his voice all business.

"What's to say? I'll visit the Hasids and take it from there."

"When are you going to see Reb Yonah?"

"I don't know. I hadn't mapped it out."

"The sooner you start the better, but get ready. The good Rabbi is not an easy man."

He kept finding ways to tick me off. "I already have started, Simon. One of us *still* hasn't slept. Sheinfeld was work, not a personal consultation."

He chuckled. "I know *Rabbi* Sheinfeld was work. But Rabbi Sheinfeld was easy work."

"What are you warning me about?" I asked.

Simon's chuckle turned sarcastic. "*I'm* not going to tell you how to do your job, Matt."

I returned to the movie but, instead of enjoying the way Richard Burton used stillness to suggest intensity, the black-and-white quiet popped a door to my uneasy anxiety. I thought about sleep, about smoking more dope, about using the little snort machine. I thought about visiting with Mrs. Sullivan, the elderly tenant I'd looked after when I'd been the super. I even thought about calling my sometime womanfriend, Boots. Unfortunately, this wasn't one of those times.

Everything registered empty until I scarfed a sliced American cheese-food sandwich, smoked a cigarette, and decided to get out of the house. I needed something other than my tail to chase. And I'd start with Simon's client, Reb Yonah.

The Rabbi's house was a skinny, nondescript brownstone on a neat, quiet block squeezed tight against its neighbor. On the walk from my parking space I noticed a child's orange chalk-drawn hopscotch board on the sidewalk three houses away from Reb Yonah's. But I didn't see any kids, odd for a mild late afternoon. As I continued toward his house I felt the hair on the back of my

neck prickle. Sometimes that meant I was being watched. Other times it meant I was stoned when I shouldn't be.

The Rabbi's home was dark and appeared empty, but I climbed a short flight of steps and rang the bell anyway. To my surprise a deep voice resonated from inside the dark. I didn't understand the language but the tone suggested enter. I grabbed the knob and found myself in a gloomy, unadorned hallway, the only light shredding from off the side.

"Nu? Nu? Ve Gaast."

By the time he finished speaking, his impatient tone contained a worried edge. I walked toward his voice, pushed at a half-closed door, and found myself standing in the entrance of a large living/dining room. A heavy brown, nicked, wooden table rested upon a rugless, scratched oak floor. A tall, austere older man with a receding hairline and a wild, gray beard stood stiffly behind the table in a circle of dull overhead light. A stack of open books rested on the table. The sleeves of his frayed white shirt were rolled, and he tugged at the right one, yanking it down to his wrist. Not quick enough to hide the flash of blue on his dark-haired forearm.

"Who are you?" he demanded in accented English.

"I'm Matthew Jacob. I work for your lawyer, Simon Roth. I'm sorry if I frightened you. I thought you invited me in."

"No," he shook his head, "I did not invite you in. I asked who you were." He paused then asked, "Jacob is a Jewish name but you don't understand Yiddish?"

"No I don't. I'm sorry to make it difficult for you."

Reb Yonah's lips tightened. His eyes were wary as he remained silent, standing, and waiting. He didn't offer me a chair.

"Do you mind if we sit?" I requested.

"Is this really necessary? I've told everything I know to the police. And to this lawyer Roth. Why don't you speak with them?"

"I've spoken with Simon, Rabbi, and if I have to I'll talk to the

police. But since I'm on your defense team it makes sense for us to go over the situation."

"Defense team," he scoffed with a swift, emphatic shake of his head. "If they want to punish me they will—with or without a defense team."

Simon was right; Reb Yonah was not an easy do. "Why would they want to punish you, Rabbi? From what I understand, you were simply trying to protect the rest of the congregation."

He stared dourly, his arms hanging at his sides. One sleeve up, another down. Braided strings from inside his pants dangled down into his pockets. A large black velvet *yarmulke* covered the back of his head. My earlier discomfort with Judaism hit me again and my head suddenly felt naked.

He caught me staring at his strings, pulled his suitcoat off the chair behind him, and put it on. "It doesn't matter what the truth is," he said. "If officials wish to punish, they punish."

I shook my head. "It's not that easy. This isn't . . ."

"Germany? That was another civilized country." His voice went flat, expressionless. "You know what happened there, don't you?"

I raised my hands. "Slow down, Rabbi. I'm not someone who often defends the government, but we're not talking Nazis here."

My unfortunate choice of words fueled his frayed temper. "What would *you* call a government that permits continuous attacks and abuse upon the Jewish people? A government that allows the assassination of our Rebbe?"

There was no need to fan the flame. "Rabbi, I'm not here to defend any government. I'm on your side. I was hired to help in the unlikely event the State *does* press charges."

He waved his hand in an abrupt, scornful gesture. As if to slap my face. "I'm not afraid of your State." Reb Yonah's voice started evenly but picked up a note of shrillness as he continued. "Anti-Semitism is not new. But Jews never learn. First, a

frantic attempt to assimilate. Then, a denial of the obvious. No matter how hard Jewish anti-Semites work to forget, they remain Jews. But they always keep quiet when their governments allow inquisitions, pogroms" — he jerked his right arm straight, the motion dragging both the suit and unbuttoned shirtsleeve up his forearm. "They were among those who kept silent about this," he snarled, exposing his blue, branded concentration camp numbers.

I stepped back, took a breath, and looked around the double room. Aside from the books on the table, everything was as cold and severe as its master. I glanced at the clear plastic that rode the living room furniture. Even in the dim light I could see its yellowed age.

"Our conversation disturbs you, doesn't it?" Yonah's hard, relentless voice interrupted.

People react in different ways after they kill someone, and Reb Yonah was still in the throes of aftershock. Perhaps he was more frightened of the legal system than he could admit. Or maybe this was who he was. No matter, today wasn't a good day for me to eat much shit. I'd already had my fill about the world's anti-Semitism.

I met his eyes and spoke firmly. "Rabbi, I can imagine how difficult all this must be for you, but attacking me won't help anything. I hate what happened to you during the war, hate what happened the other night. Simon Roth hired me to investigate and unfortunately that means I have to ask questions. My job is to gather information that will help make sense of the conflicts between your community and the White Avengers, as well as the specifics of the other night. I thought Rabbi Sheinfeld told you I planned to visit. If this is a bad time I'll gladly return."

Reb Yonah's icy stare never faltered and the mention of Sheinfeld only added fresh harshness to his voice. "Sheinfeld. Sheinfeld's worse than the *goyim*. He pretends to represent our Laws when all he does is give Jews permission to assimilate."

His body was tense and rigid, filled with wall-to-wall hate. I held little hope of getting any useful information, but his nasty prejudices bothered me. "I thought you asked Rabbi Sheinfeld for help."

"Yes." An almost cunning look darted across his stern face. "Yes. Dealing with the *goyische* world is what he does best."

"Assimilation has its function," I agreed.

Reb Yonah ran a hand across his eyes then stared past my shoulder. I watched as he let some of his anger dissipate. He looked at me thoughtfully, nodding as if a bond had somehow been formed between us. I didn't know what that bond was and his gesture only made me more uncomfortable.

"Perhaps I am being unfair toward Rabbi Sheinfeld," he finally admitted. "You must forgive me. The divisions among Jews are as ancient as they are unfortunate. It is the rest of the world who is united in their hatred of us. The grief of my Rebbe's murder has obviously been upsetting. I am very sorry if I have offended you."

His apologetic words just didn't jibe with my whiff of his personality. "I'm sure that's true," I said. "Would you care to talk about the other night?" I smiled inwardly, knowing what was certain to come. Something that never happened for me at the ponies.

"Could we meet at another time?" he asked. "Although Rabbi Sheinfeld told me you were coming, I didn't expect you today. Here." Reb Yonah leaned over the table, tore a piece of paper from an unlined pad and scribbled. "This is my telephone number."

I took the offered paper, folded it, and put it in my pocket while I thought about what I wanted to say. "Just one question, Rabbi. Can you tell me how to get to the Yeshiva from here? I know it's close but . . ."

A surprised look was replaced by a quick glance at a clock hanging on the side wall. "There will be no one available to

speak with you now. The entire Yeshiva is mourning our loss. Also, it is time for evening prayers."

"That's all right," I answered. "I just want to look around." What I wanted was to get out of this house. Fast. I'd sparred enough with the wrathful Rabbi and his gloom and doom. It was something I knew to be contagious.

CHAPTER 5

On the way back to the car I knelt and fumbled with my securely tied sneaker lace. This time I recognized the cause of my bristling hair. I glanced behind me and watched the curtain in Reb Yonah's shrouded front room draw shut. It was reassuring to have my senses accurately sniff the real world. A soft internal whisper told me I would need them.

But once behind the wheel, the interior world captured my attention. Something was gnawing.

I'd been all over Simon and rough enough with Reb Yonah to get tattoo numbers shoved in my face. I guessed the one-two punch of Simon's hopeful belief and Reb Yonah's bitterness recalled my own Age of Faith. I'd arrived in college unformed, without political leanings. But one day I listened to someone explain the Vietnam war in a way that opened my eyes to a world I instinctively "knew" to be true. Years of demonstrations, billy clubs, and the tragedy of an intractable society failed to eliminate my faith in the possibility of political change, though it shrouded it with a shell of bitter cynicism.

It took my personal disasters to excoriate the shell and crush what was left of my politics, my belief. Now, sitting alone in my car, I felt the shadow of an old loss.

I stubbed my smoke and started the engine. Peace wasn't going to descend with me sitting on the Rabbi's street, and I sure as hell wasn't reenlisting with my shrink.

Two blocks later I had to choose between illegal or parking further away than where I had started from. I thought about my drawer full of red stickers, had an apocalyptic vision of the Denver Boot, but picked illegal anyway. It was my day to tease Authority.

The inner entrance hall of the Baal Shem Yeshiva was lit with dusty fluorescent tubes hung inside dustier green boxlike holders. The air itself had a dry texture and an arid feel; a sense of antiquity — parchment stretched across an altar in a temple hidden deep within the bowels of a pyramid. Like something out of *Indiana Jones*. The walls were age-streaked gray, the paint so thoroughly chipped that past generations of institutional colors left an absurdist's signature to an otherwise somber welcome. I compared Sheinfeld's opulent Temple to the Yeshiva and imagined that class spiced Reb Yonah's venom. Inside the Yeshiva it was simple to see who occupied what niche.

I thought the place would be barricaded but, apart from muffled chanting, I heard or saw no one. I continued down the dingy hallway until I got to a door near the back. I opened it and walked onto a bare square landing. The chanting was louder, the congregation's Hebrew prayers swirling through the stairwell from down below. Occasionally a clear voice rose above the rest, carried toward the sky on the community's back. Though the language was indecipherable, there was no mistaking the emotion. These were a hurting group of people.

I thought about going downstairs but didn't want to interrupt. Or even get too close. Still, I wasn't ready to leave the Yeshiva. Something about the congregation's mournful cries reminded me of Chana's moods. Moods identified by the a cappella music of Gregorian chants ringing throughout our house. Although Jewish, Chana had been able to universalize and integrate everyone's experience.

I shook off my memories and walked up the stairs, away from the voices. I climbed until the prayers were barely audible, then walked out into another corridor not much different from the first. And just as deserted. I decided to snoop, walking quietly toward an unmarked, opaque, gray glass door that reminded me of a 1940s office entrance. All it missed was a black stenciled P-H-I-L-I-P M-A-R-L-O-W-E.

I tried the handle and initially thought the room empty. I was wrong. Behind a tall wooden lectern stood a 15- or 16-year-old kid in a long black coat, his head buried in a bucket of crossed arms. I waited silently until he lifted his covered skull. Earlocks dangled down the sides of his head despite his having wrapped them around his ears. A torn, aged, white shirt peeked out from his clean but frayed dress coat and, when he looked at me, I could see he'd been crying. I also saw a nose that had, in the boy's adolescence, grown more quickly than the rest of his face. Like the building itself, he was a fractured throwback to an immigrant time and place. A live version of a sepia photograph — an oversized, forlorn little boy wearing a grown-up suit.

Cliché or not, a protective feeling whistled through me. "I'm sorry if I startled you."

He shook his head. "You didn't. I heard you walk down the hall." His words, though spoken in perfect English, contained a hint of East European accent.

"You have good ears. I was pretty quiet."

A twisted smile crossed his face. "Did you sneak into the Yeshiva to take pictures for the newspaper? Can't you people even leave us alone while we sit *shiva*? Allow us to mourn our Holy Beloved?"

I raised my empty hands. "I'm not a reporter."

"Then what are you doing here?" Suspicion replaced distaste. "Are you with *them*? Here to continue your destruction?"

"Them?"

"The *schkutzim*." His accent grew thicker.

"The what?"

"The vermin who killed the Rebbe!" A wild, frightened look suddenly exploded in his eyes. "You're here to avenge my father!"

It took a long moment to add it up. Then another moment to consider his mother's age. There were a lot of years between this kid and his father. "Take it easy, boy. I'm no White Avenger, if that's who you're talking about. If your father is Rabbi Yonah, then I'm actually working for him."

His face shifted into a puzzled frown. "What do you mean?" he asked suspiciously.

Despite the open entrance door, it was evident the people here felt under attack. Clearly the boy did. "I work for your father's lawyer, Simon Roth. I'm Simon's private investigator." No matter how many times I identified myself as a PI, it always sounded ridiculous. Probably because Simon originally bought the license through his bureaucratic connections. "Both of us want to help your dad," I added. "I just came around to get some firsthand accounts."

"What do you mean 'firsthand'?"

His panic had subsided but not his suspicion. "I want to speak with some people who were celebrating that night. Try to get a picture of what happened. Basic stuff."

The boy thought about what I had said before he answered. "This is our mourning period. It's called *shiva*. No one will talk with you now. Not for another week." As if to apologize for the inconvenience, the boy walked across the room then stuck out his hand. "*Shalom*. My name is Yakov Saperstein."

I reached out and grasped his bony paw. "Hi. I'm Matt Jacob."

"Jacob? *Do bist a yiddescher?*"

I raised my eyebrows. "Huh?"

"You are Jewish?" he asked in English.

"You've stumbled upon the observation of the day," I replied. "What do you mean?"

I smiled. "Nothing. Just don't go diving into Yiddish on me. *Shalom* is about all I can understand."

He returned my smile. "*Shalom* is Hebrew."

"That's okay. I don't play favorites." I nodded into the rest of the room. "Do we have to stand in the doorway?"

He looked flustered then backed in. He stopped, walked to a small, chipped mahogany cabinet, opened a drawer, and returned with a *yarmulke*. "Would you mind wearing this?" he asked. "This is Reb Dov's study . . ."

At the mention of the dead Rabbi, the boy blanched. "*Was* his study," Yakov finished softly.

After a moment of vague discomfort and a tinge of embarrassment, I perched the skullcap gingerly on my head. It must have looked pretty silly because Yakov, despite his obvious bereavement, struggled to hide a small smile.

"You don't seem too familiar with *yarmulkes*," he finally said.

I tried to pat it down. "I'm not."

"You know nothing of *Halacha*, our Law?" He sounded curious. A pleasurable change after his father's condemnation.

"There hasn't been much Jewish in my life," I admitted.

Yakov shook his head then pointed silently to a set of low windows and straight-backed wooden chairs. "So Rabbi Yonah is your dad?" I asked after I settled in as best I could. The chairs were as uncomfortable as they looked.

The boy's long arms dangled, fingers close to the floor, as he nodded. "Yakov *ben* Yonah. Jacob, son of Jonah."

I kept noticing the size of his hands and feet and fleetingly wondered whether adolescent girls looked as awkward during their growth spurts. With a start I realized the kid had me thinking about Becky. "I've just come from your house," I said quickly, businesslike.

"My house?"

"Yes. I thought it might be useful to speak with your father. He didn't agree."

An uncomfortable grimace crossed the boy's face before he turned away.

"You don't seem surprised," I said to the back of his head.

"I'm not surprised. This is a time for mourning, nothing else. There is no greater horror than having one's Rebbe murdered." He turned back in my direction. "These atrocities didn't begin with the pogroms and they won't stop now. What happened to the Rebbe is a reminder of how little the world changes." His throat caught and again he looked away. "My father is not easy to talk with at any time. Since my mother died, he has become a man of very few words."

"When did she die?" I asked gently. Though we lived in different worlds and had just met, there was a shared closeness. Grief has a way of doing that.

"About five years ago," he replied tersely. "Cancer."

Given the age difference between Reb Yonah and his son, I placed Yakov's mother somewhere between the two. About the same age as Chana would have been.

The room filled with sadness. "The Rabbi's death brings it up all over again, doesn't it?"

Tears squeezed from the corners of his eyes as he nodded.

"You know that happens to everyone, don't you? One terrible thing yanks on all the rest. Makes everything hurt that much more." I flashed on Yonah's concentration camp numbers and added, "For what it's worth you aren't alone. Your father almost said the same thing."

"What do you mean?" he asked, a note of curiosity underneath his grief.

"Your dad mentioned that what happened to Rabbi Dov reminded him of other painful times in his life."

"He said that to you?" Yakov looked astonished.

"Not in so many words, but he referred to his camp experience so . . ."

Yakov stared open-mouthed.

"What's the matter?" I asked.

"He never speaks about those times with strangers." He shrugged then added, "He really doesn't talk about them with anyone except the Never Agains. Even me."

I almost asked him to explain the Never Agains, but instead sat silently while we counted our losses. Neither of us met the other's eyes until I asked, "Why are you by yourself in Rabbi Dov's study? Shouldn't you be downstairs with the rest of the Yeshiva?"

"I am different from the rest." There was no pride attached to his statement, just matter of fact. "After my mother passed away, Reb Dov chose me to learn with him. I have been his *talmid*." The boy stopped talking, then continued when he realized I didn't understand. "I was the Rebbe's private student so I spent all my time with him," he added. "I have been somewhat separate from the other *talmidem*. I'm not ready to mourn with anyone else. I'm too confused to *davin* with the Yeshiva."

"Yakov, I don't do languages, remember?"

He looked at me with annoyance. "*Davin* means to pray. How is it that you know nothing?"

"It just never came my way. Why did the Rebbe choose you?"

The boy held his head up. "A Rebbe chooses anyone he wants to chronicle his words. I was the person chosen," he said with simple pride. "My father and Reb Dov are very close."

Then his face looked stricken. "Were," he whispered. "You see why I can't go downstairs? I still don't accept that my Rebbe is no longer here."

I waited for him to calm down before I asked, "Were you Reb Dov's only student?"

"I was special," he said, his voice trailing off.

I sat quietly until Yakov continued. "I spent most of my time with the Rebbe and his family. My father is a solitary man."

Ripples of loneliness swept into the room, and with them images of a small abandoned boy. For a moment, I didn't know whether I was seeing Yakov or myself.

It was time to punt. "I've been told there has been a lot of trouble between your community and the White Avengers."

"They have *given* my community a lot of trouble," he corrected.

"I know about the other night," I said hoping to avoid the shootings. "But what happened before?"

"Where do you want me to begin?" he answered relieved by the question, despite his earlier admonition about the days of mourning. "Should I start with the broken windows? The excrement? The vicious graffiti? Or maybe the beatings at the basketball court?"

"The students here play ball?" I asked surprised.

"Of course. We aren't from another planet."

"I didn't mean it that way," I said.

A small grim frown tugged at the corners of his lips. "Yes you did. You see *payis*, the *caftan*, the *streimal*, the way we look, and believe we know nothing of modern life. You think we don't belong here."

I wasn't going to ask for a translation. "Well," I said with a smile, "I don't think Hasids reflect the avant-garde, but I wouldn't throw you off the planet. I figure there is room enough for everybody."

The boy snorted and made a skinny fist. "There is no room for the *schkutzim* who murdered my Rebbe. They don't deserve air to breath or water to drink."

"Jesus, boy, you're too young for that kind of attitude. I've been told Reb Dov was a gentle man."

Yakov looked upset. "You aren't allowed to curse in here."

"I'm sorry, I didn't know it was a curse."

"He was a false prophet. Jews should not even mention his name." Yakov's doctrine helped distance him from his horror. Horrors.

"Sorry, I'll be more careful. I can guess how hard all this is for you. Your Rabbi, your father's troubles . . ."

"What troubles?" he interjected. "I've been told there's nothing to worry about."

"That's absolutely correct," I rushed to reassure. "But it probably adds to your concern."

Although the kid didn't move, it seemed as if he had crossed the room. "I'm proud of what my father did. That animal deserved to die. He and his group are just the continuation of all the centuries of anti-Semites who have come before."

He paused. "You asked if we play basketball. Well, for the past year we haven't. Why? Because the court is public property and when we went there they would force us to play against them. If we won the game we were beaten up." He took a deep breath. "Reb Dov finally said we were no longer permitted to use the court unless we were willing to lose. He wanted to give those animals a chance to escape their nature."

"You disagreed with his decision?"

He looked at me with tears forming in his eyes. "My Rebbe is dead by their hands." Yakov twisted his body in the hard wooden chair and gazed grief-stricken out the window into the sudden dark of early night.

It wasn't a good time to push — for either of us. The kid had nestled into a raw spot somewhere inside me. I scraped my chair along the floor and placed it next to his. We sat quietly for a long while, each staring out of our own separate window while the dark turned into nighttime black.

CHAPTER 6

I thought about pressing Yakov for details about the Avengers, his Rebbe, his father, the Never Agains. Thought about it, but didn't. Didn't do anything other than sit next to the kid until it was time to go. And that time came when I could no longer tolerate the thumping of my chest in the silence of the room. I just wasn't used to the mix of protectiveness and warmth this gawky kid evoked. It had been a long, long time since I felt paternal.

It was a relief to walk into my apartment and spot the duffel bag on the kitchen table. Julius had broken in and left the rent. No matter how often I changed the locks, Julie found a way. His ingenuity and his rent never failed to lift my spirits. I rummaged through the bag hoping for a treat stronger than grass or hash, satisfied to find a plastic bottle of Valiums. Something of a surprise since Julius didn't like me doing downs.

I rolled a torpedo from the fresh, poured a double Turkey neat, and twirled the television's remote. To no avail; the usuals didn't work. I couldn't lay dead on the couch. I walked from one window of my apartment to another as if there was something important to see. Between excursions I kept a steady drain on the bourbon. I eventually realized that what I was looking for wasn't outside. But by then it was too late; I was too tired and

too high to think. I promised myself I'd work it out after I slept and sobered up.

But sleep raised the possibility of dreams. In a stumbling attempt to reduce the odds, I pried open the new plastic bottle, washed two down with my bourbon, and went horizontal on the couch. This time the television finally grabbed hold.

Too finally, I discovered, as the telephone clawed its way through my cotton brain. I slow-motioned for the receiver, suddenly realizing I'd spent the night on the couch. The TV was doing Duanne Eddy, and I was at the beginning of a big, dry, headbanger.

Before I had a chance to resist, my hand cradled the receiver. "You're home," Simon growled into my ear.

"Uh-huh." My other hand searched beneath the couch until shaky fingers found the remote. I shut down the fucking guitar but its twang kept plucking. I was frantic with thirst, my tongue plastered to the roof of my mouth. Thankfully, there was a glass of day-old aqua on the far end of the coffee table. When I looked at the Turkey bottle my stomach screamed.

"I'm waking you up?"

"Uh-huh." I stared at my fingers but they were wrapped so tightly around the glass I couldn't tell if they were still shaking.

"It's not that early," Simon said, his voice both defensive and accusatory.

"What time is it?" On my best days I had trouble reading the VCR's little clock numbers.

"Eight-thirty. What's the matter with you? You sound strange." All his defensiveness was gone.

"Nothing's the matter. I'm sluggish when I'm sleep deprived." Sluggish and stiff. I tried to stretch my back, lost the will, and sank back onto the couch.

"Or when you're fucked up."

"I'm not fucked up. Fucked up is fun and I'm not having any. What's with you? Are you trying to torture me with wake-up

calls? I want sleep." I reached back over to the table and grabbed a cigarette.

"You're not going back to sleep. I hear your hacking. You ought to stop with the cigarettes. The rest of it just makes you sick or stupid but the smokes are going to kill you."

I looked at the burning stick in my hand, took another drag, and stubbed it out. "You *are* trying to torture me," I complained.

"If you think concern is torture," Simon buttoned down. "Look, I didn't call to crap around. I got an early morning complaint. About you."

"From who? I drank alone last night."

"That's a relief," he said sarcastically. "But before your private party you apparently broke into Reb Yonah's house. Reb Yonah called Rabbi Sheinfeld; Rabbi Sheinfeld called me. Reb Yonah also accused you of barging into the Yeshiva during prayers, despite his request that you visit some other time. Do you remember any of this, Matt-man?"

"Yeah, Simon, I remember. Clearer than the Rabbi. When I knocked on Saperstein's door he responded in Yiddish. I thought he'd invited me inside."

"Reb Yonah, not Saperstein, okay?"

I held my temper. "What can I tell you, I thought the Reb invited me in."

"And the prayers," Simon grilled.

"I didn't disrupt anything. I didn't even look into the prayer room."

"Then how did he know you were there?"

I found myself reluctant to mention Yakov. "How the fuck do I know? Maybe he followed me."

My anger shut him up but his heavy breathing continued. "You're really feeling the heat, aren't you?" I asked with false sympathy. My body was pounding at me to get off the telephone.

"Yeah," he muttered grudgingly, his annoyance slowly fading.

"You get the work-ups from Downtown?"

"Don't ask. It'll just set me off again."

So I didn't. Just sat there smoking until he finished settling down.

"Look," Simon finally said. "I'm sorry I jumped on you, okay?"

"Sure. That's what I'm here for, isn't it? Just don't go believing everything a Rabbi tells you."

He tried to chuckle. "I'll try to remember. In the meantime, why don't you stay away from the Hasidim?"

I remembered Yakov's *shiva* period. "I won't go back for a while, Simon, but I'll have to return sometime. Most of the people there were at the shootings."

He couldn't argue and he knew it. "Well, wait until Reb Yonah cools down, will you?"

"I'd like to get it done before I start using senior citizen discounts."

This time the chuckle was real. "You won't have to wait that long. Why don't you lay off the Yeshiva and start nailing Kelly and the Avengers?"

"Sounds like a rock group."

"This group doesn't bite heads off rubber rats. They murder Rabbis."

"I won't forget, I promise."

"Good."

Good for him, maybe, but our conversation just added to my four-star headache. I believed Simon's anxiety related more to his emerging Jewish identity than any actual risk to his client. No matter, his misguided intensity was hard to handle.

I needed java, nicotine, and out of the house. I pushed myself off the couch, looked for some clean clothes, but settled after pulling on a fresh pair of socks. For penance, I decided to walk, not drive, to Charley's for coffee.

I had her made by the time I eased down the front steps. I liked to think my neighborhood was mixed, but young Black women

invariably came coupled with the area's music or art students. They didn't sit alone reading paperbacks in dirty green Fords. In my town, once a neighborhood was defined it stayed that way. It took a moment of painful stretching at the bottom of the stairs to make certain I was her mark. Despite an effort to cover, she almost licked her lips.

I crossed the street, strolled part way up the block, and walked to the front door of an apartment building. I blocked her view with my body while I jimmied my way inside. When I peeked out the hall window she was staring toward the door I'd entered but didn't move her Taurus. The young lady had a clear view, and what goes in also comes out.

I found the door to the basement, hurried downstairs, and climbed out a rear window looking onto the apartment building's back alley. I walked down the alley until I was behind her car, cut through a side yard, then trotted up the street and yanked the passenger door open.

"What the hell . . ." Her head snapped around, her expression flashing fear and surprise.

"Hello," I said easily. "I thought we might formally introduce ourselves, but first let me catch my breath."

"Catch it somewhere else! This here car is mine." Once she saw who was next to her, the fear ebbed from her face. "Now get the hell out," she demanded.

"Soon." Up close I realized she was not only young, she was beautiful. High cheekbones, Asian eyes, firm lips, and a head full of shiny ringlets. The lady belonged on a stage, not on a stake-out. "I'll leave as soon as you tell me what you're doing here."

"What's it look like?" she said, her large slanted eyes glittering.

"Well, it looked like you were watching me."

"Then it looked wrong. I'm just killing time."

"I don't think so."

"I'm surprised. I didn't know carjacks think at all."

"Carjack?"

"What would you call what you're doing? Unless you're after something different from money."

I resisted imagining the different, then realized I didn't care what she was doing. I even regretted frightening her. Maybe my warmth toward Yakov was spreading to include youth in general. I hoped not.

Since I wasn't going to beat any information out of her, I settled for delivering some. "You're bullshitting, but I'll let it go . . . this time. I don't like looking over my shoulder so stay away from me. I'm betting you're some kind of reporter, but I'm not news. You want information you find someone else to follow. Anyone else."

I climbed out of the car then stuck my head back inside. "And the next time you work a stake keep your doors locked." I stood and slammed the metal hard enough to add to my headache.

I didn't care whether she followed me or not. My spontaneous exercise in futility had upset my stomach. If I didn't get to Charley's soon, I'd die on the damn street.

During my walk I thought about the first time my father-in-law, Lou, tried Phil's cooking. He'd parked his bulk behind one of the signed enamel-top tables and grunted, "I should have figured. An extension of your apartment. What's with you, *boychik*? The thirties and forties do not represent all that was pure about America. I can tell you stories of the war years that would make the government's *chazarai* during Vietnam look like pabulum."

And he could. A longtime wheel in Chicago's Daley machine, Lou once had access to more garbage than Fresh Kills landfill. Still, with all his grumbling about Charley's deco/depression decor, he never left without muttering "good *traif*." No surprise, Phil cooked a mean morning meal.

Which didn't help explain why the place was usually empty. It wasn't as if Phil had no friends. Sometime before the Mayan civilization he'd been a cop, and Charley had been his partner. Phil didn't talk about why they had quit the force and opened the

restaurant. I never asked. Charley was still alive when I ate there during my former life as a social worker. In those days it was a joint where off-duty police and off-duty social workers mingled without sneers. When I finally crawled out of hibernation after Chana and Becky's deaths, Charley was also dead and Phil was doing the cooking. Despite vast improvement in the food and the city's gentrification of the area, business trickled away. Maybe the place was too funky for the new neighborhood residents or the block too fancy for the old regulars.

Phil didn't seem to care. He still had his police friends, they just didn't eat in his place. When I needed information he was one of two. The other was Julius. Between them I had legs on both sides of the law.

I opened the door to the storefront diner and walked in to empty quiet. My belly was queasy enough to make the black and white tile dance underfoot. When I got to the counter I sat on a tall round backless and grasped the heavy sugar bottle with the silvery top. The weight of the glass was reassuring.

"Look at you." A broad grin slashed through Phil's weather-beaten, craggy face. "Hard to say whether you're starting the binge or just finishing?"

I looked at him balefully, "What will you think after I ask you for six aspirin and a pot of black." My earlier four had been neutralized by my skirmish with the lady. "Oh, and maybe turn off the lights and pull the shades."

" 'Cept for the aspirin and coffee it sounds pretty sexy."

Startled, I slowly spun the stool toward the corner booth and Red's throaty purr. There were traces of lipstick on the off-white coffee mug in front of her. It didn't matter; she always wore enough to share. If Charley's was the forties, Red was fifties' costume jewelry. Serious paint, Susan Hayward red, and flattering foundation garments added up to ageless B-girl beauty. From a distance she might have been fifteen or fifty.

"Hard to be sexy when the fireworks are bursting inside your head, sweetie."

"At least somebody has fun in the dark," she pouted.

"Maybe somebody, Red. Not me."

"I didn't hear you complaining last night," Phil grunted to his ladyfriend. "You tied this on during work?" he asked me with amused curiosity.

I spun back around to face him. "Nah, after. At home. Alone." I glanced over my shoulder but Red had gone back to painting her nails over the newspaper.

"Are you working on something that's depressing you?"

The promise I'd made to think about what bothered me flickered, but the anvil in my head interfered. "No," I said with a tight throat. "An error of judgment. Valium and alcohol make for a delicate juggle."

"I wish you wouldn't talk to me about drugs."

"Why not? You haven't been a cop for twenty-five years and you wouldn't bust me if you were. When did you start walking the twelve steps?" I heard the hangover nasties in my voice.

So did Phil. He took a long look at my face then sliced a thick slab off the fresh ham he always kept skewered and slapped it on the grill.

The smell instantly aroused my already upset stomach. "I didn't order that," I protested.

"I know."

"You already had your breakfast," I accused.

"I know that too." He cut another piece then threw it on the grill.

"Maybe you are still on the fucking force, you sadist."

"You put that on for no reason?" Red's voice, no longer a purr, rammed the back of my head.

Phil rubbed his hands on his full length apron and looked over my shoulder. "I got a reason." He turned his eyes back to me. "Damn right I don't do no twelve step. I don't have to. I like a drink. A lot of drinks. But I know the line. You don't. There's never been the morning I couldn't come down here and inhale the smell of burning flesh. You oughta see your face."

My gut rocked and I tried to eliminate the need to breathe. "Hell," Phil said.

His face blurred and beads of sweat popped onto my forehead.

"Hell," he repeated. "I just threw on ham. If the she-devil hadn't been here I'da throwed on roast beef and let you watch the fat sizzle, the blood drip . . ."

I couldn't listen. I jumped off the stool and raced to the bathroom hoping I'd make it on time.

"You son of a bitch," I said when I finally returned. The meat was off the stove and the two of them were in the booth showing off their dental work. I walked over to my seat, lit a cigarette, and poured a cup from the pot of coffee he'd left on the counter.

"The aspirin are on the saucer," Red said.

I nodded but kept my eyes averted. "I don't think I need them," I said sheepishly.

They both burst out laughing and after a moment's embarrassed hesitation, so did I.

CHAPTER 7

Once the laughter died I sat quietly drinking coffee and smoking cigarettes until the rest of my headache shuddered into the background. When my residual embarrassment disappeared I took my cup and joined the merry pranksters in their booth.

"You ready to eat?" Phil asked.

"I think I'll pass," I replied with a weak grin. "I could keep it down but . . ."

They smiled at my false bravado before Red stared at the back of her hands. Phil eyed me carefully. "So what's got you messed up? You were going to lay off working the personals."

He was talking about a couple of cases that had been loaded with relationship entanglements. Both had left me battered and bruised. One also left a bullet in my thigh, an automatic airport alarm trigger.

"This one isn't personal," I said.

"So what gives?" he demanded. "What's the case?"

I'd always felt uncomfortable asking Phil for information, guilty I had nothing to trade but my appetite. Now, for an isolated moment, I had a reassuring glimpse into his side of our equation. "Jeez, Phil, a little eager, aren't you? Your fuzz-buddies stopped talking?"

Something was bothering him but before he spoke Red jumped in. "Believe me shamus, no one stopped talking. They need my Phil's thinking on things. You should of seen this place yesterday."

I turned my head too quickly for Phil to hide his displeasure. "The Rabbi thing," I guessed.

On the button. "Why do you say that?" he asked, as surprise rearranged his face.

"The police don't consult anybody if the stiff ain't white, rich, or a headline."

Phil rubbed his hands across his aproned chest. "I never could understand why you became a cop. Even private. You're almost pinko, you don't like the criminal justice system, and you're more scared of Big Brother than a thief hiding under a parked car."

I lifted my hands. "Communism is dead, cook. Don't you read the papers? And look who's talking paranoid. You're as uneasy about institutions as I am."

"For different reasons," he grumbled.

"For different reasons," I agreed.

After a moment's hesitation I volunteered, "I'm working on the same thing."

"What same thing?" Phil asked.

"The Rabbi case."

He tipped an imaginary cap, but didn't seem overwhelmed. Red glanced up from the newspaper.

"How did you get involved?" he asked.

"Simon Roth is the Rambo Rabbi's lawyer."

Phil looked at Red. "I don't know why anyone comes to see me," he said. "My mind is shot. You can't do no one no good if you can't fucking string two and two." He turned back to me. "They told me about Roth. I should have known that meant you."

I shrugged. He *should* have known. "Who told you about Simon?" I asked.

Phil ignored the question, reached into my cigarettes and helped himself.

Red stiffened. "Goddamnit, you old asshole, maybe your mind *is* shot! Just 'cause you didn't guess Dagwood the Gumshoe was working this Jew thing you gotta be double dumb and light up?" She pushed at his arm. "Let me out of here, will you?"

Phil slid off the booth and pushed at his few remaining white hairs as Red brushed past. He sat back down with a sigh but kept the cigarette. "No one preaches as good as the converted," he said, inhaling as she went through the door leading to their second-floor apartment.

"Why were the Blues here to see you?" I was still stuck on my case. Besides, I didn't like to discuss other people's drug habits.

"A big case makes them want to shoot the shit," he said, slipping around my question. "What's *your* angle?"

I saw no reason to return the slide. "Dirt digging on Kelly and the White Avengers."

Phil grinned. "Always get the good stuff, don't you? Roth likes to make you look up life's heinie."

"It's what I do best," I replied, worried it might be true.

The fucker nodded his agreement. "At least you won't have much to do," he said.

"What does that mean?"

"It means you'll get your information from the newspapers. Nobody from that neighborhood is going to talk to you. Maybe the beards, but I don't know anyone else who will."

I didn't know whether to be insulted by his term for the Hasids or surprised that I noticed. "Why won't people talk?" I asked, avoiding the dilemma. "I've lived in some pretty tight Irish neighborhoods. Hell, I even married green."

"You also divorced her. Nobody's gonna talk for three reasons. One, you're an outsider. Two, you're an outsider. You guess the third."

I tried to shake him off. "Megan divorced me. Look, it might

be hard to get to the gang, but decent people everywhere are disgusted by those kinds of hatemongers."

He nodded his agreement. "More than you'd figure if you only watched TV. Sure, there are people who can't stand the Avengers. But that don't change anything. Nobody is gonna talk to you." He glanced at my face. "Look, the neighborhood has a siege mentality. People living there are deep into Ireland and see themselves, their community, their way of life under attack."

"The Brits live pretty far away."

"Don't be smart, I'm trying to tell you something."

"Sorry, I just don't need another close-mouthed group on my dance card," I said thinking of Reb Yonah.

Phil ignored my remark in his rush to bring me down. "People living there see gentrification as a fancy word for stealing their houses, welfare a way to steal money out of their pockets. Worse, money the fucking government gives to spades."

"Blacks."

"Wait 'til you hear what they call 'em."

"Come on Phil. Aren't you a little rough? So they're white working poor. You're white, you work, and you still talk to me."

"I ain't as poor as I look."

"That's good to hear. Now I know where to come for a loan."

"You got as much chance of getting money from me as information out of them." He grabbed the coffeepot, walked across the restaurant, and let himself in behind the counter.

I chewed on his discouragement, but couldn't digest the vehemence. I ambled over to join him at the counter. "So who should I speak to over there?"

Phil kept his back to me and shook his head.

"You're not gonna leave me hung," I argued. "You must know someone. You *always* know someone."

He turned toward me with a rueful smile. "Tell you the truth, Matt, I prefer to keep quiet this time."

I raised my hands. "I don't get it, Phil. Hell, you don't care

what happens to the Avengers. All I need is a name, somewhere to start. I've got a job to do."

He pulled a tall, rickety, wooden chair over to our corner and sat down. " 'Neither rain nor snow nor sleet.' Is that the way it is? Well, why don't you tell Roth to shove his damn job?"

I stared at him.

He started to talk then shook his head and sat back in his chair, eyes glued to the coffeepot on the counter.

"What's going on?" I demanded. "What did the good old boys tell you?"

He shook his head and tried to meet my eyes, but shooting isn't the same as scoring. "Nobody told me anything," he muttered. "Something stinks with this situation. You might become part of the shit that gets swept away."

It was almost time to let him off my hook. Almost. "Maybe so, Phil. Let's hope the sweepers are looking for bigger turds. I'm doing background checks, that's all. Now come on, give me a name."

He stood up, a disgusted look on his face. "You're a fucking mule."

I faked a move to my wallet. "Okay, no is no. How much?" I asked. Something odd was happening, but Phil had helped me too many times in the past for me to be angry with him now. Hey, the man cooked "great *traif*."

"I don't charge for renting space. The coffee was on the house." He smiled. "So was the meat."

I grinned back. Maybe someday I'd learn what the problem was, but it wasn't going to be today. Today, I'd ferret for myself.

"You want a name? How about Washington Clifford."

My easygoing attitude came crashing down as his whisper broke into my thoughts. "You're shitting me." I took a deep breath and a couple of seconds to collect myself.

Washington Clifford was a heavy-duty Special Forces' cop. The Special Force lived between the cracks of my town's legit-

imate law enforcement. Every city had a similar unit. Every city denied it, and every city lied. I first met ours working on a different case for Simon. Clifford's sadistic, slab-of-beef partner played drums on my body while Clifford watched. Despite his partner's hands and feet, it was Washington Clifford's impassively cruel face that frightened me. For good reason. And Phil knew it.

"You're just kidding, right?" I finally said. "Trying to worry me?"

He stared at me. "You wanted to know what I heard? Now you know."

"Tell me more," I said, hoping there wasn't any.

"I already told you enough." Phil shook his head. "You aren't gonna quit, are you?"

"I can't walk out on Simon. The case is important to him."

Phil shrugged then added, "Hell, I knew nothing was going to stop you." He leaned over the counter. "Drop into Buzz's Tavern on Cathedral. If you tell him I sent you he might put you in touch with some of the fucking Avengers. The assholes enjoy the attention. Just don't go telling anyone you work for Roth."

I started to ask him more about Clifford but he shook his head. "Go away, I told you everything I'm going to." He waited until I had the door open before adding, "Matt, you better watch your back."

I filled the car with smoke as my headache and sick stomach returned. Only now the queasiness wasn't due to last night's overindulgence. I dug through the ashtray, frustrated by my inability to find a roach. I shook the ashes off my hand and lit another cigarette. A couple of rapid inhales left me calm enough to think. It was one thing for Simon to be jumpy about the case; his reputation within his newfound community was up for grabs. It was, however, difficult to dismiss Phil's warnings.

I leaned back onto the headrest and closed my eyes. The nicotine had softened Clifford's features in my mind, but I'd need

something stronger than Kools to remove the threat from the tough, pleasureless grin that seemed perpetually carved in his Black, granite face.

I opened my eyes in time to watch ashes fall onto my lap. Clifford's look meant exactly what it said and the possibility I'd see it again, up close and personal, worried me. I stuffed the dead butt into the overcrowded ashtray and lit another. Calmer didn't mean calm.

I leaned forward, started the car, and considered the alternatives. I could sleepwalk through the case. Like the kid who dumps leaflets in the sewer instead of delivering them. Only I was a long haul from kidland. I could take Phil's advice, drive to Simon's, and give back the job. But I didn't want to do that either. And it wasn't just loyalty. If I did let him down, friendship or no, I'd spend a lot more time around the buildings. Or worse.

I aimed the car toward the general vicinity of Cathedral. Since I wasn't going home and I wasn't quitting, I might as well visit Buzz's bar.

CHAPTER 8

A wide and open boulevard littered with garbage, Cathedral Avenue looked like yesterday's unrefrigerated Chinese takeout. It took a couple of passes before I located the dark tavern near the corner of Cathedral and Fifth. The "B" was missing from its darkened neon and the place appeared closed. Actually, the whole area looked as if it still hadn't recovered from a party the night before. Very few cars rushed down either side, the only pedestrians two old bottle hunters rolling overloaded shopping carts. We weren't talking the lush life here.

I continued driving slowly appearing, I hoped, lost but actually looking for Washington Clifford or his men. Two blocks away I spotted police. It wasn't a Lew Archer; two Blues in a parked patrol car make for an easy see.

So easy I knew they weren't Clifford's. Washington Clifford and his people were shadow men. I drove for another block but couldn't make anyone else, though my neck hairs were saluting. I looked around for another couple of minutes, still saw no one, and finally assigned my feeling to the encounter with the girl in front of my house. Still, I searched for a place to park away from the bar and out of sight of the cops.

I aimed toward a commercial lot but was rewarded for my dili-

gence with a metered space. Unwilling to thumb my nose at the ladies in uniform, I left my always handy windshield note claiming mechanical malfunction, then circumvented the Blues on my way back to the tavern. If they were going to get another look at me, they'd have to get out of their cars. Something I doubted since it was cold outside.

Despite the broken sign and gloomy entrance, Buzz's heavy, age-streaked oak door opened just fine. Though it took a moment for the silence to extend through the smoke-filled room, by the time my eyes adjusted to the gray light the few scattered customers had garroted their conversations. Lowered heads and hooded eyes snuck peeks as I walked to the large oval bar. I kept my breathing shallow as a defense against the smell of beer, perspiration, and ammonia floor cleaner. The tavern was almost as inviting as the cold, trash-strewn street.

I sat down, stared at the cigarette-scorched, sweat-darkened Formica, and listened to the conversations resume. I'd almost set a fire in the ashtray before the tall skinny bartender nodded. Unfortunately, acknowledgment was different from response, so I sat smoking another cigarette until he left his conversation at the far turn of the large circle.

"Double Daniel's. I had trouble finding your place," I said hoping he was Buzz. "The sign out front is pretty small and your 'B' is missing."

"I don't see no reason to make the electric company rich. Anyone who comes here has usually been in before," he answered. "Ain't gonna find any Jack in those," he added pointing his thumb back over his shoulder toward a tier of Jack Daniel's bottles on the shelf behind the bar.

"Just give me the best you've got." I grinned and added, "I was raised in a ginmill so thanks for the professional courtesy."

He grunted, walked away, and returned with my double. "We don't get many strangers in here and you don't sound lost," he said leaning over the Formica. "You don't look like one of those glitz reporters," he added.

I'd short-sheeted my brain and had rushed in without a damn cover story. Mr. Spontaneity had no choice but to use the bone that was thrown. And use it carefully, since I didn't imagine the bartender was alone in his opinion of the press. "Well, I am a writer, but I don't run with the pack. I'm not hot for *pigfucks*. Everyone hoping they ain't holding their nose when someone important farts." I shook my head. "You getting a lot of them in here?"

Before the bartender answered, an old man with a shock of white-blond hair spoke up. He sat a couple of stools downwind, hunching over an empty shot glass and a pint of Guinness. "A few of 'em wandered in right after the shootings but I haven't seen no one since. You work for the newspaper?" he asked.

"No way, Pop," I said. "Can't wrap fish in what I do. I'm a slick paper free-lance. National magazines. You run with the dailies you won't get anyone's name straight. When I do a story I do it right."

The full head of Warhol white turned toward me bringing a pockmarked face. "You're telling the truth there, goddamnit. The papers always got something screwed up. The television is friggin' lucky if they get the right name."

I nodded my agreement. "What's the matter with you, old-timer? You've lived long enough to know better than to read."

"Some habits are tough to break, sonny." He grinned and ducked his head back into the Stout.

I tilted my shot glass toward the bartender and nodded toward the old guy.

"What are you doing here?" asked the bartender after he served the old man his drink.

"I'm looking for Buzz," I said quietly, making certain I couldn't be overheard.

"You found him," he answered, matching my tone.

"Phil from Charley's told me to look you up. I want to do a story on the Avengers. From their perspective. I was hoping you could get me an intro," I pitched. "I don't think the Avengers

will get a fair shake with the regular media. I want an angle that's different from the beat reporters. I'm less interested in the shootings than I am in what the Avengers are really about."

I backed off the sell, ordered a Sam Adams, another Guinness for the old man, and told Buzz to buy something for himself. Before he left to fill the order, he spent a long moment looking me over then asked, "Where did you say you got my name?"

"From Phil. The guy who owns Charley's. He said you might help."

Buzz grunted his reply and walked away. Before returning he served a Budweiser to the man he'd been talking to when I'd arrived. When Buzz finally made it back with my drink, the guy tagged along as a chaser. He wore copper color wide-wale cords, a pale blue workshirt and an old, dungaree jacket. He looked in his thirties, medium build, and when he spoke I saw two gold incisors.

"Buzz says you're with the press," he said sitting down next to me.

"Not the regular media. I free-lance for national magazines."

"Which magazines?" the sandy-haired man demanded.

"Depends. First I get the story, then I pick the glossy I think will bite." I tried to remember the magazine where I'd seen the picture of the guerrilla fighter holding a human thigh bone, but Fang didn't push. Just as well; any magazine that ran Benetton ads wasn't going to help.

"These magazines pay you?"

I caught a glimpse of the old man lifting his head out of the Guinness. "Fuck, yes, they pay me. Damn good too," I said, emphatically. Matt Jacob — the Norman Mailer of a new generation. Then I caught my reflection in the mirror behind the glass shelving; better make that Hunter Thompson.

Fang slid off the stool and pointed to a booth at the back of the room. I shrugged, grabbed my beer and cigarettes, and followed. Before I wedged into my side, I motioned for another

round. My companion waited silently but grimaced gold when I lit up.

"You don't smoke?" I asked, genuinely surprised.

"We need to stay healthy."

"We?"

He stared hard as he leaned forward. "People who care about this country."

"You're not talking President's Council on Physical Fitness, are you?"

A glare of disgust followed his look of confusion. "You were joking," he finally guessed.

"It's my way, sorry."

"Well, this is fucking serious business. There's not much time left to read the funnies. You know what I'm saying?"

"If you mean that the country has gone to hell-in-a-handbasket, sure, sure I know what you're saying."

He nodded grimly. "That's exactly what I'm saying."

I chipped at the bonhomie. "So you quit smoking because the country sucks. But what's that got to do with me?"

"This country don't suck, Mister, the people who control it suck."

"You're talking about . . . ?" I asked with a friendly look.

He tilted his head to the side as if listening to a voice in his ear. Maybe he was. The voice in *my* ear was cursing for not having brought something to help me look like a fucking writer.

"Well, basically it's the Wall Street Jews." He stopped, unsure of what came next. Finally he shook his head and said, "Look. Here's the deal. I know people who want to get their story out but they've been burned so much they don't like talking to reporters."

"I'm a writer, not a reporter. Anyway, I read some stuff about Kelly. Where did it come from?" I asked.

He waved his hand. "No, no, I don't mean that. We can talk to anyone we want about Sean."

He leaned forward, dug his eyes into my face, and bared his gold. "Sean Kelly was a fucking patriot. He was a fucking genius. He understood exactly how the shit here goes down. This goddamn bearded Horn offed a true American hero. They did him just like they did Jesus. The Horns, the fucking 'liberals' with their horn-rimmed blinders on, they find a way to kill everyone who can make a difference. Sean was someone who understood things and wasn't afraid to stand up for them. You know what I mean?"

He kept his eyes on my face while I nodded my agreement. I knew exactly what Fang meant. Kelly was a manly man. A rabid, down-home, shit-kicking, beer-guzzling bigot of a man. "What's your name?" I asked fighting off the resurgence of my headache.

"Joe. What's yours?"

"Matt."

"Nice to meet you," he said.

I tried to force the action. "I understand what you're talking about, might even agree with some of it, but I still don't know why I'm talking to you. Me and the old guy were just getting acquainted."

"Fuck Pops." Joe narrowed his eyes and smirked. "You're talking to me because I can get you what you're looking for and the old man can't."

"What's that?"

"I told you, access to the top of the Avengers."

Time to pull down my skirt, play a little hard to get. "What do you take me for?" I demanded. "I'm supposed to believe you're holding the hot ticket?"

He frowned, then looked sly. "Buzz said you *might* be all right. I don't make those decisions, but I can get you to the guy who does, okay?" Joe looked proud of himself. "I can get you to someone who can tell you about the White Avengers. You can get plenty about Kelly, plus the important stuff. The shit we believe in."

"It must be my lucky day." I waved my hand dismissively. "Who is this 'we' you keep talking about? Who are those other

people? If you're connected to the Avengers, why don't you talk to me?"

He sat back on his bench. "You're pretty suspicious for someone who wants something." A sudden look of annoyance crossed his face. "I told you it ain't up to me to do the talking, especially now. But the Avengers want to educate the public. Let them know how the Horns control the fucking muds and run the government."

"Muds?"

He shook his head with exasperation. "Darkies, spics, yellows, you name it. You're a fucking reporter and you don't even know who the mud is! This is why we got to get the information out. The way the fucking country is going we don't have a lot of time." Joe's voice reeked with arrogance, topping an undercurrent of desperation. I'd found another true believer and needed a moment to dig out from his rabid prejudice.

"Writer, not reporter."

"Big fucking difference," he replied. "Anyway, we're on the lookout to see if any of you assholes will give us a fair shake."

"You really know how to grab a guy's sympathy, don't you?" I was sick of his vibes and tired of being labeled an asshole.

"What do you mean?" he asked.

It was time to close or walk so I mentally held my nose. "I mean you don't get fair treatment, do you? That's the one thing I got to give."

He snorted. "No shit, we don't get fair. Everything's slanted. Always making us out to be nuts. Only we ain't crazy. Ain't even close. Shit, we might be the only sane ones left.

"I'm telling you, I can put you next to the man who will make sense out of everything." He paused to look around. "The folks here," he waved his arm, "not just inside the bar, but the whole neighborhood, they *know* we're not crazy. Even them that don't agree."

"It'd piss me off too," I prompted. "Selling newspapers by calling you 'sickos.' "

"That's why we got to be careful."

I shrugged. "Me too."

"How much do you get for an article if you sell it?" Joe asked in a sudden jump.

"Somewhere between five and seven big ones," I made up.

He whistled appreciatively and pushed himself to his feet. "Well, wait here for a couple minutes while I get them. If they like you, we might have a proposition."

"Thanks, but I find my own women."

He started to answer but caught on. "Oh, another joke," he said.

I nodded.

"Well, wait here, anyway."

"Why not," I agreed, pushing away my growing revulsion and sudden apprehension.

CHAPTER 9

I addressed an immediate con-
cern as soon as Buzz's heavy door closed behind Joe's wiry
frame. Actually, I undressed it. I went to the john and stuffed
the bills from my wallet into my pocket. Then I unhitched my
pants. I was lucky. Today was a Jockey day. A pair with elastic
strong enough to vaguely hold its shape after adding the wallet.
I walked back to my booth feeling like a catcher wearing a
square cup, but it wasn't a day to be caught with accurate identification.

The crowd had thickened along with the gray, stale air. As the
suddenly busy waitress delivered another Sam Adams the front
door opened and I sensed it was Avenger time. I didn't see anyone until the crowd of people standing by the entrance scattered
and the atmosphere through the boisterous neighborhood tavern intensified.

I hadn't been able to see him because he wasn't very tall.
About five nine, a pugnacious face with slicked back hair, barrel
chest, barrel belly, he strode pigeon-toed from acquaintance to
acquaintance with Fang trailing behind. The man knew a lot of
people and was intent on visiting all of them. He didn't exactly
shove those in his way, just jostled past. Despite the safety of my

booth he had already jostled me; I was annoyed by the long wait and his lousy manners.

Fang and friend arrived just before my patience left. But their presence did nothing to reduce my irritation. The friend sprawled onto a chair by the booth, clipped a smoke from my pack, and drank half my untouched beer. Fang stood quietly at the end of my bench. I lit a cigarette and waited. Impatiently.

Dale Carnegie stretched a beefy leg onto another chair and draped an arm over the back. "You don't look like no writer. You do time?"

He didn't want to hear about SDS and I didn't want to tell him about the deal Simon cooked that got me out of real time and into therapy. "A couple of close encounters and a few overnights. Why? Do I look rough?"

"Not rough." He glanced out the side of his eyes. "Roughed up. You better not be a fucking cop," he said ominously, swinging his foot off the chair and turning to face me.

"I told Joe what I did. He get confused between then and now?"

"You have papers?" he asked.

"Are you crazy? Bring my wallet *here*? No thanks. Too much trouble replacing everything if it got swiped."

"No fucking credit card?"

"I'm an artist, a white man without plastic."

He grunted, looked up at his disciple, then tilted the side of his head toward the ceiling. "Go with Joe to the men's room. He isn't gonna do nothing but shake you down. I just don't want him to do it out here."

I studied the grease he used to Pat Riley his hair. Finally I nodded and stood. I slouched a little more than usual on my way to the bathroom where Joe hurried a customer, then swung the metal door hook.

As he turned to me I growled menacingly, "I keep my money in my left pocket. Don't mess with it and don't go near my johnson or I'll go fucking ballistic."

"Don't worry," he said as he ran his hands lightly and ineffec-
tually over my body. "I hate faggots worse than anybody."

He finished with my pants cuffs and stood up from his kneeling position. "Empty your pockets," he demanded.

I shrugged, shook my head, and pulled out my money and
keys. "You want me to pay for this crap?"

He looked at me blankly.

"Another joke," I frowned, shoved the money back into my
pocket, and unlocked the door. The inside of my nose was beginning to cake with urinal disinfectant and the smell of Fang's
anxiety.

By the time we returned to the table my beer was gone and
the bigshot had helped himself to more of my nicotine. "I don't
suppose you ordered me another drink?" I asked sarcastically.

"Yeah. Yeah, I did. Bass for both of us. Told 'em to put it on
your tab." He crushed out his cigarette in the cheap tin ashtray
and immediately helped himself to another.

"What about something for me?" Joe asked plaintively. His
earlier swagger was ankle high around the moocher. Even his
teeth looked less forbidding. Maybe because I could have easily
removed them in the bathroom.

"I want to talk to *writer* here in private. Why don't you wait at
the bar." It wasn't a request.

"But I want a drink," Joe protested.

"Then order a fucking drink. He has money on him, doesn't
he?"

Joe held his thumb and forefinger about a quarter inch apart.

"Put 'em on his tab."

I waited until Joe left and the drinks arrived before asking, "I
guess you don't belong to the health wing of your organization?"

He looked puzzled until he saw me staring at his cigarette.
"Oh, you mean this. Yeah, well it's probably a good idea to quit."

"Almost as good as running up my bill, right? I don't remember inviting you or *him*" — I gestured toward Fang — "to drink
on my dime."

He looked at me and shook his head. "You're a big tired-looking guy with no identification who says he's a writer. You want something, you pay for it." But some of the bigshot was gone from his voice.

I played his change of tone by gathering my stuff on the table. "Fuck this. I squash my butt for a couple hours to be frisked in a smelly head by someone with low budget Hollywood teeth. Now Mr. Big tells me I'm not done paying. To hell with this."

He put his hand on top of mine. It wasn't a caress. He was fat but there was muscle under the blubber. "Sit still, *writer*. You came here to get our story. Nothing comes free."

"So far 'nothing' is exactly what I've paid for."

"You have a tongue for a guy in the middle of a situation."

I stood. "I'm not impressed with the 'situation.' I can drink cheaper with people I know."

"You can drink anywhere," he agreed, "but you can't talk to the Avengers nowhere else."

"If you're an Avenger and you call this talking, it doesn't matter where I drink."

"I didn't want to bring my wallet in here, either," he mocked.

"If that's what's making you weird, say so." I sat back down.

He stopped the sparring, offering me a cigarette from my pack. "Look, I gotta be careful. The Avengers are taking a lot of heat right now from people who think we're off the wall. Everyone keeps forgetting that we lost our main man. The Avengers don't count. Only the Horns matter."

His lips curled. "No fucking surprise. They own the newspapers, the television, the movies. It's like Sean wasn't a human being. Like we're not human." He looked me over. "Then you come in here and I'm supposed to believe you ain't exactly like the rest? Trying to get information, then screwing us?"

It was too soon to plunge in with questions about the murder. He would just become more suspicious. Instead, I shook my head, "Don't give me that. Joe picked me out. He made it sound like you were looking to talk. If he was full of shit, say so."

"We're looking," he admitted. "I'm sitting here because . . ."

"I'm springing for drinks and smokes," I finished.

He didn't smile. In fact, he looked at me sharply. "You want to hear what I got to offer, or you want to make jokes?"

I shrugged.

"I'm trying to tell you that we might be willing to talk."

"So talk."

He scrunched up his porcine face. "Not now."

I rolled my eyes.

"Don't be an ass," he hissed, his hand curling into a fist. "This is too serious for you to keep fucking around. The goddamn country is over the edge and someone who knew what to do about it got nailed by a goddamn gun-carrying kike. No more fucking jokes!" Despite his vehemence, Mr. Burly was just not as confident without his buddy nearby.

I nodded. "Okay. No jokes, but no more games. I want the whole ten yards. On you, on Kelly, on the Avengers. On everything that happened."

I forced myself to continue, "I want to know what the Avengers believe in. If you're just another sneaker-stealing street gang, I'm not interested. If you're working for a chop-shop, I'm not interested. But, if you are political, if you believe in something and have the *cojones* to back those convictions, then I'm interested. No party lines, no fake bullshit. I'm looking for reality here. I got a built-in crap detector and if it beeps, I roller-derby out the door. *After* I get my money back."

He worked his way through my words. I drained the last of my beer, lit another cigarette, and waited patiently. I was satisfied with my lying riff.

And so was he. "Tonight," he said softly. "That's when you'll find out who we are. Then, you tell me whether we step up to our beliefs, whether we got balls." He lifted his arm, waved, and pointed at my head. It was time for me to pay.

"What's the matter with right now?" I asked. "And what's your name?"

"The name is Blue."

"Blue?"

He waved his hand for an answer. "What's yours?" he asked.

"Matt."

"Matt I knew. Matt what?"

I hesitated then rushed on. It wouldn't please him to know I struggled to find a usable. "McMurphy."

"You're a mick?" he asked, confused.

"My old man. But he disappeared when I was young. My mother was Italian and I look like a Jew. What can I tell you?"

He looked disgusted. "Bad enough to look like a kike if you're born one." Blue stood, reached back down to my cigarettes, and pulled out a handful.

"Sealing the deal?" I asked.

He raised his eyebrows, daring me to complain. "That's right, sealing the deal." He shoved the bounty into his pocket and lit another. "Tonight about one-thirty. Here. After the place closes. If it's locked, bang on the door and someone will let you in. And don't forget your papers."

"You don't trust me," I smiled.

"I don't trust anyone." He looked down at me and emphasized, "Bring the fucking papers."

He shook his head, turned, and walked away. The number of people in the place had swelled since our conversation began. The smell of workday perfume and aftershave lotion merged with the overhead blanket of smoke and the blare of multiple conversations. People were trying hard to distance themselves from their previous eight hours. Some with forced gaiety, others with anxiety-ridden relief. Blue barged into both as he pushed his way through.

I was so relieved when the overworked, tired waitress brought me the check, I didn't bother to get mad at the amount.

The fading late afternoon sun came as a shock after the lifetime I'd spent inside the bleak tavern. I rushed toward my car hungry

for a hot shower; my skin felt smarmy, coated with Joe and
Blue's hostility and hate.

I also had to speak to Simon. It was short notice, but he'd
have to pony up the phony ID. I wasn't coming back without be-
lievable plastic. When I got to the car I was pleased that my note
had staunched any flow of red. No new citations for my collection, no Denver boot. I had the door open and a foot in the air
when a tiny hand grabbed my shoulder. It startled me and I
quickly swung around bumping into the young Black lady I'd
met in front of my building.

"Sorry," I said. "You surprised me."

She had retreated a step after the bump and stood watching me.

"Another coincidence?" I asked.

"You know better." Despite her tired eyes, wrinkled black
pants suit, and general disheveled appearance, she looked even
younger than before. Playing detective for a day hadn't diminished her beauty, though. Her only jewelry, too small round silver hoops in her left ear. I leaned my head to the side looking
for right ear options.

"What are you staring at?" she asked.

"I wanted to see if your right ear was pierced."

A look of disgust crossed her face. "Is that a jungle joke?"

Her question caught me by surprise. For a knee-jerk moment
I questioned my curiosity, then shook my head. "No, I was ap-
preciating your style."

A bright white smile crossed her tired face. "Appreciate it
enough to talk with me?"

I should have been right back at her for following me. "I'm on
my way out so make it quick, okay?"

She dropped her smile and nodded her head. "I'll keep it simple. What are you doing here and what did you learn about the
Avengers?" The smile reappeared. "Quick enough for you?"

"It's direct, I'll give you that."

She looked down the street then said, "Can we sit in your car?
I don't feel comfortable standing outside like this."

Neither did I. I wasn't thrilled about the car, but we couldn't duck into a local pub for a drink. "Yeah, only you can't stay long. I told you, I'm on my way out."

I unlocked her door then climbed in on the driver's side. When I lit a cigarette and opened the ashtray, I saw her look at the overflow of discarded smokes.

"You like keeping your lungs warm, don't you?" she asked.

"And nitrites. Gotta have my nitrites. Now you know everything about me."

She grinned but shook her head. "No, sir. All I really know is that you met with a couple Avengers. I want to know what you found out. You looked pretty dangerous when you walked out of that joint."

"Dangerous? I'm held captive in my own car by a young woman without a gun, and I'm dangerous?"

"I said *looked* dangerous, and then only for a few minutes. My name is Cheryl Hampton. I'm a writer. I'm following the Horowitz/Kelly killings. And I'm not that young. I'm almost twenty-one."

"Believe me, from my perspective that's young. Who is Horowitz?"

"Who *was* Horowitz. The Rabbi who was shot." She stopped and looked at me with disdain. "Don't pretend you don't know who I'm talking about."

"Just forgot his last name. Everybody keeps referring to him as Reb Dov. Who do you write for?"

"I free-lance and have a desk at the *Record.*"

The *Roxbury Record* was a Black-owned community newspaper. "You're a little far from home, aren't you? The *Record's* circulation isn't too big in this part of town."

"I told you, I free-lance. I'm not just interested in neighborhood stories. And I knew you work for Simon Roth before you told me. That's why I've been following you."

I looked at her young, hopeful face. "You're not going to win

a prize traipsing after me, girl," I said harshly. "There's no story here."

Her eyes glittered with determination. "I don't care about prizes. That's not what I'm about. This story concerns what happens when hate is left to fester and grow. Folks have to see how deep it runs so they can change their attitudes. Someone has to hold this underbelly up to the light. Everybody, Black and White, Irish and Jew, needs to learn from this. Otherwise we'll all end up down the toilet."

Her spirit left me feeling old and tired. Too old to share her hopefulness, too tired to deflate it. Which made it time to go. "I appreciate the sentiment, but what's it got to do with me?"

"No one is releasing information and most reporters are just willing to wait. I have more at stake than they do. I want to stop this kind of hatred. To do that you have to drag it out of the night. In whatever neighborhood it shows its face. The more information you give me, the better able I'll be to do my job."

I leaned my head onto the steering wheel. "You've pegged me just about as good as you worked the stake-out. I put down my banners a long time ago. I work for money, not love. I don't care about getting any kind of story out. If I had my way I wouldn't be on this case at all, but Simon Roth is my boss and my friend. I'm willing to do him a favor, but that's as far as my generosity or my idealism goes. Sorry if I disappoint you."

My words did what I intended; she prepared to leave. Only now I wasn't sure I wanted her to go.

Cheryl nodded her head while she opened the door. "You don't disappoint me, you're just full of shit."

Before I could offer to drive her back to her car, Cheryl's silhouette disappeared into the rapidly encroaching darkness. A feeling of protectiveness swept through me and I almost jumped out after her. Almost. Instead, I lit another cigarette and fought the inexplicable anxiety her departure had left behind.

CHAPTER 10

"**M**cMurphy? For Christ's sake, Matt McMurphy. Damn, you are a trip. Why not Kerouac? Or maybe Matt Cassidy?" Simon's amusement wafted clearly through the telephone. Yea, fiberoptics.

"Well, I didn't expect to reach them so quickly. But listening to their rap made me feel like I was sitting in an asylum. Anyway, Al Ginsberg wouldn't fly with this crowd. I can't go back without identification, friend."

"No problem. I'll get you something good. Contributing Editor blah, blah, blah. Hang on to it in case you ever decide to switch professions."

"I need it by tonight."

"That's the second time you told me. Do they scare you?"

I stopped to think. "Not really. They look like bruisers but they're too stupid to scare me."

"Good. I don't have to worry."

"I always try to make things easy for you, Simon. What time should I come by?"

"Just sit tight. I'll send a messenger." He paused, then added, "Unless, of course, you feel a need to fly the nest, *McMurphy*."

After replacing the receiver, I remembered another question. I lifted the phone back to my ear and dialed his office. The line

was busy so I moved on to the subshop. A steak, onion, and cheese later I was back inside my apartment with the prospect of a long, dull wait. I tried Simon's office again, but this time there was no answer.

I gathered a couple of newspapers and leafed through, surprised to find little mention of the shootings. I flashed on Cheryl's intense desire to pursue the story and felt sheepish about the way I ran her off. Now that I was alone, her youthful optimism struck me as a refreshing relief after the hate I'd listened to. Leave it to me to chase away something I might have enjoyed.

My perversity annoyed me and I didn't want to hang around the house and dwell on it. I had plenty of time before Simon sent the plastic, so I rolled a joint and jumped into my car for an aimless ride around town.

My former shrink Gloria would have questioned my aimlessness. And rightly so since I found myself touring past the Yeshiva. I didn't intend to go back into the building until the following week, but told myself it would be nice to run into the kid. Maybe I wanted to make amends for my behavior with Cheryl. I drove by the Yeshiva twice, and Reb Yonah's house once before giving up. But while I was driving I noticed an empty basketball court, guessed it was the one Yakov had mentioned, and parked within easy sight.

I lit the joint, smoked, and let myself evening-dream. I imagined a group of kids, some Hasids, some not, playing ball, enjoying themselves. I let myself drift more deeply and saw a Rainbow team fastbreak the hell out of a bigot five. I was the coach of the Rainbows, urging them on to victory. I would see to it that nobody got hurt.

Sometimes fantasy is the only place where the good guys win. Yakov, though not on the court, kept darting in and out of my consciousness. Eventually my pleasure faded and anxiety grabbed the reins. I'd done enough shrink time to uncover the source, but I didn't want to. Instead, I started the car and

quickly pulled away from the curb. This wasn't the time to allow my imagination to run unchecked. I wasn't frightened of my late night soirée with the Avengers, but there was no need to meet them all fucked up. And I wasn't talking dope.

The banging on my office door woke me from an uneasy nap. I looked at the clock, wondered who would want me at eleven, then remembered the messenger. I pulled myself off the couch and rushed to the door.

Simon stood in the alley wearing a dug-in-for-the-duration look. A definite harbinger of his mood.

"Where the hell were you?"

"I was sleeping," I said, nodding him into the apartment. "I go to work later, remember?"

"I tried calling you earlier and there was no answer. It worried me."

"Your worry is losing its charm, Simon. I don't need bed checks." We gravitated to the kitchen and sat around my enamel-top table after I put up some coffee.

"I didn't come to harass you, Matt."

"Then what are you doing here?"

"I had trouble getting the identification."

I lifted my hands. "No ticket, no work."

He shook his head impatiently. "Don't get your hopes up. It was difficult, but I got it." He handed me a couple of plastic cards. I looked at them as he added, "You're supposed to be a free-lance so I got you a couple. Both of them are good."

That they were. I looked up. "You never have trouble with things like this."

His fingers drummed the table. "It's this damn case. I'm getting pushed from the center. Out of the loop. All my usual contacts are polite and friendly, but no one comes across." He shook his head. "I knew the situation was complicated. Hell, every Jewish organization across the globe is watching, but I can't get anything to *move*."

"Why not?"

"The State won't charge, but won't say they won't either."

"Still worried things might blow up?"

He shrugged dismally. "That doesn't explain the extent of the shutdown. I've been cut off."

I thought back to my breakfast at Charley's. It seemed like a long time ago. "This morning Phil implied that Washington Clifford might be involved."

Simon lifted his head. "Washington Clifford? What else did Phil suggest?"

"That I give back the job."

"Thank you, Phil."

I smiled. "Don't take it personal. He also told me where to make contact with the Avengers."

"What did he say about Washington Clifford?"

"Nothing." I couldn't resist. "Why don't you call Clifford up? You were friends."

Simon grimaced. "You'll never let go. I've never been friends with Washington Clifford. We used each other, that's all. Once. Just once."

"It was a helluva use, Simon. Hard to forget."

His face suddenly turned sour. "Don't lecture me. I've lived with it, not you. You were the good guy, remember? If you can't let go, just clam up about it. If Phil told you something about Clifford I want to know what it is!"

I stood up to fix our coffee. Mine black, his with sugar and cream. I opened the refrigerator and peered inside. His with sugar.

I returned to the table. "Phil didn't say anything more than I told you."

Simon slapped the air dismissively. "Phil's dreaming. This isn't something Clifford would be involved with." He raised his fist. "You have to bleed these bastards tonight, Matt! Every last drop! I want a case that no one can break."

I drained my cup and poured another. "Simon, the fix isn't in for the Avengers."

"I won't chance it."

"You're paranoid. I've met with a couple of Avengers, remember? You might have to keep an eye on them because they are mean and violent, but they aren't much use to anyone."

"The Nazis used plenty of people like the Avengers."

"Simon, please. Does joining a Temple mean you have to lose the rest of your common sense?"

"Since when do you trust the criminal justice system?"

"I'm not talking trust." I waved my hand. "I don't want to get into this with you. There will be enough dirt to make chopped liver out of 'em."

Which reminded me of my question. "Speaking of chopped liver, who are the Never Agains? Or what is it?"

For a brief moment the subject switch left him behind. Then Simon's face darkened. "The Never Agains. A worldwide Hasidic self-defense organization. They started about thirty years ago in a Jewish and Black section of Brooklyn. Protection against the high number of muggings that were taking place. They were racists then, and worse now. Vigilantes, pure and simple, only now they are international. People say they have been involved with terrorist activities against Arab consulates. They also have their own 'Nazi Watch.' The Never Agains don't get much respect throughout the wider Jewish community. Except, maybe from racist fanatics." Simon stopped and shook his head disgustedly. "As much as I despise anti-Semitism, the Never Agains make me really sick."

"I guess the Big Guy's death helps with recruitment."

Simon smiled. "The 'Big Guy,' huh?"

I grinned back. "It's hard work keeping all these Rabbis separate. They all look alike, you know."

"I hope you're still staying clear of the Yeshiva. I don't think Reb Yonah believes you'll turn Hasid."

"Well, he's got something right, anyhow."

Simon glanced at the kitchen clock and asked, "Everything in this apartment is thirties and forties so what the hell are you doing with a black cat clock?"

I shrugged. "I'm not as consistent as you, my friend."

He moved toward the office. "I have to get home. I should never have downed that shit you call coffee. I need sleep something fierce."

"So you don't want me calling until morning?"

"No," he said as he waved goodbye, "I don't want you to call at all. I'll call you."

The rest of the wait went quickly. I considered bringing my gun as part of my free-lance apparel then decided not. The Avengers were tough and no doubt mean, but I couldn't forget how vulnerable Joe had left himself in Buzz's john. I settled on a pen and small notebook.

I went for my stash and took inventory. It wasn't a complicated decision. If something unexpected went down, I wanted to be up for it. And the only up in the gymbag was inside the vial I'd snatched from Simon. Rather than use the built-in snorter I opened the bottle, poured some coke onto the back of my hand, and nosed it down. Another toot, a little more coffee, and a fair amount of nicotine put me in a fine mood to boogie.

The night had turned October cold and windy. I was glad I'd worn my leather. Collar up not only kept me warm, the look reflected my fantasy of a literary stud journalist. I just couldn't shake my man Norm.

This time around I cruised the neighborhood at a faster clip. Though I agreed with Simon's assessment of Washington Clifford's involvement, I still felt "watched" and couldn't put his mean face completely out of mind. But the area was deserted except for cats pawing through garbage.

When I arrived at the front door the tavern was still unlocked. For a moment it was a relief; the outside was so chilly and miserable that any port in a storm . . . Once I got deeper inside the dank, smelly joint, I knew the aphorism was a lie.

Buzz stood over a sink behind the bar, carefully washing a long line of glasses. He looked up when I entered and asked,

"Mind locking the door? Just twist the bolt. I don't want anyone accusing me of serving after hours. I pay off too much as it is. What'll you have?"

I locked the door, then turned. "Same as my original. Bourbon straight, no beer."

Buzz turned to make my drink, picked up a glass placed by itself on an upper shelf, turned to me, and said, "Shit, I almost forgot." He held the glass out in front of his body and let it fall to the floor where it shattered. "Had us a jig here."

I knew what he'd had because I'd seen it too many times before. A Black or Hispanic wanders into the wrong bar and drinks despite the bad vibes. As soon as they finish and leave, the glass is broken. In full sight of everyone else. But I'd never heard of a bartender forgetting, or saving it for later. Unless, of course, Buzz was sending me a message.

CHAPTER 11

I didn't have a chance to ask. "Take it with you," Buzz said handing me a generous double. "Through the door and downstairs. They're waiting in the cooler."

"The cooler?" I asked.

He tilted his head toward the back of the bar. "Nothing to worry about as long as the red light over the door is blinking," he said. I nodded, sipped the bourbon, and slid off the stool.

It didn't take long to juice my anxiety once I walked downstairs and pulled on the stainless steel bar that opened the refrigerator door. Six or seven guys stood in front of the cases and kegs that lined the walls. Even with the blinking red light and body heat, the medium-sized room was tight and uncomfortable, retaining its chill. The only thing missing was a slab of dead cow hanging from the ceiling. I pulled my leather tight around my body. And regretted not bringing my gun.

The Avengers wore long-sleeved khaki shirts and khaki pants. A cliché, but a cliché that *wasn't* on television and *was* armed with saps. Blue sat alone at a cheap card table in the middle of the room. He was dressed differently from his crew, wearing jeans and a sweater. His billy club lay on the table in front of him. I gently placed my drink next to it. For a second I ques-

tioned my decision to coke up, but knew if it came to using my
fists, forenosed was forearmed.

At a nod from Blue, three of the khakis moved in and roughly
frisked me, pulling my pen, identification, and notebook from
my jacket's pockets, tossing them down next to the bourbon.

"Where's your tape recorder?" Blue growled.

"I don't use them." I let my mind race. "Makes people uptight.
I'd rather take notes." I looked around the icebox. "No place to
plug it in, anyway."

Blue shrugged and pointed to the seat across from his.

I nodded and sat down.

Blue looked up over my head and I felt a couple of his boys
gather behind me. I resisted the desire to turn around, instead
found and held Blue's eyes. "What's going on here?" I demanded.

"We have a couple of questions, but first I want to look at
this." He lifted the plastic identification very close to his eyes. "It
looks real," he grudgingly said to his friends.

"Of course it's fucking real," I said, grabbing it from his hand
in a feigned motion of anger. "All you had to do was ask me to
show it to you — instead I get cop-house treatment! I'm fucking
out of here."

I started to stand, felt a hand clamp down on my shoulder,
and let myself be pushed back into my seat.

"I said a couple of questions," Blue commanded.

"Ask."

"What were you doing with the spear-chucker?"

Buzz *had* saved the glass for me.

"She's a writer, I'm a writer. She sees me coming out of the
bar, bang, wants to know what I'm doing. This is what you got
shoved up your ass?"

Blue stuck his face a couple of inches from mine. "I told you
this afternoon we watch our backs. You didn't say nothing about
talking to no other writer. Especially a mud."

I grabbed my pounding nerve endings. "She approached me,

asshole, not the other way around. Same as you and Joe. Fuck your freezer, Blue. I'm outta here."

This time I shook off the hand and turned to face the khaki-clad crowd. They looked tense, ready to fight.

"I told you, we have to be careful," Blue said to my back.

"Yeah, well as far as I'm concerned, you're too fucking careful."

"Just tell us what you talked about and that will be it."

I turned, lifted my drink, and slammed my palm down on the shaky table causing the pen, notebook, and billy club to jump. "I'll tell *you*. Get the live beef out and I'll stay. I'm not here for a Miller commercial."

I heard some heavy breathing and hoped I hadn't overplayed. I stared at Blue who finally nodded. "Okay," he said. "Everybody upstairs. If I need you I'll shout."

There was grumbling and sotto voce protests, still, one by one the overgrown boy scouts filed out of the refrigerator.

Which left me with Blue.

"I don't like this," I said.

"Nobody likes nothing right now. You think it's easy for them to leave me here with you?" As had happened earlier, without an audience Blue's attitude lost some of its macho. Taking its place was something like worry. He grabbed at a loose thread on his worn wool sweater.

"You gotta understand, I'm new at this. When talking needed to be done it was Sean who did it. Stepping up this way is something I got to do whether I like it or not."

"Well, lesson number one is you catch flies with honey, not bazookas."

Blue scowled. "The way the country is going we need the bazookas."

"I'm not the whole country. If this is the way you deal with people who want to get your story out, no wonder no one likes you." I caught my breath, and looked around the fridge. A bright two-hundred-watt bulb hung from the middle of the ceiling but

gave off no heat. "It's cold down here. If you have more questions, ask."

"What did the mud want?" His voice held none of its earlier
threat.

I let my hard-guy recede. "She wanted to know if I found out
how to reach you boyos."

Blue's face tightened. "And you told her?"

"Of course not. I'm not going to blow an exclusive."

"Did she see me show? She wonder what you were doing in
the bar for so long?"

I tried to lighten his concerns. "I told her I was drinking. Hell,
I have a reputation to uphold."

A small grimace, maybe a smile, shuddered across his face.
"You got any smokes?" he asked.

I pulled the Kools from my shirt pocket and flipped them on
the table. Even with three they hadn't done much of a search,
but Blue never noticed. He grabbed the pack, offered me one,
and sat back smoking with obvious pleasure.

"You trying to quit?" I asked.

"Sort of. Sean wanted us healthy. No smokes, workouts, shit
like that."

"Why?" I asked as I reached for my notebook and pen.

"He thought the whole country was going soft. Going that
way for a real long time. If we were gonna take it back we had
to be stronger than everyone else. Strong bodies, minds. He
used to tell us The Beatles said it in one of their albums. Something about get back, get back."

I didn't think "Abby Road" had much to do with fascism, but
then, I'd been surprised by Manson's affinity for "The White Al-
bum." "Who is this 'we' you keep talking about?"

Blue sat back in his metal folding chair and took a deep
breath. The interview he'd been wanting had just begun. I
clicked my pen and leaned over my notebook.

"White people is the 'we,' " he began. "Ever since the Horns
got control of immigration they opened the doors and let in any-

one who ain't White. Browns, yellows, it don't matter so long as they ain't really white."

Blue leaned forward in his chair. "I can still remember when the country wasn't like this. We had homes where women took care of kids instead of shipping them out, or letting 'em run crazy. Where sitting at the table eating together meant something. We want it like it was when I grew up. My old man worked near Gary, Indiana. He worked every fucking day and a hell of a lot of overtime. Never missed a shift. We didn't get rich but we had something. A place, enough food, some spending money." He stopped suddenly and asked, "Are you writing this down? I ain't telling you all this for nothing. I want you to understand what's going on here."

"I'm getting it," I said, vowing silently to keep scratching. His sincerity almost made me feel guilty. Almost.

"Good," he nodded. "Sean never talked about his own life but I think if we want people to understand where we're coming from they got to remember what they lost." This was Blue's attempt to assert his new leadership. He was gonna be plenty pissed when he eventually discovered he'd done it for nothing.

He looked at me with solemn round eyes. "And writer, people already lost a lot. My old man worked his ass off for nothing. As soon as they figured out they could pay muds less, my daddy was history. Let me tell you, you don't raise no family on waitress tips."

"He lost his job, huh?"

Blue's face tightened as he remembered. "He lost everything. We ended up on some relative's property, living in a fucking barn. No matter how hard we cleaned, you couldn't get rid of the smell of shit. From what Sean told us, that was about the time it really started getting bad for everybody."

"What started?"

Blue shook his head slowly and pointed to the refrigerator door. "If you talk to every guy here, you'll hear the same damn thing. Lives fucked one way or another by the Horns. Their civil

rights thing was done to get the muds to worship 'em. White family after white family pissed on or blown away." He raised his eyebrows. "Sean said we work together, meet together, pull shit together, to remember how it was to be a family. So we could get back what we all lost."

I flashed on my own losses but forcibly pushed them away. "And you think it's the fault of the Jews?" I asked dispassionately.

"Wake up, man. The Horns started with the immigration lawyer thing and then they took over the entertainment business. Especially television and movies. Gave them a chance to put out their bullshit." He waved his hand. "Sean called it propaganda. See, they started television. Some guy named Smarnoff."

"Smarnoff?"

Blue shook his head impatiently. "Something like that. What difference does his name make? He was a fucking Horn and he owned television. Newspapers, radio stations, books, everything. But it still wasn't enough for the cocksuckers. They figured once people caught on they'd be finished. They looked at what happened in Germany and knew they couldn't control everything by themselves so they started the civil rights thing. Them three Jews who were supposed to be killed in the South."

I jotted a couple of lines in the notebook. "Supposed to be?"

"Sure," Blue nodded emphatically. "It helps them get what they want. The Horns make all that shit up. Like the concentration camps."

"The Avengers don't believe there were concentration camps?" I flashed on Reb Yonah's numbers. I didn't think he branded them himself.

"Look, McMurphy, we ain't Nazis but they got a bum rap. The kikes pushed their way into power and it was up to the white Germans to get 'em out. Same as here. I'm not saying they didn't kill a few. Hell, you can't make an omelette without breaking eggs. But camps? Fuck, no. That's the kind of lies the Jew media spread to get people on their side. Made up the sto-

ries, pictures, all sorts of shit. Sean said this engineer who studied where the camps were supposed to be can prove there were no gas chambers."

He looked at me, anxious to assess my response. I kept my head down, scribbled away, seeing myself sitting in the middle of a refrigerator lit by a dangling naked bulb and a flashing red light. And I thought Alice took a pill to get to Wonderland. My synapses were exploding with the last gasps of the cocaine high and Blue's semi-organized system of ignorance had produced a sweat. Despite the icebox.

"They have that much drag, huh?" I asked, knowing I had to respond. "You guys read up on this?"

"Sean did the reading then taught the rest of us. Now, I got to." He paused. "The Horns have more drag than you could imagine. See, that's why we have to keep them off guard. The weird ones with the funny hair on the sides of their head are really the ones in charge. They want everyone to believe in their God called Yahweh. The Jews that look white work for them. But as soon as they take over they're gonna outlaw us Christians. That's why we work the Beards over. If we keep them busy they don't have time for other things."

"Sean taught you guys a lot, huh?"

"Well, when he understood what was happening he couldn't just do nothing. See, all of us knew something was wrong but we never put it together. We thought it was us. Sean showed us whose fault it really was."

"What were you into before the White Avengers?"

Blue looked at the pen in my hand and motioned for me to put it down. "I ain't gonna talk much about that and I don't want you to write any of it down."

I dropped the pen. "Fine."

"You ever notice that once in a while an armored car gets hit?"

"That's you?"

He waved his hands. "Oh no, I ain't saying that."

But he was and, at first, I didn't understand why. But he

couldn't keep the pride from his porky face and I finally got it. "You don't have to answer any of this and it's not for the story, but I'm guessing you were in charge, not Sean?"

"Bam, bam, take 'em down quick, get outa there. Leave 'em with a few knots on their heads, and a couple pounds lighter. Let's say, one of us did the planning and one of us ran the job."

"Were you busted?"

"Never." His barrel chest swelled and his voice filled with pleasure. "Look, before any of us understood this Horn thing we were just angry and acted like it. Stole from anyone. Even people who weren't no better off than us. Who gave a shit? We never figured we'd have a real chance at things. The dice were loaded but we didn't know how or who done it. Now when we do something we got a reason."

"So tell me about the shootings."

The air went out of him like a snapped popper. "I got nothing to tell. I didn't even know it was gonna happen."

"Are you kidding me?"

"Sean kept a lot of things to himself . . ."

"What do you mean?"

"I mean he didn't always tell us what he was going to do. See, Sean wasn't like the rest of us. He figured we needed a family but he was different. He learned shit on his own, did things on his own. Offing the Horn was his own thing."

Blue sounded miffed. "Don't get me wrong, if he'd a lived he'd a told us his reasons."

"You're telling me you don't know why he shot the Rabbi?"

"I'm telling you he had his reasons. After Sean understood what was what, he never did things wild." Blue smiled at the memory of Sean. "I'm telling you, McMurphy, he was a genius! Sean could figure out a plan for anything."

For a second I didn't recognize my name and almost turned to see if someone else had entered the fridge. But Blue was so intent on his deification of Kelly he didn't notice.

"I don't know what happened that night. We were supposed

to be laying low. We done a lot of stuff to the Horns since we organized and Sean was worried something negative would come down."

"What sort of stuff did you do?"

Blue spent the next twenty minutes detailing a long list of harassments: some light, some much more serious and threatening. All done with the purpose of bonding a large old-fashioned white family out of the multi-colored mess they believed America had become. I sat and listened while he regaled me with stories detailing the Avengers' commitment to scaring the bejesus out of Yeshiva students. I tried to get him to talk a little more about the armored car stickups, but here he balked. He also continued to deny any involvement or knowledge about the Rabbi's death. He preferred to turn Kelly into a prophet and martyr. A man who stood tall in the cause of White Liberation.

My high was gone and with it any desire for more information. My throat was sore from too many cigarettes and my head felt too big to squeeze back through Alice's keyhole. I was cold, tired, and disgusted. It was time to leave. But then Blue brought me back to attention.

"Why ain't you writing?" he demanded suspiciously.

I remembered the boy scouts upstairs and worded my answer carefully. "I took down the facts. Listen man, this is my first opportunity to speak with someone who wants to save the country." I had to keep talking so I threw in, "Now that Communism is gone, you know, it's easy to let down your guard . . ."

Blue was suddenly excited again. "Another fucking lie! See, that's how smart the Horns are. They got the whole world thinking Communism is dead but they're just keeping it quiet. When they get the chance they'll shove it right back up our ass!"

I stood. "Look, let me go to work and put an article together." I paused, picked up my stuff, and shook half my smokes onto the table. "One thing. I thought armored cars were impenetrable. Wells Fargo and all that. I don't want details . . ."

"Don't worry, you ain't getting any," he laughed as he scooped

up the cigarettes. "If you stake 'em out real careful, take your time and watch them right, you notice little habits the drivers and guards have." Blue stood up. "Where they like to stretch their legs, where moving the money goes slow, shit like that. Kelly was a fucking genius when it came to that stuff. The rest is like I told you. Whack, whack, bam, bam. Don't even have to shoot nobody. Shit, those companies be better off hiring us. Save themselves a couple of bucks."

"Where did the money go?"

"You gotta live."

"All of it?"

His voice dropped a notch. "We ain't the only group defending the country. What we get, we share. Sean took care of all that."

"You weren't afraid he'd rip you off?"

Blue's face darkened. "What are you thinking? We started out as thiefs but we ain't that way now. We pull for each other ever since we understood what was going on."

He stopped and stared, a mean look in his eyes. "Listen, you better not fuck up this article. If the White Avengers come across wrong, your ass is gonna be in a sling."

I quickly made amends. "Don't worry. I understand what it's like to have your family blown apart, find another, then watch that one go." I couldn't believe my words; I had just identified with Blue and his group. "I'll show you the article before I shop it around," I added dispiritedly.

His body relaxed. "That's a good idea."

"Yeah. So how do I get in touch?"

"Check with Buzz."

I followed Blue up the stairs. Everyone was bottles and eyes when we came through the door. I made my way through their hostile family. Buzz wanted to know whether Blue had turned the cooler back on but I didn't wait for the answer. I wanted the chill out, not on.

CHAPTER 12

Despite the night's drop in temperature, bone-chilled as I was from my time in the cooler, the outdoors were a flat out relief. My own white man's liberation. I took my time returning to the car; no rush to be back inside a closed space, even a cozy one. I understood how Blue and his horses got to the water, even though the pool was poison. Something I knew from my own previous dips into violence and hate. I wanted time to shake Blue's clumsy thinking, his blind rage. Time to forget my momentary identification with the Avengers' blown-out lives.

A block and a half from my parking spot a skinny black figure darted across the street. I'd been so internal I hadn't thought to watch my back. Cheryl apparently had.

"What are you doing here this time of morning?" I barked protectively.

"Tailing your honky ass, Matthew Jacobs."

"Jacob, without the s."

"Whatever."

She started to talk but I grabbed elbow and dragged her quickly toward the car.

"What are you doing?" she complained, pulling her arm.

"I'm trying to keep both our butts lead-free. If the Avengers

see us together again, I'm fucked and you won't be sitting pretty either."

"So you *have* been meeting with them," she crowed triumphantly. Then, in a more somber tone, asked, "See us *again?*"

"That's right, Cheryl, again."

She stopped resisting and matched me stride for stride. She remained quiet until I pulled away from the curb. "Where are you taking us? It's a little late, or maybe a little early, for a pleasure cruise."

I snorted but kept driving until I'd clocked a mile, then parked. "Why the hell are you still 'tailing my honky ass'?" I demanded without any real fire. Something about her vibrancy short-circuited my annoyance.

"I told you, I'm going to get this story out."

"Then why not get it out on your own instead of riding my back?"

"Are you kidding? You're as close to the White Avengers as I can get."

"Lady, I'm as close as you ever want to get."

An exuberant grin lit up her face. "Now you got it; that's why we're talking."

This time I didn't fight Cheryl's enthusiasm. It was a relief after my time with Blue. "Okay," I said with a weary smile. "What do you want from me?"

"I want to know what you know. Who you talked to, what they said. I want to know as much as you'll tell me. I want people to understand the danger of letting groups like this go unchecked. See, Matthew Jacob, I believe 'the truth will set them free.' "

"Everyone has their own version of truth, Cheryl. I just got done listening to the Avengers'."

"That's not truth; that's fear and rage. What you heard was hateful and disgusting, right?"

I looked at her bright face. Then I looked at her body. She had changed clothes and now wore a high-riding black skirt. With plenty of leg. I ripped my eyes away, lit a cigarette, and sat

quietly trying to decide what, if anything, to say. "Look, I can't talk to you until after I meet with Roth. He pays the bills."

"And you're only in it for the money."

"I'm a Frank Zappa fan."

"Who?" she asked.

"Never mind. I'll speak to Simon. Maybe he'll let me feed you what I get."

"You're not saying that just to be rid of me?"

I shook my head. "I don't want to be rid of you."

She cocked her chocolate Lena Horne head and drawled, "What's that supposed to mean?"

Her question flustered me. "I like you, that's what it means. I like your attitude. If I didn't we wouldn't be talking. And I dislike the Avengers."

I felt Cheryl's eyes on my face. "You sound different than you did earlier today."

" 'Consistency is the hobgoblin of small minds.' "

"The quote is 'foolish consistency.' Listen, Matthew, I saw the way you steamed out of that bar. Both times. Something has you by the short hairs."

I shook my head. She didn't know Zappa but had Ralph Waldo down. Or was it Thackeray? I grunted and started the car. "Where you parked?" I asked.

I dropped Cheryl off with a promise to call. To prove my sincerity, I asked for her card. I was sincere. Usually I'd rip. This time I tucked the 2-by-3 into my pocket.

On the way home I hoped for a solid eight. But when I got there my nerves didn't agree. Something tugged at the corners of my awareness while I strenuously worked to keep it out. I tried the Holy Three — but grass, whisky, and television simply added weight to the chorus. I grew worried about sleep: if I couldn't, if I could. The throbbing in my head finally settled down when I remembered the plastic bottle of Valium in the gymbag.

Which I found. And knew I'd eaten when the telephone's ring slapped me upside the head. I reached onto the night table, knocked a Crumley to the floor, and finally found the handle. "If this is a fucking computer I'm gonna hurt someone," I mumbled.

"No computer," Simon barked. "Wanted to see if you were all right."

I started to roar when I heard the phone shut down. Smart man, my friend Simon.

But not smart enough. I'd fallen back asleep and, from the look on his face, taken more than a few seconds to distinguish between the pounding on the door and the pounding in my head.

"You look terrible," Simon said as he walked to the kitchen holding a McDonald's bag between his thumb and index finger. "Time for lunch."

"I like Burger King," I complained, untwisting the sweats from around my ankles.

"Always running with the loser," he snorted.

"Not that complex. I like the King's food better."

"Bullshit. The Sox, Cleveland. Who you kidding?"

I fumbled with the coffee and hoped he hadn't noticed. I didn't like all his noticing.

"When the Dodgers moved out of Brooklyn, I rooted for the Yanks."

"Is that right?" Simon seemed genuinely surprised.

"At least until I heard Les Keiter do the Giants." None of us like to be without our images.

Simon grinned. "That's my Matt. You still look like shit."

I got the pot perking, lit a cigarette, and turned around. "Sleep deprivation can do that," I said. Simon almost answered, instead, shook his head and dumped the bag. The packages hit the table without a sound but still made me wince.

"I'm surprised you aren't here with whitefish and bagels," I said, unwrapping a sugar-coated croissant.

"Gotta take your shots, don't you?"

"Doesn't everyone? You shag me about drugs, I bang you about the 'opiate of the masses.' "

I couldn't hold my tongue. When I stopped talking, a small tremor shook my hand. I willed the coffee to hurry and puffed on my cigarette. I was not in a good mood. Despite Simon's charitable donation. Fuck it, he probably kept the receipt.

"I didn't say a word about drugs," he protested.

"I know the look."

"Come on, Matt, I didn't come here to argue. But it's evident that this afternoon you are a nasty, surly, thoroughly unlikable human. Well fuck you, then. Now what happened last night?"

"I spent a couple of hours inside a refrigerator," I growled, unable to kick my hung-up drugged-out weariness. I must have forgotten my morning Geritol.

"They locked you in a refrigerator?"

"No they met with me in one. The bar's cooler. It started as 'they,' but wound up me and their new honcho, Blue."

"Blue?"

I explained. And recounted. Even pulled the notebook and leafed through. I liked Simon's surprise. I drank my coffee, smoked my cigarettes, and spun my tale. Spicing here, flourishing there. I wanted the Avengers a done do.

It wasn't gonna be. "A good start," he said, fingering the second croissant. "This stuff edible?" he asked.

I pointed to my empty wrapper and shrugged. "You want me to meet with them again, don't you?"

He picked a corner off his roll and placed it delicately into his mouth.

"Damnit Simon, eat the fucker, will you?"

He ignored me, chewed a couple of times, then pushed the croissant away. I picked it up and shoved it in my mouth.

"Not necessarily," he said. "Why not nose around the neighborhood? With any luck we'll get more information and you won't have to freeze your chops." A nasty smile broke across his face. "A refrigerator. Those assholes belong on ice or hanging from hooks."

I flashed on Blue's pathetic sincerity. "A little unforgiving, aren't you?"

"Are you kidding? You read *me* the list of hate crimes they've committed."

"Rubbing doo doo on synagogue doors doesn't deserve the chair."

"They assassinated a Rabbi, Matt."

"According to Blue, the Avengers knew nothing about the killing. Kelly did it on his own."

"Right. And the check is in the mail." He paused, then raised his hands high. "It's one thing to root for the underdog. But these people are scum. There aren't any underdogs wearing swastikas."

I was too tired, too irritable, to be anything other than perverse. "Their wiring is fucked, but they didn't get there on their own."

"The Jews didn't push them there either. Or the Blacks. What's the matter with you?"

I'd run out of gas. I lit another smoke and shook my head. "All this faithfulness bothers me. You undergo a conversion, the Hasids do their number, even the Avengers have true belief." I almost added that I had drugs, but didn't.

Simon shook his head. "Not the same, Matt-man. My so-called conversion is not like the Avengers."

Of course not; he was liberal. And I wasn't sure what I was complaining about. Maybe I still felt lonely. I pressed my cigarette into the ashtray, lit another, and backed off. "Okay, Simon, I'll talk to the people in the neighborhood and see what I can turn up."

Simon stood and prepared to leave. "Good." He casually

added, "Listen, if you're feeling a little lonely, maybe you'd like to come with Fran and me to the Temple."

I waved him off. "No thanks. I'll see enough Jews when I go back to the Yeshiva."

"You know what's been eating you? You want to go back to the Yeshiva. This is more than just gathering information. This is about being Jewish."

I flashed on Yakov, then Yonah's stern rigidity. Inexplicably I thought of Cheryl. I pushed everyone out but her and shook my head. "Sorry, Simon. Nothing more than simple garbage collection on the Avengers. Don't worry, I won't turn it into chicken salad."

Simon nodded dubiously and moved toward the door.

"Before you go . . ."

He turned back.

"A free-lance is on to me, us. Knows who I am, who we work for."

First worry, then anger crossed his face. "Jesus, Matt. You couldn't stay clear of a fucking free-lance?"

"She must have picked me up at your office, Boss. She has a desk at the *Record* and I think it makes sense to feed her."

"The *Record*? A Black woman is crazy enough to follow you onto Avenger turf?"

"If you want integration you start with housing not schools."

"Matt, this isn't funny. I wanted you quiet. Are you sure you don't want to fuck her?"

"Don't be an asshole, Simon. I'm old enough to be her father."

I regretted my words the moment they were out. Simon's annoyance instantly disappeared and the room filled with an electric tension. A hard, painful silence engulfed us. I quickly lit another cigarette, hid behind my coffee mug, and explained the deal I'd offered Cheryl.

Simon seemed relieved when I broke the quiet. "Well, I'm sorry I blew up. Nothing goes down smooth with this case. Ev-

erybody wants to listen, nobody wants to talk." He held out his hand. "Give me her card. I'll work something out." He looked at me then added, "She'll make out okay."

He watched as I copied the telephone number onto the empty McDonald's bag before relinquishing the card. We walked to my office and he opened the door to the alley. Simon was outside when he turned back toward me. "You did good last night. I'm running into walls everywhere else. If you can keep getting me this kind of stuff, the walls won't matter."

I pounded my chest with my fists before I closed the door.

CHAPTER 13

I couldn't think of a reason to avoid the street. Most days that wouldn't matter, but today, a late afternoon colorized Cagney shoving grapefruit wasn't a strong enough bribe to keep me on the couch. I thought about visiting Julie but he'd think me too forward if I threw my arms around his legs and begged for more drugs. Lou was possible, but I didn't feel too much like a *boychik*. Truth was, I didn't want friends, I wanted out. It just took a while to recognize the feeling.

Two hours' digging through the White Avengers' neighborhood had me reconsidering the grapefruit. People were as tight as Phil had promised. As if the neighborhood was the size of Texas rather than a single square mile. Folks acknowledged a rumpus with the Jews, but no one knew anything else. "Too many strangers been here recently," was as close to an honest response as I got all afternoon. And close wasn't enough.

Along with the stonewall came the sensation of being watched. I didn't think it was Cheryl. Everyone I saw, when they weren't staring at the sidewalk or lying past my shoulder, snuck little looks. But that just made it difficult to pick out someone in particular.

Coming up empty meant another visit with Blue and the

khaki-clad Avengers. So I kept on trucking. I stopped at bars, subshops, and hole-in-the-wall variety stores that still sold penny candy and six-packs of tiny wax bottles filled with colored syrup. By the time I finished my quest I'd gained weight, but not an ounce of information.

The sun was gone, the moon still hiding, when I called Simon from a phone booth. I wanted to blow off steam about my useless day, wanted permission to return home. Before I had asked, or even gotten angry, Simon told me that he'd unsuccessfully tried to contact Cheryl. The editor at the small newspaper was frantic because she hadn't shown up for an appointment. The editor feared her absence was due to her zeal about snooping on the Avengers. Simon thought the man overwrought, assured me she was sleeping off her late night, and suggested I do the same. He promised he'd have Sadie ring her again.

I'd gotten Simon's permission to crawl back onto my couch, but Cheryl's no-show refused me mine. Her missed appointment had roused the kind of premonition that, in my life, had all too often been terribly correct. Hurting a young Black woman would not be off-limits to the White Avengers. I trusted my gut. And that meant a surprise visit to Blue.

When I got to the car I opened the door, shielded the interior with my body, and surreptitiously reached under the passenger's seat. I pulled out the small lead pipe I'd kept in every automobile I'd owned since I was a teenager. The Equalizer.

I lifted a joint from the glove compartment, smoked half, and pointed myself toward Buzz's. As I walked away from the car I noticed my muscles were bunched, tight with a tense mad.

When I saw them cross the street it took a moment to realize they were coming at me. At first I didn't recognize anyone since no one wore khaki. Maybe I should have paid more attention earlier to the hairs on the back of my neck. If I had, they wouldn't have been able to force me into the dark, garbage-can-filled alley. But once I realized who they were, I wanted to get pinched. Saved me a trip to the bar.

They stopped pushing when my back was flat against a medium-sized day-glo-orange dumpster. Irrationally, I hoped the bright shine wasn't fresh paint. I caught the glint of Fang's golden incisors. I guess he liked to work with his mouth open; easier to drool.

"Blue too much of a man to show up?" I asked, testing their mood. And mine.

"I'm here Mr. Dick-tective." Blue's high voice trilled from somewhere in the alley's shadows. He sounded happy, at home in a familiar environment.

"That's a new one, Blue. 'Dick-tective.' I'll have to remember it. Maybe I should write it down."

"You got a fresh mouth for someone whose ass is stuck up against a garbage can. When we're done with you, you might not be able to write much of anything. Of course, you don't really have to write, do you?" He stopped, then slipped an excited giggle. "But the mud needs *her* hands, don't she?"

I felt the muscles on my arms tighten. The way Fang and friends were spaced I could almost walk out of this. Unless they had a gun. Unless I wanted to stay.

And I did. All the strength I'd been using to repress and deny since the case began was transforming into a livid anger. I felt the bile well up in my stomach and into my mouth as I tried to keep control. "What are you trying to tell me, Blue?" My voice was tight with tension.

"I'm telling you you're a lying asshole. And that mud cunt won't be writing for a while. That's what I'm telling you," he shouted triumphantly.

I slipped my hands carefully to the lead pipe waiting in my pocket. I gritted my teeth. "Jesus, Blue, whacking a woman. I thought better of you. I thought Kelly taught you to be somebody."

I heard the crunch of gravel but Blue still remained out of view. "Yeah, well I thought better of you too, you lying bastard." His voice was raw with a lifetime of betrayals. "You work for the fucking Horn who shot Kelly."

Since I was the latest betrayal, he meant for me to pay for them all. "Who told you that?"

"Don't start with me, I fucking trusted you." His words quivered with rage. "You're nothing but a lying piece of shit."

He was angry. Big fucking deal. I was angry too. Angry about the betrayals in my own life. Angry enough to feel my heat slipping into a recognizable chill. A chill that had Cheryl's smile stuck in the center, somehow superimposed over an image of Yakov's lankiness. Only now the image produced no warmth, no protectiveness — just cold, hard rage.

"Okay, Blue, I work for the Rabbi. So what? According to you, you and your cattle had nothing to do with that. Now why don't you tell me where the lady is, and we'll both let bygones be bygones."

He wasn't going to let anything be gone, and neither was I.

"How the fuck do I know?" Again he giggled. "Try City Hospital. That's where they usually take muds."

My rage took the shape and gleam of a blade. I was sorry I hadn't brought my gun. "Takes a real tough man to hurt a little girl, huh, Blue?"

"About as tough as it takes to beat on a Judas. I'm tired of all this talking. Give it to the lousy fuck," he screamed, "hurt him bad!"

They tried. And tried for a very long time. But they tried without guns or knives and eventually were little match for the Equalizer. I was in a frenzy about Cheryl, about Yakov, and whatever else had been preying on me since I first talked to Simon. I enjoyed the thud and crack of lead on bone. Things moved so rapidly I couldn't see whom I was hurting but at one point Fang started crying and crawling on the ground moaning, "My teeth, my teeth, I gotta find my teeth." For a fleeting moment I wondered whether I'd panned gold, then stopped wondering and kicked him in the belly.

I didn't get off free. With five on one, even a stupid five is gonna do damage. I knew I was bleeding, that my face was eat-

ing a lot of fist, and someone kung fu'd me in the chest with their boot. I knew my rib was bruised or busted. I thought my nose was broken. Again.

But every time I focused on Cheryl's bright smile I clubbed harder. If I left them their heads they were going to have serious headaches, I exulted for one delirious, delightful moment. That's when it registered: I was binge-ing on my own violent hate spree.

And suddenly lost all taste for blood. I was lucky that a couple of uniformed police ran into the alley, or I might have let myself get really trashed. The cops quickly got control of the situation — a gun can do that. They barked their orders and lined up everyone who could stand. Everyone, that is, except Blue. He had avoided the Equalizer and disappeared.

CHAPTER 14

After the crowd was sorted and identified, one of the cops returned to his blue and white to place a call. I leaned against the dumpster listening to ten minutes of moans, curses, and commands before I was released. I wasn't sure whether the rest of them were waiting for an ambulance or a paddy wagon. I was suspicious about my quick getaway and felt like asking if it was a professional courtesy. But my adrenaline was flagging and, in its place, the first rush of the Avengers' damage. I just kept quiet and did what I was told; hell, my mouth hurt.

It was a hobbling Chester to my car, every breath followed by a small gasp caused by the pain in my chest. There was no reason to holler for Mr. Dillon since I'd be okay in a couple of days, but I decided to visit an emergency room. City's.

Four interminable, almost intolerable, hours later, I was once again released. Most of the hurt brought to heel with prescribed codeine, the rest ignored in the rekindling of my anger after I sneaked into my new friend's room. Blue had been right about the hospital. He'd also been right about Cheryl needing a vacation. The Avengers had broken bones in both her hands. She was lying on top of the steel bed's covers, her slanted eyes open but blitzed on hospital dope. Despite the drugs, pain kept flood-

ing her face, tugging at its angles. But all she would blurrily talk
about was her shame for revealing my identity, for compromising a source, for setting me up. I listened as her contrition
joined with my own. Eventually, I put my finger on her lips, sat
down on the bed, and lightly ran my hand over her forehead. I
sat with her until she stopped apologizing and fell into a deep
medicated sleep. Then I stayed stroking her head until I felt
numb.

When I limped out of the pastel-stark, false-friendly hospital,
it was light outside; my long afternoon and night finally over.
But with its conclusion came soul-rocked, apartment-locked,
days of self-recrimination. Days of almost unendurable longing
for my dead daughter.

I tried shutting everything down with my legal and illegal drugs.
They didn't do the job. After an initial dose of anesthetized stu-
por, I couldn't keep Yakov, Cheryl, or Rebecca out of the night.
Sleep turned traitor, ceaselessly jolting me with eye-opening nightmares. A cigarette, more sleep, another vignette. Sometimes about
Rebecca, sometimes about Chana, sometimes Cheryl and Yakov.
All had the same conclusion: I was always too late, too incompe-
tent to prevent the grisly horror. It didn't take a Sigmund freak to
realize what I'd been fighting off. And who had been running
barefoot behind my anxiety, my denial, my rage.

The nightmares began stretching into the day. Days. I pulled
the phone, shut down the clocks, refused visits. Part of the day
I spent high, part I spent drunk. The nights were spent drunk
and high. Every television show reminded me of walking a col-
icky baby, pushing an umbrella stroller, rolling a ball on the floor.
Of having embraced a life I never thought possible. But each
memory carried me closer to that ugly week in the hospital waiting for my family to die. Waiting helplessly, stuck to a brown
Naugahyde couch in the visitors' room, dreading the worst. And
finally getting it.

Every room I limped through, every mirror I saw, reflected my
dime-short, day-late identity.

I was tired of being the last to know. For yet another time I'd let my life's shortfall transform into hate. My fight with the Avengers had been nothing more than a rabid blood hunt. I'd *wanted* to beat their bodies. I'd brought the Equalizer *hoping* to split their ignorance, *hungry* for the pleasure in my lack of control.

I thought of Blue lurking somewhere in the city and remembered Rabbi Sheinfeld's "choose your enemies well . . ."

Maybe it was the acknowledgment of my grief for Rebecca, the sadness and shame in my violence. Maybe it was the chemicals, but I began to crawl out from my cloud of self-loathing. I started sleeping without company. Enough sleep to let the grass, codeine, and Valium meld with the solitary rhythm of recovery. I inspected my injuries, as if the light green swelling around my eyes, my splotched chest, or my painful breathing could somehow ease a troubled conscience. But it wasn't until days later, when I stood under a hot stinging shower, my tears mixing with the spigot's, that I could think of Becky without the despair I'd been fighting since this case began.

When I first heard about Simon's Temple-joining, I'd felt lonely, left out. Difficult but do-able. Only I hadn't anticipated meeting Yakov or Cheryl. Hadn't expected the case to unleash a tidal wave of paternalism. Of yearning. With no simple solution of joining the Big Brothers. When I needed to *belong*, I wanted the real thing. I wanted my family. I needed what I could never have.

I stared into the medicine chest mirror relieved that I didn't resemble Blue. I just looked like a banged-up me.

I restarted my clocks, plugged in the phone, and eased off the painkillers. I opened the door for Lou and even ate his cooking. He knew me well enough to accept my morbid silence, liked me well enough to keep everyone else at bay.

Finally, toward the end of the week, I felt patched together enough to try and explain some of what had happened to Simon.

"Always the victim or the asshole, aren't you? This time you've managed to be both." He sounded exasperated. "You get jumped by a half dozen neo-Nazis who want to stuff you into a dumpster and you're worried about being too violent?"

"The pleasure of it, Simon."

"I don't get it, Matt. No, correct that, I don't get you! You haven't been non-violent since the Vietnam war and I'm not sure you were non-violent then."

"Try 'since the days of Martin Luther King,'" I offered.

"But when you finally win a damn brawl against rednecks who want to gas Jews and fry Blacks, you're all over yourself?"

"Simon, I went looking to beat on them. I didn't even wait to see if she'd been hurt."

"You didn't wait because you know the Avengers for what they are. I was the naive one. You understand them. You rushed in because you thought the lady needed help." He paused, then added, "And because you're stupid."

"Well, you're at least half right."

"So let's drop this *mea culpa* crap. Those pieces of shit got what was coming. And they're going to get more when they realize they are going to spend the rest of their working lives earning money for a Black lady." He clicked his teeth with genuine pleasure.

"You been in touch with Cheryl?"

"Of course. She wants to know if you'll forgive her."

"Make her stop that, Simon, I can't take it. How is she?"

"About a week better. They don't need to operate on her hands, but it'll be a slow go." He stopped then asked delicately, "What about you? How long do you think it will be before you're on your feet?"

I didn't answer.

Simon waited, then pushed on, "Look, I don't want to rush you . . ."

"Yes you do," I said.

There was a second of silence, a small laugh, and a consider-

able easing of tension in his voice. "You're right, Matt-man, I do. I still can't get a lick of information out of anybody."

"So you want me back doing what?"

"More of the same. I was wrong to call you off the Hasids. Go back and get as much as you can. The news blackout doesn't change my concerns, it adds to 'em. My Jewish brethren like the silence, but want the legalities finished. They dislike the ambiguity more than I do." Simon hesitated then continued, "I don't want dime one hanging over Reb Yonah's head. Otherwise it will be an open invitation for more anti-Semitic bullshit."

What could I tell him? That I'd been blindsided by a gawky Hasidic teenager into a bone-breaking miss of my dead daughter? That I was frightened to see more of him? "I don't know, Simon, I feel all right, but my face looks like Carmen Basilo after a whupping."

"I hear."

"Who you been talking to?"

"Lou. He said you were pretty withdrawn so I didn't bother you."

"It didn't stop you from calling today."

"Yeah, well, you've been withdrawn long enough."

"You sure you weren't looking for the first opportunity to get me working? I mean you're on a mission from God here, Simon."

I couldn't bring myself to say anything about Becky. Nor could I turn him down. Most of me wanted nothing to do with Yakov, the Yeshiva, the entire case. But I was still angry about Cheryl's slender body bent and broken on the hospital bed. Also, a sliver in me still wanted more of the kid. It might not be a healthy sliver, but it was there. I wasn't finished.

"You really are stupid." Simon's voice was suddenly gruff. "I've been talking to Lou because I wanted to know how you were doing!"

I suddenly realized how incredibly difficult it must have been for Simon to stand still during my recuperation. Especially since

he knew he was waiting on a depression. "Look, Boss, I'm sorry. I'm finding this whole situation a difficult do. Give me another day and I'll jump on it. Actually, walk on it. I'm not ready to jump."

"Well, if you can't jump, you better stay the hell out of trouble."

I laughed and hung up the phone.

The laughter didn't linger. Most of the next twenty-four was metal on metal, as if the past week had suddenly slipped away and I was back to where my hurting began. But as the day trudged into another restless night, what little sleep I had was free of nightmares.

By early morning, my throat ached from too many cigarettes, my mouth dry from alcohol dehydration. It was still dark when I dragged myself from bed. I plodded into the kitchen and put up the coffee. I wanted to drown the stale, burnt, bourbon aftertaste.

I had to get the fog out of my eyes so I retreated into a shower. Standing under the hot, wet sting helped roll away the fatigue, but didn't do much for my head. I might be able to espy the causes for my lingering depression, but that was a long leap from a fix. I lifted my face into the spray and thought again about quitting the job. But the idea had me shaking like a long-hair dog after a dip in a dirty pond. I convinced myself I was just shaking awake. I also convinced myself to start working that day, just as I had promised. I was so busy convincing I almost pitched my naked butt onto the kitchen floor before I realized the large Black shadow hulking at the table was Julius.

CHAPTER 15

Instead of belly down I stood dripping, searching for my voice. Julius's heavily lined dark brown face remained impassive though I knew he enjoyed the moment. He hoisted his permanently slouched lids and tilted his head. Still too surprised to see clearly, I knew his eyes were bloodshot. His eyes were always bloodshot. Went well with his tightly curled salt and pepper hair.

Julius was one of the building's originals. Despite his vaguely menacing persona, the tenants adored him. Mrs. S. said she slept better just knowing he was around.

When I first became the super I had my doubts; Julius didn't look like any night angel to me. We boy-dogged each other for a long time before the hair on both our necks settled. Then he delivered his proposition.

"I'll slide you one of these," he said, pushing the first canvas gymbag across my kitchen table. "Instead of rent."

It took a ten-second sift. "You're overpaying."

He didn't answer, just flashed a little red-eye, and left. That had been the beginning and, slowly, over time, we became tight. He made his living brokering various enigmatic transactions. It wasn't dope. I once asked and he became seriously offended. I never asked again. It didn't matter what we knew, or didn't

know. We liked each other. Julius said we got along because we both lived a couple of steps beyond the campfire. It surprised me to think he even saw the flames.

"A little early in the morning to play Tarzan, Slumlord."

His deep voice snapped me back. Now I *knew* the scene was a smile. "Slumlord" was his term of endearment. For the second time in less than a week I pounded my chest, this time careful to keep away from the faint yellow splotches that still sectioned my body.

Julius put his hand over his eyes. "Too ugly to see all that white meat shake. And you're splashing me."

"Bullshit, you just can't stand looking at a man with a couple more inches."

He pulled his hand away from his face. "Only place you got a couple more anything is around your gut. That subshop be the death of you."

I nodded and walked toward the bedroom. "Yeah, well, the worms have an order in for a steak and onion," I said. "You know how much I like to please. Help yourself to the coffee."

By the time I returned he had two poured. "You been keeping unusual hours," he said. "Unless you turned professional pugilist, you also been keeping unusual company. You having another midlife crisis?"

I shook my head as I lit two cigarettes. "Nope. Did that already."

The corners of his mouth twitched. "I'd say a couple of times. But five minutes ago you were patting your chest and talking about the size of your iron."

I smiled. "I won the fight. It probably went to my head. Or somewhere."

"If you won, the way you look after a week on the mend, you must have fought yourself. Usually you do that *inside* your head. Nobody looks as bad as you and calls himself a winner."

"How do you know it's been a week?"

"You have a worried father-in-law. Asked me to look in once in

a while. When you get trashed you eat a prodigious amount of sleeping pills."

I shook my head. "I don't understand you. You hand me the fucking drugs, then give me shit about them."

"Ever the way, Matthew. An ancient Chinese method of medicine. Doctor be responsible for his patient's life."

I wasn't thrilled with the metaphor, but I *had* been known to call my stash the medicine chest. "Well, I've used up the sick bed. Barrister Roth wants me back on the job."

"I take it Simon's job is what prettied you up?"

"A sidebar." I gave him the play-by-play. When I finished talking I had the uneasy feeling something I couldn't see was eying me from behind a bush.

"I'd say you ran into a nasty crowd, boy."

"You couldn't tell that from my face?"

"Your face asks and every once in a while receives. It's something else to lay out a lady. Even if they're down on her pigment, breaking hands is cold."

He shook his head and continued to think out loud. "Now that the police ran in the punks, you won't be talking to *anyone*. Even the neighborhood good guys won't crack. You spend ten more years living there maybe someone'll bullshit with you over a boilermaker. Maybe."

Julie sounded a lot like Phil. Maybe he'd been the one following me while I'd been drawing blanks. "Phil thinks Washington Clifford may be involved with this case," I offered.

"That so?" The corners of Julius's mouth curved down as he shook his head. "I don't believe it. Mount Washington likes big ripples. The Avengers are not major players. Even within the hate league. You already know this, you won your fight." He backed his words with a basso profundo chuckle.

"What if it *is* a big case?"

Julie was skeptical. "Nothing Clifford-big about it. That dead Rabbi may have been important to some Higher Authority, but not to the folks Clifford answers to."

"Look," I couldn't stop trying to make that chicken salad. "What if it isn't straight up? What if Clifford really is involved and the squelch is his?"

"This kind of quiet comes down when everyone sweats a riot." He winked conspiratorially, "Even when folks think it's White on White." Julie shook his head. "Nobody wants the newspapers slobbering, television going twenty-four a day. Downtown wanted this chilled from the start. Frozen."

I kept chopping. "Why don't they just charge the Reb or completely cut him loose?"

Julius shook his head. "He's not doing time. They just waiting to formalize when it'll be three lines on page thirty-eight. You can drag yourself around by the nose, but any Kelly or Rabbi in the telephone book be too small for Washington Clifford to notice. You've already had all your excitement." A quick nod of his head. "You're better off. You won't be thumping that ugly chest of yours if you're up against Clifford."

He was right. For a brief moment I'd let myself hope for meat on the bone, forgetting who the meat was.

A small smile split the ridges of his brown lines. "You got to go back into Hymietown to dig up more dirt."

I was surprised, maybe offended. "Hymietown? Give it a rest, I heard too much of that shit in the fucking refrigerator."

Julius somehow managed to get his eyes lower. "Care to bet on the number of times you're going to hear the word *Schvartze?*"

I wasn't offended enough to argue. "What are you trying to tell me?"

He jerked his thumb back over his shoulder in a gesture I knew meant across the ocean. Any ocean. "It took but ten minutes for people to slap each other around once the Big Red Machine closed shop. Ten minutes. And we're talking Caucasians. Whites whacking Whites behind dislikes so old that nobody can remember what they are. Folks just remember the taste of blood. Hop a plane and you have the same thing in living color. South Africa. Black people taking each other out. Licking the

same boot for so long they can't stand the sight of each other's tongues.

"Back here, Jews and Blacks were soul brothers until the militants came along. But the only thing those angry Bloods did was hold a mirror to the underside of a two-faced reality. Empty a checkbook into the N double A, but write, produce, direct movies that have Stepin' Fetchit tap-dancing across the screen."

Julie stopped, stood, retrieved, and refilled. When he sat back down, he lit one of my cigarettes.

"You sure it was Jews who produced those movies?"

A momentary look of disgust crossed his face. "I don't know whether Jews did Fetchit or not. I'm saying they had clout in that industry but that didn't stop anyone from making Black folk high-stepping fools." He opened his eyes wide enough to almost glare. "You want to pretend that 'We Shall Overcome,' don't you?"

I chuckled and shook my head. "Not really. Occasionally I hope things will get better. I still have flashbacks of us against them. Seemed a little less lonely in those days."

Julius shrugged. "It's still the same, but the side of the street we're on isn't as crowded." He plunged his cigarette into the rapidly filling ashtray. "When different *groups* gang together it's for one reason. Convenience." Julie lit another cigarette. "These days, it's rarely convenient."

I stood and started for the bedroom. "So the older we get, the smaller our world. Eventually it drops to one, then nothing. Like the little dot that disappeared into a 'ping' in Zap Comics."

"Not familiar with the funny page, but sit down, S'lord. No need to fetch the gymbag." Julie lit a joint he pulled from his old, gray-on-gray vest.

He passed the marijuana. I toked, toked again, then passed it back. We sat silently until the joint worked its way into a roach. I tore off the top of a matchbook, curled it into a tight cylinder and stuck the roach into the end. Julie leaned forward with a

match. I inhaled and passed the home-brew holder. He toked and dropped the scorched dregs into the ashtray.

We both reached for the cigarettes at the same time.

"After you," Julius said, "they're yours."

" 'What's mine is yours,' " I grinned. "An old Jewish expression."

Julie grunted and lit. "What you have to understand, Matthew, is Blacks instinctively know Jews are busy 'passing' and get angry 'cause they mostly get away with it."

"Passing? Come on, Julie, that ended when they stopped ripping the 'steins' and 'bergs' off their names."

"Passing. Your Avenger homeboys told you the pecking order. Jew, Brown, and Black. That's one reason why Jews are phobic of the Arab. No one ever wants back on that bottom rung."

Julius's intensity surprised me. I'd never before heard a hint of racial identification — political or otherwise. I thought about Simon having joined Sheinfeld's Temple and felt another rush of the past week's loneliness. But before I could change the subject, Julius lit another cigarette and clamped his mouth closed.

Quiet settled in and we sat chain-smoking. I retreated to the bedroom and grabbed my stash. It was odd to find myself thrust into a situation where Jewish meant more than Lou's warmth or a little Yiddish. Jewish meant something to Simon, certainly something to Yakov. Jewish definitely meant something to the Avengers. Jewish apparently even meant something to Julius.

For me, it was something that just was. Like my size or the color of my eyes. I was Jewish when Chana told me I had a Jewish heart. Or when Lou called me *boychik*. My handles on the world were personal, occasionally political. Religion was irrelevant, Jewish culture another world.

We walked slowly toward the living room door. I asked if he would see what he could unearth about Kelly. Especially any connection to armored car heists. Julius grunted his reluctant agreement. The door was open and his foot in the hall when I

reached out and grasped his shoulder. "Julie, you make sense about the case but the other stuff puzzles me. I never feel any of that Black-Jewish rift between us."

Julius's eyes opened. Really opened. I almost fell backwards. "Slumlord, I'm truly surprised you have to ask." His eyes slowly slid back to their sleepy droop. "But then, you do have the capacity to surprise. You don't get uptight about it, and it doesn't play between us, because you always remember."

"Remember what?"

"That at your motherfucking *best* you ain't nothing but a nigger turned inside out."

CHAPTER 16

Better to be outside than inside out. After a week of hibernation, the street was more attractive than Bakelite radios, ziggurats, or Lew Archer fantasies. More interesting than my obscene fondling of the television's remote. Liberating, actually, on this side of my drunken, stoned depression. I considered movies, junking, an indoor batting cage, but rejected them all. I wanted work not play. Real case or not.

And not just for Simon. I wanted work for *me*. My newfound balance hadn't left me indifferent to Cheryl's damaged hands. I *wanted* to stick it to Sean Kelly. It didn't matter that he was six feet under. If I could, I'd push him down another twelve.

But since I couldn't, I decided to break into his apartment.

It was likely the police already had removed everything of value, but doing detective was more powerful than any "likely." Kelly's home would give me a clearer picture than the one I had. And that picture was growing important. Kelly's "political" conversion, his relationship with Blue, his distance from the Avengers, and the possibility of his acting alone on *Simchas Torah* had combined to fire my curiosity. Digging up garbage no longer felt like a dirty job, just a small payback for Cheryl's injuries. It wasn't much, but it was the best I could do. Maybe it would be enough.

My first drive-by down the tired residential street was a surprise. I had expected to see a cave in the middle of a burned out block. Kelly's address, one side of a two-family duplex, was no more rundown than the other buildings. The two- or three-flats lining both sides of the street were clapboard, asbestos shingled, or aluminum sided. There was absolutely no sign of fresh paint, though all the houses needed a coat or two. Or three. Postage-stamp backyards were used as open air closets for broken and rusted toys. The entire area had a defeated feel. No trees, no grass, the unkempt houses virtually flush with the sidewalk.

I carefully scouted for Clifford or his shadows before I pulled the car into a spot up the block from Kelly's address. The parking space afforded a view of his first-floor door and two of his small bay front windows. I rejected the idea of a joint, instead smoked a cigarette while I thought about getting into the apartment. Since light facial bruises still peeked out from behind my large sunglasses, I couldn't pass for Fuller Brush.

I was surprised by the extent I needed to work. My desire to search Kelly's apartment was less a function of potential discovery, more a release of pent-up energy. By the time I jammed the butt into the ashtray it didn't matter. There was always the possibility of finding something the cops had overlooked. Something like Blue.

The thought had me fingering my shoulder holster. I didn't plan to shoot, probably wouldn't even break his hands. But until I had him in my sights, it was possible he had me in his. I wanted to be prepared.

A slight rustle to the bay window's shade caught my attention. I took off my sunglasses, sank low behind the dashboard, and stared. I waited but nothing moved. I wondered whether my eyes had deceived, seeing perhaps the movement of a cat on the small porch. I sat up, but the shade on the other bay window shook, so I slid back down. Then the shade cracked open; someone was spying from within. I stayed very still as, almost imper-

ceptibly, the shade closed. Now I fondled the gun, not the holster.

As if on cue the door opened. I felt my adrenaline rise, but a different color and gender than the one I expected slipped out onto the porch. It wasn't Blue. A tall, leggy woman with short red hair and oversized horn-rimmed "Linda Ellerbee" sunglasses leaned forward and worked the lock. She wore a hip length dark green down jacket and black jeans. The lock took a long moment but finally surrendered. I ducked as she turned my way. After a moment's hesitation, she zipped up her coat, swiveled in the opposite direction, and casually walked away from the house.

It hadn't occurred to me that the apartment might have been re-rented.

I quieted my interior jeering and tried to figure the next move. But sometimes there is no figuring. Sometimes "action is the only reality," and this was one of those times. If I hadn't seen her play hide-and-seek, or fantasized about her difficulty with the lock, I might have gone home. Probably not. I stuffed my cigarettes and watched the woman walk. Her arms swung in easy athletic rhythm as she turned the corner.

I waited a minute before I traced her steps to the intersection and veered off in a different direction. If I was going to play, I'd play it right. When I finally looked back, the redhead was rounding the far corner onto a thoroughfare in the direction of the neighborhood's "downtown." I plotted an alternate route to where I hoped we would meet. For a moment I forgot myself and started to jog but stopped a couple of wheezes later. There was no guarantee that she'd continue on foot. Anyway, I liked to breathe.

I thought about returning to my car but stayed the course, albeit a good deal slower. Unfortunately, by the time I got to my hoped-for interstice, I thought I'd been too clever by half. The woman was nowhere to be seen. I was more surprised than

pleased when, a couple of long minutes later, I spotted her coming from a block I hadn't anticipated. I crossed the street, climbed an apartment house's set of concrete stairs, discovered a bench, and waited for her to pass by. I lit a cigarette, my patience and planning rewarded as she strolled past the steps. She walked with a relaxed gait though she kept her head cocked, her fists curled. I gave her plenty of time to switch her way up the block, and me time to quell my detective fantasies. I *should* have returned to the car but I liked feeling invisible while I watched unsuspecting strangers go about their business. I'd always known that voyeurism had partially instigated my social work career, but hadn't admitted it until I became a detective. The more things change . . .

I last-dragged, flipped my smoke, and stood. I didn't want my enjoyment to frighten an innocent woman so I stayed far behind as I kept pace. What the hell, I was out of the house and she was moving at a clip I found comfortable. Eventually she entered the large Roman Catholic church near the trolley stop. According to the broken white sign in front, there was another five minutes until Mass.

Most of me knew my imagination was grasping straws, but I sat on a stoop hidden from the church anyway. It troubled me that she had taken a long and circuitous route. Nothing to see but three-deckers, no apparent reason for her twists and turns. The route might have been chosen to shake a tail. And I might be chosen Man-Of-The-Year. Still, there was no rush; if the lady returned to Kelly's apartment, I could skip the break-in.

I was crushing my third cigarette onto the stoop — wishing I'd packed a joint — when a few elderly parishioners straggled out from the tired granite edifice. I watched while people said familiar goodbyes. They were clearly regulars who knew each other well. When everyone was finally gone, with still no sign of my redhead, I called it quits.

I was starting back to my car when the woman emerged from

the church. I kept out of sight as she hesitated before heading up the street toward Kelly's. I was dismayed. She was homeward bound and I was out of fantasies.

I watched her turn the corner before I began kicking myself up the block. I had pissed the morning away. By the time I got to the corner the woman was gone, but I couldn't guess where. Incompetence shook hands with my annoyance. Cheryl had been able to tail me to Buzz's twice, but I couldn't follow an innocent pedestrian without fucking it up.

I ran to the next corner and saw her jogging in a different direction from Kelly's block. There had to be a thousand solid reasons for her behavior, but I had a certain amount of professional dignity to restore. Despite rib ache and shortness of breath, I followed her. Followed until I watched her slow to a walk, and let herself into a three-flat five or six blocks from where we originally began. I gave her plenty of time to settle in or come back out before I walked past the house. I glanced at the address, turned, and aimed for my car.

Kelly's block was very quiet: no moving cars, no people. No Clifford. I sat behind the wheel smoking a joint until my ache retreated into a tolerable soreness. A part of me felt guilty for wasting the morning, another part kept returning to the woman's behavior. I stared at the duplex. The appetite for tradecraft was gone, but my guilty frustration needed fixing. If I broke into Kelly's, I could tell myself I'd done what I'd intended.

I entered through the back door into the kitchen, knowing instantly I'd made the right decision. The place was stuffy, with dirty dishes piled high in the sink. Kelly's bleak apartment was dark and I almost flicked on the light before changing my mind. No need to disturb the cockroaches.

The redheaded woman didn't live here, no one did. The living room was a total mess. Books, tapes, and videos were haphazardly strewn about the floor. The beat-up electrical spool that had been used for a coffee table was piled high with

pamphlets. It was evident the place had been tossed. Not exactly a surprise. The police weren't known to clean up if no one was expected to return. Let the landlord worry.

I methodically pored through the mess, intent on my original goal. Whoever Kelly was, whatever he had been, he was not an easy take. The books were primarily hate literature: *Did Six Million Really Die? The Plot Against Christianity, Protocols of the Elders of Zion*, and the like. Then, a sprinkling of unexpected titles. *The Complete Works of William Shakespeare*, an anthology of Irish poetry, *Moby Dick*, and a huge book on the history of Ireland. To my surprise they looked as worn as the others. He'd probably bought them used. The tapes were a mix of porn and hate flicks. It surprised me the cops hadn't pilfered the porn.

I kicked my way through the crap into the bedroom only to be greeted with more of the same. Kelly's dresser had been emptied, all but the bottom drawer left on the floor. Someone had emptied everything onto the bed. I pushed a space clear, sat, and started to go through a pile of stenciled hate shirts. I stopped pawing once I got to his underwear.

I started back to the living room to collect a hate sampling for Simon. On my way out of the bedroom I mindlessly stooped to push the still filled bottom drawer back into the bureau. The drawer refused to budge. I wondered why the cops had left it that way. I tried pulling but ran into resistance in that direction as well. At first I thought the wooden runners were broken, but when I squeezed my hand behind the back they were intact. I tried to quick-jerk the drawer out but failed. Frustrated, I stuck my hand inside the drawer, felt around, found nothing. If something had been there, it was gone now.

I started to gather the stuff for Simon but found myself drawn to the book of Irish poetry I'd noticed in the living room. I had once given a similar book to my first wife, Megan. She had slashed it into sections the time she destroyed every gift I had ever given her.

I scanned the front of the book for a particular poem but didn't find it. Didn't even finish looking. The moment the paper slipped onto the floor, I forgot poetry, forgot Megan. The note was dated the previous year, its content a seductive invitation. The note was unsigned but contained an address.

The same address I had just left.

CHAPTER 17

Back in my car I sat struggling with an image of Sean Kelly leafing through poetry after a long day robbing armored trucks and rubbing shit on *shules*. I also had trouble believing the redheaded snoop an Avenger groupie. I wondered how she hooked up with Kelly. Everything I was discovering about my man Sean chipped at the stereotypical image of an ignorant, racist Jew-baiter. Blue, I understood. Fang and the rest of the khakis, I understood. But Kelly was slinking further away, not closer. The facets of his life that fueled Blue's resentment and jealousy continued to ignite my professional interest.

I was pleased with my morning's haul, but the pleasure didn't send me home blind and giddy. As I drove down the alley past the rear of my building I saw the door to my office slightly ajar. I *always* locked the door.

My pleasure plummeted through the gray gravel. Fear has a way of doing that. I kept driving until I came out the alley's end all the while answering the Isley Brothers. I was gonna find out who was making love to my old lady. I parked the car and skulked into the building's front entrance accompanied by the sound of a thumping heart. I knew whose. When I got downstairs I secured the gun in my left hand, quietly unlocked the

door with my right, inhaled deeply, and dove onto the living room floor arms outstretched and ready to fire. My week-long body pain was dispatched and forgotten. Fear has a way of doing that too.

Washington Clifford showed a lot of clean white teeth across his broad, polished, ebony face. Sitting comfortably on my couch, feet on the coffee table, he didn't stop eating from my family-size bag of Fritos. "For someone as sophisticated as yourself, you sure do keep a bimbo's refrigerator," he said holding up the bag. "Why don't you put your little shooter back where it belongs and try your hind legs? You look like a whale out of water laying down there."

"Maybe I like diving into empty pools," I said without moving.

"Doesn't surprise me," he said stuffing his mouth. "But you ain't gonna shoot me and it's hard having a friendly conversation while you're kissing floor."

I slowly stood, shook my head to his generous offer of Fritos, stuck the gun away, and sat on the recliner. I didn't put my feet up. "I'm not used to friendly conversations that begin before I'm here."

"I tipped you to company," Clifford said grinning over the crinkling of the bag. "Anyway, I'm not most people. Most people wouldn't consider blowing you away for not being where you're supposed to be."

My fear hadn't dissipated, but the hurt in my body was finding its way back. The pleasure, though, was nowhere to be found. Some feelings are just more fleeting than others. "Okay, Massa, sir! What do I owe for breathing?"

Clifford shook his big head. "Always running your mouth." He pulled his legs off the table, grunted to his feet, and lumbered over to my chair. He wore a suit but you could tell he did serious time humping gym iron. He stood over me, one hand hanging onto the Fritos. Before I could ask him to save me a few, his other hand slapped me hard across the face. I felt a tiny warm

wet trickle where his ring caught the corner of my mouth, but didn't move a hair until Clifford was back across the room.

"I'm glad this is a 'friendly' conversation," I said, daring to reach into my back pocket for a handkerchief.

"I mean to get your attention."

I pressed the handkerchief up against my mouth. "Next time, all you got to do is ask."

"What did you say? I can't hear none too good when you have your mouth full of linen."

I moved my hand. "I said you got my attention, Massa!"

Clifford shook his head. "You can't help it, can you? I could turn your face into a rotten mango and you'd still spit some wisecrack."

I put my palms up. "It's a nervous reaction, that's all. You know me, Wash, no self-control."

Clifford frowned. "The Wash I don't know about, the self-control I do."

My gut froze as he reached behind the couch, lifted up my gymbag, and put it on the table between us. I tried to wipe the wooden smile from my bleeding face and sit quietly but I failed at both. "Not mine, got it on a case I was working."

"Then you wouldn't have any objection to me taking it, would you, Jacobs?"

"Of course not. Planned on turning it in myself the next time I was Downtown. It's Jacob, without the 's', Wash. We've been through that routine a couple of times."

Clifford shook his head and stood. I knew what was coming. Maybe if he hit me enough he wouldn't bust me. Or maybe I just couldn't shut up. This time he grabbed me by the front of my shirt and pulled me out of the chair. He hesitated, and for a second I hoped he'd taken pity at the sight of my fucked-up face.

He had. This time he tried putting his fist out my back. Through my belly. He let go of my shirt and I tumbled back onto the chair, tears involuntarily starting from my eyes.

"It always comes to this with you," he complained from the couch.

"I'm sorry," I grunted while I wiped my eyes. Washington Clifford was not the type to respect a grown man who cries. "Next time I'll have more food in the refrigerator."

"I'm hoping there will be no next time."

He was hoping? When the queasiness in my stomach became manageable I asked, "What are you doing here?"

"What were you doing there?"

"Where? And who's on first?"

"Buzz's, a rumble, now Kelly's. That's where." He smiled but the mean never left. "Who is on first," he added softly.

The break-in hadn't restored my professional pride, after all. I wallpapered my face with an ear-to-ear grin. "That's good, Wash . . . Mr. Clifford."

"That's all right, Jacobs. Anybody as intimate with my fist as you can call me Wash."

"Thanks. You can call me Jacobs. I'm working for Roth." He must have known; he knew everything.

"What exactly are you doing for Roth? And I mean exactly."

"My job is to investigate Kelly and the White Avengers. Exactly."

"What have you discovered, Jacobs? Exactly."

"Well the Avengers are now led by — "

"I don't give a fuck about the Avengers. What have you got on Kelly?"

"Very little," I said earnestly. "Seems like he started as a thief, graduated to armored cars, saw the light and formed the Avengers."

Clifford folded his arms across his double-barreled chest. "What did you find in his apartment?"

"Nothing. I looked through his crap but came up empty. Unless you count the half dozen hate pamphlets and tapes I scored for Roth. I got so happy when I saw your hello in the alley, I left

them in the car." I waited for him to ask about the redheaded woman but he didn't. Maybe he didn't know about the note I'd found either. Maybe he wasn't omnipotent.

"Why did you go back into his apartment a second time?"

In the excitement of discovering the note I'd returned to the car without the literature. "Look, Wash, if you know I went in a second time, you also know why. I walked out without the shit, that's all."

Clifford stared through me as if I wasn't there. I could only hope. Finally he grunted and shifted position on the couch. "What are you holding back, shamus? You gave that up too easy."

I touched my face. "Only easy for one of us, Wash. And I still don't know why you're here. You already know everything that I do. We're not covering any new ground." I paused for a psychotic break. "Your wife out of town?"

Clifford stood as I tried to guess which part of my body was going to hurt next. But to my great surprise and greater relief he only grabbed the gymbag. "Jacobs, as much as I think PIs are lower than dog shit, I figure you for smart. Not real bright, but smart. You know what I mean?"

"Yeah." From here on in, as long as he stayed out of beating range, I was gonna agree with everything.

"Well, it's not smart to lie to me."

I considered telling him about the redhead. Even considered telling him about the note. But like the man said, I wasn't too bright. "Why the fuck should I lie? All I'm doing is collecting information about a group of racist, Jew-hating punks. The job has less glamour than a divorce gig. Why the hell would I lie?"

He didn't answer my question. "What are your plans?"

"I'm going to behave myself until you're gone, then I'm going to roll a big fat joint and thank my Maker for letting me live."

Clifford closed his eyes and spoke in a measured tone. "What are your goddamn work plans?"

"A balanced portfolio for retirement . . ."

His eyes remained closed but his jaw started to grind.

"I'm sorry, Wash. I'd like to interview the Jews who were present at the shootings. Then try to drum up a little information from the Irish side of the neighborhood. Nothing fancy."

"You already been too fancy," he said opening his eyes.

"I know and I apologize, really . . ."

"Shut up, Jacobs. I don't want your voice ringing in my head the rest of the day. Go about your business, but stay away from the townies. You want to fuck with what's left of the Avengers, be my guest. Even dog shit has to earn a living. But I don't want you bothering no one except the Beards or the Avengers. And you don't go telling anyone that we talked. Not your mother, your father, or Roth. Especially not Roth. You understand?"

An insane voice protested. Hell, I understood less now than before, but a new-age respect for my body maintained control. "Nobody from the Irish side of the neighborhood will talk with me anyhow. Didn't mean to get in your way."

"I didn't say anything about getting in my way, Jacobs." As Clifford walked past me, he dropped the gymbag onto my lap. "Don't forget to bring this Downtown."

I held my breath until I heard the door shut then rifled my stash. I pulled out grass and a pipe and let the bag drop to the floor. I stuffed the pipe, lit the grass, and smoked until the first wave of calm eased my anxiety. But it wasn't until after I'd had a cigarette that I trusted my legs to carry me to the bathroom. The lip cut wasn't bad; a small Band-Aid would blend with the rest of my look.

I returned to the living room, gathered my supplies, and flopped on the couch. I reached out and pushed the bag of Fritos off the table. The sight of them brought on waves of nausea. For a while I just lay there numbly, giving my body a chance to shake the anticipation of another blow. The tea leaves read the rest of the day as a TKO between figure and forget. Between cu-

riosity about Clifford's appearance, and the memory of his fist. But before I could decide, the telephone rang and I answered the starting bell. I guess it was still too damn close to the past week for me to feel comfortable on the couch.

CHAPTER 18

"I thought you were going back to work today."

I tried keeping him distinct from Clifford by reminding myself that Simon never used his fists. "I've been working, boss. Even made some progress."

"What do we have?"

We were going to keep it simple until I had a chance to ponder, and perhaps understand, Clifford's visit. "About a half dozen pamphlets and tapes straight from the horse's barn."

"What barn? What are you talking about?"

"I'm talking about Sean Kelly. I broke into his apartment, went through his stuff, and came away with a sampler. I left the porn there."

"You broke into his apartment, huh?" Simon sounded impressed. "What did you find?"

"Wall-to-wall hate. Tee shirts, tapes, books, videos."

"Anything else?"

"Poetry. A big fat history book. Underpants." I was reluctant to mention the note. Very reluctant.

"I mean useful."

"This is useful," I protested. "You wanted confirmation that Kelly was a bigshot in the Avengers and that the Avengers terror-

ized the Jews. This stuff has them in bed with fucking neo-Nazis. You're going to have a picnic sticking it to them."

"It's not enough," Simon grumbled. "I'd like more."

I had more to give. But my more wouldn't give him what he wanted. My more would give him a migraine. And me another visit from Clifford. "Relax, friend. I'll keep working."

"It's easy for you to say, but the Jewish community has its legs around *my* head. They are going to crack it like a fucking walnut if I don't close this case soon. Right now the Never Agains are exerting enormous pressure on the traditional organizations. And believe me, I'm hearing about all of it."

"You said the Never Agains weren't big-time?"

"Like you said, this situation helps them recruit. Well, it does more than that. Reb Dov's murder and the refusal to shut the book on Reb Yonah pushes everyone's Jewish early alert system."

"Almost everyone."

"You don't have an early warning system about anything, Matt. All of a sudden Never Agains are making angry sense to people who used to be disgusted by their rhetoric. People who know better. And the Never Agains are clever enough to make the most of it."

For a moment I wondered whether this was the pot Clifford was stirring. It seemed unlikely; after all, he hadn't warned me off the Hasids. "Who are they going to blow up? Kelly's already dead."

"I don't know what they're thinking of doing and neither does anyone else. That's what has everyone worried. People who aren't soft on the vigilantes are afraid the Never Agains will do something to really bring the heat. Do something that will boomerang back onto the Jews."

I fingered the new bandage on my face. "Well, Simon, I'm getting what there is to get."

"What are your plans?"

That's what everyone wanted to know. Me too. "Well . . ."

"Come on, Matt-man. What are you going to do now?"

"The Yeshiva." I paused. "Then back to the Irish."

That placated one of us. The wrong one. Him.

"Sounds good, I suppose. I don't have anything better to suggest." Simon groaned and added, "I'll try to calm things at my end, but it would be a helluva lot easier if Downtown shits or gets off the pot."

I hesitated, then, despite Washington's warning, strung a line. "Simon, what if Clifford really is involved?"

"Use your head for a second, will you?" He sounded disgusted. "Do you see that man concerned about a Hasid's death? Or some shanty Irish? This isn't his kind of work."

"What about Never Agains? What if they are planning some sort of action?"

This time he paused. "Okay, Matt, good question."

"Thanks, Dad."

Simon ignored me. "But it's off-base. Believe me, I'm taking a crash course in their operation. Never Agains always work through local organizations. People aren't worried that something will happen up here."

"Why not?"

"Because the group doesn't have a local chapter. No, Goomba, people are afraid the assholes will do something rash, but not around here."

"I suppose," I replied dubiously.

"Look, Matt, I have enough to worry about without your paranoid fantasies. If you or Phil have something more than a rumor, tell me. If not, leave it alone."

I *had* something more than rumor. But I would tell him later, when I knew what it was. Maybe. "Okay, Barrister, I was just wondering."

"And I'm wondering how you're feeling?"

"Like a million."

He didn't ask what a million felt like. I was glad because my million felt sickly green.

The fresh joint brought a rush of serious second guesses. I had withheld fairly pertinent information. Still, Clifford seemed completely disinterested in the Rabbi or the Avengers. His focus had been on Kelly. I'd gotten there myself; but something told me Washington hadn't arrived on the same bus.

Two hours later I felt a little better. And knew it when I'd stopped thinking of my Fritos as Clifford's. But only a little. I could eat the chips but couldn't come unstuck. Something important enough to involve Washington Clifford, yet tangential to the shootings was happening around me. Something larger than the Avengers and irrelevant to any legal hassle facing Reb Yonah. I chewed on my deep-fat-fried and fervently hoped Washington Clifford was breaking The National Armored Car Theft Association.

It was a bind. I didn't intend to tell Simon about Clifford's visit until I had followed my nose and discovered something useful and connected to the case. Problem was: I wasn't too excited about following my nose into Clifford's fist.

As my frustration mounted so did the need to do something. Only there weren't all that many *somethings* staring me in the face. It took a little bourbon, darkness, and my unwillingness to remain in the house before I capitulated to the inevitable. It was time to re-visit the Yeshiva.

Walking through the door into their rundown hall was, once again, a walk back in time. Unfortunately, the retreat didn't ease the soreness in my body or cause my bruises to disappear. It only made me feel older. As my eyes adjusted to the dim light, my nose to the building's musty smell, I felt a nerve-tightening anxiety. I leaned against one of the chipped walls, closed my eyes, and forced myself to relax. The anxiety was not the fearful dread of the past week's, nor the expectation of another painful blow. My tension, I reluctantly admitted, was fathered by an undercurrent of anticipation. I wanted to see the kid.

This visit I searched for the voices. And found them in a large dining hall downstairs. I stood unseen in the shadows just out-

side the door. Like airport radar, my eyes scanned the room until I found him sitting at a corner table with a couple of older men. The men were engaged in an animated discussion but Yakov seemed content to toy with his food. The entire room boomed with boisterous conversations, creating an incomprehensible din. It didn't help that none of the words were in English.

Now that I'd managed to force myself to return, I wondered about my next move. So I just kept standing there. Aside from the population, the room was colorless, painted a plain ancient gray. Along one side was a half wall that set apart a large working kitchen. The kitchen workers, all white-aproned, *yarmulked*, and bearded, were now at rest. Once in a while someone brought their plate to the counter and one of the bearded aprons would interrupt his own meal to pile the plate high with chicken, po-tatoes, and gravy. Frequently, people carried mugs to a large metal vat where they ladled out steaming coffee. I didn't see anybody add milk, but more than a few dumped serious sugar. Even so, as soon as I noticed the jo, I could almost smell it.

When the pale white hand touched my shoulder I realized I *was* smelling it. Not from the urn across the room, but from the cup I bumped when I whirled around. "I'm sorry," I said reaching for my handkerchief. I quickly stuck it back in my pocket when I saw the blood from Clifford's visit. "You gave me a scare," I explained.

"Then I should apologize, not you." The man reached into his suit pocket for his own handkerchief. "Did any of my coffee spill on you?" he asked.

"If it had I would have licked it off."

He stuck the handkerchief back into his pocket, stroked his stringy black beard, and looked at me quizzically. He suddenly smiled. "I get it. Most people won't come into the building." He looked at me with regret. "We don't have room for people to stay here, you know."

I hoped it was my bruised face that spurred his compassion. If it wasn't I'd have to change tailors.

"Thank you, but I don't need a place to stay. Or food. I just had a sudden hankering for coffee."

"Please don't be shy. I can tell by your face things aren't easy for you. We are always happy to share our good fortune. It's called a *mitzvah*."

The GAP could rest easy about my trade. "Well, things aren't easy, but it doesn't have anything to do with eating." I smiled. "Do I look undernourished?"

He glanced past me and I turned just in time to see Yakov arrive waving his hand and speaking in rapid-fire Yiddish. The man listened intently then looked at me. He responded to Yakov who shrugged and nodded. The man shook his head, drew back a step and said, embarrassed, "I made a horrible mistake. Yakov tells me that you work for Mister Roth. I thought . . ."

I rushed to reassure him. "That's okay, lots of people make the same mistake."

He nodded without meeting my eyes and rushed past me into the dining room. I turned back to a glaring Yakov. "You didn't have to make a fool of Eliezer."

"I wasn't trying to embarrass him, Yakov."

"I saw the two of you speaking. You had plenty of time to tell him who you were."

"I was starting to when you interrupted. What's going on? The last time I left we were friends."

"Friends?" He shook his head. "We were never friends."

"Okay, Yakov, friends might be a stretch, but now you want to tear my head off."

I reminded myself of the pressure he was under. "Look, maybe I dredge up your father's legal hassle, but I'm here to help, that's all."

The mention of Yonah cut through his anger and a pained look crossed his face. It was gone by the time he said softly, "Thank you for your reassurance, but I'm not worried about my father's legal problems."

"Then what's got your back up?"

He abruptly changed the subject. "What are you doing here?" he demanded.

"I told you I was going to return. I need to interview some of the people who were at the shootings."

He nodded. "Yes, so you said." He started to add something but changed his mind, standing silent until he waved his arm. "Do you intend to interview everyone?"

"Everyone was there?"

"Yes."

"Well, I probably only need to talk with a few."

He smiled without a trace of his mad. "I can help."

It wasn't professional, but then, neither was I. If this was his way of working things through, I wasn't going to squelch it. "Thanks, I could use the help."

"Do you need a quiet room?"

"It might be easier to set up camp at a corner table here. Unless you think it will disrupt people's dinners. This way I won't feel like a high school principal calling folks into the office."

"Wait here," he commanded. He ran into another room and returned with a *yarmulke*. "Put this on," he said, shoving it into my hand.

I tried screwing it onto the top of my hair, but I still had to hold it while I followed him through the cafeteria. He led me to a table in the rear. "Would you like something to eat before we begin?"

CHAPTER 19

"**J**ust coffee, please. Black. Oh, and Yakov, I'd be really grateful if you could bring me a pencil and some paper."

He looked surprised at my request, shook his head skeptically, but left the room. This wasn't a day I inspired a whole lot of confidence. I glanced around relieved to see people smoking, reached for a small tin ashtray, and lit up. I sensed that Eliezer had passed the word since no one ran over to offer me alms. Also, the decibel level was a little lower. Now the place just sounded like Fenway during a World's Series instead of the Humphrey Dome.

I sat back in my chair smoking to the chorus of singsong voices, a constant tugging of wild beards, the de rigueur black or gray suits shiny with use, the rocking back and forth in their chairs. The men, and there were only men in the dining hall, occasionally stopped their incantations to pore through oversized, leatherbound books held on their laps. Many people were so intensely engaged by their discussions they barely touched their food. Dinner at the Baal Shem Yeshiva was not a kick-back, chill-out time.

Actually, I appreciated the din. The noise created an illusion of privacy, allowing me an opportunity to eyeball an alien world.

When I realized that it had only been a short while since I sat in a freezer interviewing neo-Nazis, the sensation deepened. I was a Stranger in a Couple of Strange Lands.

Yakov, coming back, pen and notebook in hand, reminded me of a young colt, all legs and head, as he moved toward the half wall. A couple of minutes later he was toting a tray toward me that was filled with cups and a large pot of coffee.

"Sit down," he said as I stood up to help. "This should start us off. There is more if we want it."

Though pleased by the implied partnership I said, "Aren't you a little young for coffee this time of night?"

My remark scored a dirty look. "I've been drinking coffee since my bar mitzvah. Everybody does. It keeps you awake."

"I know what it does, but why do you want to stay awake?"

"To learn."

"The last time we met you said something about this learning. What exactly are you studying?"

"Mostly *Gemorah, Halacha.*" He stopped, looked at me, then said, "Our laws." Yakov waved his hand. "You have to think about it differently. The learning itself is everything. To spend time with our Rabbis' teachings, to have the privilege of studying Holy Words is a lifetime's joy. Every moment we learn brings us a great deal of pleasure."

"So we're talking God's work here?"

Yakov smiled. "Those of us who can, will spend our lives learning." He added, "I'll spend my life here, living like I do now."

"You know that already? What if . . ."

"There is no what if."

I thought about his desire to do the interviews, and wondered whether I was an unconscious "what if." "Will hanging around here with me get you in trouble?"

"Of course not." He seemed offended by the question. "No one tells me what to do. That's up to me."

The words jumped out before I could reel them in. "What about your dad? Doesn't he have anything to say?"

Yakov's mouth tightened. "I don't question my father and he doesn't question me."

"I'm not talking about questions or explanations. I'm talking about interest."

Yakov didn't answer. I drank my coffee and lit another cigarette. I was in no rush to work. It was comfortable feeling protective without my past getting in the way. "Yakov, I get the feeling that you were closer to Rabbi Dov than you are with your dad."

The boy's face darkened. "What difference does that make to you?"

A fair question that deserved an honest answer. "Maybe it's poking in where I don't belong, but I'm a little worried about you. You seem cut off from everybody else. Earlier I saw you sitting at a table. The other people were talking and eating but you weren't doing either. I know you were close to Rabbi Dov, but who are you close with now?"

Yakov's eyes flashed, and he shook his head defensively. "You say you're worried, but why should I believe you? You also said you were coming back to Yeshiva but you waited until the lawyer Roth made you return. Anyhow, I can take care of myself." There was a hurt, bitter tone to his voice.

I finally understood his anger. The boy felt trapped; caught between his hunger for, and fear of, contact. "Yakov, I'm sorry if you expected me back sooner, but Simon did not order me back to the Yeshiva."

"Then why has it taken so long? I expected you after our *shiva*."

I considered telling him about Becky but couldn't begin. Didn't want to begin. Instead, I let go of my breath. "I ran into a little trouble on the case."

"Your bruises are from my father's case?"

"Yeah. The Avengers stopped talking to me."

"What do you mean 'talking to you'?"

"I masqueraded as a writer to get information."

"Isn't that dangerous? Is that what you always do on a case?" He might spend the rest of his life hauling heavy Jewish, but

right now he had the excitement of a kid curious about the world.

"Slow down, boy. Detective work is mostly boring, plodding research. Believe me, I spend more time in libraries than on the street. The impersonation stuff is unusual."

"But it must be dangerous," he offered. "Look what happened to you. What if the Avengers had guns?"

"Nothing so exciting, Yakov," I dodged. "Just a couple goons who jumped me. No big deal." I couldn't help myself and added, "They got the worst of it."

Yakov nearly rose from his chair and said something in Yiddish.

"What's gotten into you?" I asked.

"You were the person who beat up the Avengers!" he said excitedly. "We heard a rumor about that but no one knew if it was really true. Now it turns out you were the one who did it." He wore a huge grin and looked around the room as if he wanted to shout the news.

I reached across the table and pulled on his suit cuff. "I'm telling you, Yakov, it wasn't a big deal. And I'm not sure it's something to be proud of. There are better ways to take care of business than fighting."

Yakov's head snapped back. "A moment ago you sounded pleased, now you sound like a teacher. This 'better way' didn't work for my Rebbe."

I'd struck another nerve. "No it didn't, but that doesn't change what I said. It reinforces it. Proud is part of the problem. All of us are brought up believing we're strong and powerful if we can 'beat' the other guy. That's tough to shake. Hey, when you told me about the basketball court I understood your frustration, but maybe your Rebbe had it right."

"Or maybe Rebbe had it wrong," Yakov said stridently. "At least about this," he added quickly. "Nothing is gained by allowing yourself to be abused. Or by running."

He drank from his cup and made a sour face when he discov-

ered the coffee cold. I waited while he freshened both our cups, and then he continued. "Jews feel proud about the people who were killed in the Warsaw ghetto. We feel pride in those who would not die quietly. Even the atheist Zionists understand this. The rest of the world respects them because they refuse to be intimidated. We need the same attitude here so people will stop pushing us around."

"I don't agree with you, Yakov. Respect doesn't mean much if it's gotten through blood." I paused then added, "Anyway, who are you going to stand up to? Right now the Avengers are out of circulation."

He shook his head stubbornly. "They weren't the first and won't be the last. Anyhow, you say one thing but do another. You fought the Avengers. Our community must learn to protect itself. This, at least, is something my father and I agree upon."

"Your father?"

"Yes. If the Rebbe had listened he would not have been sacrificed. My father has always wanted us to stand up for ourselves."

"You're talking like the Never Again people, aren't you?"

"What do you know about them?"

"I've just heard stories. Yakov, they don't sound very cool."

"Cool? We don't care about cool. We care about safety. The Yeshiva needs to be safe for us to have our life. We are different from everyone else and if we don't take care of ourselves, no one will. The Never Agains provide strength and protection!"

"And you and your dad want them here?"

"Yes, but the Rebbe did not agree. Just like the basketball court."

"What do the other Yeshiva people think about the Never Agains?"

"In the past most agreed with the Rebbe. Since his death it isn't so clear."

I shook my head, "I've heard that they do more than protect. I've been told they are a vigilante group."

Yakov waved his young hand dismissively. "Are you a vigilante?

What is the difference between what the Never Agains do and what you do? You work for people who need protection. If you have to fight, you fight. It's the same, except the Never Agains is an organization for Hasidim. And you are an individual who can be bought by anyone."

"Not anyone, Yakov," I said mildly. "I don't know enough about the group to argue with you, but when I first began working your father's case someone quoted, 'Choose your enemies carefully for eventually you'll resemble them.' Well, it probably applies to friends as well."

He started to retort but I didn't want to continue the disagreement. "It's time for us to work. It would be a big help if you could start with people who were right around the shootings. Maybe begin with the two or three who you think will be comfortable talking to me."

For a second Yakov looked as if I had blown it. But his interest in the assignment grabbed hold. He nodded and left the table.

I lit another cigarette, and tried to get my head into the job. I felt good about Yakov and me, though I found his allegiance to the Never Agains disturbing. But right now I needed to put it away until some other time. I wanted to make up for having forgotten a pen and paper. I wanted the boy to see a pro.

Maybe I was showing off, or maybe I was still smarting from being ID'd as a homeless, but I interviewed the hell out of the Hasids. People, describing the night of the shootings, said basically the same thing: Kelly caught their attention while he was screaming anti-Semitic slogans and curses; the crowd was too surprised and confused to react; given the chaos of the celebration, and the darkness of the night, no one had seen Kelly's gun.

No one realized there was danger, or even that the Rebbe had been shot until Reb Yonah ran toward Kelly with his own gun. By then it was too late.

Eventually I changed horses and focused on the Avengers' history of attacks on the Hasids. I had no trouble getting more specifics to bring to Simon. At one point I glanced up from my pen

and notebook, surprised to see my table surrounded by a dozen Hasids, each intent on recounting still one more harassment. I struggled to keep up with my notes.

After the last person had finally finished his story, the crowd dispersed and I wearily dropped the pen on the table and closed the notebook. "The Avengers really worked you guys over, didn't they?" I said to Yakov.

"Why do you think they have finished? These stories are the reasons we need to involve the Never Agains."

"I'm too talked out to argue, Yakov."

A sudden smile broke across his serious face. "You do this work well."

I felt a flash of rare pleasure. "It wasn't real difficult, kid. Everybody wanted to speak."

"They wanted to speak because you wanted to listen."

"That's my job."

"Will this help my father?"

"Simon says it will and he is a terrific lawyer."

Yakov stood up and looked away, as if embarrassed about his concern.

"Look, kid, it makes sense that you're worried."

A small sour look darted across his adolescent face. "My worries leave sense in the dust."

I waited but nothing more came. "What do you mean?"

"Nothing, Mr. Jacob."

"Now that we've worked together, do you think you can call me Matt?"

"Sure, Mis ... Matt." The boy looked around the now deserted dining hall. "Is there more you need to do?"

"Not tonight. Sometime I'd like to talk to your dad, and I may want to find someone who actually saw Kelly's gun go off, but 'that's all for now, folks.' "

"So you will or won't be coming back?"

He wasn't asking about interviews. "I'll be back, Yakov. You can count on it."

"I have to leave now." But he hesitated. "The lawyer Roth. Everyone says he is very good at what he does?"

"Simon leaves good in the dust."

"Do you want me to show you out?"

"I know the way. Anyhow, I want to have another smoke."

"Okay," he said reluctantly. He started to walk away then turned back. "You know, cigarettes aren't good for you."

I smiled. "I know. Thanks for the concern."

He blushed and mumbled, "Thank you for yours."

I watched as he left the room, poured myself the dregs of cold coffee, and had just returned the pot to the tray when I heard someone enter the room from a door in back of me. I turned, somehow expecting to see the kid, but was met by his father.

His angry father. "Are you finished with your intrusion?" Yonah stood glaring, fists on hips.

"Pretty much. I'd like to talk to you, though."

He mumbled something in Jewish.

"What did you say?"

"I said I haven't the time right now."

"That's what you said in your house."

He ignored me. "Why are you sitting here if you are finished with your questions?"

I piled the social debris onto the tray and stood.

"Leave all that there," Reb Yonah commanded.

I nodded, slipped into my jacket, and stuffed the notebook into my pocket. I held the pen toward Yonah. "Would you give this back to Yakov? It's his."

Reb Yonah gestured as if to slap the pen from my hand but held himself in check.

"What's the rub, Rabbi? How did I manage to get onto your bad side?"

"This is our Yeshiva, Mr. Jacob. Everyone here has work to do. Now that the Rebbe is no longer living the work is more important than ever. You waste our time."

I started to move slowly toward the door. "It's hard to under-

stand why you think helping you is a waste of time. That's what the people here were doing tonight. It wasn't a party."

"I don't need any help!" He kept pace with me, making certain I was really leaving.

"You sound like your son."

When we got to the dining room door Yonah suddenly reached out and grabbed my arm. "I don't need you to tell me how my son sounds. I don't need you filling his head with *goyische* ideas. I want you to leave him alone!"

I pulled my arm from his grasp. "I wasn't filling his head with any ideas, Reb Yonah. I like him, that's all. And my guess is he likes me. Is that what has you so upset?"

Yonah stared at me with venomous eyes. "*You* make me upset, not my son. You barged into my house without an invitation, you barge in here." He glared. "I don't need this help of yours!" Yonah pointed toward the steps. "The door to your world is that way. Leave ours alone!"

CHAPTER 20

By noon the next day I'd finished my job. Using newspaper morgues and police complaint files, I'd corroborated enough Hasid and Avenger hostilities to call it quits. There was no reason to listen to Simon's sermons or fear Washington Clifford. There was no need to exacerbate the tension between Reb Yonah and Yakov. No real reason to locate Blue. I could tinker with my Bakelite radios, go junking, visit with my tenants, or just get high. I was back in my own private New Jerusalem.

I settled down for the one o'clock movie—grass, cigarettes, and leftover Fritos close at hand. I was in luck, a non-colorized version of *Out of the Past*. Unfortunately, Mitchum had trouble holding me. I found myself wandering around the apartment, looking for, then rejecting things to do. My antsiness refused to quit until I finally decided to visit Cheryl.

Simon wasn't in his office when I dropped off the material. Once I yanked Sadie away from reading Alice Walker she was friendly as ever and gladly gave me Cheryl's home address. She mentioned that Simon wanted to talk. I asked her when he didn't.

Cheryl lived in an apartment building on the border of Dorchester and Mattapan. Her mother, a chubby, youthful-

looking, beaded-haired woman in her late fifties, let me through the door. I watched her large backside roll beneath an oversized flowered skirt as she went to get her daughter. The television voices from "Hard Copy" stopped in mid-sentence and a moment later the two of them emerged from a room in the back. With her fro'd-out hair Cheryl looked like a young Angela Davis. Though her rich skin was drawn and her hands in casts, when she saw me her lightly sedated eyes brightened and a smile lit her face. "This is the guy I told you about, Ma. You know, the man who kicked butt when he found out I was in trouble."

The chunky woman, already on her way out of the room, turned back. "You were a little late, weren't you?" But there was no recrimination in her voice.

"I'm sorry, Mrs. Hampton."

She inclined her head. "No need to apologize. You did what you could, I'm sure. I tell this young lady that journalism is dangerous work these days, but she won't listen."

"Ma," Cheryl complained, "do you have to start that again?"

The woman glared at her daughter. "I never stopped, girl."

"I know, Ma. How about putting it on hold for a little while?"

Mrs. Hampton shook her head and asked me, "Is there something I could get you?"

"Maybe a glass of water, ma'am."

"Listen up, young man. Don't be calling me ma'am. In fact, don't call me Mrs. or Ms. My name is Charlene and if my daughter had remembered her manners, we'd have been properly introduced."

"Matt, Mrs . . . , I mean Charlene."

"All you want is water? Something your size . . ."

Cheryl interrupted. "The man said a glass of water, Ma. If he wanted something else he'd ask."

"How do you know, girl? This is his first visit. Maybe he's bashful. Matthew, I cook a mean homemade ham."

I tried to keep the sudden rush of hunger from my voice. "No ma'am, I mean Charlene. I'm not shy. I'm really not hungry."

"See?" Cheryl said.

Her mom didn't answer, just strode toward the kitchen.

After a moment's awkward hesitation, Cheryl said, "Why don't you come with me?" She led us to a small, fake-wooden-paneled room and pointed to a large couch.

I sat and looked around. The room was dominated by a furniture model television and a modern stereo system. Records were piled high along each side of the television and on either side of the speakers. "Someone likes music," I said.

Cheryl smiled ruefully, "Yeah, both of us. She likes the big old bands, Ellington, Basie, stuff like that. I like different groups."

"Like who?"

"Like Eddie Palmieri. You ever hear of him?"

"Sure. I have 'La Verdida' and a 'Best of.' "

Another grin split her delicate features. "That must be why I do better with you than her."

I felt another bolt of desire. And this time it wasn't hunger. "Well, you both like good music," I said lamely.

Cheryl frowned. "I guess. But cooped up together like this makes us crazy."

"That's the damn truth." Mrs. Hampton entered the room carrying a serving dish piled with sandwiches. She also carried a pitcher of iced tea.

"Ma, Matt said he wasn't hungry."

"He said one thing, his face said another. Sheesh, girl, you're supposed to be the reporter." She winked at me. "This is my homemade. You're not going to get ham like it anywhere else."

"Leave him alone, Ma."

"Now quiet, Cheryl. You were talking about us driving each other crazy, well, you're doing it to me right now. I'm getting out before you succeed." With that she snatched a sandwich from the plate, smiled, and left the room.

Cheryl shook her head. "She means well."

I grabbed a sandwich and munched. "She cooks good too. This tastes terrific."

"Making a liar out of me?" Cheryl grunted.

"I'm a sucker for pig. *You've* been inside too long."

"No maybe about it. I haven't thanked you for stopping by."

"There's no need to thank me, I wanted to see you."

My words hung taut in the air between us. Cheryl glanced at me. "Are you still working on the case?" she asked finally, breaking the uncomfortable silence.

"Off the record?"

"Okay," she agreed.

"You promise?"

"You're talking to me like I was a child."

So I told her. Told her about everything except the depression. When I told her about the redheaded woman I could see the curiosity in her eyes. When I told her about Clifford's visit she grew indignant.

"Basically, he told you to make yourself scarce, to get off the case?"

"Not really. He told me to stay away from a piece of it, that's all. I think we just overlapped. My guess is he's working the armored car angle. Nothing to do with the Hasids and the Avengers."

"Bullshit," she said, her eyes flashing. "There's no such thing as an overlap. If he told you to stay away from Kelly, he's telling you not to do your job. Running you off."

"I don't think so, Cher. Anyway, Simon has everything he needs to plaster the Avengers to the wall. That was my job."

"And you're not the least bit curious? About the woman? About Kelly calling attention to himself? About what's got your friend Clifford slapping you around?"

"He isn't a friend."

"You really don't give a damn about what's going on, do you?"

"I understand Kelly's outburst, Cheryl. The area was crawling with people. To get a decent shot he had to clear people out of the line of fire."

"You're selling, Matt. Hard selling. Only you wouldn't be sit-

ting here telling me all this if you didn't smell the stink. Sheet, when you talk I smell it."

"Hey, I brushed my teeth this morning."

"Hey yourself, White Man. Roth said you're good at this. Hell, I know you're good. You got to the Avengers and got them to talk. Matt, you know something strange is happening here?"

I'd spent the first half hour of my movie shoving all that knowing aside. "Let's pretend there is. Who will it help if I stick my nose where it doesn't belong?"

"Where Washington Clifford tells you it don't belong!"

I shrugged.

"You're scared of that man."

"Sure I'm scared. He could pull my license, beat on me again, or worse."

"You'll wade into a group of vicious punks but you won't mess with a cop?"

"Cops, not just Washington Clifford. I feel more comfortable with punks than Blues."

"What are you talking about? You're a detective."

"I'm not in the business for the same reasons as the police. I don't much care about 'law and order.' "

"Then what *do* you care about? It sure doesn't sound like you give a damn about getting at the truth."

I groped for words. "I'm interested in people and I like looking for things," I finally said. I didn't say "looking for myself," which was what I thought.

"Well, you ain't showing much interest, and you surely ain't looking hard."

"I told you, Cheryl, I don't cross cops."

"Even when it means leaving your friend Simon flapping in the breeze."

"I gave Simon everything he needs to walk the Rabbi. That was my job and I did it. Curiosity didn't win you the Pulitzer, sweetie." She'd gotten me annoyed.

Cheryl raised her hands. "I'd do it again."

"Maybe the twenty years between us makes the difference."

She shook her head. "Doesn't have anything to do with age. It has to do with changing the way things work." She paused, then said regretfully, "Damn, I wish I could be out there. I'd show you what's what."

"Don't even think about it young lady." Mrs. Hampton strode through the doorway.

"You've been eavesdropping," Cheryl accused.

"No, I've been listening," Charlene corrected. "From what I heard this man makes good sense. Stop pushing your face where it don't belong. Why can't that sink into your thick, woolly head?" Mrs. Hampton swung around in my direction and I expected a blast but all she said was, "Did you enjoy the ham?"

"It was terrific, Charlene."

"Charley."

"Charley."

She turned back to her daughter. "I want you to stop this foolishness. If this man thinks something is too risky you have no right urging him on. None at all."

Cheryl shook her head sadly. "I wish I could do it myself."

"And thank the Lord you can't. Girl, you're lucky to be standing here. Look at yourself, both hands in casts."

I'd worn my welcome a little thin. "I have to leave, Cheryl. How long do the casts stay on?"

"A month tops," said Cheryl.

"A minimum of six weeks," said Charlene.

I stood. "Would it be all right if I dropped in again?"

"Of course." The two women spoke at once.

"Be a better visit if you do what you ought to," cracked Cheryl.

"Now don't you pay any attention to her," Mrs. Hampton instructed.

I had a dismal thought. "Cheryl, I know you feel strongly about this, but what I told you was off the record and confidential."

"You mean don't go talking at the paper?"

"Anywhere. *Even* Simon. I don't want you to talk to anyone."

"I'll think about it," Cheryl answered.

Before Mrs. Hampton could dress her down I said, "Listen, you respect my confidentiality and I'll think about what you said."

"You'll stay on the case?"

"I'll think about it."

This time it was Charlene who shook her head.

A mischievous smile broke across Cheryl's face as she stood. "Fair enough," she said. "Now I'll walk you out."

When we arrived at the door that tense silence descended once more. There was no mistaking what it was and it made me uncomfortable. I nodded and skipped out of the house.

The ride home was a breeze — no traffic, no car trouble. At one point I found myself tapping my hand on the steering wheel to Dire Straits' "MTV." I was surprised; I hadn't expected the doorway tension to lighten my mood. Up till now I'd bundled Cheryl in with Yakov as a finished job. By the time I was sitting at my kitchen table the bundle was breaking apart. Without Cheryl's prodding I might have let things slide. But Cheryl *had* pushed and I was going back to work.

I debated telling everything to Simon. Hell, if I was going to disobey Clifford's first commandment, there was no reason to uphold his second. But I was concerned that an anxious Simon would shake trees that would tumble me to Washington. Also, despite Cheryl's scorn, the odds still favored an overlap. I decided to go easy and break one commandment at a time.

I rolled a joint and considered my next move. Despite hazy purpose and clear risk, I enjoyed returning to the hunt. I took a couple of tokes to somber up. I'd already done too much mindless to add more now. I thought about trying, again, to ferret out information from the neighborhood, but wasn't quite ready to spit in Clifford's face.

I walked into the bedroom, pulled the gun case from under the bed, and brought it back to the kitchen table. I lit a cigarette, opened the box, and stared. After a couple of minutes I dragged out the holster, strapped it on, then cleaned the gun. I wasn't planning to use it but the equipment helped me feel like a real gumshoe. I glanced at the clock, nodded to the cat's shifting eyes, and shoved the .38 into its leather. It was time to visit my redhead.

CHAPTER 21

Clifford hadn't known that I'd followed her — at least he hadn't hit me for it. So the woman seemed like a relatively safe place to begin. Especially if I didn't run her to the police.

I worked hard to shake any potential tail before I drove to the address on the note I found in Kelly's apartment. The same three-flat I had followed the redhead to. I pulled into a parking space up the block in case she wasn't home. *If* this was her home. On the short walk to her building I cursed myself for not having brought something to read; I hadn't considered the possibility of a wait.

There were names attached to the three mailboxes on the front porch. Two of the tags suggested *Kirche und kinder*; the third-floor box read D. RYAN. I pushed the bell and waited. After a couple of disappointing minutes I tried again, ready to give myself a reaming. But just before my foot hit the step the front door jerked open and I stood facing my quarry.

"Can I help you?"

Though her face glistened with fresh sweat, the woman's tone was neutral, her breath steady. She wore a long-sleeved, perspiration-dampened, white tee shirt low riding over black

spandex leggings. "I think so. I'm trying to gather information on the White Avengers."

"What does that have to do with me?" Rubbing her sleeve across her face in a short, choppy gesture.

"Well, it's come to our attention that you knew Sean Kelly."

"Our? Who is 'our'?" she asked, dropping her arm back down to her side.

"Kelly was shot in self-defense after he assassinated an important local Rabbi. I work on the defense team for that person, a Rabbi Yonah Saperstein, who killed Kelly."

"Do you have any identification?"

I handed her the photostat of my ticket.

She handed it back. "From the way you describe the incident it's difficult to see the need for a private investigator. Anyway, this has nothing to do with me. Where did you get your misinformation?"

"Perhaps we could go inside? I'm cold so you must be freezing."

The woman hesitated. "Sure. I forgot my manners. Come on in."

I followed her up the stairs. Occasionally she took two steps at a time and a pair of dark red gym shorts peeked out from under the long shirt. By the time we got to her apartment I was breathing heavy but it wasn't just from the view. It had been a long three flights.

Ms. Ryan watched me catch my breath, an amused look on her face. "Don't work out much, do you?" she asked.

I saw a large all-in-one gym on one side of the room. "Every once in a while. How much did that thing set you back?"

She shook her head. "You don't want to know."

"I see them advertised on late night television but they never give the price. Anyway, I'm afraid it would end up in the basement next to the rowing machine and the fanny-flattener."

She smiled slightly. "The type they sell on television isn't very well made."

"That's okay, neither am I."

She squinted her eyes. "I can't imagine why you're questioning me. I really don't have any information about the shootings."

"None?"

"Only what I read in the papers."

"Well, that's not entirely true, is it? By the way, what does the D stand for?"

Her questioning look disappeared and she glanced at me coolly. "Deirdre. You sound pretty confident for someone who doesn't even know my name."

I shrugged. "Some things I know, some I don't."

"That's not good enough, Mr. Jacobs."

"Jacob, without the s."

"With or without the s, it's not good enough."

"Then please call me Matt." Deirdre wasn't hostile or angry, just rock firm. I stood for a moment and took my first hard look. She was older than I'd thought, though you couldn't tell it by her supple body. Only the tiny crow's-feet at the corners of her green eyes, the slight roughness of skin on the back of her hands, and the darkening of some of her face's freckles, gave her away. All but the nail on her left ring finger were closely cropped. That one extended a quarter inch beyond her finger. She wore no polish. Kelly's age and the seductive tone of Deirdre's note reminded me of Doris Lessing's notion that the sweetest morsel in the smorgasbord of love was the one between an older woman and a younger man. Standing six inches away from Deirdre, older man, older woman didn't seem half bad either.

"Would you mind excusing me for a second?" she said interrupting my thoughts. "I don't feel comfortable talking to you in these clothes. I was in the middle of my exercises when you rang the bell."

Before I answered she had spun toward a door that led to the bathroom while I regretted the length of her tee shirt. Despite

the flatness of her demeanor there was an undercurrent of hard. Or maybe distance. I couldn't tell. When the door closed I looked around the living room. A large bookcase on one wall was filled with modern literature. Her collection included the Vintage Contemporary Fiction Series. So did mine; I liked the covers. But even with the bookcase, the room had a transient feel. The beat-up and scratched oak floors were without rugs, the windowshades without curtains, the wall paint a faded off-white. Somewhere to stay but no place to call home.

"A detective who reads." Deirdre had silently reentered the room.

"I couldn't find the television," I grinned. She wore a very loose pair of army-green canvas pants with open ankle zippers over the spandex, but had left her shirt alone. I hadn't heard a toilet flush and wondered why it had taken her as long as it had.

"I don't own a television. A radio is enough."

"Enough what?" I replied with another grin.

"Enough of this. Why are you here, Mr. Jacob?"

"Matt. Look, Deirdre, I *know* you knew Kelly. Why play games?"

She smiled glumly. "No games. It wasn't common knowledge that we knew each other. It surprises me you found out." She paused and added, "I didn't know him very long. A couple of months, maybe."

According to the date on the note, a couple of months meant more like a year and a half. "Then why the denial?"

"Frankly, once I read about the shootings I didn't want to get involved. It doesn't help a single woman's reputation to have police visits." She held her palms to the sky then waved toward the chairs spread out in the room. "Why don't we sit down?"

Deirdre chose a straight-backed chair while I found one I hoped wouldn't collapse under my weight. I pulled it across the room close to her. "What do you do for a living?" I asked, sitting gingerly.

"I'm a teacher but right now I work as a temp."

"Why does a teacher work as a temp?"

Her left hand had balled into a fist. "Where do *you* live? They haven't hired a new teacher in this city for years. Anyway, what does my job have to do with Sean Kelly?"

"It's difficult to picture the two of you friends," I said by way of an answer.

"I didn't say we were friends."

"Then what were you?"

"I said I knew him."

"I know what you said. I'm asking about what you won't say."

Deirdre sat quietly thinking. "We were acquaintances, if you will," she said.

"Which brings me back to what I said before. It's a little hard to imagine."

"Perhaps there is a problem with your imagination."

"The man was a neo-Nazi. You too?"

"Don't be ridiculous," she said evenly. "That had nothing to do with me."

"Then what did? From what I gather the Avengers were his life."

"Not his entire life. We met because he wanted a high school diploma. I am an unemployed teacher, so he hired me to tutor him. We never discussed politics. It was simply a way for me to teach."

Hammer time. "Come on, Red. Put away the shovel. You were closer than that. Why are you still bullshitting me?"

Maybe the crow's-feet deepened and her fist tightened, but I couldn't swear to it. The woman was cool. She kept her eyes locked to mine. "You're beginning to be rude."

"And you are continuing to withhold information."

Deirdre slowly stood. "Mr. Jacob, I've told you the truth. I didn't want to get involved with those horrible shootings, and your attitude is precisely why. I refuse to listen to anyone's insinuations. If you don't mind I'd like to get back to my workout."

I didn't know how to press the envelope so I left it open. "If

the information I received was wrong, Ms. Ryan, then I apologize for disturbing you," I said getting to my feet, relieved to be off the chair.

She smiled but her eyes remained watchful. "You have a way of putting words in someone's mouth, don't you? I never said I was disturbed."

I returned the smile and sauntered toward the wrong door. "It's a projection thing, that's all."

She walked alongside me, gripped my upper arm, and steered me in the proper direction. Despite my leather jacket, her fingers dug deep. "Sometimes that 'projection thing' is all anything is."

We were at the door before she let go. I opened it and walked out to the landing before I said, "Sometimes."

"That's what I said," she replied closing the door behind me.

I lit a cigarette as soon as I got back to the car. I didn't bother sticking the key in the ignition since I planned to hang around. Every shamus has his fantasies. Right now, the hope that Deirdre was going to lead me to something useful was mine. I settled in without really expecting anything to happen. This dick was still able to separate fantasy from reality.

But occasionally the two coincided. When Deirdre's front door suddenly swung open, I dove down onto the car seat so fast I dropped the cigarette. With my nose buried in torn upholstery, I blindly fingered the floor. And got burned for my trouble.

I swallowed a swear, yanked my hand away, and hoped the butt didn't burn through the floor rust. I let a minute pass before untwisting from a position reserved for teenagers in love and lifted my sweaty head high enough to peek out the window. Deirdre hadn't stayed upstairs doing pushups.

This time I followed her very carefully. Despite her overt nonchalance, Deirdre was alert. But I did good tail, and followed her unseen all the way to the same Roman Catholic church she had

visited the last time. Only this time, if the broken sign was to be believed, there was no Mass for her to attend.

I sat across the street on a stoop in full view of anyone leaving the church. I was squashing my third smoke underfoot when I saw a black-clad arm push the church door open. Deirdre was accompanied by a tall blond crewcut in full priest regalia. Both were frowning. The priest was talking when Deirdre spotted me. Her frown quickly disappeared. When she said something and nodded in my direction, his frown momentarily deepened. But by the time they had crossed the street and stood in front of me, both wore friendly looks.

"Hello again," said Deirdre. "You're a bit early for Mass."

"It takes me a while to screw up enough courage. Short workout, huh?"

The priest stepped forward. "I don't think we've met. My name is Brady Collins," he said forcefully. "Deirdre told me that you're working on the Kelly situation?"

"Well, Kelly's situation seems clear. I'm working for Rabbi Saperstein. My name is Matt Jacob. Matt is fine."

"Good, good. Formalities bug me too. Please call me Brady."

Brady stuck out his hand and I stood to grasp it. Up close it was possible to see more than the blond crewcut and white teeth. In fact, it was a crewcut with sneaky sideburns. I didn't know whether the style was fifties, or the nineties had a new thing happening. Collins emitted a visible tension despite his forced friendliness. I couldn't tell whether his worry was constant or caused by me.

"Deirdre mentioned that she's spoken to you about her reclamation project," Father Collins said smoothly.

"Reclamation project?"

He chuckled. "That's what I called her work with Sean Kelly."

"She mentioned it. Sounds like you had your doubts."

He nodded his head vigorously. "More than a few. Frankly, I harbored little hope of that boy accomplishing anything." Col-

lins waved a long tapered finger. "Don't get me wrong, it would have been wonderful but . . ." He let his words drift away.

"Brady," Deidre filled in the space. "You weren't as pessimistic as you're making yourself out to be." She faced me. "He encouraged me to tutor Sean, if you want to know the truth."

"I'm always interested in the truth," I said, meeting her eyes.

"You seem a little hostile, Matt. Or are you naturally abrasive?" Brady observed with a sharp look.

I retreated a half-tone. "What you're hearing is frustration. I'm having an impossible time getting anyone around here to talk with me."

Father Collins shook his head. "That I understand. It took me a while to make friends, even though a certain amount of trust comes with the job — if you know what I mean."

"Well, maybe I could borrow your collar or give you a list of questions."

He flashed another automatic smile. "I'm afraid we wear different sizes and, unfortunately, my time is quite spoken for." He glanced at my face. "You were poking fun, weren't you?" Father Collins turned toward Deirdre. "Deirdre constantly accuses me of being too serious. She admonishes me to lighten up." He said the words "lighten up" as if they were foreign. Maybe for a priest they were.

"I don't admonish you about anything, Brady."

"I chose the wrong word," he assured her with gusto. "Deirdre is heaven's gift to our church. She really makes things happen around here. An incredible volunteer. I pray the archdiocese assigns us an intern before she finds a permanent teaching job." Brady shook his head gloomily. "I don't want to think what will happen if no one takes her place. There is little enough time as it is."

The mention of time dragged his arm out from beneath his flowing black robe. He read the Timex and jerked his head back up. "I apologize for looking at my watch but I just remembered an appointment. Do you see what I mean about time?"

I nodded understandingly. "I have a couple of days a year like that."

"But none of this really helps you, does it?" He turned toward Deirdre. "What can we do to make Matt's job a little easier?"

Deirdre shrugged. I didn't get the feeling she wanted to make my job easier.

Father Collins suddenly clapped his hands. "What about the lecture?" He pivoted away from Deirdre and back to me. "We get terrific speakers at our Thursday night forum. This week we have someone who spent his summer touring Ireland. It should really be fascinating and any time someone brings back firsthand news of the Island, we pull a crowd. I can't promise you how much time I'll have, but I'm sure between the two of us we can get you started."

Deirdre wasn't jumping for joy. "I've already started," I said blandly. Couldn't help myself; Deirdre hadn't jumped for joy.

"Well, whatever you decide," Father Collins said. "I think you'll find *some* people a little more gregarious if they meet you through the church."

"I'm sure you're right, Father. I'd love to come."

Brady smiled, nodded, and shook my hand. "Good. You might even find the program interesting. We begin at seven-thirty and serve light refreshments after the Q&A." He dropped my hand and turned to Deirdre, "I have to run."

"I know," Deirdre said. "Mr. Jacob will walk me home."

It wasn't a question. "I'm going the same way," I acknowledged.

The priest, apparently satisfied with this little corner of the world, bowed toward the two of us, twirled, and strode vigorously back into the hulking church.

CHAPTER 22

I broke the awkward silence. "Is he always so aggressive, intense?"

Deirdre looked startled. "Father Collins isn't usually described as aggressive."

"How would you describe him?" I asked.

She started toward home. "Enthusiastic. Committed and enthusiastic."

I fell in step. "Committed? To what?"

"To his parish. To the well-being of the people in the community." Deirdre glanced at me from the corner of her eye. "And you? What is it that you are committed to?"

"I don't understand what you're asking."

"When you first arrived at my apartment you made your case sound cut-and-dry. So where does your persistence come from?"

I shrugged. "It's not very complicated. My boss wants as much information as possible about Sean Kelly and the rest of the Avengers. It's my job to get it."

Deirdre stopped walking and smiled. "Are you always so determined?"

I met her eyes. "When a case gets under my skin."

"And this case is?"

"It's starting to."

We continued our walk back to her apartment in silence, until Deirdre said, "Brady's comment that Sean was a reclamation project was true."

I nodded. She clasped my arm in her strong hand. "I knew about Sean's anti-Semitism and gang activities. But there were other things about him, as well. He grew up without any guidance, without anyone caring. Had there been alternatives to the street, Sean might have made a success of himself. I saw that potential and wanted to give it an opportunity to flourish."

"The padre didn't think much of your chances."

Deirdre ran her free hand through her short hair. "I believe Brady had more faith than I did. But he was afraid I would become hopelessly disappointed if it didn't work out. He was protecting me."

"From disappointment?"

"Mr. Jacob . . ."

"Matt."

"Matt. When I met Father Collins I was quite different than I am today. I was totally depressed about my inability to find a job. About my life in general. When Brady realized what I was going through, he urged me to recruit private students. He was proud that I was able to involve someone like Sean. Someone everyone else had given up on."

"It looks like everyone else was right."

Deirdre, eyes down, nodded. "I really can't explain it. I was certain Sean was separating himself from that gang. I guess they had a stronger hold on him than I realized."

"Why the lies?" I asked quietly.

"What I told you in my apartment was true. I didn't, I *don't* want to be dragged into this mess. I'm embarrassed about my failure. I actually believed that once Sean had a different focus, he'd give up all those ugly ideas."

Deirdre glanced at me with a small smile. "I haven't been withholding as much as you think. Sean had me promise never to tell anyone but Brady about our work. He was afraid to be hu-

miliated by the rest of those awful Avengers. I wanted him to be proud of what he was doing, but no amount of talk or reason would change his mind. It was a condition he set. I've really told you more than I should."

"Deirdre, Sean is dead."

We were at her house. The temperature had dropped, and when she let go of my arm she tugged her coat tighter around her body. She looked up at me. "Have you ever made a promise to someone who died? It's harder to break, not easier."

I nodded sympathetically, but flattened my tone. "Deirdre, you didn't run to the church after we talked because you broke a promise to a dead man."

She sat down on the steps to the porch and closed her fist. "Mr. Jacob, have you ever done things you knew were wrong but were helpless to stop?" She didn't meet my eyes.

Given enough time, most of my life might have flashed by. "I've had the experience."

The redhead took a deep breath. "You asked if Father Collins was always this intense. Well, the truth is, he was very upset when we left the church just now."

I stood still, waiting for her to continue.

"This makes me very uncomfortable," she said.

"If it's any solace, I'm pretty good at keeping quiet."

"The reason I went to the church had to do with your potential to discover the reality about Sean and myself. Once I realized that you knew something about us, I was frightened you would discover the rest." Deirdre took a deep breath. "You see, Mr. Jacob, Sean and I were having an affair." She rushed on, "I was alone and lonely and thought there was something special about his desire to better himself.

"I couldn't take the chance that Brady would learn about it from someone else. He has incredible trust in me, and I let him down. It was important to tell him myself. When you met him, he was still quite upset."

I sifted through her admission. "Well, now that that's out of the way, perhaps you could answer a couple of questions? I'm not interested in your sexual relationship with Kelly. Only his connection to the Avengers and the armored car burglaries."

She covered her face with her hands and shook her head. "Unfortunately, it's not out of the way for me. I'm still asking myself about what happened." She dropped her hands and twisted her face into a sour grimace. "You aren't a therapist as well as a detective, are you, Mr. Jacob?"

"Matt. No, but I can refer you to a good one. Don't be too hard on yourself, Deirdre. Needs play out in many different ways."

"Thanks for the reassurance." Her face lost a little of the lemon. "Now, I really do have to work out. I guess I'll see you Thursday night?"

"What about my questions?"

"Oh, I'm sorry. What I told you earlier was the truth. Sean and I never discussed the Avengers. I tried to talk with him about it many times but he refused to say anything about them. Ever. As far as armored car robberies, well, this is the first I've heard about that." She started up the stairs. "I really have to run, Mr., uh, Matt. I'm due back at the church in a couple of hours."

"One last thing."

She already had the front door open but turned back toward me. "What is it?"

"Didn't you ever wonder where he got the money to pay you for his school lessons?"

She stared past me. "I wouldn't touch a dime. I felt enough like a slut without taking money."

I drove home on auto. Deirdre's story explained her actions and might also explain why Washington Clifford wouldn't much care about her. Still, my discomfort remained. Perhaps it was due to an inability to picture Deirdre and Kelly in *any* relationship,

much less a sexual one. Or maybe it was the circuitous walk to the church the first time I saw her.

I told myself to be patient. Told myself I'd learn more on Thursday night. Nevertheless, it wasn't until I drove past the front of my building that Deirdre really left my mind.

Yakov was sitting on the front steps, his face buried in a thick book.

I pulled into the nearest parking space and walked over. "Easy reading?" The book's cover was dotted with Hebrew lettering.

Yakov looked up, startled by my voice. "I didn't hear you," he said nervously. Then, as if he had just registered my question said, "This is the *Talmud*. It's not easy reading."

I smiled. "I take it you aren't lost?"

"Of course not."

"Have you been here long? Someone should have let you into my apartment."

"Someone offered but I didn't want to go inside with him."

"Why not?"

Yakov looked at me suspiciously. "I think he was a *faigeleh*. A homo."

The Yeshiva needed a new-age rabbi. "I know what a *faigeleh* is. Do you know it's an insulting term?"

"I know that a man with makeup on and a woman's babushka on asked me inside. That's what I know."

Understandable but amusing coming from a kid with earlocks and fringes. "That's Charles. He's the superintendent of the buildings."

"Who would hire *him*?" Yakov asked incredulously.

"Me," I smiled. "Charles is a terrific person. Sometimes it helps to look past the first page."

Yakov shrugged dubiously and stood up. "Perhaps it was a mistake to come here?" he said.

"I don't know. Let's go inside and find out." I started up the outside steps and added, "You don't have to be afraid, I'm not wearing any makeup."

"I didn't say I was afraid," he retorted, following me into the building and downstairs to the basement. "Where are you taking me?" he asked.

"To my apartment."

"You live in the cellar?"

I unlocked my door, opened it, and waved him in. He walked inside, albeit tentatively. I pointed toward the chair. "Make yourself comfortable."

Instead of sitting down Yakov walked around the room looking at the art deco radios.

"There are radios like this in my grandmother's house," he said.

"Are they for sale?" I asked half-seriously.

"I don't think so," Yakov replied. "Why do you want to know?"

"I collect stuff like this."

"Why?"

"I like the way they look."

"Don't you listen to them?"

"No. Some of them don't even work."

He stared at me as if he didn't understand. "Then what good are they?" He didn't understand.

"Doesn't anybody you know at the Yeshiva collect things? Baseball cards, maybe?"

"Of course not. We have a huge collection of books but they are there for a purpose, for learning."

I nodded and asked, "Are you hungry? Can I get you anything to eat?"

"No," he said sharply.

I snapped my fingers. "I get it; I'm not kosher."

He nodded, relieved I think, for not being forced to criticize.

"How 'bout a glass of water?"

"I can't use your glass."

I started to protest but realized he wasn't talking about sloppy housekeeping. "How did you get my address?" I asked.

"I called the lawyer Roth's office and explained who I was."

"That would do it."

Yakov nodded and finally sat down staring uncomfortably at his oversize hands and big feet. I lit a cigarette and gave him a little time before I asked gently, "So why are you here?"

"My father told me about his conversation with you. I wanted to explain."

"You don't have to explain, Yakov. I wasn't insulted or anything."

"My father has not been himself."

"I can understand that."

"No, I don't mean the shootings." He faltered and stopped.

I finished my smoke and waited patiently.

"Since my mother died my father has thrown himself into the Yeshiva. He spends all his time making it a better place to learn. When the *schkutzim* — you know? Lowlife *goyim* — started with their Nazi hate, my father redoubled his efforts to ensure our safety."

Something piqued my interest but I didn't want to break his chain of thought. It was difficult enough for him as it was.

"It sounds like your dad used his grief in productive ways," I nudged.

Yakov bobbed his head. "Yes, that's it exactly." His voice dropped an octave, "But it leaves little time for anything else."

"Like you," I said softly.

"I didn't mean that."

"Sorry, I misunderstood."

"It's just, well, the Yeshiva doesn't leave much time for anything else." Yakov rubbed his eyes with the back of his hand. "It's not as if I've been uncared for. What I'm trying to say is that Rebbe's murder makes him wonder whether he has done enough for the Yeshiva."

"It seems he did all he could."

Tears filled Yakov's eyes, desperation flooded his face. Something was trying to fight its way to light, but he pressed his lips

together. I knew better than to push. We both sat quietly while he regained his composure.

"You own a basketball," he finally said, pointing toward the corner.

"Yeah. When we renovated the buildings we built a small court."

The kid's face lit up. "You have a court right here?"

"Between the buildings."

He didn't ask so I did. "Would you like to shoot around?"

"It's getting dark."

"We'll put on the lights."

"You can play at night?" He was excited about the court . . . relieved to stop talking about his father. The combination made for a happy boy.

"Not great, but do-able."

"Could we? Just for a little while?"

"As long as you'd like." He had more to say and I had more to ask, but both of us could wait.

"Come on."

He jumped to his feet, walked directly to the basketball, tapped the top with a practiced touch, and caught it on the way up. I grinned and led us out to the alley through the office door.

"You have a nice apartment," he said once we were outside.

"You didn't expect it?"

"I didn't know what to expect," he said honestly. "You always wear jeans and when you went to the basement . . ."

We got to the end of my building and I watched as he placed the ball at his feet and took off his suit jacket.

"Aren't you going to be cold?"

"Can't play ball in a coat," he scoffed.

I didn't want to expose my gun so I left my jacket alone. "Well, it's too cold for me," I said flicking the switch for the floodlight. The kid ran onto the court with a springing little jump. Almost magically his awkwardness disappeared. He dribbled toward the basket, his lanky body curved forward, looking a

little like a young Hasidic Pistol Pete. Suddenly he stopped and popped.

"Yes!" he yelled in a perfect imitation of Marv Alpert as the ball whistled through the net. Apparently all that learning still left time to sneak a little N.B.A.

While he ran after the ball, I ambled onto the court.

"Here," he called, then hit my palm with a perfect one-handed bounce pass. The kid could play.

I fed him underneath the hoop where he upfaked, swiveled, and laid it in. I moved toward the loose ball, grabbed it, and passed it behind my back to Yakov who had faded to the foul line. "Shoot," I said, then watched the ball arch with perfect spin toward the net. "Two," I called as the twine rippled.

"Again!" he demanded cutting to the hoop. Gone was the diffident, insecure Yakov. I bounced one into his hands and he soared, finally flipping the ball off his fingertips as he approached the rim. When he grew a couple more inches he'd have a perfect finger roll. I watched the ball slip over the iron and fall softly through the ropes. It was a damn good finger roll right now.

I stopped admiring his game and focused on my own. I planted myself halfway between the foul line and the basket at the edge of the lane, kept my back to the hoop, and raised my hand for the ball. Yakov immediately understood and for the next half hour we ran an assortment of pick and rolls, cuts and pull-ups. We were so engrossed that neither of us noticed the two figures standing at the corner of the building until we heard their applause.

Mrs. S. and Charles had big grins on their faces when we looked up.

"Just beautiful, Matthew. Poetry in motion."

"Why, thank you, Charles," I said.

"Not you darling," he smirked. "Your young friend. S-o-o-o graceful."

"Hush, Charles," said Mrs. S. gallantly. "Don't believe him, Matthew, you looked very good too."

I smiled, bowed, pulled out my handkerchief, and wiped my face. It was odd, I hated to run but I could chase a ball all day long. "What are you guys doing out here?"

Charles cocked his head. "I heard noise coming from the court and when I saw you playing, I simply had to tell Mrs. S. We just had to watch you close up. The young man is a terrific athlete. If only it was summer and we could see the two of you in tiny gym shorts."

Before I answered Mrs. S. jumped in with, "Stop that, Charles! The boy doesn't know you're joking!"

"Am I?" he said coyly.

"If you don't stop I'll tell Richard," I warned.

"My lips are sealed, Matthew, I promise. Now will you introduce us to your young friend?"

"Sure. Yakov, this is Charles and Mrs. Sullivan. Like I told you, Charles manages the buildings and Mrs. S. manages Charles."

Mrs. S. smiled, "Not just Charles, Matthew."

I laughed. "Not just Charles."

My laughter stopped when I glanced at Yakov's face. His exuberance was gone. In its place, a worried frown.

"What's the matter?" I asked.

"I've overstayed my visit," he said curtly.

"Not by my account," I replied.

"By mine," he said. He walked over to his jacket and shrugged it on. "Can you let me back inside? I left my book."

I signaled to my neighbors. They understood and started to leave. After Mrs. S. was inside, Charles turned back and called to Yakov, "Please come back. I can't remember the last time Matthew played basketball. It's good for you, isn't it, darling?"

I smiled. "Yes, Charles, it's good for me."

CHAPTER 23

It had been a long time since I'd used the basketball court. Even longer since I'd gotten any pleasure from my body. The remaining soreness from the Avengers' beating and Clifford's love taps had worked itself out during the scrimmage with Yakov. Thankfully, very little returned after my shower.

In a moment of lightheaded spontaneity, I dialed Boots's number only to be met with a taped message announcing the date of her return. I hadn't known she was leaving. I waited for the line to die before I hung the phone back up. I don't know why I had expected a personal postscript. Or even hoped for one.

Still, I felt too good to let it get to me. The time till Thursday created a delicious hiatus in the midst of hectic. A chance to think things through and read the Sporting News. A chance to sleep without dreams.

It surprised me that Simon didn't call until early Thursday morning.

"What the hell did you pull at the Yeshiva?" he asked exasperatedly.

"I didn't pull anything. I did what I said I was going to do. Interviews. And got what you wanted. Didn't you read my report?"

"The report was fine." Simon hesitated then said abruptly, "The Hasidim don't want you working on the case anymore."

I felt my body stiffen. "Which Hasids and why?"

"Reb Yonah. I'm still not entirely sure why."

A shot of anger ripped through my morning drowsy. "Well, *fuck* him. It was Cheryl's hands that were broken, my ass that was kicked. Reb Yonah wouldn't even bother to talk to me."

"Look, Matt" — Simon dropped his belligerence — "he's the client. If it's any consolation, you've given me everything I need. Just let the rest go. I'm not sure how much more there is to get, anyway. You did good. I told that to Reb Yonah, but he wouldn't listen. He called you a disruptive force to the Yeshiva students."

"Disruptive? People there were falling all over themselves to tell me about the geeks." I had a hunch about what Reb Yonah really thought disruptive. And that was bullshit too. "What other crap did he sell you?"

"He wasn't selling, Matt. He was too angry. He said that as long as the courts left him alone, he didn't care about the legalities. He told me he was hopeful of having the Yeshiva protected very shortly. I don't know what he meant by that."

"He meant muscle."

"What are you talking about?"

"The Never Agains."

"How would you know that?"

"Reb Yonah's kid, Yakov, told me."

"He told you his father wanted to use muscle?"

"Not in so many words. He was explaining the conflict in the Yeshiva about the Never Agains . . ."

"Why were you talking to his kid about them? Why were you talking to the kid at all?"

Simon's interruption slowed me down. After a second I replied, "I ran into him the first time I went to the Yeshiva. He's been my unofficial guide. He's a good kid. Was the Big Guy's hand-picked student."

Simon heard the pride in my voice. "No wonder Reb Yonah wants you off the case. That's why the boy called the other day looking for your number. Did he get in touch with you?"

"He came by. We played a little basketball."

"Jesus, Matt. Hasidim don't like people fucking with their children. The boy went to your house to play ball? That's a long way to travel to tickle the twine, babe. Come on, Matt, what's going on?"

"He came over to apologize for his old man's rude behavior."

"I know those Yeshiva kids. They don't just drop in on somebody like you."

" 'Somebody like me'?"

"Don't be a schmuck. An atheist Jew. Christ, they won't even drink a glass of water unless they're absolutely certain the house is kosher."

"Tell me. You don't sound so gung-ho Jewish this morning."

"I've never been big on the Middle Ages. Rabbi Sheinfeld's temple is Reformed, for Christ sake."

I felt a little of my anger subside. "Reb Yonah gave you a hard time, didn't he?"

"I don't take kindly to being treated like a dog. *Por favor*, what's really happening between you and the kid?"

"The boy is lonely. His mother is dead and Reb Yonah funnels all his energy into the Yeshiva. Near as I can tell, when the Big Guy died, Yakov lost the closest thing he had to a parent."

"How old is this kid?"

"I'm not sure, maybe fifteen, sixteen." His question stretched my nerves.

"And you're going to take Reb Dov's place?" Simon asked softly, without sarcasm.

A week ago his question would have hit the core of my depression. Today, I just felt angry and guarded. "No, Simon. But I like him. You'd like him."

Simon grunted. He had long since given up hope of children. Something I'd always associated with Fran's lack of desire.

"I'm sorry, Matt, I still have to pull you off."

"Why? Your client isn't footing the bill."

"It's not just Reb Yonah. I'm catching it from all sides. Hey, I don't like this situation any more than you. Probably less. It took me a couple of days to even call about it. But I've got to try and settle this in a way that keeps everyone calm."

It was senseless to continue. I had planned to tell Simon about Clifford and my uneasy feeling about Deirdre, but now I was just too angry. I was sick of people questioning or complaining about every step I took. Anyhow, Simon was under too much pressure from too many directions to concern himself with something that wasn't in the middle of his plate. Something that might not be on the menu.

And maybe he was right. Maybe there wasn't anything left to do, but I wasn't going to let Reb Yonah leash me to a tree.

"You understand why I have to do this?" he asked.

"I don't like it, but I understand. I'll send you the bill for my time."

"No, don't. I'm keeping you on the meter until everything is completely squared away."

"You don't have to do that."

"I want to. They're going to pay for the privilege of telling me how to run my office."

Good old Simon. Runs with the herd until the herd steps on his foot. Sometimes it just took a while for him to notice.

"Sounds like an early Christmas. Let me know how everything works out, okay?"

"Sure." He paused. "Matt, you aren't thinking of flying solo on any of this, are you?"

"What's left?"

"I'm talking about you and the kid." He took a deep breath. "I'm thinking that your rapport with Yonah's son has something to do with Becky."

"Maybe it does, Simon, but not to worry. I won't get between Reb Yonah and Yakov."

"Good," he said with an air of finality.

Why not? As far as he was concerned, it was finished.

"Keep in touch," I said.

"Sure," he said, his mind already on his next task.

I hung up the phone more determined than ever to discover what had Washington Clifford by the nose. Yonah's attitude about me, about the Never Agains, had piggybacked onto my suspicions of Deirdre. I had trouble when something supposedly finished left me with more questions than when I began.

Hell, if I was careful enough, I'd even get paid.

Only, how careful was careful? I wanted more information about Kelly and his organization. Unless I found Blue — and by now I had a hunch he was nowhere to be found — there weren't too many places to look for answers.

Except, perhaps at the Yeshiva. Or, if Father Collins meant what he said, back in the neighborhood.

Terrific. Now I had both Clifford *and* Simon to dodge. I sat in the office reviewing my notes, trying to spur my thinking. All it spurred was a couple of joints. As much as I tried to spin open-ended scenarios, I couldn't see a connection between the Deirdre–Kelly relationship and Reb Dov's shooting. I had nothing to grasp but uneasy feelings and doobies. Not exactly foundation stones on which to build an investigation.

I retired to the couch, frustrated and fatigued by my useless endeavor. I kept smoking, added a little bourbon to the mix, and tried to relieve the anger I'd felt since I was fired. Unfortunately, I fell asleep before I discovered whether it worked.

CHAPTER 24

My eyes shot open to the forlorn music of a "M.A.S.H." rerun on the television. It took a hard try to remember why I felt rushed. Rolling onto my feet cursing, I grabbed the couch's arm for support. This bum wasn't getting to the church on time.

And I didn't. By the time I slipped inside the church's meeting room, a sandy-haired college kid was re-living the middle of his summer vacation. A projected picture of green fields covered the top half of the front wall. Father Collins sat at a table off to the side in front of the room. Collins had an intense expression on his face and his eyes kept flicking toward the first row of spectators. All I could see was the back of a gray head between a couple of caps.

The priest caught me peeking and abruptly interrupted the presentation. "Welcome to our program, Mr. Jacob. I'm glad you could join us." He aimed his next words to the crowd. "Before I knew about our guests I invited Mr. Jacob to attend tonight's talk. He is gathering information about that horrible double shooting. I know he has already been around to see some of you. I want him to learn that our neighborhood has no tolerance for violence, that we are willing to help in any way we can."

He turned toward the speaker. "Brian, I'm sorry for the interruption. Please continue with your presentation."

The padre's buckshot greeting slammed me against the door. As soon as the slides recaptured the room's attention I quietly retreated into the hall. I looked hard for an ashtray, found none, and kept going until I landed outside.

I almost went home, then reminded myself why I had come. It didn't obliterate my claustrophobia, but it calmed me enough to light my smoke. I was exhaling into the cold night air when the church door swung open and Deirdre joined me on the steps.

"You ran out of there pretty quickly," she said.

"I hadn't expected a twenty-one-gun salute."

"I thought you might have been embarrassed by Brady's introduction. I'm sure if you had been here on time he would have been less obvious and word would have spread."

I was calming down. I flicked the cigarette onto the street. "Yeah, well I'll remember that the next time I plan a meet with the padre." I flashed on Collins sitting in the front of the room. "Who was he staring at?"

Deirdre looked puzzled. "What are you talking about?"

"Father Collins. Right before he nailed me he kept looking at the front row. Visitors from Rome?"

"From Ireland." Deirdre spoke quickly, pulling at a button on her heavy sweater. "For the past three or four years the parish has been raising money and donating goods to the Color It Green program. The program collects food, medical supplies, and donations for people in Northern Ireland. Basic aid for the victims caught in the middle of that horrible conflict. There are a few representatives visiting. Maybe you noticed Brady looking at them." She shrugged. "I think they were in the front row."

Her mention of Northern Ireland disturbed me, but you can't play a card you couldn't see. "You're freezing out here, aren't you?" I asked.

"To the bone. The formal program is probably finished. Would

you like to join me inside? I'm sure Father Collins will be help-ful to you. And quieter," she smiled.

I followed her into the building and back to the meeting room. Collins's table was now covered with homemade food and the crowd was milling around. Some sat at small tables that had been placed around the room. But the real action centered on three men.

Each stood inside a circle of excited parishioners. My earlier sighting had been correct: two wore caps, and the one facing in my direction was gray-haired. Ramrod straight, he was a pale, thin man with a stern, pinched face and closely cropped hair. Al-though he spoke to the folks in his circle, his eyes were jumping warily about the room.

I couldn't hear what Mr. Relief was saying so I started moving closer. Deirdre nonchalantly stepped in front of me. "I'm sure Brady will join us as soon as he gets a chance."

I waited while the gray-haired man backed away from his well-wishers and nodded to the caps. I watched the different groups reluctantly part, to give the three men a path to the front of the room. Father Collins joined them at the door and each took turns shaking the priest's hand. The two caps looked less like re-lief than the original. Burly guys, the type Lenny Bruce said wore wool suits with no underwear. Their coarseness didn't seem to bother anyone else in the room as the parishioners gave the men a raucous round of applause. All three nodded toward Brady and acknowledged the acclaim with modest waves of their hands. When they were gone their wake contained a palpable buzz of disappointment. For one uncomfortable moment I thought IRA—then jammed the thought away. I had enough worries.

Father Collins looked around the room, urged people to treat themselves to the refreshments, and reminded everyone that Brian could only stay another hour. When he noticed Deirdre and me in the corner he grinned, bobbed his head, and briskly walked over. "I hope it didn't bother you when I stopped our

meeting," he said to me without any preamble. "This is a close-knit community and I was afraid that . . ."

"I'd make everyone uptight." I finished. "I should apologize for coming late."

"No need, no need. Sometimes things happen unexpectedly," he said half to himself.

Deirdre spoke up quickly. "I've explained our visitors to Mr. Jacob, Brady. Father Collins is especially proud of the Color It Green program." Resolutely she brought the priest back to my purpose. "Brady, who did you have in mind for Mr. Jacob to speak to?"

The priest appeared relieved by Deirdre's question. "Why don't you come with me?" he asked, though he left little room for an answer as he pulled on my arm. "I'll be back as soon as possible," he called over his shoulder.

I recognized the man Father Collins picked out as the owner of a local variety store. It had a reputation as a gossip barn, but I hadn't gotten more than a few monosyllabic grunts when I'd visited during my rounds.

"Mr. Pearse, this is the gentleman I spoke to you about." Father Collins turned toward me. "Mr. Pearse owns a local store and knows everything that happens in the neighborhood. If you don't mind I'll leave the two of you to get acquainted while I mix."

Pearse nodded me to a chair at his small table and stared. For a second I thought we were going to have a repeat of our last meeting but Pearse leaned his ruddy face across the table. "You didn't look like a teetotaler when you came into the store, and you don't look like one now."

"I don't believe in tea."

"Gratifying to hear. Then you wouldn't mind if I added a bit of sacrilege to our conversation, now would you?"

I watched him reach under the table and surreptitiously lift a small brown bag.

"I didn't know you weren't allowed to drink in a church," I said.

"The good Father disapproves so I'm careful about it." Pearse reached into the pocket of his spacious winter coat, withdrew a shot glass, poured, and gulped. "He's tried to get me to swear off the stuff, but I can't. You won't run and tell him, will you?"

"Of course not."

"Will you be having any?" he asked.

It was a miracle what a priestly blessing can bestow. "Sure."

I expected him to hand me his glass, but he pulled another one from his coat pocket. "You never know who you might run into," he murmured by way of an explanation as he slipped me the glass and bag underneath the table.

I kept the whisky off my pants and into the small glass, then returned the bag. I checked to make sure Father Collins wasn't looking and chugged. "Good," I gasped as harsh heat filled my throat and chest. "What is it?"

"Single malt," Pearse answered before quickly swallowing his refill. He looked to see if I wanted another but I demurred. Pearse, on the other hand, downed his third.

"See, people around here stick to themselves," he said, almost leaving me behind. "But the Father asked me to talk to you so I don't mind saying that around these parts most people didn't know *what* to make of Sean Kelly."

Pearse leaned back in his chair and almost disappeared into his tweed overcoat. "They knew what to make of his father, a born thief if there ever was. But people felt different about Sean even though he ran the street from the time he wore knickers. He was surely up to no good, but then, you could say that about most of the boys around here. Hell, you could say it about everyone in this room." He sighed. "Everyone thought he'd end up right alongside the rest of us," he said absently.

"What do you mean?"

Pearse poked his head out of the coat, a blank look on his

face. "Nothing in particular. He was a very bright boy though he never went to school. People hoped he would outgrow his mischievousness. Use his God-given intelligence for something useful."

"Isn't it stretching things to call the Avengers mischievous?"

Pearse rubbed his nose. "I'm not referring to *them*." There was no mistaking the disgust in his voice. "No one understood Sean's behavior as far as they were concerned. People were surprised when he went in that direction. Our neighborhood wants no trouble with the Jewish people. People might call them names, throw the occasional stone. But most everyone here, I'll tell you, fought against the damn Nazis. I personally know people on both sides of the pond who died with great bravery. No one wanted anything to do with Sean when he started with his brown uniforms. Except those dummies who looked up to him."

"Like Blue?"

"Not exactly. Blue isn't quite as stupid as the rest." He cackled, looked around the room, and carefully poured himself another shot. Pearse continued to describe the scorn the neighborhood held for the Avengers. He told me stories confirming what I'd heard at the Yeshiva, and even added a couple of new ones. But when I asked how the group financed itself he grew guarded, and even more so when I pressed for details about Kelly's pre-Avenger life.

I motioned for another shot, gulped it down, and looked around the rapidly emptying room. I'd talked to Pearse longer than I'd realized. In the interim, Father Collins had mixed his way back to Deirdre and the two were engaged in a quiet conversation. Pearse offered me another drink but I refused. When I told him how much I appreciated his willingness to speak with me he realized I was about to leave.

"Now don't you go talking to the Father about our nips, you hear?" he said, handing me a couple of breath mints.

"Are you kidding? I'd like to visit you at your store and do it

again." I popped the mints into my mouth. "I know a homeboy when I drink with one."

"Well, I would certainly enjoy the company. I want you to know that nobody wanted or liked what those Avengers were doing." He lowered his voice, "Forgive my blasphemy, but perhaps there was a bit of relief with the boy's death. It's an honor to fight for what's rightfully yours. But to use violence for enjoyment, to bully, well, no one in this neighborhood is comfortable with that."

I started to ask Pearse about the church's visitors, but decided to leave well enough alone. Instead I thanked him for his time, his single malt, and left the table while he snuck himself another drink.

CHAPTER 25

Father Collins saw me rise from the table and waved me over. Deirdre, her forehead's fair skin furrowed, silently nodded her greeting.

"Well, Mr. Jacob," Brady asked, "was Mr. Pearse able to shed a bit of light?" There was no mistaking his tense undertone.

"Did Joshua blow the walls away?"

"Ah, do you hear that, Deirdre? Perhaps our church is beginning to rub off on our friend, here." He smiled ingratiatingly. "Deirdre was worried that I'd falsely raised your hopes."

"No, not at all. Mr. Pearse was quite forthcoming. I appreciate your help."

"No appreciation necessary." His eyes scanned the room. "If I can be useful again, don't hesitate to call. Right now I have to close up, so if you will excuse me?"

"Sure." I turned toward Deirdre. "Would you like me to walk you home?"

She smiled but the creases never left her face. "I think not. I want to stay around to help."

"Sure."

"Mr. Jacob, Matthew, I'm pleased that tonight was helpful. I don't know what you must think of me since our conversation

this afternoon, but I'm certain the Rabbi you work for only did what he thought necessary. I want you to know that."

"You sound like there won't be another opportunity to tell me?"

Deirdre looked startled. "That's not what I meant at all. I rather hope we'll meet again."

"I'm sure we will. I guess I'll leave you to your work."

When I got to my car I sat and smoked a cigarette. Aside from my time with the Avengers and my depression about Rebecca, the more information I accumulated the less I understood. My instincts screamed "Sharks!" but I still hadn't found the ocean.

I finished the cigarette, fingered through the ashtray, found a roach. I was tired, but unwilling to go home and back to sleep. I hoped a ride around town would clear some of the fog.

I drove around aimlessly for about a half hour before I started toward my house. If I hadn't been trying to guess about things outside of my vision I might have seen what was happening under my nose. Maybe.

I don't know how long the car without headlights had been following and, when I first noticed, I remained unconcerned. There was nothing like quality work. When the next car filled the lane on my left, my first thought wasn't about danger, but about the problems of driving on the Jamaicaway when cars traveled side by side. I squeezed over to give the car on my left room to pass, but when it got to my fender the car slowed down and just kept pace. I took my foot off the accelerator but jammed it back as the car without headlights rapidly moved up behind. The car on my left now drove up parallel and I saw an arm waving behind a dark passenger window.

Still stupid, I thought he was trying to signal so I started to unroll my window. Suddenly the waver's window opened and I stared into the long frightening barrel of a Magnum. And Blue's face behind it. Day-late Matt was back in town: I hadn't brought my gun. I left the window where it was and pounded the gas

pedal into the floor. Barely in time, as my rear-door window shattered pelting me with spraying glass. I thought about jumping on the brakes but the unlighted car was crawling up my ass.

The two just kept pace while I fought my panic and kept the corner of my eye on the car to my left. It pressed me closer to the inside of the road as we banked down the rounded curve and steep hill leading to the abandoned Bynner Street ice skating rink. For a moment I thought I could make the turnoff, but my hope was smashed as Blue's car drew up alongside. Again I crushed the accelerator. It bought me a second or two, but not enough time to get to Bynner. When I saw Blue prepare for another shot, I slammed the brake and felt the crunch of the car behind. I floored the gas pedal and wheeled sharply to the right. I hoped I'd traveled enough distance to avoid the hill that lined the right side of the J-way. If I hadn't I'd be one dead dumb detective.

I had. At least most of it. As my car bounced over the curb, the passenger side lifted up until I thought I'd overturn. But my lead held long enough for me to drag the steering wheel left, race down to the base of the hill, and listen thankfully to the screech of brakes and tires somewhere in the background.

The moment my tires hit the gravel of the ball field's parking lot, I spun sideways in the direction I thought they'd be approaching. I stood on the brake then scrambled out the door using the car for cover. It was harder to quash my hysteria in the open air and, for a moment, I couldn't decide which way to run. Then a slug ripped into the side of my car. I bolted across Bynner to the back of the rink and threw myself down the hill, rolling to the bottom. I wasted no time burrowing into a long row of huge bushes off to the left, oblivious to the thorns tearing at my skin. I hunched down like a catcher, fighting my panic. If they noticed a trembling bush, I'd be dead meat.

I spotted four men huddling along the Bynner side of the skating rink. For a second I wondered if I'd made a mistake not breaking into the abandoned building. Then one of the men

smashed through some rotting plywood and climbed inside. The other three stood waiting and talking, but the only voice I heard was Blue's.

"He's fucking around here somewhere and I want him . . ."

One of the men kept peering down in my direction but the moon was well hidden and so, apparently, was I. I watched the man inside the rink tear more thin plywood off a window and climb back outside. My knees were starting to lock but I kept myself rigid and held my breath while the men regrouped.

"Why stop now?" Blue pleaded loudly. "We spread out and find the cocksucker. I told him to stay away from the neighborhood but the lousy prick wouldn't listen. I want to find him and blow him away once and for all. Jesus, you told me I'd get a chance."

If they continued to look, I'd be found. Simple as that. But I had pulled an ace. Despite Blue's whining. Slowly, each of the shadowy figures turned away from the slope and started back toward Bynner. Just when I thought I could unkink my legs, Blue dashed away from the rest, ran back to the top of the hill, and blindly fired into the bush on my immediate right. I felt like a pheasant: stay still and die, fly and die — the ultimate rock or hard place. I gritted my teeth and waited for his next attempt.

But caught another break. One of the other men came up behind Blue and knocked him to the ground with a short sweet forearm. I damn near cheered. Then the man knelt, picked up the gun, grabbed Blue by his peacoat, and dragged him to his feet. This time when they started for Bynner, the Forearm kept hold of Blue while I held onto my nerves.

And kept on holding until I heard the sound of car ignitions. I wanted to move but I was still scared. I breathed rapidly, quietly. I listened to the roar of what I hoped was their engines, and waited in my prickly hideout for another five. Finally, when the only thing audible was the distant hum of traffic, I scratched my way out of the thorns. Down on my hands and knees, I started to shake uncontrollably. Every time I caught a near-death expe-

rience I rediscovered just how much I wanted to live. I wished I could remember it when I was depressed.

As soon as the panic subsided, I realized I was an easy target if they had left anyone behind. I quickly pressed my belly to the ground and crept up the hill. I crawled to the top then hurled my body through the newly opened rink window. I heard something move in the dank, pitch-black structure, and for a nauseating moment thought I'd just rolled into my grave — a fucking cavernous abandoned ice skating rink. And I didn't even root for the Bruins.

Suddenly, soft fur brushed against my face and the screaming in my head quieted enough for me to hear the purr of a mangy cat. I stood up to a chorus of hungry meows, wished I could oblige, but instead felt my way to the Bynner side of the abandoned ice rink. I peered through gashes in the building's side. No one was walking around, and there were no parked cars other than my own.

I went to the hole, climbed out, and walked carefully back to the car. I still had the shakes but forced myself to inspect the damage. The rear fender was ripped from the body where I'd been rammed, the bumper mangled. Shattered glass blanketed the interior and I briefly looked for the offending bullet until I realized Blue's shot had blown through both rear door windows. The driver's door was dented from the shot it had taken, and I spent a moment trying to pry the bullet free. When it refused to budge, I did. Hanging around was starting to dent my control.

As soon as my hands were steady enough to grip the steering wheel I climbed inside, started the car, and pulled away. I slowly drove to a well-lit street and limped toward my house. This time my eyes were wide open for anything that seemed out of the ordinary. It wasn't difficult to do; I couldn't close them.

Edges of panic returned when I realized they could be waiting for me. So instead of home I aimed toward Manuel's Auto-Caribe where I left the car in front of his metal shuttered garage

doors. I stuffed the key in the ashtray. Manuel would know what to do.

Which was more than I could say for myself. I had keys to Boots's apartment and could go to ground there if I wanted. I didn't want. The panic was sharing space with a flicker of anger and I loathed the idea of hiding, of leaving my home vulnerable to hit men.

I ducked through backyards between the Auto-Caribe and my building, careful to stay quiet and out of sight. I scoured the nearby streets searching for suspicious cars or persons but saw nothing unusual. I finally snuck into my alley hugging the back walls as I approached my apartment. With a sick stomach and a fresh jolt of dread I saw a light that hadn't been on when I left. Stifling a powerful urge to run, I crept on my hands and knees across the gravel, determined to peek in through the kitchen window. I squatted, lifted my head, and looked inside. Unfortunately, Cheryl chose exactly that moment to look outside and scream loud enough to heart-stop us both.

CHAPTER 26

I let myself in the office door and quickly ran my hand down the open wooden venetian slats. Cheryl came running, looked for the light switch, and nudged it on with her elbow.

"Turn it off," I ordered curtly.

I had just enough time to see her frightened look of apprehension. "Look," Cheryl explained, "I didn't break in here. A really sweet guy with beautiful eyeshadow on let me in." Her laugh was forced.

"Not now," I said in a low, tight voice. "There might be trouble. We have to shut all the lights and pull the blinds."

We went from room to room in what felt like a methadrine stoked tour of my apartment. I was tempted to point out various items; like the fucking gun hanging on the back of a kitchen chair.

"Which room should we stay in?" Cheryl asked in a whisper.

"Here." I pointed to the enamel-top kitchen table.

"Why the kitchen? The living room is further from the alley?"

"Yeah, but I want to hear if someone comes down the back way. Wait a second while I make a call." Two calls, actually. One to Charles thanking him for letting Cheryl in, then asking him to throw all the locks on the front door, including the bolt that

only opened from inside. I heard him talk to someone and for a frantic moment thought he was held hostage. The frantic relaxed when Richard came on the line.

"Matt, Richard here. Charles is shutting things down. What's going on?"

"I hope nothing, but there's a possibility some people may come looking for me. I don't think they'll bother anyone else, but I wouldn't urge you to stick around."

"Don't be absurd. Do you need any help?"

"I could use eyes in the front of the building, but if you do that you have to stay dark. They are pros."

"What should we be looking for?"

"Rich, you don't have to do this."

"I know. Charles is back and the front door is secure."

"Good. Look for anyone eyeballing the buildings, or cars just cruising the street. Call me even if you think it's a paranoid flash. Also, let me know if anyone legit goes in or out."

"Should we warn Lou? The rest of the building?"

I took a moment to think. "Not yet. I'm not sure anyone is really coming."

"These the goons who worked you over?"

"One of them." I felt Cheryl's eyes comb my face. "But it's not the same group."

"Okay. Let us know if you need anything else."

"Rich, thanks." I dialed Julius's number and let it ring a long time before giving up. Cheryl had disappeared into the bathroom and I slumped onto one of the kitchen chairs. When I opened my eyes she was standing at my side, washcloth in cast.

"You're filthy and all scratched up."

"Here, give me that. You'll get your cast wet." I took the warm cloth, wiped my hands and face, then lit a cigarette. Cheryl walked around the table and sat down across from me. Despite the closed blinds, amber streaks from the grocery store's anti-crime lights leaked into the room casting a dark orange glow on her smooth black face.

"What are you doing here?" I asked. "How did you drive?"

"My mother brought me. You turn this place into a bunker and ask *me* questions? First things first, White Man. What's going on? How do you know it wasn't the Avengers?"

Her energy rattled against my self-control. "I get the feeling that if you could write, you'd have a notebook open."

"If I could write I wouldn't be here."

She saw something cross my face because she amended, "*Might* not be here."

I recounted Simon's call and my evening's activity. Somehow the last half overshadowed the first.

"Why are you so certain they weren't Avengers?" Cheryl asked. "You saw Blue."

"I don't believe they could coordinate an attack like that. The Avengers are a bunch of fucking losers. Anyhow, Blue wasn't the Big Enchilada."

"You think since you trashed the Avengers you have a national supremacy group looking for revenge?"

"I think it's possible."

We remained quiet for the next few minutes while I contemplated Salmon Rushdie's life, but Cheryl stomped on the romance. Hard.

"What about the Irish?"

"Say what?"

"That Color It Green program sounds like a front. Plus, your description of the church's visitors. They don't sound like social workers."

Cheryl's verbalization of my earlier suspicion sent a chill through my emotional restraint. I tried to match my assailants with the men at the church, but the bush hadn't given me a clear view. I hoped it had been the bush. It might have been the fear. "What would Color It Green front for?"

"I don't know. Guns. How does the IRA grab you? That neighborhood has always been involved in the war."

It was common knowledge that an underground existed be-

tween my city and different factions in the struggle to liberate Ireland. But common knowledge is not the same as fact. Especially one I didn't want to hear. I shrugged and fought the idea, but my dread was listening hard.

"What difference does it make if it's white supremacists or the IRA?" Cheryl asked, accurately perceiving my rising tension.

"The IRA doesn't make sense," I said stubbornly.

"But a national white supremacist group does?"

"I don't know." I stood, walked softly to the window, pulled a slat of the blind, and looked into the alley.

"Do you hear something?" Cheryl whispered. She didn't sound scared.

I patted the slat back down and returned to the table. "Just the sound of my panic." I forced a smile and said, "Let's say Color It Green is a front and I did brush up against the IRA. Why would they come after me? Hell, I'm just working the Avengers and everyone knows it. What connection could the IRA have with Kelly? No, sweetie, odds are I got real Americans here."

I wasn't willing to lay mortgage money on my logic, but somehow neo-Nazis seemed like the easier do. "Can I get you anything?" I said, debating whether to retrieve bourbon or grass. I decided on both.

When I returned to the table Cheryl shook her head. "Cigarettes, dope, booze. Shit, you're a walking death wish. I don't know why you're scared of anyone else."

I finished rolling the joint before I looked up. "Walking is the operative word. I almost buy it and you're hassling me about dope?"

Cheryl's voice grew soft. "I like you, Matt."

Her simple words broke through the numb and cunning I'd been using to hold myself together. I tried to light the joint but my hand wouldn't stop trembling. My body broke into a clammy sweat and I felt bathed in layers of fear. I tried to speak, couldn't, and dropped the joint on the table. I covered my face

with shaking hands as the entire evening's tension exploded, my body twitching like I'd just plugged into 220. For the first time since this endless night began, I stopped holding on and burst into tears.

Cheryl stayed where she was and let me sob myself out. Eventually the crying and shaking eased. I took deep breaths until I regained a semblance of calm.

Then Cheryl stood, walked close behind me, and cradled my head against her breasts. I felt my pulse quicken, closed my eyes, and let my hands reach back and slide down her flanks. I pictured her naked, lying across my outstretched body, replenishing my fear and fatigue with her youth and vitality.

I rose from my seat and faced her with open eyes. All my fear, my desperation, was replaced by a burning desire. The rest of my kitchen was gone and the only thing I could see was the welcome of her stance, the invitation of her body, the pulse of a tiny vein in her neck. I reached out to pull her into me but stopped when the casts on her hands curled onto my chest. I immediately felt awkward, silly, and confused. Suddenly more protective than impassioned.

And almost jumped out of my skin when the telephone's bell slashed through the moment.

I grabbed the receiver with a mixture of disappointment and relief. It was Richard. "We just spotted Julius. Charles is going to open the door and I wanted to let you know."

"Thanks." My throat was dry but I forced the words. "Will you ask him to come down?"

"Sure. You sound strange. Are you okay?"

I looked at Cheryl. "I'm okay."

"You never told me why you came over," I said, after I hung up the phone.

"Yes I did. I told you that I like you."

"Yeah, well there's problems with that," I answered gruffly, retreating. "Like twenty-some years' worth."

"Those years disappeared pretty fast a minute ago." She

smiled. "You make yourself out to be an old man and me a young kid. Neither is exactly true."

I lowered my shield and tried to return her smile. "We probably have to talk but now ain't exactly the time or place. My friend Julius will be here any second and I'm going to ask him to take you home."

I was spared her protest by a light tapping. I motioned for Cheryl to sit, grabbed the gun from the holster, and opened the front door.

Julie stared balefully at the barrel, stuck his finger out, and gently pushed the gun aside. He stepped inside the door and stood motionless while I locked up.

"Dug in pretty deep, here," he said. "Who you waiting on?"

"I'm not sure. I got run off the road by professionals. They wanted to take me out. And they had an Avenger with them."

"He thinks white supremacists, I'm thinking Irish. Maybe the IRA," Cheryl called from the kitchen.

Julius glanced at me. "Sounds like you got the fort well supplied."

"I've had enough problems for one night," I said. "Cheryl was here when I got back. I want you to take her home."

"You expecting more trouble?"

"Not expecting, but anything is possible."

Cheryl stepped out of the kitchen shadows. "I haven't agreed to leave." She lifted her casts. "These don't mean I'm a quitter."

I shook my head. "Cheryl, you can't pull this now. If I'm going to get out of this jam I can't be concentrating on your safety. Please? Let Julius take you home. As soon as I find out what's going on I'll tell you. Promise."

For a moment I thought she was going to resist but suddenly a smile cracked wide across her face. "Guess I'd have trouble with a trigger anyway. Okay, big bad Black man, I'll get my coat."

I started to explain who Cheryl was. Julie waved me quiet. "The casts speak for themselves, Slumlord. You just keep your head down while I'm gone."

I called Richard to tell him that Julie and Cheryl were on their way out. He told me they would check the street from their window. Smart man, my neighbor.

As soon as Cheryl and Julius left, the apartment felt cold and empty. I was momentarily sorry they had listened to me, but better judgment prevailed. I went through the house, gun in hand, checking the windows. The third time through I began to relax.

By the time Julius returned I was fairly certain the night's surprises were over. Almost had me wishing I hadn't sent the lady home. Then I flashed on her casts and my awkwardness and wasn't so sure.

I nodded us to the kitchen table and lit the joint. "Cheryl fill you in about the night?" I asked.

"Enough."

"What do you think?"

"I think the sister makes sense. According to Phil, Washington Clifford was involved *before* you trashed the Avengers. Easy to see him sinking his ugly teeth into the Irish business." Julius liked Washington even less than me and without having tasted Clifford's fist. Less afraid of him, too.

"Well, that could be true." I glumly told him about Clifford's visit and warnings.

Julius nodded. "Then I'd bet she does have it right. Here's a little more. I looked into your boy Kelly. His conversion was a relatively recent event. Not even a couple of years."

"And before?"

"Before is interesting. He was behind a long trail of burglaries."

"Armored cars?"

"Predominantly."

"So he was a thief."

"A long string of complicated *successful* burglaries."

"A thief with talent?"

"A whole lot of talent, Matthew. But since The White Avengers, people never saw much sign of the same successes."

"He stopped his heists?"

"Not completely. But cut way back once he started the Avengers." Julie pulled two cigarettes from his pack and handed me one. "Something else strange. These White Avengers came out of nowhere. Like Kelly got hit with religion and the next day he was out preaching."

"Were the Avengers the same pack he'd been running with?"

"I don't know."

We sat quietly while I tried to make sense out of his information. What stuck was Clifford. The IRA, or some other renegade faction, would indeed garner his interest. "If Kelly were involved with the IRA why the hell start the Avengers? Why would he want that kind of attention?"

Julius just grunted and shrugged.

Occasionally, different aspects of a case present themselves like puzzle pieces. Information to shift around until it fits. This case was different. I had been jumped, fired from my job, shot at, and still couldn't find the damn game board. "I'm floundering, bro. If Kelly was connected to the IRA while he was involved with the Avengers, then the Avengers' actions toward the Hasids somehow figure in. Hell, the shootings figure in." I shook my head. "It's a whole lot clearer if my pros are Nazis."

"Indeed. Only you don't know enough to be clear about anything. Or even linear. Slumlord, if you're serious about tracking this shit down you got to change the way you usually think. You look for a *person's* reasons when something happens. This isn't like that. These folk act for *organizational* reasons. Whether we be talking swastikas or initials. Nothing personal going on here."

"I don't know, man, the night felt plenty personal. Julie, what fucking connection could the IRA have with a Hasidic Yeshiva?"

Julius looked out from under his half-masts. "I'm guessing that's what you're gonna find out."

CHAPTER 27

I telephoned Charles and Richard and called off the alert. Julie lived on their side of the building and I knew he wasn't going to sleep.

After he left, my apartment once again felt empty. Somewhat surprising — given its usual configuration of one. Of course, this wasn't a usual night. As time continued to drift and I trudged through a series of window checks, my fear of invasion lessened. And with it, the clutch of alone.

Enough to take a long hot shower. I was filthy from my dirt-eating forage behind the abandoned ice skating rink, my body caked with dry sweat and blood where the thorns had ripped skin. At first, the hot sting of water against the scratches conspired with rivulets of dirt to revive my anxiety. Especially when I picked tiny glass splinters from my hair. But as the dirt dripped to the tub floor and the tiny cuts numbed in the wet heat, I broke through the shell of fear that had invaded me since I'd looked down the barrel of Blue's gun. I got pissed.

The thought of Blue led the way. That little prick kept me freezing in a tavern's cooler, broke a nice kid's hands, and came within a bush of sending me to the Great Beyond. No matter who was pulling his strings, Blue had overreached.

But the notion of a nameless, faceless enemy sent me on an-

other intense window patrol: the idea of IRA involvement, or even a supremacist organization, was sobering. Too sobering, so once I finished the last safety check, I gathered my stash, bourbon, and .38, settling in for a hard night on the easy chair.

Maybe it was the adrenaline drain or the cul de sac ending each bright idea, but my eyes grew heavy. The closer I drew to doze, the less I worried about invasion ... the more I thought about Cheryl.

The room was familiar though reminiscent of another age, another lifetime. The hint of something unpleasant hid nearby but, as I looked around and saw twin beds, a blond wooden dresser with stenciled flowers, a shelf overloaded with tiny glass figurines, the unpleasantness drifted away. I saw myself lying on the far bed when the door opened and Cheryl stepped quietly into the room, finger to her lips. The next I knew she had slipped in lightly beside me. I thought she was wearing something sheer, something gray, but now, lying next to me, the only contrast with her dark skin was my large white body.

I started to speak but she put her fingers against my lips, leaned forward, and kissed me gently on my forehead. I opened my mouth and captured the tips of her fingers between my lips. She rested her mouth against my head. "They're free," I heard her say. "They're finally free."

I kept her hand in my mouth exploring the skin between her fingers with the tip of my tongue. I opened my eyes, saw her other hand slide over my body, and watched myself harden as her fingernails dug into my flesh. I took her hand from my mouth, stretched it past my head, and traced the graceful, inside curve of her arm with a string of gentle kisses. Her eyes were closed and her hand had stopped its relentless squeezing. I thought she had grown frightened, but she shifted her slender body and we were suddenly breast to breast, belly to belly.

Heat spread between our legs bathing our bodies with a thin layer of sweat. I leaned forward, kissed her closed eyes, then

gently wiped away the perspiration just above her mouth. I felt her tremble so I wrapped my arm around her back and pulled her closer, tighter. She opened her eyes and moved her lips against mine.

We lay there, eyes open, motionless, for a long moment. Then the unpleasantness beckoned, its voice a thick ugly whisper. A whisper that I silenced by closing my eyes and letting my tongue slide across the fullness of Cheryl's mouth. I heard her breath quicken, felt her hard nipples push against my chest. Again Cheryl's hand searched my body, though now her fingers were light, fluttery, eager to discover, touch, continue. My tongue explored the inside of her mouth while I roamed down her smooth back until my hand rested at the top of her tight round buttocks. Cheryl's mouth opened wider, her lips and tongue in sudden sync with her thrusting body. I felt a burst of added desire as she hungrily bit at my lips. I slid my hand lower.

She pulled her head back and for another moment we stared into each other's eyes. Again I heard the disquieting call; again I ignored it, waiting for the sound of our breathing to fill the room. I knew somehow that I should be paying attention to my growing unease, but I sight-feasted on the hills and valleys of Cheryl's lush, slim torso. So young, so black, so beautiful. Her long legs, her smooth belly, her breasts marked by dark aureoles and nipples semi-sweet in her sleek chocolate skin. Together we watched my fingers dance lightly, whitely, over her sweat-dampened front. Cheryl's mouth was open, moaning, as my hand stretched toward the stiff curled hair between her legs.

She grabbed my hair and pulled my head tight to her breast, her rush of moistness drenching my hand. I shifted my body and slid to the foot of the bed. Off the bed, knees on the floor, I lifted her feet, pressing her soles against my face. Listening in the darkness to her loud gasps and my silent desire. . . .

We stayed foot to face until I could no longer stand the blindness. I opened her legs and pulled her down to the edge of the bed. I heard a louder cry that reverberated but just closed my eyes.

When I opened them, Cheryl was sucking her fingers. But her skin somehow seemed lighter, her body smaller.

I leaned forward and squinted. Cheryl's body had grown even ti-nier and her pubic hair had changed from black to blonde. I strug-gled to my feet wiping at the crazy film in front of my eyes, but the transformation refused to disappear. Horrified, I watched the rest of her body whiten. Cheryl's hair, fanning across the pillow, straightened before my eyes. In a desperate attempt to silence my screaming mind, arrest my hallucinating vision, I jerked my body from the bed and looked away. But something forced me to turn back, forced me to look at her face . . .

I bolted upright on my easy chair, my body shaking and sweat-ing, my gun clattering onto the floor. I grabbed my cigarettes, lit one, and tried to calm down. Damn. I just kept getting jumped by ghosts of my dead daughter.

Ghosts I'd hoped I had left behind. . . .

I jumped to my feet, swiped at my forehead with my damp tee shirt, and trotted from window to window. I had trouble enough without sharing the night with Electra. Eventually, the dream's after-images dissipated, leaving just the cold and uneasy sweat.

I stood at the window and stared. The sky had a pre-dawn gray, and I had the beginning of the blues. Something I couldn't possibly afford. There was a difference between dreams and re-ality, and my situation hollered for action, not depression. Prob-lem was, my rest had left me depleted rather than refreshed.

I walked into the bedroom strung between fatigue and fear of another dream. I searched the night table's ashtray, and found a decent sized roach. Valium would be better for sleep, but if I slept I wanted to be able to wake. I smoked the roach, then filled a pipe with more. I swung my legs onto the bed, smoked the pipe, then slid onto my back holding the gun on my chest.

I was shocked back to consciousness by the trill of the tele-phone. I shoved it next to my ear before the second ring. "Who?" I barked, slapping the night table for smokes.

There was no answer. Just the faint hollowness of an open line. "Who the fuck is this?" I demanded. Again no one answered, just a click.

I swung out of bed, lit a cigarette, and thought about evacuating the building. Someone had checked to see if I was home — though they had stayed on the line longer than necessary. Before I'd arrived at any decision, the phone rang again. I lifted the receiver and heard Cheryl ask, "Matt, are you there?"

Her voice instantly recalled my dream and I took a long pull on my smoke. "I'm here," I said glumly.

"You don't sound too good."

"Yeah, well, I didn't sleep much."

"It wasn't a criticism, Matt. I'm worried about you, that's all."

"Well, don't be. Right now I don't need your worry. I need to be left alone."

I understood her silence and immediately felt guilty. It wasn't Cheryl's fault I was a sick puppy. "Look, I'm sorry I snapped. Someone just called and hung up on me. Was it you?"

"Why would I hang up?" she asked. "I want to know if everything's okay. If anyone showed up."

"No one showed."

She waited for me to speak but I didn't. After a minute she asked, "You want me to go away, don't you? I'm disturbing you?"

Other than the gunmen, the only person who really disturbed me was me. "I need a little room to get out of this mess, that's all."

"So I *am* bothering you?"

I didn't answer.

"Well," she said, "at least call once in a while so I know you're alive, okay?"

"Sure, Cheryl, I'll call."

"Thanks," she said sarcastically, slamming down the phone.

I replaced the receiver and was stubbing out the cigarette in the ashtray with an angry twist of my wrist when the phone

rang again. I imagined it Cheryl, thought about ignoring it, then yanked it to my ear. "Yes. Who is it?"

The thin voice surprised me. "Mr. Jacob? Matt? Is this Matt?"

"Uh-huh." I had a sudden hope and asked, "Yakov, did you call earlier and hang up?"

"I did," he answered. "I thought I woke you and I got nervous. I'm sorry."

He'd gotten the two of us nervous. "No problem, Yakov." No problem, no evacuation. I thought about my crawl up the hill behind the rink. What was I thinking, no problem? "What can I do for you?"

"Can I come over? I'd like to talk to you about something."

It wasn't how I needed to spend my time, but there was something in his voice that made it impossible to refuse. "We can get together. How about the Yeshiva? I don't want to meet here."

"If you come to the Yeshiva word will get back to my father."

I chuckled grimly. "I don't want that to happen either."

"Even though he's out of town he would find out. Somebody would tell him that we met."

I was curious about Yonah's trip but didn't want to ask. "Then we'll meet somewhere else." I thought for a moment, "How about the main library? If it's warm enough we can sit in the courtyard."

"I've never been there," he said.

"The courtyard?"

"No. Inside that library." He sounded dubious.

"Do you know where it is?"

"Yes."

I looked at the clock. "Can you meet me on the Boylston Street steps in about an hour?" That would leave me the rest of the day to do something about staying alive.

"Good," he said. "Mr. Jacob . . ."

"Matt."

"Thank you."

He hung up the phone as the recorded voice of Ma Bell demanded more silver. I wondered what drove the kid to a public telephone. I replaced the receiver and lit another cigarette. I'd find out.

Sooner or later I had to confront the mess I was in. But right now, mañana seemed soon enough to me.

CHAPTER 28

I telephoned Julius and asked him to hang around the house. Then a call to Charles and Richard to suggest they do their normal boogie. Charles begged me to define normal. I couldn't, but told him to relax anyway; Julie was staying home. That worked better than any definition and he asked what I was planning to do. When I told him I had no plans he giggled nervously before wishing me luck. I appreciated it.

The skin-tingling traces of my freaky dream receded as the reality of my situation grabbed center stage. I pushed aside my automatic panic and forced myself to think like a detective rather than a prisoner on Death Row. It helped that I managed an idea or two before leaving the apartment to meet Yakov.

The trek to the library was an exercise in stealth. Forward, back, around, back again, then forward. Like an acid-injected rat let loose in a labyrinth. It took nearly forty minutes to travel the fifteen-minute walk. By the time I approached the Copley Square library I was pretty sure I hadn't been followed. Any other time I'd have been certain.

Yakov was an easy spot. Once again he was reading his large leatherbound book. But this time he kept raising his head, look-

ing uncomfortably at the derelicts who called the broad concrete steps home. Every now and again he'd combine his nervous sideways glances with a stand-up gaze down the block.

I stayed out of sight until his head was buried, walked quickly next to him where I knelt tying my shoe. "Don't look at me," I warned softly. "Just get up and go into the new building. There is a men's room downstairs. I'll meet you there."

"I can't do that," he whispered. "It's forbidden to take this book into a bathroom."

"Then once you're inside just go to the information desk," I said impatiently.

He glanced at me with the same expression he'd had when he looked at the bums. "You can't take the *Talmud* into a toilet. It's a . . . a . . ."

"Sacrilege, Yakov," I supplied in a gruff, quiet voice. "Just go inside. Now! I don't want to party on the steps."

Yakov shook his head as if to argue, but closed the book and retreated into the library. I turned, sat on the steps, and lit a cigarette. Halfway through I tossed the cigarette and entered the Philip Johnson building.

I found the boy where he was supposed to be, placed my hand on his shoulder, and watched the door. No one sat in the chair inside the information booth. The library couldn't afford it. After a moment or two I removed my hand from his shoulder. "Hello."

Yakov had it figured. "We went through a detective routine like somebody was after you?"

"Someone may be following me and I wanted us to be alone." I held up my hand to stop his flood of questions. "You've never been in here, right?"

"What's that got to do with anything?"

It had to do with ridding him of his growing nervousness. "Not too much, but the place is worth a quick look. Is there any other room besides the john your book can't travel?" I asked with a grin.

Yakov began to protest but changed his mind. "Just bathrooms and churches."

We walked through the new building, across the courtyard, and into the old. Yakov tried to appear disinterested, but I caught him sneaking looks at the different pictures on the walls. "Check out the ceiling," I suggested, as we walked through the Elliot Room.

He glanced upward then blushed. "Are you teasing me?"

"What are you talking about?"

"Telling me to look at a naked woman."

He was serious. "We're talking art, here, Yakov. It's called *The Triumph of Time*. Been here since the turn of the century."

The boy shook his head. "Art," he sneered. "What's the difference how long it's been here? Naked is naked."

I'd intended to show him the Edwin Austin Abby murals, but *The Quest of the Holy Grail* would only goose his anger. I glanced up the stairs toward the Sargent Hall and rejected that idea as well. It was easier to just lead him to the outdoor courtyard. The air was chilly but the sun bright, so we sat on a corner bench where I kept an eye on both entrances. Yakov looked around, an amazed expression on his face. "Yeshiva students who go to night school sometimes use this library, but I never imagined this."

"What do you mean?" I asked.

"Our library doesn't look anything like this. It's just a large room with *shtendals* and books."

"What's a *shtendal*?"

"You know, tall wooden bookrests where you stand and learn. How does anyone keep their mind on what they're doing when they are surrounded by all this beauty."

I'd never thought of beauty as a deterrent but it was a treat to look around through Yakov's fresh eyes. Tall marbleized columns, a stone walkway alongside the center square garden —the garden's last green hangers-on protected by the double building's walls.

"Why are there long nails in the tops of the pillars?" Yakov asked.

"To keep the pigeons from landing."

"The animals aren't allowed to rest?"

"So people can."

Yakov shrugged unconvinced. We sat quietly watching an occasional passerby stroll between buildings. It was cold enough to keep anyone from stopping.

"What's bothering you, boy?" I finally asked.

He wasn't ready to say. "Why couldn't we meet at your house? Is it the way I look?"

I reached over and tousled his bristly, crewcut hair, almost knocking his velvet *yarmulke* from his head. "I don't even notice the way you look anymore."

"What did you mean when you said someone may be following you? Are you on another case?"

"Not really."

"Then why are you acting so mysterious?"

"I ran into a little trouble last night and have to be careful. Right now my house isn't completely safe."

"What kind of trouble?"

I compromised with the truth. "Some guys in a car hassled me."

"Because of my father? The Avengers?"

I looked at his face and said, "Probably not. I haven't figured everything out yet."

Yakov looked at me with a worried expression. "Are you frightened?"

"Not at the moment."

"Were you frightened last night?"

I hesitated. "Yeah. I'm scared whenever I'm involved in a confrontation."

"Did you use your gun?"

"No. I didn't have my gun."

"I bet you have it now, don't you?"

I smiled ruefully as his enthusiasm and curiosity overcame his usual seriousness. I'd have preferred this response when we were looking at the murals.

"Do you think they'll find us here?"

"No. Tell you the truth, I really don't think anyone is bothering to look."

"If that's so, why did you do all that on the steps?"

"Yakov, my friend, we didn't meet to talk about the detective business. Come on, why did you call?"

But he wasn't finished with his questions. "Do you believe this had something to do with my father's case?"

"I don't think so."

"Are you working on something else?"

"Yakov."

He looked earnest. "It's important to me. Did the people in the car look Jewish?"

"Jewish?" I asked, astonished. "What do you mean?"

"Did they look like Hasidim?"

"No, of course not."

Relief crossed his face.

"Yakov, why are you asking me this? What are you thinking?"

His worried look deepened and he anxiously rubbed the book in his hand. "Do you remember our conversation about the Never Agains?" he asked.

"Yes."

"I've been thinking about what you said. About them being vigilantes and how maybe that wasn't okay."

I sat quietly, giving him time. He was trying to tell me something but right now he could only skirt the edge.

"What you said made me think. It bothers me," he said worriedly.

"Say more."

The kid's complexion was pale and drawn, his mouth a rigid line carved into his face. "I told you that my father was involved

with the Never Agains. But I don't think I really said how much. I've begun to worry about it."

"Why?"

"He's spending more and more time with it. Now that the Rebbe is no longer with us, my father is using all of his energy to convince people of the necessity for self-protection."

"That makes sense, Yakov. You told me he wanted them in the neighborhood before Rabbi Dov was shot. I'm sure he believes it's even more crucial now. Not too long ago you were saying the same thing."

"You don't understand. This has started to take *all* his attention. It's all he talks with anyone about, all he thinks about. This is the first time in my life that I've ever seen him devote so little time to learning, to the *Halacha*. It's almost like he's not a Rabbi anymore."

I buried my antipathy toward Reb Yonah in my affection for the kid. "I see why you're concerned, but I have a different take. Remember when I told you your father had mentioned the camps? Well, I think Rabbi Dov's murder has stirred all those memories. He's frightened and trying to combat it the only way he knows. It makes sense that he would turn to a group he trusts. From what you tell me, he trusts the Never Agains."

Yakov shook his head. "He doesn't act scared. He is angry all the time. He even uses you and the lawyer Roth as examples of why we need the Never Agains. Why we need to watch out for ourselves," Yakov blurted, a stricken look on his face. He hunched his skinny body forward, pulling his arms in tight as if to ward off a millennia-old blow.

"I'm not upset that he uses us as examples, Yakov," I said gently.

"He says the fancy lawyer and detective haven't been able to help him. That all you can do is disrupt the Yeshiva and cause trouble. We would be better off if you went away and we learned to take care of ourselves." By the time the boy finished his voice was a mixture of guilt and relief.

"Look, there are a lot of ways people mask their fears. Especially from themselves. It's not unusual to turn it into anger. So he lashes out. No big deal. Simon and I make for nearby targets, that's all. Eventually, maybe with the help of these people, he'll settle down. Leave some of his fears behind. Yakov, the camps left deeper scars than only the numbers." I paused, then asked, "You were worried it was Never Again people who hassled me last night, weren't you?"

Yakov nodded keeping his face averted. "I don't know what I was thinking. You don't understand how angry my father is at you and the lawyer Simon."

For an instant I sensed he had more to say but he remained silent. "Listen, kid, the Never Agains had nothing to do with last night. Put it out of your mind. Where did your father go, by the way?"

"New York."

"New York? Why?"

"*Berucha und Mazel.*"

"What is that?"

The boy looked perplexed. "I keep forgetting that you are a Jew who knows nothing."

"Thanks, kid."

"You know what I mean. About Jewishness."

"So, *nu?*" I asked with a smile. "What does it mean?"

"My father went to New York to return diamonds."

"Diamonds?"

"Yes."

"Is your father in the business?" I knew the Hasids had an enormous foothold in the diamond industry and New York was the center.

"Not really."

"So he had diamonds to return?"

"Yes."

"Do you know why he had them in the first place?"

"No."

"But something about it bothers you."

"Of course not." His answer was swift and emphatic. And untrue.

"Okay," I said, backing off.

We sat quietly watching the occasional pigeon approach the tops of the pillars and fly away. I felt the churning of my own loneliness, but I was free of the foggy depression that usually accompanied it. Yakov leaned forward as if to speak, changed his mind, and sat back.

"What is it?" I asked.

Yakov hesitated then shook his head. "Nothing."

It wasn't true, but this talk had been difficult enough for the kid. I felt the warmth of our increased closeness and realized our talk was difficult for me too. "It's time to go, boy. You all right?"

He nodded despite a worried frown. I waited to see if he was going to add anything. When he didn't I stood up. "Do you remember the way out of here?" I asked.

Yakov nodded.

"Good. It's time to get your butt back to the Yeshiva."

"You're staying here?"

"I'll leave in a few minutes. I don't want us to walk out together."

"Are you going to be okay?" Yakov asked.

"I'm going to be fine," I smiled.

Yakov stood and clutched his book tight against his gawky body. "Are you sure?" he asked.

"Of course I'm sure," I replied with more confidence than I actually felt. Now that our conversation was coming to a close, the rest of my life was circling.

The boy started toward the entrance then turned back. "Can I call you again if I want?"

"Anytime. Hey, we got hoops to shoot."

Yakov tried to smile, gave up, and left the courtyard to me and a frustrated pigeon.

CHAPTER 29

I deked, feinted, and deked my way to the Auto-Caribe. And while I didn't spot anyone who looked ready to kiss me a fond farewell, I couldn't escape the sensation of eyes on the back of my neck. Anyway, I hoped it was eyes. If it was a scope, I'd never have a chance to play that game of hoops.

I finally understood what it meant to feel truly "under the gun," but it was growing impossible to draw a distinction between fact and fantasy. Right now, to imagine was to believe. The best I could do was continue evasive maneuvers and pretend to pray. If a conservative is a liberal who got mugged, a religious convert had to be someone almost finished off the night before.

The news I received at Manuel's did nothing to buoy my optimism. He'd moved my car to the lot behind his garage and the two of us stood staring sadly at the damage. Manuel waggled his head though he didn't ask any questions. He told me that it would take time to fix and offered me a loaner. That was the good news. The bad came when I asked if he had removed the bullet from the door and he said no. I rushed Manuel back to his office then played Green Beret, trying to spot sniper positions. I found positions but no snipers, returned to the lot,

and hunted the grounds fruitlessly. I expected to come up empty; my gut told me the bullet hadn't simply fallen out. Eventually I got sick of crawling around on my hands and knees, thanked Manuel for his tired, oversized sedan, and drove out of the lot.

There was no comfort inside the big gray metal box. I still felt naked. Only now it was time to do something about it. But if I was going to function effectively, I needed to rid myself of long-range rifle fantasies. I had enough trouble with my normal life to imagine living like this. Always on guard, fearful that my head was a centerpiece in anonymous crosshairs. I pulled a joint from my pocket and smoked until my nerves settled into a dull background rumble.

Quiet enough to allow focus, loud enough to keep me from huddling on my couch. Quiet enough to hear my anger. Loud enough to force the action.

I stopped at a fancy liquor store, took a short course on single malts, then bought two of the best. I knew if I had somehow slipped my attackers' net, I might be waltzing right back in. I just didn't see any alternative. The dull nerve noise mushroomed into a roar when I parked a block from the variety store. Before leaving the car I checked the safety on my gun and gripped my bag of presents tighter.

Pearse kept his attention on the customers in front of the counter as I walked through the door. I nervously paced the entire store twice before the place emptied. When the door finally closed on the last customer, Pearse called from the front, "Surely you can do something better than strut around my business like a rooster in the henhouse?"

I felt more like a chicken in the coop with a fox, but I grunted appreciatively and returned to the counter. "How are you feeling?" I asked, estimating the amount of liquor he must have drunk the night before.

Mr. Pearse looked at me strangely from behind his large red-veined nose, and pulled a bottle up from behind his counter.

"You're asking me how I feel? Take a gander in the mirror, son. You don't look none too well yourself. A fight with a she-cat?" he asked, nodding toward my scratched face.

"No," I managed a smile. "Fell into a bush."

Pearse dipped his head and shoulders. "Had to be a big bush. Or, a very long fall."

"Big bush," I muttered.

"Perhaps some of this will ease the pain."

"No pain, but it will definitely help with the memory."

Pearse produced two clean water glasses but I stopped him from pouring. "We drank yours last night." I eased my grip on the brown paper bag, reached inside with my other hand, and placed one of the bottles on the counter. Then I clanked the bag down about six inches away.

"You are a surprising find, young man. Not the sort of person Father Collins usually introduces me to." Pearse came out from behind the counter, walked to the door, turned the hanging sign around, and pulled the shade. "I don't want to chance the good Father strolling by," he said on his way back. "We have this tussle, you know. It would be a shame to get caught."

His resentment was real. I grunted my support and forced myself to look forward to the drink.

"This is a fine Scotch you've brought," he commented, holding the glass in front of his eyes.

I nodded and lit a cigarette.

"I don't imagine you brought it here just to have drinking company?"

I nodded again.

"And, if I am willing to help you, I will be rewarded with the contents of that brown paper bag. I hope it's as good as this?"

"Better."

"I suppose I'll have to try, then. It's a sinful thing, to play upon a man's weakness. A person's vice."

I smiled at his enjoyment of our game. "I don't know you well enough to play on your virtues."

"That's always the rub, isn't it? Our worst is the first thing anyone observes."

"I don't know" — I winked — "I'm sure you have more going for you than whisky."

Pearse shot me a glum look as he downed his double and poured another. "If you are a gambling man I'd advise you not to take the bet," he said. He stared pointedly at my untouched drink. "It's troubling to talk when I'm drinking alone."

I hoisted my glass and took a healthy swallow. It was smoother than last night's, but the chest-filling burn was the same.

"What is it you want to know?" Pearse asked.

"I want to find Blue."

He looked disgusted. "That's what everybody wants. I was hoping for better. Or at least different."

"Who else has been asking?"

"That wouldn't be right, would it? I'll tell you what I told the others. Ask around Buzz's. Now, does that get me the mysterious bag?"

I shook my head.

"Ah," he said, "I didn't think so. I'd best drink more of this." He topped his glass, waited until I'd drunk more of mine, then replenished my drink. "Why is it you want to know Blue's whereabouts?"

"We have some unfinished business."

"And what might that business be?"

I had to think about that one. Pearse hadn't sent me packing, but I'd be out the door if he nailed me in a lie. "He broke a friend's hands. I want to return the favor."

It was his turn to pause. He looked into my face then drank from his glass. "You mean that literally, don't you?"

I nodded. "Maybe. I don't know for sure."

"So you think I'll inform on Blue because his gang broke a Negro's bones?"

"A young Black female, Mr. Pearse." I gritted my teeth and sucked oxygen. "She's a kid, no threat to anyone. Blue had her

hands broken to send me a message. We're not talking informing," I said pointedly. "This isn't betrayal. We're talking about a twenty-one-year-old girl. This isn't the kind of incident that helps this neighborhood's reputation."

I had hit a soft spot. Scatter enough shot, something has to land. Pearse filled up his glass while I drained mine. This time I reloaded for myself. The warmth felt invigorating after a couple doses.

"I hadn't known the girl was as young as that," he replied grimly.

"As young as that, Mr. Pearse. Let's face it, you don't like those animals any more than I do. That's why you've been willing to talk to me. I could tell that last night and I can tell it now." I paused then guessed, "I have a feeling it wasn't because Father Collins asked you to."

"That's for damn sure," he growled. "He's made it impossible for me to enjoy a drink in public. That's why I sneak it in the church."

Everybody has their own way of saying fuck you. "It's not me, it's not Collins, and it's not my bottles that's gonna get you to talk." I pulled the bag next to the open bottle between us. "It's who you are and your concern for the neighborhood." I paused and cast another line. "Listen, I know what people around here are willing to fight for and it isn't scum like Blue."

Pearse nodded his agreement. "It surely isn't. There are real battles to be fought."

"I'd guess Ireland is pretty important to folks living here."

Pearse's face closed down. I'd hooked an old boot and rushed to throw it back. "That's why telling me about Blue has nothing to do with informing. He doesn't stand for anything worth supporting. Look, Mr. Pearse, I know you have no reason to trust me. I'm an outsider, a stranger. But I won't let a punk like Blue stomp on a friend. Especially a young woman. The gift is yours whether you tell me where to find him or not. And I'll come back sometime and help you use it. But I *will* find Blue, Mr. Pearse, with or without your help."

Pearse's tension eased as he made his decision. "I believe you will, I believe you will."

For a moment I thought he was finished. Then he added, "He won't be easy to corner even if you do locate him."

"Why is that?"

Pearse hesitated, tore off a piece of the bag, reached under the counter, and emerged with a pen. He scribbled on the brown paper and pushed it toward me. I glanced at the address then stuffed it into my pocket. "Why will it be hard to get to him?" I asked.

"He has himself barricaded in the cellar of an abandoned warehouse. The address is in your pocket."

"Is he alone?"

"I would expect. Right now none of his old friends want to be around him."

If he knew about Blue's new friends he wasn't talking. "You really don't like the Avengers, do you?"

Pearse rubbed his red nose. "I surely don't, but I don't want to be a party to a murder either."

"I won't kill him. You already know that." I thanked him, and waited until he hid the bottles before we walked to the door. I was on the street when he said, "Take care of yourself, will you? Way things are, I don't have many people to share a nip with."

I pumped his hand and promised.

The whisky's warmth had spread to my head. I realized that the moment I considered storming Blue's bunker. I didn't think it likely, but Pearse might be walking me into an IRA trap. I didn't need a welcome wagon. Especially one without Tupperware.

I lit a cigarette and thought about returning home. But, by the time I finished the smoke, my blood had thinned enough for me to *use* my head. Home meant living with an extra layer of paranoia. And my couch just wasn't that comfortable.

I drove around the neighborhood looking for eyes, saw none, then motored past the address Pearse had given me. The disin-

tegrating warehouse was semi-boarded-up with chicken wire and cheap plywood covering its doors and broken windows. The place was about as inviting as an abandoned ice skating rink.

I drove back to a local hardware store, purchased a couple of tools, and shoved them into the sedan. I was pulling my head out of the rear door when I felt a heavy tap on my shoulder.

"Whoa, Matthew. Sorry to have startled you," Father Collins said as I swung around. "A bit jumpy, aren't you?"

"I guess," I muttered as soon as my breath returned. "You look different?"

"It's the street clothes."

"I'm not used to seeing you this way."

His mouth twisted into an empty smile. "What are you doing here?"

"Buying some supplies. I help take care of a couple of buildings."

"This hardware store is a little far from home, isn't it?" His words were clipped.

"I don't remember telling you where I lived." So were mine.

The question threw him off guard, but only for a second. "You're right. I just know that you don't live here." Collins immediately adjusted his attitude. "You do seem on edge today. Is something the matter? Your face is cut."

I lowered my throttle. "Bad day shaving."

"Perhaps it's time to change the blade. What really happened?"

I just didn't trust his friendliness. But my suspicion might only be guilt by association since I believed the assassination caravan had followed me from the church. "I had a small car accident."

"Last night?"

"On my way home from your church, actually."

"I'm sorry to hear it. I hope no one was hurt."

"No one was hurt."

I tried to think of a way to draw him out but the padre sud-

denly looked at his watch. "Part of my clerical *and* civilian garb, unfortunately. I'm glad you're okay."

I nodded, carefully watching his face.

"I've got to run. Oh," he added casually, "are you still busy with your case?"

"Sure, why do you ask?" He didn't make it easy to restrain my suspicions.

"I'd hoped you'd gotten enough information from Mr. Pearse to allow you to finish your work," he replied easily. "I'm sorry, Matthew, but I really must go. Please call on me if I can be of further assistance."

"Thanks, I might take you up on that."

I climbed back into the car and tried to reason with my distrust. When I couldn't, I contented myself with a long drive as the last of the late afternoon faded into evening. By now, I assumed the feeling of being followed was going to last until everything was over. It was still not understanding anything about the "everything" that bothered me. All I had was one thin string written on a bag scrap. And, as the evening drew into inevitable darkness, I knew it was getting time to pull.

CHAPTER 30

The whole block looked like a picture postcard of Berlin in 1945. Smashed streetlights; ramshackle, falling asbestos-shingled housing; padlocked, rundown streetside garages; broken and abandoned fire hydrants. It was lucky I'd driven by earlier while there had still been daylight. Otherwise, I'd need to scour the entire block, flashlight in hand, to locate the address. Even knowing the correct building didn't jump-start my confidence. So I used the little glass bottle and finished the last of the cocaine.

I climbed out of the car from the passenger's side, knelt on the sidewalk, and organized my equipment. Manuel's sedan was tall enough for me to slip the tool belt around my waist without showing much of my head over the roof. Once I had the tools in place and the safety off my gun, I scurried up the street, crossed, and doubled back.

Skinny concrete driveways separated each of the old large buildings or garages. A few hosted small, rusted pickups. Others were empty, their tar tops cracked and pitted. A beat-up Plymouth without plates sat deep in the driveway next to my target building. I considered disabling the engine, then didn't bother. If Blue made it outside, I wouldn't be chasing.

I quietly walked to the back of the abandoned warehouse. I as-

sumed the basement was underground and, as expected, saw no light from any of the boarded, wired, or shattered back windows. I studied the rear of the four-story before picking a ground-floor window. Better to get inside without being heard, but if not, no great loss; I planned on inviting Blue to my party.

I raced to the building's far side and ducked when a light flashed from a nearby building. No need for a nosy neighbor to spot me and call the police. I stayed squatted until the light snapped off, then returned to the window. I cautiously clipped the chicken wire and bent it back. Unfortunately, the window still had large shards of glass stuck in the frame so I pulled on my new work gloves to gingerly pry the pieces loose. I'd had it with cuts and scratches. I piled the glass neatly alongside the building, pulled the gloves off my hands, and hoisted myself up and over.

And in. I held my breath and stood motionless until my eyes adjusted to the dusty darkness. For an instant the huge floor space revived memories of last night's skating rink — with one major difference. Tonight, I was the hunter.

I pulled the small metal flashlight from the belt, the gun from the holster, and began to explore. Heavy steel shelving lined most of the walls and, to my initial dismay, were bolted into the concrete.

All except the one I needed. Next to a rear window, a large stand-alone shelf assembly stood on wheels. I scouted the cavern and returned with an old *Herald*. The date read '88. No surprise. Lots of warehouse closings that year. I slid a few sheets under the metal wheels and slowly rolled the shelf across a padded newspaper trail. Splotches of moonlight snuck into the room from around the crooked plywood window slats. The place had a dank, rank stench. As if a truckload of ratty sneakers and dead squirrels had been left to rot and meld into the dirty atmosphere. Might not be as easy to get Blue up here as I had hoped.

By the time I dragged the metal across the room I'd worked up a nervous sweat. Despite the ability to see my breath. It

hadn't been easy to do everything with my right, but my left hand wasn't letting go of the gun. I walked back to the rear of the building, stopped next to a half-shattered window, and lit a cigarette. I didn't much care about the smoke. Might help entice him into the stinking cave.

I used the cigarette break to memorize the room. If the oldest trick in the book worked, it wouldn't be necessary. But coke rush or no, I wasn't betting on the book. I finished the cigarette and stamped it underfoot. Showtime.

I trotted to one side of the door, grabbed hold of the shelving, and threw the whole damn thing to the floor. It landed with a terrific crash sending up a storm of dirt and dust. A couple of shelves twisted and broke loose, adding to the din. If the fucker hadn't built himself a bomb shelter, he heard the racket.

I stuck my head through the debris and pushed the whole unit a couple more inches to allow the nearby metal door about half its normal swing. Then I took my position and waited. For a few long minutes I went neurotic. He wasn't there. A *bunch* of them were there. *They* weren't going to investigate the crash. *He* wasn't going to investigate.

I could have kept grinding, but, as so often is the case, my worry turned worthless: I heard a single set of metal heel taps click sharply against concrete. I started to generate a new set of concerns but pushed them aside when I saw the door swing in its obstructed arc. I listened to a grunt when it banged against my barrier. Then the door drifted back.

I heard Blue mutter, "I'm sick of chasing fucking cats in that stink." I tensed while I waited for someone to answer. When no one did, I reminded myself that talking aloud was the earmark of being alone for too long a time. Just as I reached out to rattle the steel and up the ante, the metal door suddenly banged against the shelves.

I pulled my hand back as Blue leaned, grunted, and pushed the door. The steel shelves slowly scraped along the floor and I lightly grasped the knob. Blue kept grunting and pushing. As

soon as the door swung free, I yanked, then slammed his exposed head as hard as I could with the side of my gun.

He fell right on top of the shelves. I leaned down, wiped off his blood from the revolver onto his shirt, and dragged him off the metal. I rolled him onto his back, put my shoe on his throat, and waited for possible reinforcements. With my free hand I reached inside my pocket, extracted a cigarette and lit up. Fuck it, if anyone else came through the door, I'd just shoot.

I felt my mean ride a cocaine rush through my bloodstream, and it took plenty of restraint not to stomp when I felt Blue wriggle. Enough time had elapsed so that I was no longer worried about backup punks or pros so I balled my fist and added to his upcoming dental bill. If he made it to a dentist. He stopped moving and just lay there moaning.

"Open your fucking eyes," I said throwing the cigarette to the floor.

When he didn't respond I placed a little more weight on my good foot. The one on top of his throat.

Blue's eyes opened but it took him a minute to focus. I wanted him to know who belonged to the foot so I shone the flashlight on my face, then plunged the back end into his belly. When he started to double up, I pressed my shoe down harder. I remembered staring into the long barrel of his Magnum and wasn't going to let him forget what helpless felt like. My time in the bush called for some heavy payback.

"Hello, Blue, I happened to be in the neighborhood."

He tried to talk but all that emerged was blood and teeth. I used my foot to push his head and kept it on the side of his face. I waited patiently while he spat onto the floor before I slipped my shoe back down to his throat.

Blue turned his head up and mumbled something that took me a moment to understand.

I was pumped and knew it, but most of me didn't care. "I don't know whether I'm going to kill you or not," I chuckled and hoped he could see my nice white teeth. "I feel like it."

I reached down and grabbed him by the front of his shirt. He flinched but kept his eyes open while I dragged him across the greasy, filthy floor and propped him up against one of the bolted wall units. He started to raise his hand to wipe the trickling blood but I slapped it back down.

"Just like the movies, asshole. You move when I tell you. With one difference. In this movie the gun has real bullets." I pulled back the hammer and placed the barrel against his forehead. We both listened as the urine trickled down his leg.

I pulled my arm back a couple of inches and gently put the hammer back down. I didn't want a sweat slip. At least not yet. Blue opened his dripping red gash and gasped for air. I was glad he hadn't eaten dinner.

"We're going to have a little talk. Who were your friends last night?"

He shook his head. "Don't know," he mumbled.

I made sure his hand was flat on the floor, dug my heel into the back of it, and waited for him to stop moaning before I asked, "You want to try a different answer?"

He rolled his head from side to side, tears coming out of his eyes. "I swear."

"A couple of men stop you on the street and invite you on a joy ride to kill me? You expect me to buy that?"

"They knew where I was staying," he gasped. "They came and got me. I swear."

"I don't fucking believe you." I did the toe and heel on his other hand, but my heart wasn't in it. "Let's try something else, Blue. Why did Kelly start the Avengers?"

Blue, relieved by the question, answered quickly. "He said the country needed a racial cleansing. Those were his exact words."

"I'm not asking for the party line. I want to know why one day he runs a regular gang of thieves then turns it into a Hitler organization the next."

"It wasn't just one day," he answered with a little too much sarcasm.

I grabbed his hair and slammed the back of his head into the steel shelves.

"I don't know exactly what got Sean started," Blue groaned through his tears. "I heard he had something going with a broad. Ask her, maybe. He always kept part of his trip hidden from the rest of us. I don't know what made him do it. All I know is that it made sense to me."

"Did you ever meet this girlfriend?"

"Never." He worried his answer wouldn't fly and added, "Sean didn't talk to no one about her. I mean no one. I asked him about her once, and he told me it was none of my business. He told me to shut the fuck up about it."

"And you just did what he told you to do, is that it?"

He nodded his head as best he could.

"And it didn't bother you that Kelly took from the top?"

"Everyone saw money. Enough to live okay and enough to run the Avengers."

"But you were stealing more than that, weren't you?"

"Sean made sure the rest got to the nationals. Anyhow, without him, there was no money. Nobody could plan jobs like him."

"He sent money to the same folks who ran with you last night?"

"I swear — I don't know who they are!"

It would be easy for Blue to say they were from some national neo-Nazi group, but he didn't. Either he was still covering, or he really didn't know.

I balled my fist again and backhanded him across his face. "You're covering for your Nazi friends, you lying bastard."

Blue rolled his head. "No, no. They would have told me if they were with us."

"What else, Blue? You have other reasons to believe they weren't fellow travelers. What are they?"

He lifted his head and I began to notice the damage I'd inflicted. "At least one of the guys was Irish," he said.

I felt like hitting him again for causing the involuntary lurch in my stomach. "Just one?"

"Only one guy talked."

I thought for a minute, then asked, "Before the Avengers, when you and Kelly took down armored cars, did you give money to the IRA? Is that where your money has been going?"

Blue leaned forward painfully. "Before the Avengers we'd do a job and Sean would take money off the top for pay-offs. Drivers, someone in the car barn, maybe a cop. I don't know. Sean always ran the money. He coulda been paying anyone."

He hesitated and dredged a little more energy. "Listen," he mumbled, "I been thinking the same thing. After those guys left I couldn't figure why some Irish guy wanted you. But if Sean was giving our money to them, it meant he was lying to me. He wouldn't do that!"

Blue had to believe in something. I looked at his slumped body and twisted face. Sure, Sean wouldn't lie. And I wouldn't do this.

Blue was beginning to fade in and out of consciousness, so I didn't think he heard the faint scraping outside the door. But I did. I moved quickly to his side and curled my forearm around his throat. I didn't want the intruder to know I'd heard the noise so I asked another question, "You dug the bullet out of the car door, didn't you?"

"No," he moaned with what little strength he had left.

"Don't lie to me, you cocksucker," I almost shouted, as I slammed my foot hard on the floor. I hoped it sounded like a body blow as I kept my eyes and gun on the open door. "Don't lie to me!"

"He isn't lying, Jacobs," a voice barked from somewhere in the corridor. "He isn't lying! This is Washington Clifford. You don't sound wrapped too tight and I don't want you to kill him or shoot me. Now, I'm coming through the door and I'll flash a light on my face so you know that it's me."

"Should I slide my gun across the room like a good little doobie?"

"I know better than to ask. Now listen up, I'm coming in."

"Save the fucking batteries. I recognize your voice."

"Good, Jacobs. That's good."

But he flashed the light anyway as he walked carefully into the room.

"Over here," I said.

Clifford pointed the light in our direction and I had to turn my head when it caught my eyes. No low-power job for my man Washington.

"Jesus, Jacobs, put the fucking gun away."

I guess the light also caught my left fist.

Clifford followed his request with a slow walk toward the two of us. Blue had passed out but I was still holding him in front of me. I let go and pushed him on his side so he wouldn't choke. I was turning soft.

Clifford knelt and pushed my gun hand off to the side. "If you're not going to put it away, at least keep it out of my face." He flashed the light into Blue's eyes and prodded his body. Clifford relaxed when he discovered that Blue's death wasn't imminent.

"You did a real bad-ass number on this boy, Jacobs. Maybe you ought to thank me for showing up when I did. You might have killed the little prick."

"You going to bust me for beating on him or for what I might have done? And the fucking name is Jacob."

"I'm not going to bust you at all, you poor asshole." He flashed his light onto my face but this time I squinted it down. "You are either very high, *Jacobs*, or you enjoy the work. Now go home, take some tranqs, and get it together. Your party is over."

"Bullshit! Nothing is over! I'm a clay pigeon for shooters, *Wash*. There's one down, more to go."

Clifford hesitated then tried to pacify me. "You got nothing to be worried about."

I fairly shouted, "Fuck you, nothing to be worried about? At least three guys want me dead. I understand that don't worry you."

"You don't understand nothing," Clifford snarled. "I'm telling you that you don't have to be worried about your shooters. Nobody is going to try to kill you again, except maybe me."

His message finally twisted its way through my high-voltage head. Then I remembered his words from the hall. "You've been tailing me, haven't you? You found out about the scene on Bynner and went to the garage?"

"You think I have nothing better to do than run around after you?"

"You said you had the bullet. Do you?"

Clifford hesitated again, stood, and offered his hand to help me up. I spurned the offer and pushed myself to my feet.

"Yes," he finally admitted.

"What about him?" I nodded toward the now sleeping Blue.

"I'll worry about him. Listen to me, Jacobs. It's time for you to go on home. And tie your ass to a chair before you really do something stupid."

CHAPTER 31

I *had* nowhere else to go but home. And when I looked at my reflection in the car's rearview mirror, it was clear no other place would take me. I was lucky Manuel's box-on-wheels had Florida-tinted windows. If a cop caught a glimpse I'd be run in immediately, no questions asked. I glanced into the mirror again, flashed on Blue's moaning, prone body, and, for the first time, bit on Clifford's scathing remarks. I *might* have killed Blue. And for what? Revenge?

My coked adrenaline rush was fading, leaving in its place a yawning emotional fatigue. I white-knuckled the skinny steering wheel and pointed the car toward my apartment. Clifford's assurance that I was no longer a potential road kill was a relief. But the relief was shadowed by an undertow of dissatisfaction. Clifford was shutting down my case before I knew what my case had been. It didn't exactly depress me, just left me feeling empty. What would fill the empty when the cocaine completely wore off?

I parked the car in my back alley, crunched across the gravel, and let myself inside. I didn't know whether I was pleased or pressured to hear Lou call from the kitchen, "*Boychik*, is that you?"

"Uh-huh." I walked down the hall and joined him.

"Oh my God, what the hell happened?" Lou hoisted his considerable bulk with surprising speed. "Was there an explosion? Are you injured?"

I winced as his urgency collided with my growing lethargy. "I'm fine. I did the exploding."

"You look like you were crawling around in the dirt. Jesus, *boychik*, your eyes look insane. I'm going to get you a drink."

"Thanks. Would you bring the stash too? I gotta make a couple of calls."

Lou shook his head, but did what I asked while I went into the office and spoke with Julie, then Richard. Richard was relieved to hear we were no longer under siege. Julius sounded disappointed. Both had a handful of questions, but I wasn't in an answer-man mood.

I returned to the kitchen table and took a long pull of bourbon. Then another. Lou wouldn't meet my eyes. I tried grinning to break the tension. It must have looked strange because once I finished twisting my lips Lou asked nervously, "Matt, did you kill someone?" He whispered the question, afraid of the answer.

"No, Lou. I didn't kill anyone."

He finally came out with it. "You have blood all over yourself. Is it yours? Are you sure you weren't stabbed or grazed? Sometimes the body goes into shock and a person doesn't even know they've been hurt."

This time my grin seemed more genuine. At least to me. "Sounds like you're talking from personal experience."

His anxiety found an angry outlet. "Damn right personal, Matty. You think the early days of union work meant walking around with cardboard signs? Or my Daley years in Chicago were a quiet piece of cake?"

"I'm just kidding you, Lou."

He wasn't placated. "You think I don't know what you're doing? By you, *boychik*, everything is a joke. Your face is black like a coal miner, blood all over your clothes, and you don't even know if you're hurt. But you can sit there kidding me."

"Believe me, Lou, I didn't get hurt."

"Well, if you're not hurt go to the goddamn bathroom and clean yourself up. You look like a piece of *dreck*."

I grabbed an empty plastic bag, retreated to the bathroom, and avoided the mirror until after the shower. My clothes were garbage so I stuffed them into the bag. I wanted to throw my skin in after, but as hard as I'd scrubbed under the scalding water, it just wouldn't shed.

The bulging plastic did little to assuage my father-in-law's fears. "You act like you're getting rid of evidence," he said.

"I am, but not because of the law. I don't want to be reminded about tonight every time I step into these clothes."

Lou's worry broke through his protective anger. "*Boychik*, what the hell happened? I've never seen your face look like that, especially your eyes."

"Yeah, well, I can't throw my eyes out."

A resigned expression crossed his face. "Okay, I get the message. You're not going to talk. But what the hell is going on around here? Charles and Richard have been acting strange all day. Even Julius was different — walking around like a bigshot, like he was guarding the buildings. We're partners here, Matty. If something isn't right, I want to know about it."

Partners was a generous term. His money, our familial bond and friendship. "Everything is okay, Lou. I was afraid some toughs might show up looking for me. I wanted to leave the buildings so I asked Julie, Charles, and Richard to keep their eyes open." There was no need to frighten him with my ice rink escapade.

Lou was quiet. "If you asked all three to keep watch you must have expected serious trouble."

"It was possible."

"But no longer?"

"That's right." If Clifford was to be believed.

"You think I'm a fat useless old man, don't you?" Lou asked.

"Just fat, why?"

"You ask the *faigeleh* to help you with trouble but you don't ask me?"

A part of me was annoyed; I had enough lousy feelings without adding extra guilt. But another part relaxed in the face of his familiar attitude and concern. "I thought about it but it was very late at night and I didn't want to disturb you. Charles and Richard are always awake."

"Doing God knows what," he grumbled, softening.

"See Lou-e-gee, I was just protecting our society from immoral, perverted deviance."

"Just protecting me is what you mean," he said with a trace of pleasure.

"Are you kidding? No need to protect someone with your experience."

"Don't be a smart guy. That was true."

"I know, Lou."

"Are you finished?" Lou asked.

I glanced at my drink. "Don't get up. I still have some."

"Not the drink, Matty. I'm talking about whatever it is you're involved in. What you've been doing."

"Yeah, it's over." I said it, but wasn't ready to believe.

"Did it have something to do with the Yeshiva case?"

I didn't know how to answer. "Tangentially," I finally said. "Nothing direct."

"Were you successful?"

"I don't know what success means with this one. Everyone, including Simon, thinks it would be better if I just drop out." I rolled a joint and lit it. Though the worst images of my night's sadism were slowly receding, the emptiness of concluding the case with only my memories of abandoned rinks and warehouses grated on me.

Lou looked puzzled but struggled not to pry. He poured himself a small shot and downed it quickly.

"What's that going to do to your sugar?" I asked.

"It can't do any worse than what you do to my heart," he replied.

I gave him a tired smile. "Come on, tough guy, I don't get into too many of these scrapes."

He thought about it. "No, but when you do . . ." He chopped his words in mid-sentence, then looked at me. "I heard you had one of the Hasids over to the house."

"Yeah, Reb Yonah's kid wanted to talk. We played some ball."

"This was before Simon asked you to drop out?"

"Yeah, but I'll have him over again anyway."

The worry left his face, replaced by a sad look of kindness. "You like this boy, don't you?" he asked softly, distantly.

I felt his sadness resonate inside me. "Yeah." I paused. "You're thinking about Chana, aren't you?"

"I'm thinking about many people, if you want to know the truth. I'm getting old, *boychik*. I'm starting to outlive everyone I know." He met my eyes. "This Yeshiva-*bocher* reminds you of Rebecca?"

I nodded. "At first it blindsided me. That's really what last week's depression was about. Now, well, he sort of gives me an opportunity to feel like a father." I flashed on my night's activities. Just what the world of boys needed, me as a role model.

I realized I'd spaced out and rushed through the rest of my thought. "It hurts when I think of Becky, but I like helping him out. Since Reb Dov's death, the kid's been like an orphan. Everybody is so busy working for God and community, he's fallen through the cracks."

"The father is too wound up with his legal *tsouris*?"

"The good Rabbi is apparently too occupied organizing to worry about his case."

"Organizing?"

"Yeah. There is this Jewish defense thing called . . ."

"The Never Agains," he interjected.

"That's right. You've heard of them?"

"What Jew hasn't? They're thugs."

"This Jew hadn't. You're a little harsh, aren't you? Some of the Hasids see them as a shield against anti-Semitism."

Lou said angrily, "At its best, Never Again gives people an opportunity to hold their pecker on nights other than Friday."

"What's with Friday?"

"*Mitzvah* night. Religious Jews are supposed to *schtup* their wives on Friday. Mitzvah night they call it. So when they become Never Agains they can feel like men on other nights too."

"I'll remember this conversation if I ever date a Hasid. You don't like these people, do you?"

"If the Hasids want to piss their lives away, who am I to say no? The Never Agains are another story. They are bullies who hide behind their beards and *payis*. To my way of thinking they incite more anti-Semitism than they stop. And they do it in the worst possible way. These people are thugs. You're telling me Reb Yonah is one of them?"

"Wants to be. The Big Guy wouldn't let the group near the place but now that he's dead . . ."

Lou sighed. "They aren't decent, those people, those Never Agains. The boy is bothered by all this?"

"Mixed." A piece of the conversation with Yakov came to mind. "Lou, what exactly does *Mazel* and *Berucha* mean?"

"*Mazel*, like ma, not may," he corrected. "It means luck and blessings. Who do you know in the diamond business?"

I was surprised. "How do you know it has to do with diamonds?"

"It's a traditional saying at the conclusion of a deal. Goes with the handshake. Among the Jews in the industry there are rituals to close a buy or consignment."

"Consignment?"

"Everybody fronts all the time. It's a way of life."

"Is it usual for people up here to go to New York to do business?"

"New York is New York, you know what I mean? I know some-one who has been in the business forever, a *macher* in the Dia-mond Club. You thinking of changing trades?"

"It might not be a bad idea, but no. I'm interested because the kid's father seems to be involved. What's this Diamond Club?"

"It's like a self-regulating commission. They settle disputes that come up between traders. Like I said, very few deals are written down." A thoughtful look crossed Lou's face but he re-mained silent.

"What are you thinking?"

"This Rabbi has fingers in many pies, is all."

"Too many. Might be better if he saved one for his son."

Lou nodded and we sat quietly for a couple of minutes giving my fatigue a chance to catch up. Lou noticed the yawn and pushed himself to his feet. "You're exhausted, Matty. Talk about tonight can wait."

I walked him to the door where he turned and gave me a hug. "I'm glad you weren't hurt," he said. "I can't stand the thought of outliving you."

I hugged him back. "Get used to it, old man. You're an ox." I let go and wagged my finger, "As long as you watch the sugar."

He smiled as I closed the door. I leaned my head against the wooden frame. I was tired. I bypassed the couch, grabbed my cigarettes, stash, and retired to the bedroom. I kept the light off and stared into the shadows.

I wasn't proud of my night's violent behavior but I wasn't ready to accept that my job was finished. Finished without any resolution. Okay, psychotic break complete, now back to regular life. As if all the beatings and broken bones had been tossed into a meaningless void. I went into the kitchen, grabbed the bottle of bourbon, and washed down a couple of Valium. A way to toss myself in along with everything else.

CHAPTER 32

Ride, Matty, ride, still had its spurs dug deep when I awoke the next morning. If only I had a horse. What I had was bacon and eggs. And, of course, coffee, and tobacco, and newspapers, and eventually television and dope. As long as I lingered over the first few I was okay. Trouble started when I resisted the eventuallys.

It started small. As promised, I called the building's protective society. But when I explained the situation, and why we were no longer under siege, their questions simply collided with more of my own. By the time I lamely finished each conversation mouthing Washington Clifford's assurance, I could taste my annoyance along with the nitrite.

This wasn't gonna be a day to lump on the couch. Instead, I found myself at the kitchen table when the telephone dragged me out of mental gridlock.

"Yo, bro," the voice boomed inside my head.

"Let the air out, Simon, will you? I want this ear," I grumbled testily. "You just discover another trust in Fran's inheritance?"

"Aren't we a little surly today?" He was in one of his moods where nothing could disturb or deter.

"What's so different about today?"

"Well, for one thing, it's time to tote up your abacus."

"The Reb walked?" I asked covering a sudden bolt of suspicion.

"Sprung. Just a matter of bureaucracy and paper pushing. Got the call this morning, Matt-man."

"And you trust it?"

"Why not?"

"You haven't floated a bone for the criminal justice system up 'til now."

"Up 'til now they haven't said the right things. This morning they did. Very apologetically, let me add."

"And the explanation?"

"What'd you'd expect. Wanted everything to ice down before they made their move — yada, yada, yada."

"You're stealing my vocabulary."

"Well, I'm not going to steal your time. It didn't hurt for them to know I was planning to bust chops. If I had a chance to use the information you gave me, the anti-Semites would be holding their groins for a real long time."

"You mean I'm not on your shit list for alienating the Jews?"

"Not all the Jews, Matt, just my client. Now, it would be different if you pissed off Rabbi Sheinfeld, but you didn't. And, I don't plan on working with the Hasidim again."

I was reluctant to puddle on his shoes but finally said, "I still think there is something wrong with this case."

Instant uptight. "What's the matter with you? Don't you ever like to *win*? I'm telling you we did it. Reb Yonah won't even have a paper trail. The Jewish organizations are taking a deep breath, happy for Yonah and relieved . . ."

"There won't be another pogrom."

"You don't get it, do you? This is a good thing."

I almost told him just how good it really was. Almost. But I knew that Simon wasn't going to snuff his victory cigar over an incoherent assortment of miscellaneous facts. Or even shootings.

"I thought you'd be pleased," he complained, interrupting my thoughts.

"I am, Simon," I lied.

"You're lying," he retorted. "You're still pissed about Reb Yonah pulling you off the case. Is that it?"

I half-heartedly gave it another shot. "A little, but that's not what bothers me. Something is working under the surface."

"Come on, Matt. Shit, you were the one who insisted this was a no sweat deal. Well, you were dead right!"

No, I was *almost* dead wrong. "Simon, what kind of information did Downtown finally send you?"

"What are you asking?" he snapped, his annoyance showing.

"Did you get the usual package?"

"No."

"What do you think that means?"

"It means no case against my client," he replied curtly.

"It doesn't bother you a little?"

"It bothered me a lot. What do you think I've been bitching about all this time? But it doesn't bother me now. Reb Yonah's case is finished, done."

He added, "You are a piece of work. We finally sew it up and you complain. Look, I wasn't born yesterday. If they try to put something past me I'll be over them like a bad suit."

I let it go for both our sakes. Hell, I was supposed to put the case behind me too. "You're right, friend. It's probably nothing. I just need to get a life."

He hesitated, apparently mollified by my retreat. "Look, I know you said you weren't interested, but maybe you would like to come with me to the Temple sometime?"

I stifled my snort but he got the message.

"Don't be an asshole, Matt. It sounds like you're looking for something to sink your teeth in, that's all," he said defensively. "How many hours a day can you watch TV?"

"Television works twenty-four, Bwahna. God's show doesn't

cut it for me. If there was a question, I got it answered with my close-up of Saperstein."

"The Hasidim aren't all Reb Yonahs. You like his kid, don't you? Anyway, Sheinfeld's temple is nothing like the Yeshiva. The focus is on social and political issues."

"Yeah, like fundraising for Israel. Sorry, it's not my side of the street."

"If Israel didn't bother you, Matt, you would find something else that did. The truth is, you're like the Groucho joke. You won't join a club that will take you."

"I'm not the marching type."

"Well, what type are you? Listen, we can continue this over a beer. Right now, I'm gone. Send me the numbers."

I hung up and lit up. It was another good question: what type was I? If you went by my Cheryl dream and drug habits I was just a passive middle-aged primitive. But Simon's case had aired other aspects. Revengeful, violent, sadistic. For no fucking reason. Now I was supposed to relax on the couch, worse for wear, but satisfied. Hell no.

I thought about smothering my surge of anger with smoke, but instead decided to stay with the job. Groucho had me nailed about enlisting in the search for Big Truths, but I sure as hell could join myself in looking for the little ones.

I lit a cigarette, cleaned my gun, and decided on the only path available. I couldn't wait for things to come to me. I had to squeeze the tube. Both ends if necessary.

Word would toboggan back to Simon if I looked for the link between Clifford's case and Simon's client at the Yeshiva. I might be forced there eventually, but it didn't have to be first out of the box. I had other suspicions to diddle.

Driving to Deirdre's three-flat, I realized that both Cheryl and Yakov hovered in the outskirts of my mind. My resolve to keep truckin' was, in some measure, a reply to both of them. To show *my* vision. Yakov had his strict religion, Cheryl her desire to el-

evate people's thinking. Well, Matt Jacob finished what he started.

This time I picked my way into the downstairs door and rapped loudly on hers. I listened as the door chain locked into the holder, then stared eye to eye with a wary Deirdre. The heavy links of metal looked like a tarnished slash across her throat. She didn't jump to invite me inside and kept the chain where it was.

"How did you get in the building?" she asked, her crow's-feet cracked deep with unhappy surprise.

"Someone left the door open."

"That's strange. I was the last to come inside. I don't usually forget to lock up." Deirdre worked to keep the suspicion from her face.

I smiled politely past her braided necklace. "Well, maybe you should thank me, then. I locked it before I hiked upstairs."

She returned my empty smile with a grimace. "This isn't a very good time for me."

I wasn't ready to walk. "Deirdre, during the past two weeks I've fought in a brawl, been a target for hit men, and beat the living hell out of someone. This isn't a *very good* time for me either."

My troubles didn't melt her heart. "It sounds terrible," she lied. "Any other time I'd invite you in, but right now I'm tied up. Would you mind coming back? I don't know what any of those things have to do with me, but I'll be glad to discuss them with you. Just not now. I'm sorry, Mr. Jacob."

The necklace sagged as she shut the door in my face. For a moment I considered shouldering through but didn't think it would help our relationship. I trudged downstairs, locked the front door behind me, and walked back to the car chewing through my options. The other end of my tube was Reb Yonah, but I just wasn't ready to jump in Simon's face.

I drove around the block, parked, and walked back to a small apartment building stoop near the corner of Deirdre's block. I

had a decent view of the house from behind a high hedge. I'd trade a Bakelite radio for more information and my gut told me Deirdre had some.

I couldn't stop my nod of satisfaction when I saw a jeaned and jacketed Father Collins step out of her building. He wasted no time leaving the porch and headed quickly, on foot, in the direction of the church. For an instant, I wondered whether I'd interrupted a forbidden affair. Unlikely. Deirdre hadn't looked or acted like someone in the middle of a religious experience.

I waited another forty-five minutes before I gave it up. I ground out my cigarette underfoot, then immediately sank back down as her door opened. Deirdre stepped out and took a cold, hard look up and down the block before she left the porch. I was well hidden but *still* breathed a sigh of relief when she chose the opposite direction. That look was nasty.

It was a good thing I stayed where I was. Deirdre disappeared around the corner, then doubled back and acted like she was waiting for someone, peering intently in all directions. I still-lifed until she took off again. I imposed patience, then delayed a little longer, before I stretched and crossed the street.

For the second time that day I let myself into her building. For the first time, her apartment. I stood and smelled for recent sex, but the apartment was as close-mouthed as its tenant. And her belongings just as sparse. The kitchen wasn't in the paper-plate-and-plastic-fork category, but close. It did have a well used Mr. Coffee machine.

I walked rapidly through the apartment to see if the other rooms matched the kitchen's minimalism. By the time I returned to the living room I was certain I'd b&e'd an underfurnished furnished apartment.

At least it was easy to keep my foraging neat. I had begun worrying about Deirdre's return, so I worked quickly. It wasn't difficult. Her personal belongings were as meager as the apartment furniture. And just as neutral. Her clothes were simple; one black skirt, one gray. A long down coat, some jeans, canvas

work pants, three white blouses. A few winter sweaters on a shelf in the closet, a pair of black flats and a pair of cross-trainers on the closet floor. This was not a woman who went sport shopping. Even for basics. Her dresser turned up a half dozen army/navy woolen socks, underwear, heavy leggings, and a few pairs of black sweatpants, sweatshirts, and tights. Nothing from Victoria's Secret. The top drawer held her jewelry, highlighted by subdued clip-on earrings.

A small sitting room off her bedroom doubled as a makeshift office. Though jumpy about getting caught, I carefully went through each drawer of the small student desk. Other than a few cheap pens, all I found was the same stationery I had discovered in rifling Kelly's apartment. Without any interesting notes. I also found a writing pad imprinted with a bright Color It Green. I didn't find a checkbook.

I returned to the living room and sat on the bench of her body building torture machine. Despite my buzz of frustration, I urged myself to search her john. Hell, I might find a couple aspirin for my burgeoning headache. I pushed myself into the bathroom but emerged without the pills. Without needing the pills. Simple, friendly, unassuming Deirdre kept a loaded .380 Backup and a Maxim Subsonic silencer taped to her toilet's interior.

CHAPTER 33

The gun didn't answer any questions. But seeing the careful tape job, looking at the beautifully crafted stainless steel, imagining it combined with the silencer, had instantly renewed my intensity for the hunt. Raw red meat in front of a hungry dog.

Headache all but gone, I recalled Deirdre's trip to the bathroom and change of clothes the first time I'd visited. Nickel to dime bags she'd come out holding; and I didn't mean dope. Her palm-sized weapon would barely wrinkle skintight pantyhose. But the gun was powerful enough to put a permanent wrinkle in anyone's mortality. We were talking modern firearms here.

I walked to the front windows, lifted a shade, and looked carefully in both directions. The street was empty so I returned to the exercise bench, sitting there scanning the apartment, looking for places I hadn't searched. In a moment of curiosity, I swung a leg over to the other side of the body builder and pulled on the weight handle. The first thing I noticed was the heavy poundage. The second was the loose grip under my left hand. I quickly worked the rubber off, stuck my finger inside, and felt it rub against a ball of paper. I went to the kitchen, returned with a knife, and slowly edged the ball free. I unwrapped the unusual paper and stared at two dull stones, each covered with a grayish film. I hoped they

were diamonds, but had trouble believing jewels could appear as lifeless as the pebbles in my hand. These stones looked like they belonged in a fishtank, not floating in Liz Taylor's cleavage.

Thoughtful, I replaced the rocks, then the rubber grip. After another rapid, fruitless run through the apartment, I left the building and trotted to my car. As I lit a cigarette I looked at my shining eyes in the mirror. Part of me wanted to rush the good padre and keep the pressure on, but I forced myself home. I wanted to give Deirdre time to discover that her rooms had been searched. I had left small items out of place but hopefully no clue that anything had been found. Though worried that my action reopened the possibility of another hit, I figured raising the stakes was the play. Anyway, Washington Clifford *had* vouched for my safety, hadn't he?

I paid close attention as I took a long, circuitous route. I couldn't shake the tingle on the back of my neck, but made it home and inside without mishap. Even had the courage to score a large Italian from the corner subshop. It would be supper time in a couple of hours and I wasn't going to cook. I preferred my cholesterol straight out of wax paper. I placed the sub in the refrigerator and grabbed a bottle of Negro Modelo. I had hours to kill before I paid a return visit to Deirdre, or went looking for Father Collins.

For the first time in a long, long while I enjoyed the late afternoon movie. Though Bogey's face was the color of pink putty, his search for the black bird reminded me of my situation. Sam Spade hadn't known or understood what he was involved with either. Still, *he* came out on top. Of course, Sammy busted someone he had fallen in love with, but hey, I didn't fall that easy. Lucky me.

I was sitting at the kitchen table eating Italian and drinking Mexican when the telephone rang. "You're a real fuck, you know that?" Cheryl snarled the moment I lifted the receiver. "You think I can ask my mamma to chauffeur me around town to look for a dead man? You might have been, for all I knew."

After a moment's guilt I scratched for something to say. But I just couldn't bring myself to tell her I'd been spooked by her middle-of-the-night transformation into Rebecca. "I'm sorry, kid, I blew it. I should have called. I'm okay."

"No, you are most certainly not okay, *Kid*," she mocked me.

"I'm not going to get anything right today, am I?"

"You're still alive, you fucker, I'll give you that," she replied, her tone softening. "Where the hell have you been?"

I told her about Reb Yonah's walk, my encounter with Blue and Clifford, the gun I found at Deirdre's apartment. I almost told her about the pebbles, but wanted to speak with Lou first. As I listened to myself rattle I wondered why I kept talking. It wasn't her reprimand; over time, I'd been battered with enough recounts of my inconsiderate behavior to no longer feel forced to explain or rebut. Truth was, I had no reason to tell her anything. I just wanted to. I wanted her to know I wasn't sitting around watching Bogart and drinking beer.

It would be an exaggeration to suggest she became entirely forgiving, but her tone lost its sarcasm. "Jesus. You're not talking about a Saturday night special, are you?"

"I've never heard of folks using a silencer for protection. You ever see an AMT Backup? Very slick, very small. Very sweet."

"I didn't know you were a card carrying member of the NRA, White Man."

I chuckled. "Professional interest, that's all."

"You say professional but you sound enthralled."

"Impressed. And gratified that my instincts cashed in."

"*Your* instincts? I had to blackmail you to stay on the damn case. So now you're convinced the lady is shady. Do you understand any of it?"

"I think you had it right. The padre and Deirdre use the Color It Green organization as a local front for the IRA. My nosing around the Avengers threatened them so they tried to scare me away."

"They weren't trying to kill you?"

"I don't think they cared one way or another."

"And Blue?"

"He gives them a protective layer if he does the shooting."

"What do you think threatened them?"

"I don't know."

"How does your friend Clifford figure?"

"I think he's moving in."

"What's taking him?"

"I don't know that either. Maybe he doesn't have enough evidence, maybe he wants bigger fish."

She took her time thinking about my explanations before she said, "What are you going to do now that you're out of work?"

I grimaced and lit a cigarette. "Who said anything about done?"

"Stick a fork in yourself. The Rabbi is free and Clifford's closing down the Provos. What's left for you?"

She sounded like Simon. "I'm surprised at you," I chided. "You're smarter than that. Hell, you asked the question."

"About the Avengers?"

"Yes."

"You think it's important?"

"There's a crossover that I just don't understand, Cheryl. Kelly was connected to the Color It Green through Deirdre. Kelly starts the Avengers and shoots the Big Rabbi. What the fuck is *that* about?"

"Matthew, Kelly's dead, you've put the Avengers out of business, the Rabbi's free. Even if you're right and a few things are still cloudy, what difference does it make?"

"This doesn't seem like you, Cheryl. What happened to the importance of giving the people the truth, the whole truth? Didn't I hear you once say something about pulling facts out of the dark?"

"Yes, I said it. But I'm not sure *these* facts are worth anyone else dying for. Hasn't there been enough blood?"

"Too damn much. That's why it's important to get to the bottom. To at least understand why Rabbi Dov died."

"All of a sudden you're hearing the angels sing? Or is it ego?"

"No angels, no mission." I was still confused by her attitude, only now my confusion wore a cuff of annoyance. "Sure there's ego. The case isn't finished and I'm a detective."

"You sound like a different detective than the one I first met."

"It just takes me a while to get started. What's bothering you? I apologized for not calling."

"You apologized, but I was the one picturing your body bleeding on the floor." She paused then said quietly, "This isn't simply a story for me anymore. I thought it stopped being a job when they broke my hands, but it hadn't. I was working when I had my mom drive me to your apartment the other night. But today, listening to hours of no answers on the phone gave me a few, anyhow. Matthew, the biggest regret I have about my broken hands is not being able to touch the lines in your face."

I pictured the casts on her hands and didn't know what to say. Or even feel. "I'm a little lost for words," I admitted.

"Just don't bring up the age difference, okay."

I hadn't, she had. But it gave me something to hold onto. "You just did." I rushed on before she could interrupt. "And it's not just the years, Cheryl. Back in another life I had a wife and daughter who died in a car accident. Rebecca would be a teenager if she were alive. You play some of those chords and it complicates things between us."

There was another long silence then, "You said your wife died too. Does that mean you can't have relationships because all women remind you of her?"

It wasn't a question and I knew it. But that didn't stop me from flashing on my arm's-length connection to Boots, and her similar imputations. "I don't know what it means."

"Anyway," she continued, "no one on this here planet will ever think of us as kin."

I smiled despite myself. There was something about this girl, woman, that snuck through my Russian winter.

Cheryl broke into my thoughts. "Are you being honest when you say you don't know what it means?"

"Yes."

"Are you willing to find out?"

"I don't know."

After a moment's hesitation she started to laugh. "You don't make it easy, you know that?"

"I can believe it."

"And of course you're going to stay on the case."

"Of course."

"But we're going to talk about all this when you're finished. You know that, don't you?"

"I guess."

"No guesses about it. And no more guessing whether you're dead or alive. Right?"

"Right."

"Take care of yourself, Matt. But you best keep in touch."

I always took care of myself. Only sometimes I did it better than others. Despite our having the kinds of conversations I usually abhorred and avoided, my feelings for Cheryl were warm and confused. Hopefully, a puzzle to solve without the standard coat of Teflon I usually wore to relationships.

But only after I solved the case. At least I hadn't told Cheryl I'd left a card at Deirdre's. But *I* knew it, and also knew I had to keep the heat up.

And *on*. Night had descended and the apartment was chilly. I roused myself from the kitchen table and tried Lou's number. The line was busy so I found a clean shirt and jeans and changed clothes. I tried his number again but it was just as busy. As I replaced the receiver the telephone rang and I imagined it was Lou.

"Lou, I've been trying to get you."

"This isn't Lou."

Yakov's voice caught me short. "Hello, boy. Back for another tour of a public institution? Or are you hankering for a little one-on-one?"

"Matt, please don't joke around. I have to see you."

I heard the tension in his voice but my first rush was impatience. I wanted to get on with my job. "It's Saturday night, Yakov. Can't it wait? I'm in the middle of something I'd like to finish."

"I can't wait any longer than I already have. It's been a terrible *Shabbos*."

I couldn't ignore the urgency in his voice. "Okay, Yakov, we can get together. How about the Yeshiva in a half hour?" If Simon heard, he heard. At least I'd have a reason for the visit.

"No, not the Yeshiva," Yakov said. "I want to come to your house."

"Well, how about outside? The park you told me about, the one with the courts."

"No. I won't meet anywhere but your house," he said stubbornly. "It's the only place I can be certain not to be seen."

"Can you tell me what this is about?"

"When I see you. I must get off the telephone now. Goodbye."

No one had reason to harm him on his way into the building, but I didn't want him in my apartment if someone came after me. I called Lou and asked if I could meet with Yakov in his place. Lou agreed but rushed me off the phone before I could ask him about the rocks. He was baking for Mrs. S. and had to tend to it. He told me to call when I finished using his apartment. He sounded pleased to have a reason to stay upstairs.

Me? I was not pleased about sitting around. And less so when I realized the kid was probably taking public transportation. I couldn't remember ever seeing a Hasid step out of a cab.

CHAPTER 34

I puffed on a joint to slow my growing irritation. As the grass soothed my jitters I thought about parenting in a way I had long forgotten. I thought about the unceasing demand to park my personal needs in the back of the bus. Rebecca's death had completely overshadowed memories of dirty diapers, wet beds, late night crying jags. Marriage with Chana had been a real attempt to share our lives, our child, our work. But sitting at the table battling my impatience reminded me that a lot of that sharing had simply meant a perpetual stream of housework.

Instead of throwing me, the revisionist thinking actually helped stem my annoyance. I considered a bourbon but went brew instead. The house was completely dark because I kept the lights off. Not for protection; the lights were off because it was comfortable to sit in the black, sip my cold beer, and think about the way my life had really been, not the way I usually painted it.

Yakov's insistent finger on the doorbell sliced through my head like a bloody Texas chain-saw. I hopped from the chair and nearly ran to the building's front door.

"You have a heavy hand, my boy," I said, leading him back downstairs.

"I walked around to the alley but didn't see any lights. I thought you left."

"I haven't budged since your call," I said reassuringly.

"Why were you sitting in the dark?"

He was reluctant to enter the unlit rooms so I pulled the lamp chain. "Come inside for a moment. I want to get my things. Aren't you cold just wearing that suit?"

"I don't think about the cold. Why can't we stay here?" he complained to my back. "I told you I didn't want to go anywhere else."

I didn't want to add to his tension with my concerns. "We're not going far. Just upstairs to my father-in-law's place. If I sit here any longer I'll go nuts."

Yakov looked thoughtful. "Your apartment is still not safe, is it? That's why the lights were off and why you're taking me upstairs?"

"That's not why the lights were off. It is why I'm taking you upstairs. I don't think there is any danger. But as long as I'm responsible for you I can't take chances."

"You are not responsible for me," he flared. "No one is but me, and *Hashem*."

"*Hashem?*"

"God." He spoke a very quick sentence in Hebrew or Yiddish then blurted out, "This is an incredible mistake. I should never have come here."

I stopped gathering my cigarettes and keys, turned, and took my first real look. His face was pale and exhausted, as if he hadn't slept. A slight tremble danced along his lower lip and he kept pulling at the strings that ran down his pant sides.

"Well, I don't know whether you made the right decision or not," I said gently. "But you're here and we might as well go upstairs while you decide."

Yakov nodded stiffly. I thought he was afraid to trust his voice. I resisted a temptation to place my hand on his shoulder as I passed by. I didn't know what clawed at him, but I did know

he'd resent any hint of condescension. Yakov deep-breathed to regain his composure as I led us up the hall steps. I made sure not to turn around until we were inside Lou's apartment.

"Do you have a preference? Kitchen? Living room?"

"Which room looks most like yours?"

"The kitchen." I smiled. "Does that mean we go to the living room?"

"No."

I walked toward Lou's kitchen, Yakov in tow. Despite the empty oven, the room was fragrant with the delicious smell of a bakery in overdrive.

"Somebody was cooking here?" Yakov asked once we were seated at the table.

"Lou was baking."

"My coming has sent him from his house?"

"Stop being paranoid. He's delivering the goods to a friend upstairs. You're not putting anybody out."

"Lou is your father-in-law?" he asked as if he had just understood what I'd said downstairs. "I didn't know you were married."

For the second time that night I spoke of my past. And for the second time, spoke of it without my usual quake, tremor, or defensive shell. I wasn't exactly eloquent, but my relative ease and his recognition of some parallel experiences proved settling. For both of us.

"I didn't know any of that about you."

"I don't talk about it very often." Or as well.

"I still don't know if I belong here," he said.

I looked at his shiny black suit, his quarter-inch crewcut, his earlocks. I looked at his faded open-necked white shirt, his black velvet *yarmulke*. "Belong, you don't," I said with a grin. "But that doesn't mean being here is a bad idea."

"I don't know," he answered shaking his head. A small smile played at the corners of his mouth.

"Neither do I. And won't, unless you tell me what's going on."

His trace of a smile disappeared. "I've been worrying about my father."

I waited, but he sat silent.

"Simon, the lawyer Roth," I teased, "called me today." I thought it was today; my days were still running together. "Except for the paperwork, everything is okay for your dad. He has absolutely nothing to worry about."

"Your friend is a good lawyer?"

"I told you, he's the best."

Yakov stood up and paced the kitchen, moving his lips silently all the while. If my news dented his anxiety, it sure didn't show.

"Yakov, your father has nothing to worry about. Do you hear me?"

He stopped his silent chanting but kept walking back and forth. "I hear you. My father no longer has *that* to worry about."

"What else is he worrying about?"

The boy stopped pacing and rocketed me with a withering look. "You have no conception of our Yeshiva's loss! No idea of the weight that has fallen on Reb Yonah's shoulders. We have become a community in disarray."

He surprised me by calling his father Reb Yonah. "Of course your Yeshiva is confused. No one anticipated Rabbi Dov's death. You have to give it time to settle. Your dad is a smart man. As soon as things get back to normal, he'll realize how much he needs you."

Yakov returned to the table but stood behind his chair. "I'm having a terrible time sleeping," he said.

I waved toward the chair. "I can tell. Why don't you sit down?" I lit a cigarette and waited while he decided. Good old Lou. A reformed smoker, he still left an ashtray on the table. "Are you having trouble fitting back in with the rest of the students?" I asked once he was sitting.

"No, no" — waving his skinny hand dismissively — "I'm not here for any of those reasons."

"Then why, Yakov? What's got you so upset?"

He rubbed his hand across his face and left it in front of his eyes. "Do you remember our discussion about the Never Agains?"

"Sure."

"Well, the Yeshiva is starting one."

"You mean your father is finished setting it up, don't you?" I asked softly, making certain there was no recrimination in my tone.

He kept his hand over his eyes and nodded.

"Why does this keep tearing at you, Yakov? Your father has wanted them around for a long while." I stopped, then added with a smile, "Even the last time we talked you didn't think the Never Agains were a totally lousy idea."

"It's not them exactly." He stood up again, grabbed the back of the chair to steady himself, then walked toward the kitchen door. For an astonished second I thought he planned to keep on going. But when he got to the door he leaned face first into the frame, and started to sob.

I walked up behind him and placed my hands lightly on his shoulders, half expecting him to shrug them away. He didn't. Instead, he leaned back against me.

"I think my father was involved in the Rebbe's murder," he cried out between sobs.

Though some of my mind catapulted into furious activity, I forced the rest to stay in the eye of the storm. I hugged Yakov closer, kept my arms around his chest, and rested my chin on his velvet *yarmulke*. We stood like this through his tears, through his long, tortured gasps of breath, through the shudders and shakes of his skinny body. We waited until he was steady enough to walk and I was able to talk through the cacophony in my head. We may have been there a long time.

I walked him, hand in mine, back to the table. My cigarette had long since extinguished itself so I lit another. It wasn't going to be my last.

"You're hitched to a heavy piece of luggage there."

He nodded.

"Been carrying it long?"

Another downcast nod and more silence.

"Does your suspicion have anything to do with your father's diamond business?"

He kept his eyes on the table. "No. I don't know, maybe." His head tilted south but he glanced at me from under hooded eyelids. "What do you know about his diamond business?"

"Only what you told me. I just don't know what else to ask." Truth was, I was torn about asking anything. I wanted to comfort him. To absorb the fear and dread from his scrawny body and add it to my own. I was older, bigger, and suddenly aware of extra room. I wanted to find guiltless words to explain "projection," grant permission for his anger, blow away his tears. I wanted to send him home relieved, a well-adjusted Hasid looking forward to the rest of his Hasidic life.

Trouble was, there might be something to what he said.

I told myself the kid would rather have the truth, wherever it led. Then I told the truth to myself. I was the one with the preference. I was the one who needed to know.

"Why don't you tell me why you're frightened." Maybe I'd get lucky and be wrong about my hunch.

"I almost said something to you about it in the library."

"It seemed like there was more on your mind."

"My father has known people from the Never Agains for many years," Yakov began. "He and the Rebbe argued about his association all the time until the Rebbe finally forbade it."

"Where did your dad know them from? They didn't have a group here."

"He met them in New York. Through his trading."

"How could Rabbi Dov forbid it? He didn't follow your father to New York."

"The Rebbe would know. Anyway, my father wouldn't lie."

I let the irony of his conviction pass. "He continued traveling to New York for business?"

"No. He stopped trading. He'd never done much to begin with. Every once in a while, that's all."

I waited as he gathered his thoughts. "Maybe a year ago some of the Never Agains visited the house. I was sent to the Yeshiva. Very soon afterward there were more arguments between my father and the Rebbe."

"You think they were arguing about the Never Agains?"

"I know they were. The White Avengers had begun to terrorize us and my father was beside himself. One time, the Rebbe told me about a particularly big fight. The Rebbe was still upset and I think he forgot who I was. My father wasn't supposed to meet with the Never Agains but during this past year he ignored the Rebbe's command."

"More visits to your house?"

"Not that I know of. Telephone conversations. But many."

"And you're certain the conversations were with Never Again people?"

He nodded.

I waited for him to continue but he sat silent, finished.

I felt disappointment for me and relief for him. His admission hadn't given me any new avenues to explore after all. Well, if he couldn't help me, I could still help him.

"Yakov, I know your relationship with your father is extremely difficult, especially now when you need him the most. I think your worry comes out of that difficulty. You're angry at him and your anger has you thinking the worst. He might have desperately wanted the Never Agains to be a part of the Yeshiva, might have started talking to their people again, but Sean Kelly murdered Rabbi Dov. Not a stranger, not someone from the Never Agains, not your father. No one knows why Kelly did what he did. But he did do it."

"I know it was that monster Kelly who shot the Rebbe," Yakov whispered hoarsely, his voice brittle with tension. "I know it was Kelly. This is why I'm so afraid. My father had dealings with that *schvantz*!"

CHAPTER 35

The information rearranged the playing field in my head like a cat's paw rearranges bees in a hive. I tried to catch a few of my thoughts but they darted out of reach like quicksilver. I settled instead for another cigarette and Herculean restraint. "*Schvantz?*"

"It's an insult too unfit to explain. I meant Kelly the murderer." Now that Yakov had finally spilled the heart of his anguish, he appeared slightly less ready to break.

"What do you mean by dealings?"

"I don't know what their business was, only that they knew each other."

"I'd understand better if you tell me everything you know."

"There were telephone calls between them."

"How do you know the calls were from Sean Kelly?"

"One night last summer I overheard my father speaking English on the telephone. You must try and understand, this was unusual. Especially since it was very late. My father often receives calls in the middle of the night asking about a section of the *Talmud* or the Laws. Yeshiva students study without regard to time. To be called on to explain a difficult portion is a sign of respect. My father would never refuse such a call, no matter how late."

There was a note of pride that disappeared once he continued. "Only Yeshiva calls were never in English."

"So you listened in?"

"Sort of. I didn't want to eavesdrop, I was just very surprised to hear him speaking English. I wanted to be sure."

"Did you hear what they talked about?"

"No."

"So why do you think it was Kelly?"

"That call was only the beginning. There were more telephone calls, more English. I didn't really listen in on the conversations, but I always knew when they occurred. My father would be disturbed afterward."

"I still don't see how you can assume it was Kelly?"

"During the late summer, after another of the English telephone calls, my father left the house. He returned about an hour later. I came downstairs pretending I'd just awakened. He was more upset than I'd ever seen him. When he saw me he tried to cover it up but couldn't. He told me to go back to sleep."

"He say anything else?"

"No. Just *gae schluffen* — Go to sleep. The next time he left the house after one of those conversations I followed him."

Yakov's anxiety was mounting, but I was too engrossed to settle him down. "You followed him?" I prodded.

"Yes. He didn't walk very far. You know the small park attached to the basketball courts? I followed him there and saw him meet with Kelly."

"You're sure it was Kelly?"

"At the time I didn't know who he was. I could only see that it wasn't one of us. A *goy*! I thought I recognized the face, but I didn't know from where. I never imagined he might be one of the Avengers who had been harassing the Yeshiva.

"I had no reason to." He lifted his thin shoulders helplessly. "It was not conceivable to me that my father would meet with someone like that. I only realized who it was when I saw him

again on *Simchas Torah*. I didn't even learn Kelly's name until after the shootings."

His face clouded over, so I steered away from the killings and back to the past. "Did you hear what they talked about in the park?"

"No, nothing."

"Did you see anything unusual?"

"Only that my father was meeting a Gentile in the middle of the night. I just stayed for a minute or two then went home."

"Why so short a time? Weren't you curious?"

"Curious?" He looked at me strangely. "I don't think so. I was worried." He turned his head away. "I felt very guilty so I returned home." His voice dropped into the atonal rhythm he used when talking God. "A child must be certain never to wake his father unless it is an extreme emergency. This is the manner of respect a Hasid learns to have for parents."

His flatness cracked and jumped an octave. "I trespassed when I listened to my father's conversations on the telephone! I trespassed when I followed him. My suspicions, especially telling them to you behind his back, is an enormous act of disrespect."

His hand trembled as guilt washed through his slumped, slight frame. I was split wide: one voice insisted I continue my questions. But that voice was being drowned out in the realization that this was the moment to use my newly discovered interior room. This was the moment to touch, absorb, step away. The moment to take his weight, his fatigue, his suffering.

But in that instant I also saw a little girl taking her first, halting steps. Though the steps were aimed toward me, they were really her first giant strides away. Right then, I knew *this* moment was the beginning of another goodbye.

"You're being much too hard on yourself, Yakov. You are incredibly concerned about your father. There is no sin in that. You listened and followed out of love, out of respect. You wanted to help him. Your religion can't condemn that."

Yakov's shaking slowed but his voice lashed back, at himself,

at me. "And here? Now? Telling you all this? This is not respect, this is weakness. I could no longer keep thoughts to myself. What I'm doing is *betrayal*."

I gave him a moment to catch his breath. "Yakov, stop trashing yourself long enough to listen up." I paused to make sure my words could sink in. "You came here to talk because I am someone who, in a very small way, filled the gap left by Reb Dov's death. The same gap Reb Dov had been filling since your mother died. For whatever reason, your father couldn't or didn't."

I met and held his eyes. "Truth is, your father hasn't done much good by you and that's a tough nut to swallow. You have a lot of anger toward your dad about it. Anger you turn on yourself.

"Boy, you're sitting here because you want to help your father. And you want me to help him as well. You're afraid that you're here out of rage but, fact is, you're here out of love. You imagine the worst, but want the best. You came to me because I'm someone you trust and because you want me to find out what those calls and meetings were about. At least you think you do." There was a whole lot more gray, but gray was for middle-age, not adolescence.

Seeing a different row of ducks gave him back some bone. "Why do you say I think I do?"

"Because I don't know if it's always a good idea to search for irrelevant information." I looked him directly in the eye and lied, "I am absolutely certain that your father was in no way involved with Rabbi Dov's death. I don't know what he was doing in the park or on the telephone with Kelly, but if I had to guess I'd say it had something to do with his diamond trading."

A surprised, hopeful look crossed his face. "Why do you think that?"

"Because both of us flat out know your father could never hurt his Rebbe. And diamonds are something people like the Avengers are interested in."

"Those are your only reasons?" He sounded disappointed.

In for an ounce, in for a pound. "No. When I searched Kelly's apartment I found diamonds."

"You think he was blackmailing my father?" He seemed almost happy about the idea.

Why shouldn't he be happy? That had been the intent of my lies. "I don't know. But what difference does it make? Kelly's dead. You haven't seen your old man sneaking out in the middle of the night recently, have you?"

I heard my harshness, but Yakov was oblivious to it. "No. Except for the Never Agains, everything is the same as it used to be."

"See?" I bit back the beginnings of a mad. "If you can deal with the fact that you're really very angry at your old man, you won't be plagued by these fantasies."

"You're saying that I thought my father was involved with the Rebbe's death because I'm angry at him?"

"That's exactly what I'm saying."

"So you're telling me not to worry about him knowing Kelly?"

"Whatever went on between them was their business. Maybe some day he'll tell you." I had a flash of Reb Yonah standing behind his table, his stern face frozen in a sneer. Sure he'd tell him. "I'd just leave it alone if I were you, Yakov. You'd do better to work on the relationship."

"I don't know what you mean by that."

I forced myself to smile. "Go home, get some sleep. When you wake up, help pull the Yeshiva back together. Do your learning and be a loving son. That's what I mean."

Yakov stared at me. He looked relieved but depleted. I lit a cigarette and got up. "It's late, kid, I'll drive you back."

Yakov jumped to his feet. "No, no, you've already done enough."

I smiled again and motioned him to follow.

If you didn't count Yakov's increasing cheerfulness and my corresponding withdrawal, the ride to Reb Yonah's house was un-

eventful. Despite my forebodings of loss, I had few regrets. This way, only one of us was counting. We said goodbye about a block from his house. His, an enthusiastic promise of another one-on-one. Mine, the imminent certainty that there were no more games to be played.

Well, I'd shouldered his load, all right. What a guy.

When I arrived back at my apartment, there was a note from Lou inviting me upstairs. I crumpled the paper and threw it into the garbage; I wasn't going anywhere. I sat at the kitchen table, poured a couple of fingers' worth of 'Turkey and sipped.

The night trickled away while I thought about Yakov's spill. All the ambiguities I'd neatly sidestepped in my earlier explanations rushed back to their rightful places leaving me worried and confused. Worse, my suspicions and dislike of Reb Yonah clashed with my decision to send Yakov home.

I was still sitting, still sipping, when the first streaks of morning brightened the sky over the yellow crime lights. By the time I noticed the change I no longer thought Yonah's involvement possible. I thought it likely. I also figured it likely that the Never Agains had been manipulating the Rabbi.

What I couldn't figure was the other side of the pond. Kelly was the bridge, but the bridge to what? And why? What the hell did the IRA, Father Collins, and Deirdre have to gain by joining forces with the Never Agains in an internecine struggle within a local Hasidic community?

I also thought about my conversation with Julius, finally understanding his warning about organizational agendas. Despite our discussion I had continued to view the case in personal and personality terms. No surprise; it was the way I saw my life, my work. I'd even reduced the IRA to the specific pugs who had run me off the road.

But the spilled blood here wasn't the drippings of dysfunctional families, personality disorders, psychosis. This blood was the result of ideology in action. The goosesteps of religious, political, and social visions. The fucking IRA. The Never Agains.

The Church, the Avengers, the Yeshiva. These were the forces at play, pressing their goals and desires onto a small, isolated city patch. To understand what had been happening during the last few weeks meant comprehending that Collins, Deirdre, Yonah, even the bastards who tried to kill me were nothing more than tools. Now that I'd sent Yakov home, the only personal left was me. And maybe Blue. Not a pleasant comparison.

Throughout the course of the night, I occasionally tried to convince myself to drop the case. Belay my questions, silence my conjectures, stop my investigation. Even if Yonah had somehow been involved with Dov's death, nobody else was going to pursue it. Hell, I didn't *want* anyone else to pursue it. Legitimately reopening the case inevitably meant turning Yakov against his father, against himself.

If I let it slide now, there would be nothing more. The kid might have a shot at a life, Yonah his beloved organization, Deirdre and the priest their IRA gunfest. The books would close and life would go on.

But I *had* absorbed Yakov's suspicions, his worry, even his sleeplessness. And more. Added to my list of unanswered questions, my feelings of confusion and loss, was the outside possibility that I'd sent Yakov home to someone involved with murder.

By morning I knew there was no possibility of ending my hunt. Though I might be forced to cast a drooped eyelid on what I discovered, I had to know what I was winking at.

CHAPTER 36

My eyes had to open to wink at anything and that didn't happen until early Monday morning. And they weren't open long before I decided it was time to hammer the Holy Man. Rabbi or no, I had to grab his nuts and twist until he told the truth. The connective tissue among the Never Agains, the Avengers, and Color It Green was still missing, still out of sight. The Rabbi was my best chance at that tissue, the weakest link in a chain I now knew existed. But there was little hope of getting to him; none if I tried by myself.

Sadie took one look at me coming through the door and pointed silently to the rear office. Simon lifted his head from the mess on his desk. "Oh Christ," he groaned. "This ain't gonna be good."

"It's rotten. Lousy. The whole case stinks."

"Sit down, Matt. You look like you just rolled out of bed. You still carrying on about Reb Yonah?"

"Damn right. The fucker was up to his ears in the Big Guy's murder."

"Slow down! What the hell do you mean? Did Julius give you bad drugs?" Despite his sarcasm, Simon leaned forward.

"It's a trip, all right, but there's no dope." I laid it out. Every bit of it. Deirdre, Collins, the hit, Clifford and Blue, Yakov. I

went over each detail, angle, theory, intuition. At the beginning of my story he had Sadie hold his calls. In the middle, he had her break his appointments. I took both as encouraging signs.

When I finally finished he sat beating on his head. "What a fucking story," Simon said. "All this shit happening and I don't know the first thing about it. Why didn't you tell me any of this before?"

"Tell you what? You wouldn't have believed the different pieces were connected. You're having trouble believing me now."

He waved his hand. "No, no, you're wrong. It's your conclusions I have trouble with. The ice rink has you distorting things, blowing them up."

"Blowing them up? Is that a joke? How much bigger than the IRA do you want?"

"That's exactly what I mean. Who says they were IRA? A freelance writer and a literate dope dealer. The goons were probably more Avengers."

"Blue says no. He said he didn't know them, that one spoke with a brogue."

"Blue says. Cheryl says. What about Lou? What does he say?"

"And the kid? What do you think about him?"

"I think he's telling the truth. In fact, I happen to think the explanation is damn close to the one you gave him. Hell, Matt, you can theorize forever. Maybe Washington Clifford is just interested in the Avengers. Maybe Reb Dov's death was accidental. Maybe Kelly's bullet was really meant for Yonah. The point is — there are a lot of maybes."

"The diamonds in Deirdre's apartment?"

"You don't even know for a fact they were diamonds." He thought a moment. "Okay, let's say they were diamonds. She was fucking Kelly, right? Maybe he gave her a gift. See what I mean about maybes?"

I lit a cigarette, and grabbed a tighter grip on my frustration. *Maybe* Simon was right and this wasn't Spy vs. Spy. *Maybe* the attempted hit had left me susceptible to Cheryl and Julie's

flights of fantasy. But there was no *maybe* about Father Collins's artificial friendliness, the professional way I'd been run off the road, the small sleek pistol in Deirdre's apartment.

"I only have to be right once to make my paranoia worthwhile."

"I didn't call you paranoid," Simon quickly interjected. "I don't know how I would react if a couple of thugs ran me off the road and took shots at me. I'm just saying that something like that tends to skew your thinking."

"Okay, Simon, say I'm skewed about the IRA. You don't think I'm skewed about Reb Yonah, do you?"

He hesitated a long time before he responded. "Truthfully, no. I think you're onto something. Rabbi or not, I don't like or trust him." Simon leaned back in his chair and put his feet on the desk. "But it's a long spit to tie him into a conspiracy with the White Avengers or the IRA. Personally, I like your idea about blackmail. The Avengers get something ugly on Reb Yonah and hit him up. He pays off with diamonds."

"With Rabbi Dov dead, the Never Agains waltz through open doors."

"Shit happens," Simon agreed.

"That's not what I mean."

He swung his feet down and rolled his leather chair out from behind the desk. "I know exactly what you mean and I think it's crazy. Reb Yonah might be a Never Again groupie, but a Hasid doesn't kill a Rebbe. They don't pay to have it done either. I have to call you on this one. Hell, you've always been phobic about religion and right now you're grabbing a face to hang it on."

"I don't feel good sending the boy back home without knowing the truth."

"Matt, get real. You don't feel good about sending the boy home, period."

Everything he said seemed sensible. I'd fallen off enough bar stools to know that truth rarely comes wrapped in a tightly rib-

boned package, all questions asked, all answered. But I *had* seen the gun, believed Blue, and worried about sending Yakov home. I might not find all the answers, might end up agreeing that IRA footsteps were a product of overheated fear. But I couldn't quit until I resolved my concern for Yakov; I still clung to a world of real people.

"Let's find out."

"Find out what?" he asked with exasperation.

"Let's find out about our Reb Yonah. Let's see if he knows something that clears things up. At least we can learn whether I sent the kid back to a safe situation."

Simon shook his head skeptically. "This isn't a detective talking, Matt. You're back to social work."

"So what? I don't believe you'd feel real comfortable hearing something happened to the boy. I'm not talking about his father hurting him, I'm worried about the Never Agains. If they believe he knows something damaging . . ."

"No one from the Never Agains is going to harm Reb Yonah's kid."

"I'm not arguing the odds, just the possibility. Let's make sure. Simon, I'm not going to rest easy until I know what really happened between Kelly and Yonah."

"And how are we supposed to find all this out?"

"We'll ask him. I have enough information to lean pretty hard."

Simon looked amused and interested. "And if he doesn't talk?"

"Then we're in no worse shape than we are now."

He placed his hands on either side of his head. "You aren't paranoid, you're completely crazy. You want us to toast a Hasidic Rabbi and hope he has something to hide. If he does, we learn what and he keeps quiet. But if he doesn't break or has nothing to hide, you say we're no worse off."

Simon groaned again. "*You're* no worse off. It's *my* ass that gets hung from a tree. The second we leave, Reb Yonah screams

persecution, and every Jewish organization lands on me like I was a fucking airport. My name will be Judas."

"I know where you can get new business cards."

"I like my cards. I like having a business. All Reb Yonah has to do is say you're crazy. He'd be right."

I shrugged. "If you don't help you're fucked anyway. I'll go to the cops and they'll work on him. Believe me, Reb Yonah will know who sent them. If it's us and not the police, you can always say we were clearing up loose ends and Yonah misinterpreted. But if Downtown asks the questions, you'll be dealing with more than miscommunication. I don't think the organizations that are squeezing your chops will distinguish between you and your trusted employee."

Simon's face broke into a sardonic smile. "I knew it was coming. You always hold an ace, don't you?"

"This is the only one I have. From here on in it's a bluff."

"Blind man's bluff, you prick."

"So you'll help?"

"What choice do I have?"

"Don't bullshit me, Simon. You don't cave this easy unless you want to."

Simon rolled his chair slowly back behind his desk. "I already told you I despise the Never Agains and I don't like Reb Yonah. I'll take some heat for holding their feet to the fire, but I think you are going to come up short and foolish."

"I'll break him."

Simon ran his hand through his hair. "I don't know what you'll do, but even if he gives you what you think you want, you'll end up frustrated and dissatisfied. That's my Matt." He pushed his hair away from his eyes but this time smiled mischievously. "Now what is it you want me to do?"

After I told him, his smile turned sour. "You don't want the kid there?" he asked incredulously. "Why not? He's your crowbar."

"I wouldn't be doing this if I wasn't worried about him. I'm not trying to ruin his fucking life."

"Maybe you care about the boy but this 'ruin his life' routine is rationalized bullshit. A minute ago you were threatening to send the troops. How would that have helped the kid? Call it the way it really is: you don't quit until you're good and ready. You were the same way with your first goddamn marriage and the same way about everything that happened between us."

"I wasn't going to call the cops; I knew you were going to help."

"Damn right you knew. And, I'm sure you have some real feelings about the boy. But don't lie to yourself about *you*." He lifted the phone but kept his hand on a button. "You're absolutely certain you don't want Yakov there? It's the best chance of getting Reb Yonah to talk."

"I'm sure."

It took about a half hour of telephone calls, call backs, and heated discussions before a meeting time was finally arranged. We would gather at Reb Yonah's house after nightly prayers, a time when the Yeshiva students ate dinner. Simon didn't mention me throughout any of the conversations. Given the heated exchanges, it seemed like a wise omission. Once I arrived Yonah would find it impossible to slam the door in my face.

After Simon finished the setup he sent me home. He was angry, already regretting his participation. We were better off by ourselves. I agreed to meet him in front of the Rabbi's house a couple of minutes before the meeting.

It wasn't a triumphant ride back to my apartment, but it had its moments. Though I was still flying blind, there was a smell of finish in the air. I had to be careful not to allow that smell to slow me down or drag me back to the couch.

As soon as I got home I went upstairs. Lou glanced up from the kitchen table when I entered his apartment. "You look better than the last time I saw you, Matty, but not by much. You could use three more days of solid sleep."

"That bad, huh? Well, do you have any caffeine?"

"The water is hot for tea." He bustled about adding a piece of his pie to the offer. I sat quietly, trying to maintain the satisfaction I'd felt while driving home. But the heady hint of finish kept slipping away, obscured by pangs of doubt. I told myself that doing right by me meant doing right for Yakov, only the mantra didn't work: I felt like shit, and it showed.

"What's the matter, *boychik*?" Lou asked once he was seated. "This is more than tired."

I tried a smile but quit halfway through. Instead, I hurriedly recounted Yakov's visit.

Lou's face sobered but he waited for me to continue.

"The boy was sick about it. Really trapped. He didn't know what to do, keep it a secret, tell, or what."

"He trusted enough to come to you?"

"Sort of. It was like he was committing patricide. I tried to calm his fears and make it possible for him to return home."

"Do you actually think Reb Yonah had a hand in the Rebbe's death? Or in what happened to you the other night?"

"I don't know, Lou. He had something working. At the very least he's a pulling guard for Never Agains. I keep wondering if I did the right thing by sending Yakov back."

Lou grunted, refilled our cups with more hot water, dipped the used teabags, and returned with the cups to the table. I didn't say anything about the three squares of sugar he dropped into his tea.

"But you don't really believe Reb Yonah was involved in the shooting, do you?"

"You keep asking me that," I said. "He knew Kelly, he shot Kelly. Makes you wonder, doesn't it?"

Lou looked at me and carefully chose his words. "Are you going to tell me about the other night? The blood, the dirt?"

"Sometime. Not right now."

Lou let it pass then trapped me with a right hook. "This

friendship you have with the boy puts you in a difficult position, doesn't it?"

"Seems to. I thought I was finished mixing him up with Becky, but now I'm not even sure of that."

Lou smiled. "It's never possible to be certain about something like that, *boychik*."

I rubbed my face. "I'm finding out. So I run over to Simon and convince him we have to grill the Rabbi. He sets up a meet for tonight. Driving home I'm cheering. Now I'm thinking, what the fuck did I get myself into? If I break the Rabbi down and find out he's been up to something, what'll I have? If I do something I hurt the kid. If I don't, I'm left with an unhappy me. The situation isn't only difficult, Lou. The situation sucks."

Lou shook his head. "What's the difference, Matty?" he said sharply. "You're not going to stop. You won't let it rest until you're satisfied. It doesn't matter who will be unhappy or who won't be."

Lou's echo of Simon's earlier accusation stung. "Including the kid?"

"Including the kid. Will he be there?"

"No. At least I made sure of that."

"But Reb Yonah could go to jail?"

"I'll tell you something, Lou. I doubt I'd go to the police even if he was guilty."

"Because . . . ?"

"Because I don't think I could take the kid's father away from him and live with myself. Believe it or not, I have some limits."

"I don't think you want to hurt the boy, Matty." Lou sat thinking then said, "Anyway, why should you know now what you will do later? Find out what's going on, then make your decisions."

"A little fast and loose, no?"

"Everything in life is fast and loose, *boychik*. We just pretend it isn't."

"I could use a little help."

His eyes lit up. "What kind of help?"

"First, you can tell me something. I found a couple of gray, I don't know, stones I guess, wrapped in a lined origami-like envelope. They looked like dirty lumps of frosted ice. It would make case sense if they were diamonds, but they looked like dull pebbles."

"I can't tell you for certain unless I looked at them, but they could be roughs. Before the gem cutters clean and shape. It's possible you saw industrial diamonds, but those usually aren't wrapped in diamond paper."

"Good. Could you call your friend in New York and see if he knows anything about Reb Yonah's dealings?"

Lou shook his head dubiously. "I'll call, but don't expect much useful information. People in that business keep their hands very close to the vest and their mouths sealed."

I chugged the rest of my tea and stood. "You don't mind trying?"

"Of course not. It will give me pleasure."

"Thanks, Lou. I'll be downstairs. Give me a ring if you dig something up?"

He didn't bother to say goodbye. He just nodded while he hoisted himself from the kitchen chair and headed toward the telephone.

CHAPTER 37

I should have stayed upstairs with my father-in-law. As soon as I walked back into my apartment, the couch sang its siren's song, seducing me horizontal. I resisted as long as I could by smoking in the kitchen but finally succumbed. Though the song whispered sleep, horizontal had me rolling around with fresh waves of doubt. I smoked a little dope and tried television, but things were heading south. I had time to kill but if I spent it like this, the time was gonna kill me first.

Thankfully, a couple of television reruns, nicotine, and a little more marijuana later, Lou's telephone call dragged me vertical.

"Matty, I spoke to my friend." His excitement eliminated any pause between words. "He took a while to track down but I finally caught him. I spent a lot of time shmoozing about the old days, but whenever I brought up Reb Yonah he became very guarded. He told me everyone was still talking about Reb Dov's murder and Reb Yonah's reaction. But as hard as I tried, my friend was very reluctant to discuss Reb Yonah's diamond dealing."

"Did he say anything specific? Anything at all?" I heard the

bite in my voice and instantly regretted it. "I'm sorry, Lou. It's already been a long day and it's only late afternoon."

"Don't apologize, Matty, you have plenty on your mind. My friend doesn't like the diamond people Yonah deals with. I'm sorry but that was the most I could get."

"That's enough," I lied. "Every little bit of information will help when I put on the screws."

"*Boychik*, stop goosing me. You were hoping for more details."

"Yeah. But I've been hoping for that ever since I got this damn case. You'd think I'd stop hoping already."

"Why? It doesn't cost you."

"Says who? Damn, I wish I knew for certain I'd seen diamonds."

"Oh, *boychik*, I nearly forgot. God, how I hate that! Promise me something, Matty. If I get too old to remember which hand I use to wipe my tush, you'll shoot me."

"I'll shoot you today if you don't tell me what he said."

Lou chuckled, delighting in his usefulness. "My *lanzmann* said that lately Reb Yonah traded in New York but brought the stones home to get cut locally. He said it was unusual for people to front for something like that."

"What was he trying to say?"

"I'm not sure. That's when he clammed up. I'd guess the roughs you saw were on consignment."

"It makes sense. Listen, Lou, this helps, no bull."

"Matty, you still have a couple of hours until your meeting, don't you?" His excitement was gone.

"Yeah. Do you need something?"

"No, I'm fine. But I can tell you need to get out. Come up here if you'd like. You'll only make yourself miserable if you lay around your apartment."

"Thanks, Lou. Maybe I'll take you up on your offer."

But I didn't. As much as I felt supported by Lou's concern, the day already had too many ghosts. I didn't want more stories

about the old days. Instead, I debated visiting Deirdre and Collins. I had hoped that leaving little signs in Deirdre's apartment would apply pressure; now I thought it a dumb do. A tip to simply remove the gun and gems. Sometimes I paid extra for buying my license.

It made sense to crack the Rabbi before confronting Deirdre or the priest since I had no leverage to stop a simple stonewall. Problem was, I was impatient to push their side of the street. I called the question by getting to my feet and strapping on my holster. There was no reason not to do a little leaning. Call it a short prelude to a real meal. Anyway, Lou was right; if I stayed home I'd make myself miserable.

On my way to their neighborhood I realized fall's brisk chill had aged into winter's uncomfortable cold. The past week's blurring of days and nights, its difficult emotional roller-coaster had robbed me of my habituated certainties. No matter how many years slipped by, the oranges, yellows, and rust red leaves always held promise of change. Then, each winter, I would reluctantly discover there was nothing to the promise. This year I hadn't even noticed the colors.

Overcast and gray, the early evening darkness added a gloomy and desolate pall to the world outside my car's tinted windows. Everything looked old and shabby and swiped at my energy. The grime reminded me of the first or second day on the case. The day I went looking for the White Avengers at Buzz's.

I drove past Deirdre's house hoping for lights, saw none, and kept on driving. No way I was going to porch it in the wind and cold. I considered letting myself into her apartment, but instead drove to the church and parked up the block. I fished a cigarette from my pack and smoked. With half an eye I watched a couple of cars speed by, one parking behind a van close to the church. I didn't pay much attention. I was too busy regretting that I'd finished all the coke.

But finished it I had. Every little granule. I walked toward the church and planned my approach to Father Collins. Lost in

thought, I didn't even recognize the car I'd seen park until its passenger door slammed into my passing body.

I doubled over with a grunt of surprised pain. Before I could resist, a hand groped my unzipped jacket and dragged me back toward the open door. I started to squirm away, but as soon as I saw who was attached to the hand, I stopped flailing. When he saw my nod of recognition, he let go, slid behind the wheel, and pointed to the seat. I reluctantly forced myself inside and closed the door.

He didn't give me time to buckle up. I grabbed the roof grip as he shot down the street a block or two before screeching to a stop, the car's right front wheel scraping against the curb.

"How you manage to stay alive is beyond me," Washington Clifford said without hiding his disgust.

"I'm not the one driving," I answered as soon as I caught my breath. "Anyway, I told you we have to stop meeting like this."

"What's your ass doing here?" he demanded.

"Sitting on your car seat. It's a sucker for a free ride."

Clifford reached under his seat and pulled up something that looked like a telephone operator's headset. He slipped it over his head and fiddled with a switch at his ear.

"When did you start moonlighting with Ma Bell?"

"Shut up, Jacobs." Clifford turned his body away and mumbled into the attached microphone. When he turned back he slid one of the electronic muffs sideways off his ear. His mean smile looked pasted onto his broad face. "Let's start again, Jacobs. What are you doing here?"

"I was thinking of volunteering for the Color It Green program."

"Damn your mouth." Clifford turned his head and looked out his side window. "How much do you know?"

"About what?"

"About Collins." Clifford kept staring into the night.

I didn't see the percentage in lying. Or in getting hit. I didn't want to show up at the Rabbi's house covered with blood.

"Nothing certain, but I think he's running a front for the IRA. Somehow they got mixed up with the Avengers and the Rabbi murder. When I began poking around they tried to take me out. But you already know that, don't you? Anyhow, I think the goons who came after me are connected to the priest. I don't know how the woman fits."

Clifford turned his head back in my direction. "Just like a dumb private dick. You make some of the players, but get the wrong team. Why don't you ever listen? I told you twice to stay out of my face."

"Yeah, but you never told me why, Wash. I'm not good at taking orders if I don't know the reason."

A squawk escaped the headset and Clifford pulled the earphone back down. "Good," he said into the mike, making no effort to whisper. He glanced at his watch. "I'll tell you when to move."

Clifford pulled the set off his head. "You're lucky I talk to you at all, shamus. Did you manage to notice a van on your way to the church?"

"Yours?"

"We have the church lit up. The last of your fan club just entered. All of them are going down."

It took one glance at his glittering eyes to know that any hope I had of questioning Brady Collins and Deirdre was gone. No matter what I learned from Reb Yonah, Clifford wasn't going to risk his operation. The best I could do was weasel information without accruing more damage to my body.

"You tell me I have everything twisted, but you're here with a high-tech posse. Gee, I wonder if it's the IRA?"

"Interesting, isn't it? Someone thinks Irish, they always think IRA," he said, almost admiringly. "That was the beauty of it."

"The beauty of what?" I couldn't keep the frustration out of my voice.

Clifford stared at me for a long time before answering. "You don't know it, Jacobs, but you did me a favor. You've been run-

ning interference ever since you began flouncing around this neighborhood. Half the time you don't know that your skirt's up around your ass, but you always attract a fuckload of attention.

"We've been watching the Color It Green organization for a long time. But until you played hide and seek in the bushes, we couldn't make their Irish connections. We knew Color It Green received money from neighborhood donations, and we knew it collected skim from Kelly's armed car jobs. Only we never saw a nickel in any IRA pipeline. The only thing we could snare was their donations to legitimate Ulster charities."

"You said they used to collect skim. Do you mean before Kelly died?"

"Yes. The people Kelly ran with couldn't tie their shoes if he didn't show them how. They remind me of you."

"Yeah, well, pipeline and Ulster reminds me of the IRA. Couldn't they have a gate you don't know about?"

Clifford nodded. "That's what we've been searching for. Now we know better."

"And exactly what is it you know?"

Clifford's face crinkled. "Jacobs, there are two sides to the Irish war. Tell you the truth, until we made the faces we never thought about the other side."

"What the hell are you talking about, Clifford? The other side of that war is Protestant, not Catholic."

"If you're going to stick your mouth where it don't belong, shamus, do your homework. There are Catholics who don't want to separate from England. Catholics who despise the idea of a United Ireland and hate the IRA. Our Father Collins belongs to *them*."

Clifford saw the confusion and surprise on my face because he smiled and added, "Pretty fucking cute, isn't it? I'm betting everyone who donated a dime to Color It Green thought it was going to the charities or the IRA. Including Kelly." He looked at his watch and held the mike from the headset up to his mouth.

"Okay boys, it's yours. Tell me when you have them in the schoolbus."

I knew he'd just given the signal to take everyone down. I had a momentary image of his squad jumping from the van, vanishing into the shadows. But my mind couldn't let go of what he was saying. "You're telling me the priest is a plant?"

"I'm telling you he works for people who are in a bloody war with the IRA. I don't know what Collins is. His background checks out. Either he is a believer or someone has him by the short hairs."

"Jesus." My head was running in circles. "I never heard of *any* Catholics who support the Orange."

"You see why we didn't figure it? We've known about the skim since dirt, but couldn't get it past the church." For a moment Clifford dropped his patronizing. "This one had both sides of the ocean scratching their heads."

"You want to tell me how I helped clear up your confusion?" I was stalling, trying to let his information catch up. Despite Clifford's revelations, the questions driving *me* remained unanswered. Collins's allegiance didn't explain the connection to the Never Agains. Unless, of course, I really did have it twisted and there wasn't one.

"Sure, Jacobs. You were your stubborn fucking self. I was on you as soon as you started working the neighborhood. When they tried to take you out we got a good look. You helped drive a couple of foreign pros out from under their rocks. Gotta hand it to you, Jacobs, you got away from them real good. Almost looked like you knew what you were doing."

Anger began to shatter my amazement. "You motherfucker, you could have stopped them. You didn't give a shit whether they killed me or not as long as you got your look!"

Clifford raised his eyebrows. "I gave you fair warning to stay away, Jacobs. Anyhow, you didn't need any help."

I almost got lost in my mad but something he'd said nibbled

at my attention. "So you made the assholes who came at me as part of this anti-IRA group?"

The nibble would have disappeared if he had lied, but he didn't lie. He equivocated. "Something like that."

More of my incredulousness about Collins moved into the background as I quickly patched things together. "What was special about tonight?"

"We finally have the priest and all the muscle together."

"Who is here?"

"I told you. The priest and the beef."

"What about the girl?"

His face was blank, his voice neutral. "What girl?"

I told him about my encounters with Deirdre, her relationship with Kelly and the priest, what I'd seen inside her apartment. When I finished Clifford didn't seem either impressed or concerned. "I see what you're trying to do," he said. "Don't bother. There's no connection between this operation and the Jew kill."

"The 'Jew kill' is what got me involved, Washington. My 'Jew kill' investigation got your pros after me."

"You don't know that."

I reached into my pocket and pulled out my cigarettes. Clifford made a face but it didn't stop me from lighting up. I opened his ashtray and puffed for a few seconds before I said, "You know what I think, Washington? I think you're leaving something out. I think the redhead works for you."

CHAPTER 38

Clifford heard something in his earpiece he liked because he pumped his fist and spoke into the mike. "Any noise? Nice. Wait in the truck until I get back." He rotated his fire-hydrant body in the car seat until he faced me. "No," he said across his slab of thigh. "I told you that you have everything screwed up. Your girlfriend doesn't work for me."

"Bullshit. I'm playing Diane Keaton to your Al Pacino."

"What are you talking about, Jacobs?"

"*The Godfather*, Clifford. You're lying to me about Deirdre Ryan. You still haven't told me how you finally identified the pros. So how did you learn *what* side Collins is on?"

"Once we saw who we had, everything came into focus."

"You sound worse than a politician, Wash. You found out about the priest through Deirdre Ryan."

He grimaced. "Use your fucking head for something other than running your mouth, will you? Do you think I'd have been holding my iron if I'd had someone inside? You think I would have needed you to pigeon? I'd have been all over them like a fly on shit if she was working for me."

His answer brought me up short. Not just the content. It floored me he answered at all. Clifford was never generous with information. "Look, Washington, things don't fit together. I in-

vestigate Kelly and the Avengers, then Collins sends the troops. You're trying to tell me that the one person connected to both Collins and Kelly isn't involved? It doesn't add up."

"You need all the numbers to get things to add up, shamus." He shifted his body and stared pointedly over the steering wheel.

"What are you trying to tell me?" I asked quietly.

He kept his eyes straight ahead while he snarled, "I'm not trying to tell you a damn thing. You're trying to tell me something, but as usual it's half-assed."

He shook his head. "You don't have nothing except a wild imagination and a fast mouth. I'm telling you the girl isn't mine or one of the priest's."

"Clifford, you ever hear of the Never Agains? They're a vigilante organization made up of Hasidic Jews."

"I know what they are," he growled. "A bunch of strange old men trying to apologize for rolling over some fifty years ago."

"Maybe, but with the Rabbi's death, they're now rolling through the door."

"Remind me to pack a gun the next time I visit the Yids."

His attitude bothered me. Not the Jew-baiting. I knew he was just trying to piss me off. But Clifford was a shark about his turf. Any vigilante group would provoke more of a response. I considered telling him about my conversation with Yakov, but wasn't willing to chance my body. He was busy dismissing and one of his dismissals might slap me across the face.

Still, I couldn't help feeling he was signaling something. "I keep thinking if I stay here long enough I'll understand what you're trying to tell me."

Clifford looked at me. "We're done with show and tell, Jacobs. My mamma didn't grunt and groan for twelve hours to put me on this world to feed *you*. She don't know about you and I don't want to know about your Rabbis."

He reached across my body and I instinctively shriveled in my seat. "Relax, shamus, I'm not planning to change your looks. I

can't tell you what to do, only that it won't change nothing. Deirdre Ryan is not involved with Collins's organization and we're not going to touch her."

He finished leaning and opened the car door. I climbed out and gently closed it. I didn't want to accidentally catch his fingers and bring him back to reality. Since when couldn't Clifford tell me what to do?

I made it back to the church just as the van was pulling away. Though the two back-door windows were blacked out, I imagined Brady's face pressed against the glass. Part of me felt relieved, knowing the priest's shooters were shackled inside the van. Part of me was impressed; it took balls to scam for the Orange in the middle of Green. No wonder Brady was always anxious.

I drove back to my apartment no more able to close the circle than I'd been before speaking to Clifford. It didn't matter. I was glad Clifford closed Collins and his crew. I was sick of True Believers working their will on unsuspecting people. It didn't matter whether they were Green, Orange, or Jewish. It didn't matter whether they were Churches, Temples, or Governments. Right now they all filled me with the same revulsion I'd felt sitting in Buzz's cooler with Blue.

I might not discover the connection between Dov's death and Collins' do, but before I quit working, that small square mile was going to be free of manipulating groups. Clifford took care of one, and when I finished with the Rabbi, I planned to take care of the rest.

And I would take care of a redheaded woman — once I knew where she fit.

Clifford's neon "we won't touch her" was still flashing when I saw Lou's note on the kitchen table. After I'd read it, the neon and most of my exhilaration were gone. Simon had tried to reach me and, when he couldn't, left a message with Lou for me to call. My gut said ignore, but I was loathe to show up at Reb

Yonah's house alone. I didn't know whether to be worried or relieved when I heard his answering machine.

I had to hustle if I was going to get to Yonah's on time. The ride was unpleasant. Thinking about talking my way through the Rabbi's door without Simon enervated me, pulled at my resolve. But my adrenaline found its pump when I saw my friend's fancy car sitting on Reb Yonah's block.

I parked near the corner, snuck up to the rear of his pearl-white 7-Series BMW, rapped sharply on the back glass, and watched him turn a startled face. A surprised but unamused Simon leaned across the other bucket to open the passenger door.

"Doesn't your boat do that for you?" I asked once I climbed inside. "You had to stretch."

"And you had to Ginger Baker my back window. What's the matter with you?"

"You ask that a lot," I said shifting my body on his comfortable leather. I reached into my pocket and pulled out my cigarettes.

"I ask because I keep hoping you'll have an answer. Do you have to smoke in here?" he complained, but opened the ashtray on the dashboard.

"Get your aim straight, Esquire. We want answers from the Rabbi. You can use the rest of our lives to badger me."

"Just the way I want to spend my retirement. You know, I'm not feeling too good about this meeting."

I shrugged and cracked my window. "I figured as much when I saw your message. How do these windows work with the engine off?"

"I don't know, I just drive the damn thing. All afternoon I'm thinking: this case is locked and loaded. Everybody is satisfied — Downtown, the Jewish organizations, Rabbi Sheinfeld, everyone."

"Not everyone."

He stared balefully in my direction. "Excuse me. Everyone but you." He looked at my jacket. "Why the hell did you bring a gun? Are you delusional? You can't really think it will come to that?"

"I forgot to take it off, that's all. I was walking the Irish beat. Man, Clifford *was* involved. Wait until I tell you about the priest."

Simon waved me quiet. "I don't want to know about anything if it doesn't change our plans." He glanced at his watch. "I just want to get this over with. You can fill me in later."

He suddenly banged his fist on the fat, leather-wrapped steering wheel. "I should have canceled this damn meeting when I couldn't get in touch with you." He pointed to his car phone. "We still can, Matt?"

"We don't want to. Look, Simon, you didn't close down the meeting, because *you* want to know what really went on with Dov's murder. Give yourself some credit, you haven't become a complete shyster."

"Thanks. I'll try to remember that when the shit hits the fan. Okay, how do you want to work this?"

"You get us in the door, I take it from there. You're absolutely certain Yakov is at the Yeshiva?"

"You think the Rabbi wants his kid involved with more meetings about the shootings? He said the boy will be at the Yeshiva. I didn't go there to check, goddamnit."

The door to Reb Yonah's house flew open before we were up the front steps. "You said nothing about bringing him!" Yonah thundered, black eyes flashing. He stepped back onto the small front porch and slammed the house door.

Simon held his ground. "This man is my closest associate. Had we been forced to go to court with your case, Rabbi, it would have been Matt's work that got you off."

Reb Yonah's hand cut at the air. "But we are not going to the courts, are we, Mr. Roth? You told me that the legal matters are settled, so what are you doing here? What is *he* doing here?"

Simon's mouth tightened stubbornly. "I think it's time to invite us inside, Rabbi. I don't intend to have this conversation outside on your porch."

Reb Yonah looked as if he were going to refuse, but changed

his mind, abruptly jerking the door open. "Come inside if you must," he said disagreeably.

The interior of the house looked just as uninviting as its owner. If possible, darker and gloomier than the last time I was there. Yonah led us to the large old table in the middle of his dining room but didn't offer us chairs.

"Perhaps we can all sit down, Reb Yonah?" Simon asked.

"Sit if you must. But be quick about this, please."

Everybody settled into wooden chairs as Simon handed off. "Matt has come across information that raises new questions about Reb Dov's murder."

Yonah glared at me. "What sort of information, what questions?"

"Why don't I start at the beginning?"

"Only if the beginning is not too far from the end," he snapped. "You are wasting valuable time for no useful purpose. I'm sure there are other people who could better answer your questions."

"Maybe," I agreed, "but I don't know anyone else associated with the Never Agains."

Yonah sat back in his chair, folded his arms across his chest, and waited.

"But I do know you. I also know you've wanted them up here for a long time but Rabbi Dov forbade it."

Yonah pulled at his earlocks. "The Rebbe disagreed with me. That is quite different than forbid. You see, sir, your information is already inaccurate. This was something that was settled between Reb Dov and myself long ago. It has nothing to do with my legal situation."

"Not to be disrespectful, but I didn't think it permissible for a Rabbi to lie. The disagreement between you and Rabbi Dov may have begun a long time ago, but it didn't really end until he was dead. It certainly didn't end when he forbade you to meet with the Never Agains."

Yonah stroked his long gray beard with trembling fingers. "You

speak to a Rabbi like this? You are supposed to be Jewish, Mr. Jacob. I told you, Reb Dov never forbade me to meet with anyone." He turned to Simon. "Why do you allow this man to insult me?"

"He knows what he's talking about, Rabbi," Simon answered simply. "We'll finish much sooner if you answer his questions instead of just trying to get rid of us."

I nodded appreciatively but kept my eyes on the Rabbi's face. "There was a period of time when you stopped meeting with the Never Agains, but then you resumed. Why?"

Yonah unfolded his arms and planted them on the table. "I met with friends because the very life of our Yeshiva was endangered by the anti-Semites. Anti-Semites who surround and abuse us."

"Rabbi Dov didn't think so," I pressed.

"The Rebbe didn't understand the seriousness of the threat."

"Come on, Reb Yonah, of course he understood. He just didn't exaggerate it the way you did."

"There have been Jews like you throughout all of history," he sneered. "Hating themselves for being Jewish! Scorning those who maintain a link with the *real* Judaism."

"We aren't talking religion here, Rabbi. Reb Dov didn't think it necessary to enlist vigilantes in this never-ending war. Why don't you stop your wriggling? You continued your involvement with the Never Agains behind Rabbi Dov's back."

Reb Yonah's lips cut a tight line through his gray facial hair. "The Yeshiva had once again come under attack. But this abuse was not individual anti-Semites taking it on themselves to rid the neighborhood of Hasidim. This was the work of an organized hate group who made it their avowed purpose."

His mouth opened showing tobacco-stained teeth and it took me a second to realize I was looking at a painful smile. "What do you expect?" he asked with a little less hostility. "In his goodness, in his warmth, the Rebbe couldn't see what was right in front of him. I had no choice but to find help." He paused and stared at

me venomously. "I have no need to explain myself to you. I have no need to tell you any of this. But, do you think it was easy for me? Do you imagine it pleased me to disagree with my Rebbe?"

"It didn't stop you from sneaking behind his back."

An involuntary tic just under Reb Yonah's eye started up. "It was impossible to stop the Avengers by ourselves."

"You took it on yourself to disobey your Chief Rabbi's decision not to allow the Yeshiva to become involved with the Never Agains?" I wanted to keep the tic working, spread it to the rest of his body.

"Reb Dov believed the attacks would stop by themselves. He didn't understand these people. We could not wait for a miracle. Our Law grants certain exceptions to many of its edicts. A Jew is never allowed to eat food which is not kosher. But if his life is in danger, he is instructed, *by our own law*, to eat that *traif*. There was no comfort in finding myself at odds with Reb Dov. There would be no pleasure if I were forced to break our Laws. Our lives, our community's very existence, was in danger."

Reb Yonah tried to regroup and turned to Simon. "I still can't comprehend why you're letting this man question me. Nor do I understand why my relationship to Never Again, to my Rebbe, has anything to do with either of you."

Before Simon could ease the tension I interjected, "It has to do with us if the Never Agains were involved with your Rebbe's death."

Yonah reacted like I'd slapped his face. He jumped up from his chair, and motioned for us to do the same. Simon obeyed but I stayed where I was.

"This is a complete *shonda*. You have the nerve to enter my house and make these insane accusations? To insult our religion, to insult me? To insult all Hasidim? I want you to leave immediately! Even your, your . . . *Sheinfeld* would know enough to be disgusted by this."

"Matt, maybe . . ." Simon began.

I ignored him and kept jabbing. "Then call Rabbi Sheinfeld.

Tell him to come over and join us because I'm not going anywhere until my questions are answered. Honestly answered.
Where did you get the gun, Rabbi? Who fronted your diamonds?"

Reb Yonah kept working Simon. "Mr. Roth, you have done a
good job for me. Until now you have treated me with respect.
Don't you think this outrage is enough? We are not like the Jews
you associate with, but how can you allow these defamations to
continue?"

"You don't see him running to the telephone, do you, Simon?
He's not going to call Sheinfeld because there are too many
facts he doesn't want known."

Yonah couldn't stop himself from retorting. "Mr. Jacob, I don't
believe you hear your own words. You find the worst possible interpretation for my meetings with the Never Agains. Then you
accuse them of having something to do with the Rebbe's death.
Do you know how deeply you must hate us? The insult of your
accusations? You have taken our Rebbe's death and twisted the
blame to fall upon Hasidim. I told Sheinfeld this would happen,
but I didn't expect this virulence from another Jew."

"Then call and tell him to come over, Rabbi. I don't care
where the blame falls. I just want the truth. The timing of the
emergence of the Avengers and your decision to play ball with
the Never Agains was just too close to be coincidence." It was
jugular time. "Look, I haven't gone to the authorities. Neither
has Simon. But both of us are going to find out why you met
with Kelly before the shootings. Why you were paying him off
with diamonds."

The room had already been crackling with anger and hostility. Now, Reb Yonah's features almost disappeared behind his
beard and rimless glasses. He stood stock still, arms rigid,
hands fisted at his side. I didn't dare glance at Simon so I
forced myself to watch Yonah's color return in blotches of pur-
ple rage. His fist smashed down on the table causing the reli-

gious books to jump. He kept shouting something in Yiddish until I kicked through.

"Nice act, Rabbi, but you'll have to use English for us to really get it. It's time to stop your bullshit. You had numerous conversations with Kelly and met with him at least once before *Simchas Torah*. I know he ended up with your diamonds. What we have, Rabbi, are Avengers, Never Agains, you and Kelly, diamonds, and a dead Rebbe who didn't want a vigilante group anywhere near his Yeshiva. But your vigilante pals are here now, aren't they? You want to sell Rabbi Sheinfeld on all these coincidences?"

Reb Yonah's face was gray again and he looked imploringly toward Simon who still stood, pale, his eyes staring at the floor. "How can you let him slander me like this, Roth? How can you? I am a Rabbi, you are a Jew. How dare you let him make these attacks? Did you see the diamonds he talks about?"

Simon kept his eyes averted and shook his head.

Yonah's voice quieted but contained an edge of desperation. "I met with the Never Agains and yes, I did so without Reb Dov's knowledge. But to then imagine I had met with the likes of Kelly is blasphemy. You are suggesting that I had something to do with my Rebbe's slaughter."

Strengthened by his quasi-admission he turned on me. "You sit there like a *k'nocker* and spew out one lie after another. You are the very worst kind of Jew. I saw you in the camps. You stayed alive by shoveling our dead brothers' and sisters' bones . . ."

"I'm not the one with the shovel, Rabbi. You had telephone conversations with Kelly and you met him at least once in the park," I repeated. "Calling me a liar doesn't change the truth."

"The truth. A Jew who despises everything Jewish but somehow owns the truth. How is it you came by this truth? What proof do you have? Show me the diamonds. Show them to Roth. This truth you speak of is nothing more than your Jew-

hating imagination. Were you there when these so-called conversations with Kelly took place? Were you there when we
supposedly met? Well, were you?"

There was a moment of excruciating silence before a small,
firm voice spoke from the doorway's gloomy shadow. "He wasn't
there, Papa, I was."

CHAPTER 39

Yakov's thin, reedy voice riveted everyone in the room. My stomach lurched as I turned in his direction; this was everything I'd wanted to avoid. I glanced at the Rabbi and saw a stricken look chip into his stony face then pass as his anger regained its footing. Reb Yonah raised his voice and spoke harshly in Yiddish, wagging his finger toward the door.

"No, Father, I'm not leaving. I won't return to the Yeshiva," Yakov answered evenly. Then he looked toward me. "You lied to me, Matt. You said there was nothing to my fears, but you yourself weren't telling the truth."

I gritted my teeth and kept silent.

Yonah shouted in rapid-fire Yiddish but Yakov shook his head vehemently. "I will not leave. And you must speak in English. This conversation is not just between us two."

Yonah turned to me. "This is your doing! You have succeeded in turning my only child against me!"

"I didn't want this to happen, Yonah. I tried to keep this private."

"Lies, nothing but lies." Yonah couldn't stop his hands from shaking. "You put these lies in Yakov's head. From the beginning you wanted to take him from us, from me."

"No, *Abba*, it was the opposite. Matt lied to protect you. He

told me what I had seen and heard was of no importance so I could return home with peace of mind." Yakov shook his head at me. "You thought too little of me, Matt. You treated me like a kid who couldn't hear the truth."

Simon walked over to my seat and tapped my shoulder. "Matt, maybe we ought to come back another time?"

I thrust his hand away. "It's too late, Simon." I refocused on the boy. "I didn't lie about everything, Yakov. I don't believe your father was responsible for Rabbi Dov's death. But I believe he has information that can make sense out of what happened. And you're right, I do want to give the two of you a chance together. A clean chance."

"Listen to him, Roth. Do you hear how he seduces my son?"

Simon returned to his chair. "I don't hear seduction, Reb Yonah. I hear care and protection. If this conversation had been left up to me I would have called in the boy. Yakov approached Matt with his suspicions, not the other way around. Matt wouldn't allow me to involve him."

"After which he would have gone directly back to Yakov," Yonah cried out bitterly. "This man's entire reason for being here is to drive a stake between me and my son."

I looked at Yakov while I responded. "The stake was planted long before I landed in your life, Yonah. When Yakov's mother died you backed off and allowed Rabbi Dov to play father. And when Dov died, you let Yakov dangle. I wasn't, and am not, trying to tear Yakov away from you or your religion. Yakov was looking for help to find his way back. It's pretty difficult when you're young, all alone, and mixed up in the middle of something you don't understand."

I turned to see Reb Yonah drag his chair back to the table and sit down. "I am used to being surrounded by hatred. My entire life has been spent warding off attacks. Even before the Nazis occupied Poland we were always preparing for an assault. Everyone lived in constant fear. We were Saturday-night sport for the

drunken *goyim*. But this, this is different. This comes from my own son."

"I'm not attacking you, Papa," Yakov said from the doorway. "I could never hate you. I didn't come to the house to blame, but to find answers. I don't think the lawyer Roth is here from hate, nor Matt."

The sound of my name rolling from Yakov's lips re-ignited Reb Yonah's temper. "You call this anti-Semite by his first name? You go to him with your concerns and fears but not to your own father? This is not what you've been taught! Where did you get these ideas if not from this *schkutz*?"

"You want to beat on the kid for your failures, don't you?" I challenged. "I understand your anger. I'm forcing you to admit what you are and what you did. I also understand why you think I'm here to stick it to you. But your son is here out of love and respect. If you want to attack someone, attack me or yourself. Leave the boy alone."

"I don't need your protection, Mr. Jacob." I was stung by Yakov's use of my surname but listened while he spoke to Reb Yonah. "I love you, Papa, no matter what has happened, but I want to know the truth."

"How is it you've come to be involved?" Reb Yonah demanded. "I haven't pushed you into any of this. This man is the one who did that."

"No, Papa, it's not true. I was the one who overheard your telephone conversations. I was the one who followed you to the park and saw you meet with this Kelly. I was the one who told Mr. Jacob about all of it."

Simon opened his mouth but I stopped him from speaking with a curt wave of my hand. Yonah had slumped forward, the wrath seeping slowly from his face. I watched him mouth silent words and tug at his beard. He removed his glasses, placing them carefully on the table. I felt my body relax as the intensity in the room slackened.

Reb Yonah said something in Yiddish but Yakov interrupted. "You must speak in English, Father. Everyone has to understand what you are saying."

Yonah looked as if he was going to argue and I thought we were back to battle. But he restrained himself and rubbed his eyes. "I never wanted you to spend your life living with the same fear as I have."

"You never spoke with me about any of those fears," Yakov answered. "You only talk to the Never Agains."

Yonah shook his head and gestured with his hands. "I couldn't. Your life was difficult enough. We are encircled by a world that begs, entices us to turn away from our beliefs. And beats us when we don't. To speak with you about the atrocities that happened in my life meant exposing you to my fear. I could not do that and expect you to take from me the strength and courage to be a Jew. Our kind of Jew."

Yonah paused and when he spoke again his note of despair had deepened. "After your mother died my aggravations were so great I could barely speak to you at all. When I looked upon you I saw her. I saw another piece of my life that had been stolen."

He dropped his head to his chest. "I had to do something, anything, to free myself of this affliction. It was after her death that I first met the Never Agains. These were not people frozen in fear. These were not Jews who walked quietly to their graves. I believed I could learn, that the entire Yeshiva could learn. That was why I met with them.

"But our Rebbe, with all his wisdom, all his knowledge, could not understand. He, Merciful God, had been spared the horrors of the camps. He had not seen firsthand the blood and bones of dying relatives in piles in front of open trenches. Our Rebbe had not been forced to wonder whether a beloved had been used to make the thin sliver of soap the guards occasionally handed out. Or whether a child's skin had been molded into a lampshade."

Yonah groaned. "Of course our Rebbe knew of the horror, but he did not witness it the way I and the Never Agains had wit-

nessed it. We saw these things with our eyes. With our own starvation, our own death staring at us each day."

"But why, Father?" Yakov's voice was a hoarse whisper. "Why did you continue to meet with them after the Rebbe forbade it. Why did you meet with Kelly?"

Yonah looked at each of us in turn. "I stopped the meetings. I explained to the Never Agains that the Rebbe would not allow me to bring the organization to the Yeshiva. They were not pleased with my information. Nor were they pleased when I refused to continue my efforts without Reb Dov's knowledge. In the past they had confronted similar objections, but always continued their work. I would not allow that here. I could not ignore my Rebbe and I could not let anyone else ignore him."

There was a long pause while each of us digested what he had said. Yakov emerged from the doorway's shadow and took a seat a couple feet from the table. Silent tears dripped from his eyes. When I looked at Yonah he too was awkwardly crying. Simon was white-faced and staring in my direction but I didn't think he actually saw me. I let the silence ride then went on.

"But you picked up with the Never Agains later, Rabbi. Why?"

Reb Yonah spread his hands helplessly. "An important Rabbi, a friend from within the organization, contacted me shortly after these White Avengers began their systematic attacks upon the Yeshiva. Though I was at first reluctant, I became convinced there would be little harm if we met."

"What was the meeting about?"

Some of his feistiness returned. "It was about the horror that has confronted Jews since we first became a people. Our conversation reminded me of why I had originally sought them out. These were people who understood what organized antiSemitism led to. They understood that the abuse would never disappear on its own. It would end with the destruction of our Yeshiva, our community. My friends understand the world as it truly is."

"But the meetings didn't stop with just one," I suggested in an even tone. We were moving into the present and I didn't want to trigger his temper.

I needn't have worried. Reb Yonah was no longer interested in me or Simon. Throughout his explanation he continually glanced at his son. Finally convinced there was no condemnation to be found, he looked directly at Yakov while he answered my questions. "It was the first of many meetings," he admitted. "I did not want to end my association."

"What was their intent, Reb Yonah? How did they want to use you?"

He took his eyes from Yakov's face, glanced toward me, then went back to talking to his son. "I had no sense of being used. I'm not certain they *have* used me. I have made my own judgments throughout this ordeal."

He stared down at the table. "They asked me to approach the Rebbe again. They felt the Rebbe might feel differently since it was no longer isolated acts of hatred, but an organized system of anti-Semitism. I *wanted* to talk to the Rebbe about this." He returned his gaze to his son. "People with numbers burned into their arms see all too clearly the nature of appeasement."

"But Rabbi Dov still refused to let them recruit?" Simon found his voice.

"He said no."

I stole a look at Yakov before I asked, "What was the Never Agains' next idea, Rabbi?"

Reb Yonah lowered his eyes. "When my friends heard that I had been unable to convince Reb Dov, they asked me to recruit behind his back." He lifted his head momentarily. "Again I refused. But as the attacks from the Avengers increased, they insisted something needed to be done to change the Rebbe's mind."

Reb Yonah took a deep shaky breath as anguish contorted his face. "This is when everything terrible really began. I met with my friend in New York and we talked through the night. If the Rebbe

truly *understood* the gravity of the Avenger threat . . . If Reb Dov *saw* our vulnerability, he might finally understand. My friend suggested a disruption at the *Simchas Torah* celebration — thugs would interfere when everyone was out on the street. The Rebbe would clearly *see* how easy it was to be in harm's way. He would *want* our Yeshiva protected. Protected by our own." Reb Yonah covered his face with a hand and spoke from behind it. "To this day I don't know why I countenanced this idea."

"But you did," I said.

Now that he'd begun telling the truth, Reb Yonah seemed determined to tell all of it. Maybe the Catholics were on to something with their confessionals. Yonah removed his hand. "Yes. But I returned from New York uneasy about our discussion so I put it from my mind. Eventually it became as if I had dreamt it. Such a long time passed before I heard from him, I hoped my friend had also forgotten."

"But he hadn't?" asked Simon.

I heard Yakov's chair scrape along the floor, sliding closer to the table. I didn't look his way.

"No," Reb Yonah said. "He had not forgotten. Worse. He told me that through various contacts the Never Agains had been able to do the impossible. They had arranged for this Sean Kelly to disrupt our holiday! He said the Rebbe would taste our danger! After the disruption, if Kelly were caught, he would be identified as an Avenger. The Rebbe would now be certain to change his mind . . ."

"What were you supposed to do?" Simon's eyes shot sparks as he leaned into the Rabbi's words.

"Everything. I was told that my friend could no longer be contacted. It was important the Never Agains remain hidden, out of sight. They would call me after everything was finished. After *Simchas Torah*. I tried to remove myself but it was impossible. Everything had gone too far and I was the only one left to exercise any control over what was to occur. It was too late to stop Kelly. My friend gave me a time to meet with him."

"Where were you supposed to meet?" I asked.

"I was given an address in the neighborhood. It was a church. When I got there I believed it to be the wrong address."

"Why?"

"Because a Hasid would never go inside any church. I started to leave when Kelly ran over. We spoke for a little while and set times to meet again."

"When did he start blackmailing you?" I asked.

Yonah lifted his shoulders tiredly. "I'm not certain of when. By then *everything* seemed as a dream. A terrible nightmare. This was not a Rabbi's work."

"But he did blackmail you?" I pressed.

"Yes, he blackmailed me. He had tape recordings of our conversations. He wanted twenty thousand dollars. I grew frantic and found myself negotiating, but I had nothing with which to negotiate. No matter what price he fixed, I would not be able to pay."

"What did you do?" Yakov asked.

"I called my friend in New York. Then I went there, only to be given rough diamonds to push onto Kelly. I was told to refuse him any cash or any more diamonds until after the disruption." Yonah looked at me. "This is when I was given a gun and instructed to pretend to protect the Rebbe on *Simchas Torah*. I was to chase Kelly from our midst."

"Kelly went for the jewels?"

"He wanted cash. Also, rough diamonds do not appear valuable. I explained that when everything was finished, I would see that they were cut into gems. He was unhappy, but he finally understood I could do no more."

Once again everyone lapsed back into silence, the only sound Reb Yonah's labored breath. "Everything went wrong that night, didn't it?" I asked softly.

Reb Yonah didn't need to be told which night. "Yes, everything went wrong. Kelly was to have screamed and cursed while he threatened with his gun. He would stand in full view when

the Rebbe came out of the building to be sure the Rebbe saw the threat."

Reb Dov stared over my head. "It began as planned. I saw Kelly scream and curse. I made certain Reb Dov saw the disruption. When I turned my attention back to Kelly he was waving his gun. I took mine from my pocket and started toward him. Then I heard an explosion. I turned back to see my Rebbe fall to the ground."

Tears washed over Yonah's face, his arms and hands shaking uncontrollably. Inside his black suit he looked small and lost. He looked old. "Something happened within me. Something that would not allow another loved one to be taken away without revenge. I ran at Kelly. He continued to wave his gun. The next I knew I had pulled the trigger."

Yonah slumped forward resting his head on his arms and sobbed. I heard Yakov leave his chair and watched him circle the table to his father. Yakov was ashen but dry-faced. He tentatively placed his hands on his father's heaving shoulders, leaned forward, and kissed Yonah's black *yarmulke*.

Simon sat quietly, a grim, hard look on his face. I kept myself from squirming in my chair.

Sometime in the future I would be comfortable with my role in having opened a path for Yonah and Yakov. Comfortable, even, with forcing Yonah's *Simchas Torah* participation into the light. But right then I had a heavy heart. Right then, Yonah's tears and Yakov's gain were exposing my losses.

CHAPTER 40

I fought the numbing the only way I knew. I crawled in deeper, insisting to myself there was a job left to do. A case that was still unfinished. I silently urged myself to press on. But for the next few minutes there was only me to prod. Reb Yonah stood and clutched his son. Yakov returned the embrace with equal fervor. The two held each other speaking singsong Yiddish in soft murmurs. Simon stared at the floor and I stared past Simon.

When Yakov and Reb Yonah finished their private conversation, Yonah sat back down and faced us. Yakov remained standing, hand on his father's shoulder. I tried to be happy for the kid, failed, so turned my attention back to Reb Yonah's story. "Rabbi, you said Kelly was still waving his gun just before you fired. Are you certain?"

The Rabbi spoke with a husky voice. "Yes, I am certain. In that moment everything had slowed down. It was as if the darkness disappeared and he stood apart from everyone else in his own circle of evil."

"Did you actually see him shoot the gun?"

"I saw him waving it over his head. There were people between us when I first ran toward him. I heard the explosion then looked back to the Rebbe."

"Could you see Kelly's face after that?"

"Yes. I saw his face just before I shot my weapon. I will go to my grave seeing his face."

"What did it look like right before you fired? Was he happy, worried, what?"

Reb Yonah answered after a painful silence. "His mouth hung open but I no longer heard his curses. He looked surprised, frightened, as if he hadn't expected to do what he had done."

"Did he try to run away?"

"He just stood there."

"Did he appear frightened of you, of your reaction?"

"I don't think he even saw me."

"Did you see anyone else near him? Anyone who might have been there with him?"

"No. I saw only Kelly. The people around him were our own people. Everyone was confused, running in all directions."

"What are you driving at, Matt?" Simon asked.

"I don't know, Simon. The Rabbi didn't see Kelly shoot." So far I hadn't found anyone who had. "I don't want to leave without making sure I've got everything, that's all."

"There were people in Reb Yonah's way, Matt," Simon explained.

"I believe him." I turned back to Yonah and abruptly changed the subject. "So now the Never Agains have you in their pocket?"

"In their pocket?"

"That's right. You recruit, send them money, do whatever they want. You're boxed in worse than you were before *Simchas Torah*."

He shook his head. "Why would they want to trap me?"

"You're their guarantee. Their assurance."

"Assurance for what?"

"Reb Yonah, as long as they own you, they can do what they damn well please up here. That's what their scheming was all about. The Never Agains want another launching pad from which to fight their holy war."

I expected another rip at my character but Reb Yonah had nothing left but dogma. "My friends have no need to trap anyone. They protect us, help us maintain our lives against the threat of another holocaust."

"Reb Yonah, Never Again is involved with more than the protection of helpless Jews. I'm no expert, but Simon can tell you all about your so-called friends. This was no defense against anti-Semites. What happened on *Simchas Torah* was directed against your Rabbi. My guess is the Never Agains were flat out partners with the White Avengers."

Although the shattered dogma left him with nothing, Reb Yonah didn't protest. The blush had long been chiseled from the rose, but until tonight the Rabbi had been unwilling to notice. "Then I too was a partner with the Avengers. I was a partner with Kelly."

"A manipulated partner, Rabbi. You were jerked around. Used. Vigilante groups turn fear into hate, then find enemies to aim it on. Like all vigilantes, like the White Avengers, the Never Agains feed on the fears of its members. And they had a dinner party with yours."

I rushed on, embarrassed by my own passion. "Look what the Never Agains did to you. They turned you, Reb Dov, even Kelly, into victims. They *created* a moment in time which you had spent your life running from. And they manipulated you into helping them do it. Do you really feel any safer now?"

Reb Yonah turned and pulled Yakov closer to his side. "It is difficult to accept that all this suffering, all this death, was in vain."

I started to respond but Yakov surreptitiously waved me silent. "Papa, what Mr. Jacob says is true. The Never Agains pushed you into something that became much worse than any possible Avenger attack upon the Yeshiva. These aren't friends."

The Rabbi looked at his son and shrugged despondently. "Even if Jacob is correct, there is nothing to be done. The people in New York are very insistent about starting their organiza-

tion right now. I have no means to stop them, especially if what he says is true."

Simon's one hand slapped at the table, the other ran through his hair. "I'm not so sure of that, Rabbi."

I had seen the livid look on my friend's face before. He was enraged by what he had been hearing and clearly knew whom he was angry at. "I can do something about the Never Agains. I *will* do something." He leaned forward glaring at Reb Yonah. "But you will stop your recruiting. You will give up on this hate group." Simon lowered his voice. "And you'll give me the names of these people you are still calling your friends."

I saw Yonah stiffen but Yakov intervened. "Father, to allow these people to continue their work is to honor those who forced you to turn against the Rebbe."

"I'm not oblivious to your worries about anti-Semitism," Simon added. "But the Never Agains are not going to stamp it out. They just invite more. If I help with this situation, you will have to find better ways to deal with your fears."

I didn't catch Reb Yonah's answer. In fact, I was starting to tune out. Simon was Simon and the Never Agains would never be. At least up here. Yakov was home and Reb Yonah was glad to have him there. Simon wasn't even pissed that I had put him through this wringer. Me? I just wanted out.

"Simon," I interrupted, "do you need me for the rest of this? I'm absolutely beat. I want to go home."

Simon shot a quick look at Yakov, then back to me. I saw a troubled expression cross his face. "You ought to be thanked before you go anywhere," he said.

I got up and smiled wearily in his direction. "No need, boss." I waited for a moment hoping, I think, for Yakov to say something. I didn't expect him to thank me, but it would be nice to hear a goodbye. When all I heard was silence, I glanced across the table and saw him staring at the floor.

I walked over to Simon. "Are you going to have any trouble with this, with the rest of it?"

His eyes were gleaming. "Are you kidding? When I'm finished the Never Again will be sorry they ever heard of Reb Yonah. Hell, they're going to be sorry they exist."

"Then I'm history."

Simon accompanied me to the front door. "Listen," he said in a quiet voice. "You were right to make this happen. Right to make me do it with you. Sooner or later the boy will realize what you meant to him and Reb Yonah. When he does he'll thank you. Right now, the only thing he sees is his old man. Maybe for the first time. And believe me, I'll get everything else straightened out."

"I believe you, Bwahna. Thanks." I started to leave, remembered something I'd forgotten to ask, and walked back to the dining room doorway. "I have one last question, Rabbi. In all the time you've been associated with the Never Agains, have you ever met a woman member?"

He looked at me as if I were from another planet. "A woman?"

"Have you ever even heard a woman mentioned?"

Reb Yonah shook his head. "There are no women in the Never Agains."

I shrugged my thanks, nodded to Simon, and found my way to the car.

I thought I went home to sleep but deep, delicious, dopeless sleep was something from a past life. The best I could do was get tangled in the bedcovers. The more I twisted, the closer I came to eating some V. But images from the night kept whipping through my head and I was reluctant to chance drugged out dreams. I didn't need to find myself locked into something I couldn't escape. I finally gave up, gathered my cigarettes and grass, and retreated to the couch. If a depression was coming I wanted to be in position.

The depression never came. Instead, I found myself fiddling with the night's revelations. At first it felt like helplessly picking at an open wound. A pyro playing with fire. But as I picked, my

ruptured relationship with Yakov imperceptibly drifted into the background and I found myself trying to weave Clifford and Reb Yonah's stories into one. The more I tried, the more frustrated I became. And with the frustration came a deeper fatigue. Eventually, the exhaustion, a well-made joint, and the familiarity of my living room couch caught me.

I awoke the next day angry. Positive that Clifford wanted *me* to bring down Deirdre Ryan. That's what he'd been trying to signal. That's what he meant when he'd invited me to dig. What he'd meant when he told me he couldn't touch her. He couldn't but *I* could. Clifford had used me as a Trojan horse right from the beginning and wanted to keep on using me until the very end.

And I didn't care; I wanted to bring her down. Deirdre was the only card left in the deck. If Clifford couldn't finish the hand, I would.

I pulled the telephone off the hook and spent the day at my desk pushing paper like a government bureaucrat on speed. I hammered the case from every angle and perspective. I looked at the events through the eyes of each player, searching for objectives, hunting for means. I took Washington Clifford's advice and ran all the numbers. I added, subtracted, and added some more. I smoked, paced my rooms, and smoked some more.

By the time the apartment needed its lamps, I was ready to leave. I strapped the holster and gun across my shoulder, threw on my leather, and walked into the alley for Manuel's car. It wasn't gonna be a carnival, but I had tickets for one more ride.

CHAPTER 41

I'd spent the entire day getting it wrong, but that's not what I discovered when I first got to Deirdre's apartment. Instead, I discovered her sleek modern gun pointed toward my belly from under the dangling door chain. At that moment I was absolutely certain I had it right.

"Come inside, Mr. Jacob, but keep your hands away from your body." She opened the door to allow me to enter as she motioned her pistol invitingly.

"Matt, Deirdre. Call me Matt," I said, gingerly stepping into the apartment.

"I think not" — backing deeper into the room — "I prefer Mr. Jacob."

"Tough to be intimate with someone standing in front of your gun. Is that the problem?"

"Just turn around and face the wall. We'll talk in a minute."

Unless she lied I wasn't going to be shot in the back. Of course, she'd been lying since we met. The room looked different, more spacious, as I turned to face the wall. Her torture machine was missing. "Stop working out, Deirdre?"

"Right now be quiet and do what I say. Place your fingertips flat on the wall, Mr. Jacob."

I leaned into the white wall at a slight angle as her foot kicked

each ankle in rapid succession. My head banged against the painted Sheetrock. Lucky me, a new way to assume the position. Deirdre ran a professional hand over my body extracting the .38 along the way. When her fingers slid over the back of my legs I considered a short hard kick, but better sense prevailed: the hard silencer was brushing against my leather.

"You don't have to remain against the wall," Deirdre said.

I turned to see her crow's-feet crinkle from the scornful smile on her face. "A little old-fashioned, don't you think?" she asked kneeling. Deirdre placed my gun on her hardwood floor and slid it across the room.

"I'm an old-fashioned guy. You know how it is, love the gun you're with."

"I thought you might visit," she said, waving me to a chair.

"Thought? Only thought? Damn, doesn't the CIA know everything?"

She ran her fingers through her short red hair. "The CIA, Mr. Jacob? Is that what you think? Why the CIA?"

I sat down, but Deirdre remained on her feet, gun in hand. "That's my question, lady. But when Washington Clifford behaves like a good doobie, it gets me wondering. There aren't too many institutions or agencies that can plant a pacifier between his teeth." I paused then asked, "I don't have to tell you who Washington Clifford is, do I?"

"No, you don't." Deirdre dragged a wooden chair opposite me and sat on it backwards, one arm across the top of its back, gun hand on her knee. "He worked well with my agency. Reluctantly, but efficiently."

"Are you smiling at my sharp deductions?" I asked looking around the room. A couple of packing crates were open in front of her kitchen and bedroom.

"Sorry to disappoint you. I'm smiling because you deduced it wrong."

"Come on, Deirdre, you're holding the gun. Do you really have to play plausible denial?"

Her smile widened. " 'Plausible denial'? Please, Mr. Jacob, you've read too many exposés. I'm afraid the books haven't been helpful. Don't feel badly, the writers usually screw it up too."

"Come on, *Ms.* Ryan, I'd hoped we could be honest with each other."

"We are, Mr. Jacob. You're being honest when you accuse me of working for the CIA. I'm being honest when I tell you I do not." She was enjoying the cat-and-mouse. Why not? She wore the longer fur.

Despite her gun I grew irked. "I'm tired of the runaround, Deirdre — or whatever your real name is. You started the Avengers, helped the Never Agains set up Reb Yonah, then manipulated Kelly into the shootings. I know that and I believe Washington Clifford knows it. But you're here, gun in hand, while everyone else is either fucked up, dead, jailed, or sitting on their butts. That takes drag, lady, serious drag."

"You would do well at horseshoes, Mr. Jacob. You definitely win points for getting close. Unfortunately, you have the wrong service and wrong country."

I heard her but it didn't register. I pointed to the boxes. "Whatever your game, it's over, so you're out of here. What area will be fucked up with your shadow next? I didn't think the CIA was allowed to work in the States."

"I'm not staying in the States. I'm going home."

"Home? You mean the Agency brought you in from overseas? Ireland?"

"I only look Irish, Mr. Jacob. My home is in Israel."

Her words finally landed. Slashed right through my annoyance, mistaken analysis, and into my gut. My mouth dropped open and I floundered for something to say. Israel. Redheaded, reserved, Deirdre Ryan was from Israel. "You work for Israeli Intelligence?"

"Draw your own conclusions, Mr. Jacob." Deirdre added with another brittle smile, "Perhaps Mr. Jacob is too formal. May I call you Matthew?"

I was too busy rearranging everything in my head to answer.

"You look perplexed, Matthew. What are you thinking?"

I shrugged. "I don't know what I'm thinking. I couldn't figure out why the CIA was involved, and this makes even less sense."

"Why do you say that?" she asked with interest.

"You created the Avengers, had them murder a Rabbi, and now tell me you work for Israel. You don't see something wrong with the picture?"

"Truthfully," she said, "I see someone way out of his league. You are naive, Matthew, far too naive to be mixed up in this."

I started to talk then pressed my lips closed. I wasn't sure I wanted my cherry busted. I didn't know my odds on staying alive but worried that they dropped with every new revelation.

It wasn't my choice. "To understand why I'm here, why I was sent here, you have to look at the larger picture," Deirdre broke the silence. "Year after year your government's financial and moral support have diminished. We understand this. Oil, changing alliances, new world order." She paused then asked, "As a Jew, Matthew, doesn't the term 'new world order' bother you?"

"Most order bothers me."

"That doesn't come as a complete surprise. On the other hand, you've been quite orderly in your persistence."

"It's been order through ignorance."

She nodded. "That's partially true. But don't underestimate yourself. You were on to me very quickly. What made you suspicious?"

"I found a note from you in Kelly's apartment."

Her smile disappeared and her hairline wrinkles deepened. "Surprising. I turned his apartment but didn't find any note. Where was it?"

"In a book of love poems."

Deirdre made a sour face. "How did you know it was me?"

"I saw you leave Kelly's, followed you to Collins's church, then back to your house. Same address as the one on the note."

Deirdre's smile returned, though not as wide. "You're better than I thought, Matthew. I'm not used to surprises."

"Let's stop the boogie, Deirdre." I pointed to the gun on her knee. "Toss the bun and get to the meat. It's confusing enough without the bullshit."

"It's really not complicated, Matthew. My country simply won't let American support fade away. Our existence depends on your public and private monies. Anti-Semitism in the United States keeps the money channels flowing."

The hamburger was tough to swallow. "You're telling me you created the Avengers to promote Jew-baiting?"

"You sound shocked, Matthew?"

I was shocked. "Sean Kelly worked for Israel too?"

"First of all, Matthew, I work for the *good* of Israel. You won't find my agency listed on any bureaucratic flow-chart. Does that shock you as well? Sean's allegiance was to Ireland. *He* thought he was working for the IRA."

"But you convinced him to start the Avengers and terrorize the Hasids?"

"I helped convince him," she corrected. "Brady Collins had a lot to do with it."

I started to swallow the meat. "And you owned Collins?" I shook my head in perverse appreciation. Once you got on the bus it was easy to keep rolling.

Deirdre returned the admiration. "Now you're catching on. Brady Collins had been in deep cover for more than twenty years. Since he'd been a teenager. Over the years he had siphoned a great deal of money *thought* to be going to the IRA. It was a truly brilliant operation. Unfortunately for him, we knew about it. Knew about it for a long time before we decided to use it. How could he possibly refuse? He either worked with us or went out of business. Life's a bitch, isn't it? Always a choice between the lesser of two evils."

"Illusion of choice. Collins worked with you but still got burned."

"It's a pity how some things just don't work out. Still, he's much better off this way. If the IRA had found him out ..."

I couldn't rip my eyes off her gun, but found it impossible to stop talking. "So you and Collins had Kelly trash the Hasids?"

"Trash isn't the word I would choose."

"And every time another anti-Semitic incident hits the newspapers, Israel plants more trees."

"You've got a rich sense of humor, Matthew."

"I'm not feeling very funny." My irritation and amazement were shifting into a deeper anger. "So why bother with the Never Agains? Why set up *Simchas Torah*? The Avengers were already doing what you wanted."

"If I may use your metaphor, local newspaper stories don't plant many trees. We have a long-standing relationship with the Never Agains. Once we learned about Reb Yonah's overtures ..."

"So you cooked up the holiday celebration?"

"An incident like that is heard around the world. It wasn't an opportunity to pass up."

My confusion was gone, my amazement with it. But my anger was just starting to perk. I felt my body harden, my insides begin to chill. "Do you hear yourself? What are you? Who are you, anyway?"

"I'm a Jew, Matthew. I'm someone who believes in the primacy of a Jewish homeland. Committed to the defense and life of my country. I'm a patriot."

"Open your eyes, Patriot, you're not in your fucking country. Since when is the first line of Israeli defense located in the United States?"

Deirdre chuckled. "From our inception, actually. But you miss the point. We go where circumstance dictates, act when the time is right. This particular opportunity happened to be here and I was the person sent." Deirdre's green eyes blazed with the passion of her commitment. "Only Israel can truly guarantee the continued existence of the Jewish people."

"Some Jewish people."

She ignored me. "Our survival depends on my country's willingness and ability to effectively use the openings we're given. We came to this community because our knowledge about Collins gave us entry. Rabbi Saperstein unwittingly handed us a chance to build upon what we had."

"You sound like a goddamn textbook, lady. Those were real people pumping red on the street. Rabbi Dov will never make it to your homeland, will he? Or Sean Kelly to his?"

Her endorphins downshifted. "You are old-fashioned. It's becoming."

"And you're one cold spy. No coming in for you, is there? Were the diamonds part of your fundraising effort?"

She shrugged. "I couldn't decide if you *wanted* me to discover you had been here or had just fucked up. But I hadn't realized you found the roughs." She shook her head. "The shakedown was Kelly's independent contribution to the program. When he saw he couldn't get cash from Saperstein, he accepted the diamonds. Roughs," she sneered, "he wanted to give them to me."

"Don't sound so disparaging. Romance convinced him to pull the trigger, didn't it? See, Deirdre, I don't think Kelly shot the Rabbi on his own. Thief, extortionist, willing anti-Semite, sure. But without you, without loving you, I don't believe he'd have played kamikaze. It's one thing if he's busted for packing, another if he uses. You saw bigger headlines, more trees, and played Kelly like a Clapton guitar riff."

As I finished speaking something scratched at my head but I couldn't pinpoint it. I couldn't even try. It took all my control and focus to keep from raging. I didn't like my chances as is. If I lost my temper, I'd like them less.

"Kelly thought he was cunning," Deirdre said flatly. Her eyes suddenly became hard, opaque. "But he was stupid."

I thought she was getting ready to use her gun and I froze in my seat. I let out my breath when she continued to talk.

"Sean was a sponge. You dripped on him and he soaked it up,

squeezed him and everything dribbled back out," Deirdre sneered.

"You did some heavy dripping, lady." I ran my eyes up and down her lithe, tight body. Maybe she hadn't liked fucking him for Israel's greater good. "And I bet you're a champ. Good enough to find people's weakness and shark them. Only you don't eat, just nibble until they do what you want.

"And I bet your marks even like the nibble. Was it you or Collins who wanted me dead?" I was only half interested in her answer. Kelly still picked at my attention. Kelly, and the gun in Deirdre's hand.

"Does it matter?" She must have seen some emotion cross my face because she added, "I didn't order you killed. Collins panicked. He hadn't expected his visitors when he invited you to the meeting. You simply chose the wrong time to add to his anxiety."

"It doesn't sound like you worked very hard to stop him?"

She looked at me like I was a stupid schoolboy. "Please, Matthew. You really do personalize too much."

"Hey lady, you don't get personal about anything. You have a jones about your homeland. But who do you want a homeland for? Jews? You instigate hatred against Jews. Rabbis? You left one dead on the street and vultured Reb Yonah. Even Kelly cared more about his own than that."

"You're quite eloquent, Matthew. Eloquent but shortsighted. You sound like the social worker you once were.

"Don't look surprised, we have our sources," she added. "The world is more complex than the simple right or wrong you make it out to be. There are larger tides — of much greater importance — than any particular individual. More important than any particular tragedy. I regret the Rabbi's death but Kelly got carried away. I told you, Sean was stupid. Stupid and hotheaded."

I finally knew what was bothering me. Almost everything Deirdre said about Kelly contradicted what I had learned about him.

He was a planner, a detail man, not someone prone to self-destruction. Not even for love. Tell me Blue got carried away and I'd believe it. But I didn't believe Sean Kelly spontaneously murdered Reb Dov. I didn't think he had murdered the Rabbi at all.

I took a deep breath as the final fragment of my confusion cleared. "You were there that night, weren't you? If you can do Irish, you can certainly act like an Orthodox Jewish woman. Hell, you can do anyone you want because there ain't no real you! You shot Rabbi Dov, didn't you? Sean wasn't a hothead. He was as surprised as everyone else when a gun went off. Let me ask you, did you kill them both?"

Deirdre stared at me long and hard before she answered. "I guess it's grow-up time for you, Matthew Jacob." Her mouth was drawn tight across her teeth, her eyes unyielding. "I didn't have the luxury of waiting until I was an adult." Deirdre's face twisted into a mirthless grin. "And I had no one to teach me the facts of life, either. You see, Matthew, my parents survived the camps but not the experience. They escaped the ovens but never, for a moment, the fear. And from the fear came only silence."

Deirdre ground her jaw and ran her free hand rapidly through her hair. "I read a study once that placed a dog in a cage and randomly zapped different parts of the cage with electricity. After a short while the dog quit trying to out-guess the pain and just sat waiting for the shocks. No matter that they stopped the electricity, the dog kept sitting and waiting. That's what happened to my parents."

She stared at me. "Can you imagine living in a house where the shades were never up? Windows never opened more than a crack? Where conversations, all conversations, were held in whispers? Where the only visitors, and I mean *only*, were those who also survived the camps but not the fear? I don't think you can understand what it means to grow up surrounded by the living dead. Too ashamed to have friends, since friends might want to visit my house. The gloom, Matthew, I grew up in perpetual gloom."

Deirdre gave a hard shake of her head, as if to rid it of mem-

ories. "I willed myself to resist that fear. I refused to become like that dog. I swore that my life would be dedicated to making certain that no Jewish child would ever be forced to grow up in the gloom again. There were limits to the usefulness of the *Simchas Torah* operation. It was my decision to extend the benefits. If you pull your head out of the sand, think like a Jew, and look around, you'd see how enormous those benefits are."

I felt nauseous and my hand gripped the seat of my chair. "Extend the benefits? Is that how you explained it to the cops? Or was that someone else's job?"

She dismissed the question with a quick wave of the gun. "There hasn't been much to explain. Pandemonium is the perfect operational cover. By the time I disappeared, Kelly was holding the gun that killed Dov. Rabbi Saperstein's decision to fire his own gun made things even simpler. He was wonderful television while arrangements were processed through private channels. Like I told you, Clifford is a professional." Deirdre shrugged. "My agency had no choice but to protect me. And frankly, your officials were quite grateful for our information concerning Brady Collins."

Deirdre stood, stretched, and walked across the room. She raised her left hand and flashed her long fingernail. "I dislike lying, Matthew. But I dig this sharp fingernail into my palm to remember our people's history, our suffering. I'm not a social worker. There are things about my work I don't enjoy, but I do them. Sometimes those things are ugly and distasteful. But I do them anyway. I do them because I believe in something larger, something more important than myself. Something that will still exist long after I join the Rabbi and Kelly."

She bent down, picked up my gun, and walked back in my direction. "There are two commandments in my job. Believe in the cause. Be the last one standing."

I felt my body brace and my mind bolted in a thousand different directions. None of them led to a way out. "Are you going to find killing me distasteful?" I asked in a hoarse voice.

She motioned me to get up and I willed my legs to obey.

"Distasteful," she said raising my gun. "Of course I'd find killing you distasteful." She smiled. "I don't often speak as personally as I have with you. But I'm not going to kill you, Matthew. You can't cause me any trouble and you're not in my way. I have no *reason* to kill you." She made a sudden motion and tossed my gun. To my undying credit, I recovered in time to catch it before it landed on the floor.

CHAPTER 42

I grasped the cold metal in my damp palm, my rage and fright momentarily smothered by relief. But when my safety dug in, the anger blew out. "So I'm supposed to walk away pretending you don't exist?"

"For all intents and purposes, Matthew, by tomorrow I *won't* exist. I don't understand your dissatisfaction. We helped your friend Washington Clifford close down Collins's operation, and I've already been told your other friend, Roth, will be able to keep the Never Agains from moving up here. What's your complaint? Do you still carry around some antiquated fantasy about crime and punishment, guilt and innocence?"

Deirdre unhooked the silencer from her pistol, placing it along with the gun on the seat of her chair. "I couldn't chance your being irrational," she explained. "I apologize if it led to the wrong conclusion and made you uncomfortable."

I don't know if it was the words or her matter-of-fact delivery. My rage screamed for action. Deirdre might be gone tomorrow, but she was here now. And very real. If I let her disappear she would just turn up somewhere else wearing a different name and hair color. Someplace where more unsuspecting people would be manipulated, and perhaps killed, in the name of her commitment. I lifted my arm and pointed my gun at her face.

"Washington Clifford has a job, Roth has a reputation and career. I just work for myself."

My gun hand trembled. "I'm glad about Collins and the Never Agains, but someone has to pay for Dov and Kelly. Someone has to pay for the nightmare you've put people through." My voice quivered and I blinked rapidly to clear my vision.

"Whose nightmare are you talking about, Matthew, yours?" Deirdre asked sarcastically. "Go home to your friends, go back to being a private detective. It's the right job for someone who sees the world split between good and evil, right and wrong."

I cocked the hammer of my gun, the tiny click booming like a thunderclap. "Move away from your chair, Deirdre."

She stood where she was. "We look at the same world through different lenses, Matthew. I didn't use my gun on you because I had no reason. You aren't going to use yours because it would place you on the wrong side of your dividing line. Two different pairs of eyes, two different sets of lenses, but the same conclusion. Says something about life, doesn't it?"

Deirdre scowled. "It's time for you to leave, Matthew Jacob, time for you to go back to your safe, American world."

My teeth clenched and a newer wave of cold sweat bathed my body. I closed my eyes, exhaled, and shut down my one-man army. With shaking hands I stuffed my gun back into its holster, nodded silently, grimly, and shuffled out of the apartment.

Deirdre's laughter cascaded around my ears as I closed the door. I heard her laughter while I walked down her steps, crossed the porch, trudged back to my car. I heard her laughter while I hit the ignition and stomped the accelerator. When I continued to hear it a block or two away I swerved into the nearest parking spot and killed the engine. I was afraid it would never go away.

I put my back up against the door, stretched my legs across the seat, and lit a cigarette. The laughter didn't entirely disappear but my trembling was easing. I leaned against the window

glass and watched a montage of faces and listened to snatches of conversations replay in my head. Yakov's gawky body; Collins's slick, hearty handshake; Cheryl's casts; Blue spitting blood. Too many had been bruised, broken, or left dead on the altars of belief. Deirdre's, Never Agains', Blue's, Collins's, Yonah's.

Maybe my own. There was a finer line than I had imagined between victim and victimizer.

I turned my head and stared at the lighted houses on the pleasant residential street. This one square mile had been a converging point for disparate fears, a battlefield for divergent ideologies. Blind to the suffering, inured to the cost, their invisible presence left lifeless bodies, shattered lives.

I pushed the spent cigarette into the ashtray and lit another. I'd wanted to stop Deirdre from finding another neighborhood, town, city, country, to work her ugly magic, leave her trace.

But I hadn't uncocked the hammer with my right finger. Hadn't been willing to keep her from her appointed rounds. It wasn't fear or self-preservation that stopped me. I just wasn't willing to be another walking ideology blinded by commitment to my own dubious vision of right and wrong. The gun was stuffed back into my holster because there weren't enough bullets to stop Deirdre, to stop whoever followed her, and whoever came after that. There were never enough bullets. History swore to that.

Simon had asked if I was tired of living without belief. His question had recalled the sixties when belief had been my food, when a vision of a new age had consumed my life. But right now, with Deirdre's mocking laughter only an echo, I was relieved. *I* had no higher guide or guideline dictating where to go, what to do, who to be. Without any organized belief I had to find out for myself. And right now, I liked that. Deirdre *wasn't* the last one standing.

I swung my legs off the seat, stubbed the cigarette, and thought about home. Then I heard my stomach growl with hun-

ger and saw my grin in the rearview mirror. I didn't want to go home. I didn't want the couch, the television, the stash, or the Wild Turkey.

I started the car and pulled into the street, smile still in place. Right now I wanted more of Mrs. Hampton's, Charlene's, home-made ham.

ABOUT THE AUTHOR

A former VISTA volunteer and founder of the Peoples' School in Chicago, ZACHARY KLEIN moved to Boston, Massachusetts, in 1971 to work at the Project Place Collective, an employee-run social service agency. Since 1976, he has been a therapist and consultant to individuals, couples, and nonprofit social service agencies. He lives in Boston with his sons, Matthew and Jacob, and his partner, Susan Goodman.

IROQUOIS-13